Brilliance and Betrayal
A Diamond of the Ton Regency Mystery
Book 1

Lynn Morrison

Anne Radcliffe

Marketing Chair Press

Cover design by The Killion Group, Inc

Published by

The Marketing Chair Press, Oxford, England

LynnMorrisonWriter.com

ISBN (paperback): 9781917361071

Contents

Dedication

Are you going to write the dedication?

I thought you were going to do it. It's your turn.

I can't think of anything funny to write.

So just write that.

Fine, but it's your turn to pick dinner.

Prologue
London, Late June, 1813

*"To wed is to tread the respectable halls of matrimony.
Conveniently timed widowhood, however, ascends one to the
gallery above, offering a commanding view—and influence—over
all below."*
—Reflections of Grace: A Guide to Etiquette

L ady Charity Cresswell recited the mantra in her mind as she
stopped at the precise distance from the throne and sank
into a curtsy deep enough to make her mother proud.

*Confident steps. Head held high. Chin dipped in perfect
obeisance.*

"My diamond," Queen Charlotte purred, her voice sharp
enough to cut glass. "What a surprise to see you today."

Charity kept her gaze on the intricate parquet floor, not taking
the bait. Torturous hours under Mama's eagle-eyed scrutiny had
finally borne fruit. Even now, Mama's voice echoed in her mind.
*One does not lift her gaze until bid to do so. Nor speak, nor
twitch.*

"Stand, and explain the purpose of your visit."

Charity rose smoothly, her slippered foot sliding across the polished wooden boards.

This was the only way forward.

This parlance would determine Charity's entire future. Forcing this meeting was a bold move, but what came next was even riskier. To ask the Queen to forgive her for ending her carefully arranged engagement was nigh unthinkable.

A pang struck her as she recalled Lord Roland Percy's confused, stricken expression when she told him she was breaking off her engagement to him mere minutes ago.

Lord Percy would be the next Duke of Northumberland. He had wealth. A title. Darkly handsome looks. Perhaps most unusually, he seemed to be a good-hearted man. By all aristocratic accounts, it was a splendid match for the both of them, especially since she was this season's diamond of the first water.

Yet her brilliance had dulled. After her audacious kidnapping from the Fitzroy estate earlier in the season, her reputation had been saved from ruin only by the boldest of lies made by the Queen, and a subsequent engagement to Lord Percy—the man who had so unexpectedly fallen in love with her best friend, Lady Grace.

Her family had no inkling of her whereabouts. When they discovered she was here to end that engagement, their fury would be volcanic. Her mother, most of all, utterly incapable of comprehending her reasons.

Her footing was still not firm enough to survive more scandal. Everyone who knew the truth of her situation believed Charity needed to marry Lord Percy quickly.

That included her loyal best friend, who had begged him to protect Charity at the expense of their own happiness.

Now is not the time to focus on feelings, she chastised herself. The Queen's aid would not come without a cost. It was tantamount to playing chess against an opponent who could topple the board at will. And yet, the Queen didn't simply play the game—she held the pieces, the board, and the rules firmly in her grasp.

Charity assumed a pose of cool deference, ignoring the retainers and guards around Charlotte as if it were only herself and the Queen in the room. "Your Majesty, you and Lord Percy have done me a great service this year. He is a perfect gentleman, and any woman should be lucky to marry him."

Queen Charlotte, no one's fool, sat straighter on her throne. "Why do I hear a 'but' in your unspoken words, Lady Charity?"

"Because Your Majesty is perceptive. I fear he has a weakness which I cannot overlook. He is in love."

The Queen waited, perplexed, expecting Charity to say more.

"I cannot marry him, Your Majesty."

The Queen huffed and she waved a hand in the air. "Love is a gift, Lady Charity, but certainly not something which warrants our attention nor the dissolution of a betrothal. Especially for a lady in *your* predicament. Allow me to guess. He is smitten with the little mouse who assisted him in those escapades to find you."

Charity did not answer, watching the Queen through her lowered eyelashes, which was answer enough.

"How very curious," Charlotte continued. As she leaned forward slightly, the light of a hundred candles in the golden chandelier sent the tiara on her head ablaze. "He was committed to this course, and now you are against it. I wonder why. She is your friend, is she not? Lady Grace Tilbury, hmm?"

At the small incline of Charity's head, the Queen's tone soured. "I am disappointed in you. A diamond must be as unyielding as it is dazzling, yet here you stand, ready to fling your cap over the windmill—either in a fit of romantic folly or misguided loyalty. The former would be foolhardy, and the latter would be cowardice. Perhaps you can understand why it displeases me to consider either option!" The Queen's voice was strident, just shy of a shout.

You should apologise and leave, her mother's voice suggested. It was always there, reminding her at every turn how to walk, look, and even breathe.

But ever more frequently, there was a new voice inside of Charity, a coolly logical one, that warned her to harden her spine. Loyalty it was, but hardly misguided. If she went through with the marriage, at best her best friend would eventually grow to despise her. More likely, the two would eventually betray her.

The worst part was, she would be the first to encourage them to find what happiness they could. But as soon as word got out—and it would—she would be the laughingstock of the *ton*. The Queen would not come to her rescue. Charity would find herself missing from all the best guest lists.

That damage to her standing would not do. Not when the strongest reason she had for courting Percy had been for his connections and title. Power was the one thing Charity craved above all—even if a desire to grant a small favour of happiness to her best friend was a close second.

Charity stilled her hands to keep from plucking at her skirts. *Show no signs of fear*, the logical voice said.

"I am surprised you have not raised the concern I have taken leave of my senses, ma'am. Rest assured, my ambitions do not include falling in love."

She gave the Queen a small smile. "I have little to gain by thwarting Cupid's arrow. I will not consign myself to a match with a man who does not understand the subtleties of court—not merely to quell rumours of my virtue. Magnanimity does not have to harm our interests. We could secure both the friendship and gratitude of the next Duke of Northumberland—not to mention Lady Grace's—for the price of a simple broken engagement. And that would be a bargain, would it not?"

Queen Charlotte's brows drew lower, but underneath them, Charity could see the Queen thinking. If the Queen was thinking, then Charity had a chance of succeeding.

"A bargain," the Queen repeated as she mulled this over, but her face grew suspicious. "A broken betrothal would be only half of the deal, Lady Charity. If you think you might negotiate with me for the chance to remain unwed and unattached, I will disabuse you of the notion."

As if that was an option. Once she broke this engagement, Charity would have to marry someone else—at once. "Of course, Your Majesty. There are better matches to be made."

"Are there? The unfortunate truth is I have no idea who. What person of standing might be willing to overlook both your disappearance *and* a broken betrothal? If you do not have a plausible alternative, I am sure I need not tell you how very troubled I will be."

Charity had spent countless hours before her debut poring over the noble families of England, charting matches with the precision of a military strategist.

"Lord Percy was only the best of those in London," Charity began slowly. "I can not settle for anything less than his station, or Lady Fitzroy will have won. She will have succeeded in ruining my prospects, and secured a victory over you."

Queen Charlotte scowled at that, then softened. "You suggest someone who is outside of London, then. For a moment, I feared you were about to propose marriage to one of mine. I am not cruel enough to allow that."

"I would not dream of such a presumption, Your Majesty, though I will have to venture farther afield—to Scotland, to be precise. Duke Atholl is a widower. Again."

Charlotte's tapping fingers paused. "Atholl is three breaths shy of the grave. And he already has an heir."

"A *young* heir," Charity countered.

"No one will accept you as a steward until he comes of age."

No one will accept a woman, she meant. Beneath Queen Charlotte's words was a world of frustration. With her husband indisposed, she was forced to bow down to her son, when by all other rights she should have ruled.

"Duke Atholl is a reasonable man who will want his heir protected and cared for. His vast Scottish holdings are tempting prizes for many. Your Majesty, I suggest we might solve both his problems with one blow."

The Queen's gaze slid to the side as she considered Charity's words. "Duchess Atholl… it is possible."

"Mayhap Prince Edward might offer his services as guardian for the lad?" Charity ventured. "His Grace could go to his death in peace for the future of his family line."

"He would be grateful to me. And his son as well." The Queen touched her lip and then motioned for a footman to approach. "Fetch a lady's maid and have them bring a quill and paper. I am of the mind to dictate a letter."

Her relief was so great that Charity needed to imagine herself as a Grecian goddess carved from stone. Immoveable. Unfeeling.

"You did not mention the inevitable matter of a mourning period. Some might view that as hiding, but cutting the time short would not be respectful either."

Was that all? That would be simple. "If Your Majesty had some need of me here, I could hardly disobey a command to appear. The princess will be making her formal debut next season, I believe?"

Queen Charlotte's mouth twisted into a smile. "Indeed. The benefits to this course of action may appear to outweigh the detriments. So if this is your wish, Lady Charity, I suggest you think hard about how you will be of use to the throne when I recall you. Use the time of your ride to Scotland wisely."

1

London, Early May, 1814

"*The trappings of power, like the finest wine, are best savoured in company; for what value does it have if it cannot be paraded amidst a throng of admirers?*"
—Charity's diary

A trill of laughter floated over the meticulously pruned hedges of the gardens of Carlton House. It was as false as the carefully arranged expression gracing Charity's face, her lips curved in a serene smile that felt as stiff and unnatural as the whalebone stays pressing against her ribs. A fête hosted by the Prince Regent was not an event at which one let down their guard, and it was thrice as important for Charity to remain vigilant.

Smile, nod, and listen closely.

And place yourself in the correct position to watch, Charity added to the imagined voice of her mother. Mama's advice didn't pop into her head nearly as often as it used to. Then again, her mother had not been preparing Charity for the life she was living now.

The title? Yes. The cloud of disapproving suspicion that occasionally surrounded her? Not even close. Fortunately, her rank and favour to the Queen held the worst of the gossip at bay. So far, she had heard not one word that suggested the Fitzroy family had been responsible for her disappearance last year.

Perhaps Charity could finally put her worst fear to rest.

Still, the advice was sound. Giving no hint of the thoughts churning in her mind, Charity parted her lips in a vacant smile, nodding along as the people around her chatted. With one ear attuned to their chin wagging, ready to respond at the first hint of her name, she let her gaze follow the movements of the important guests.

"Excuse me." Charity gave a polite nod as she retreated from the group with the precision of a general. Her silk skirts brushed over the stone as she manoeuvred around the clusters of guests crowding the terrace, her mind focused on her next target. Laughter and chatter and heavy perfumes warred for attention, but she paid them no mind.

Her satin slippers crunched over the tiny white pebbles on the path, each one a sharp reminder that style and comfort rarely coexisted in high fashion. She kept her pace without winces or sighs.

Pain was a small price to pay for dignity—or, as her mother might have said, for avoiding the indignity of limping like a lame duck.

As she passed under the ivy-covered arch, she spotted Queen Charlotte ahead. Charity adjusted her stride to match the royal pace, falling into step beside her, a silent companion to Her Majesty's stately progress around the social event.

The older woman stopped when the central fountain came into view, its cascading water catching the sunlight in shimmering arcs, framed by beds of irises and primroses that perfumed the warm spring air.

Charity kept her gaze forward. She had always admired Queen Charlotte's composure, the regal tilt of her head and the unyielding elegance in her posture, but today it felt like trying to emulate a marble bust—an exercise in impossible stillness. The Queen's gaze, sharp and assessing, studied the scene before them as though every detail were a riddle she intended to solve.

"Your Grace. I trust the princess has not caused too much chaos yet?" the older woman asked in a low murmur, surveying the season's fawning debutantes with a practiced eye. "Though judging by this season's crop of fresh faces, chaos might be an improvement."

Charity chose her words with care, mindful that others might be listening. "She has been pleasant and exchanged kind words with all who have crossed her path—"

"But she has not gone looking for anyone off that path. She has not approached Prince William," the Queen said, finishing Charity's sentence. "If he had any sense, he would have approached her himself by now—or perhaps he is smarter than he looks."

In all the lands, there were few reasonable blue-blooded options of an age for the Queen's namesake, Princess Charlotte. Even the princess had conceded that point. The Queen's gaze slid to the cluster of foreigners from the Netherlands lingering along the garden path.

Negotiations for Prince William of Orange to secure the princess's hand had moved at a pace that could generously be called sluggish. Still, most agreed the announcement was days away. As with all arranged marriages, whether to foreign princes or not, it required an abundance of diplomacy—and apparently an equal measure of discomfort.

"It is early in the event, Your Majesty. All eyes are upon the pair. Another round of champagne, and I am certain both will find the courage to say hello."

"I require a sincere greeting and a kind word between the pair, at minimum, Your Grace," the Queen reminded her. "And if you detect even the faintest hint of willfulness brewing in my namesake, you are to redirect her immediately—preferably before she dismantles the entire wedding negotiation. She must marry Prince William. If needed, I will personally escort her down the aisle myself."

When the Queen spoke in that tone, all of England leapt to do her bidding, Charity included.

Everyone, that was, except for Princess Charlotte of Wales, who stood not ten feet away, doe-eyed and pink-cheeked, as English as the roses blooming behind her. She appeared to be enjoying the party, talking to everyone—except the one person her father and grandmother had ordered her to.

"I will uphold my duty, Your Majesty," Charity promised, holding perfectly still under the Queen's searching gaze.

Never mind the exquisite gown, or the pearls and sapphires adorning her person. Lady Charity Cresswell—now the Dowager Duchess Atholl—was as much at the Queen's beck and call as the liveried footmen balancing trays of champagne.

She didn't complain, of course. There were far worse fates than being an 'honoured guest' at society's most exclusive events.

The Queen allowed a faint hint of satisfaction to brighten her expression, and she turned to walk away. But another woman came to a halt before her, bobbing the appropriate curtsey, before Charlotte could take a step.

Charity recognised her at once as Lady Pelham. Viscountess, wealth aplenty, mother to four healthy sons—and a vicious harpy with a penchant for gossip. Especially when it came to Charity's presence. Her gown was a bright riot of purple satin and feathers, as ostentatious as her personality.

Lady Pelham ignored Charity, flashing a bright smile in the Queen's direction. "Well met, Your Majesty. It is a beautiful day for a garden party, is it not? The spring blossoms are nearly as lovely as our fair princess."

"My granddaughter is particularly becoming today," the Queen agreed. "I was about to say as much to Duchess Atholl. You have had the pleasure of meeting her? If not, do let me know so I can rectify your oversight."

Lady Pelham's smile faltered, thinning into a line as she raked her eyes down Charity's gown, which was decidedly not in any colours of mourning. "I heard she was here, but have not had a chance to speak with her, of course," she replied, her tone clipped. "I heard word of your return, Your Grace, but I assumed it to be mistaken. To re-enter society so soon after the death of your spouse is… unusual, is it not, Your Majesty?"

Lady Pelham was hardly the first to say so. Charity's own mother had insisted, "A year in mourning, at a minimum. Give society time to forget about your debut. In a year—or even two— with your title and wealth, they will be more than happy to welcome you back."

Charity ignored that advice. Though they shared the same blonde hair and bright blue eyes, her mother was soft where Charity had grown hard. Lady Cresswell clung to a belief that beauty and loyalty could conquer all.

But Charity knew better—both were meaningless without the wit to wield them as weapons. Ten months in the north, feigning grief for the ancient Duke of Atholl—a man whom Charity had barely known for two weeks—had given her ample time to hone both plans and resolve. She instructed her parents to remain in the country this year. Better they spend the season in pastoral ignorance than fret over every snide whisper.

Thus far, Charity had no trouble handling women like Lady Pelham. Everything was calculated… and properly done.

"I am upholding the duke's final wishes. My dear husband insisted upon my return to London on his deathbed."

"So you say…" Lady Pelham's voice trailed off disdainfully. It left no question as to her opinion on the matter.

"So *I* say." The Queen's stinging words took both Charity and Lady Pelham by surprise, and Queen Charlotte looked down her nose at the viscountess. "Even before they married, the duke knew my wishes—his wife was to accompany the princess during her debut. I am sure I remember my own request."

The venomous woman's mouth fell open, but no retort escaped her lips.

Charity maintained a composed expression. It wouldn't do to gloat. Lady Pelham wasn't an enemy, merely an irritant—a fly to be swatted when necessary. "My husband was a great supporter of the crown. Her Majesty's wish is our command, Lady Pelham, is it not?"

"Good day, Lady Pelham," the Queen said in an imperious tone. The woman bobbed a curtsey and then backed away as fast as she could without losing her balance.

Queen Charlotte flicked open her lace fan and waved it lazily in the air. "Lady Pelham would do well to remember that one does not rise to the top only by stepping on those around her. Perhaps she should redirect her energies toward proving her usefulness. To me, specifically."

"Excellent advice, as always," Charity murmured. "And on that note, I would ask for your leave to check on the princess."

With the Queen's approval, she walked deeper into the garden. She held her head high as would befit the wealthy duchess, now lady-in-waiting, and presumed confidante of the princess.

Charity was fast on her way to reclaiming her status as a diamond of the first water. Had she not known just how easily all that could be lost, she might have revelled in this accomplishment. Today, however, duty took precedence. Her task was to ensure the princess behaved amicably with her intended beau.

At present, the princess was leisurely strolling arm in arm with one of her aunts, clearly in no rush to fulfill her obligation.

Charity gathered her skirts, gliding forward until she slid neatly into place at the princess's other side. Then she feigned a dry cough. "All these conversations have left me in desperate need of a glass of lemonade. Are you not parched, Your Highness? Come, allow me to escort you to the refreshments table."

Releasing her aunt, the princess looped an arm through Charity's and tugged her in the opposite direction. "Your Grace, your timing is perfect. I want your court knowledge. There is a handsome man in the French contingent, and I am curious as to his antecedents."

Not fooled, Charity did not look to see who the princess meant. The stranger's identity was irrelevant. The highest ranking foreigner at the event was Prince William of Orange, who happened to be positioned near the refreshments. Charity made a second attempt to suggest they go the right way, but once again, the princess dragged her feet.

"Please, Your Grace, must we go that way? My intended is so very…"

"Generous?" Charity offered. "He gifted you the bracelet around your wrist, did he not?"

The princess sniffed, not quite pouting. "It is a plain golden band, as dull as his conversation. The man could make the weather sound dire—and he never becomes remotely interesting until he has had three glasses of wine, at which point he is positively incoherent."

The Dutch prince had many fine qualities, but his tolerance for drink was not one. Nor was conversation, unfortunately. Still, Charity had to get the princess and prince talking to one another.

Else they would be finding themselves with a stranger on their wedding night.

It was rather an unpleasant experience, and Charity had learnt that lesson the hard way, enduring her wedding night beneath the fumbling hands of an octogenarian she'd only met hours before. Once had been sufficient to validate their union—mercifully brief and, by some stroke of fortune, not fruitful. It was a memory she carried with grim clarity.

The princess would be required to submit to much more than that. As soon as she married, she would have the duty to birth the heirs to two thrones.

Charity straightened, her tone firm as she pressed her point. "We must at least make our introductions. I will be right beside you. No harm will come of a simple hello."

"Fine," the princess sighed, with all the exaggerated resignation of a young girl gravely inconvenienced. "But first, just one more turn around the garden. I know Papa insists I marry him, but surely I am entitled to a harmless flirtation or two before I am officially doomed. Please, Your Grace. Wait for me here? I swear, I will be back before you can even lament my lack of sense."

Charity checked to ensure the Queen was not looking their way before nodding her agreement. "Do not tarry, or your grandmother might take the matter into her own imperial hands— and no one will want that."

The princess waved aside the threat and sauntered off with her aunt again.

In truth, Charity did not begrudge the charming but rebellious girl her moments of fancy. She remembered her first society events all too well. Wishing to be prepared, she had arrived in London with a short list of acceptable suitors in mind, and went to work matching the names with faces. Though she had always planned to marry to best advantage, she had also not been any more immune to aquiline noses, firm chins, and muscled arms than the next woman.

Lord Percy had been nearly the sum of all Charity could wish for. People thought she was mad for breaking the engagement.

Freeing him from their engagement wasn't as altruistic a gesture as most thought. A man with no appetite for society made him a poor choice indeed for a woman bent on standing at its pinnacle.

Now, however, she was a widow, unshackled from the constraints of maidenly virtue. There was pleasure to be had in the act, Grace had assured her, though Charity was unconvinced of its value. Perhaps, in time, Charity might consider a discreet lover. Not immediately, of course, but perhaps by the end of the season.

Her gaze swept over the gathered men, assessing them with cool detachment. She sought someone worthy of her attention— someone she could control.

Across the lawn, a flash of blonde hair captured her attention —a colour that bordered upon white, it was so fair. Her whole body froze, and it felt as though the sky clamped down upon her, suffocating her with its nearness.

Stop. The world is not closing in, she ordered herself sternly. *Stand tall. Graceful. You cannot faint here in front of the guests. You must stay with the princess—*

The wrench of her gut at the thought of her dereliction, a knife-hot pain, forced her to breathe shallowly again. That, and the sparkles of light and dark that began to edge her vision.

It was not possible. Not at Carlton House. She must surely be mistaken.

No, not a mistake. A Fitzroy is at the party. A Fitzroy is here!

The voice in her thoughts, the one that sounded suspiciously like her mother, made a screech like nails on dark slate and fell silent. Charity halted in her steps, steadying herself with a hand upon an ornamental rail. It was a miracle she did not gasp for air, but she did not think the iron bands around her chest would allow it anyway.

It must be true. Only one family in London bore those hallmark locks, brighter than the spun gold of tales of angels or fairies. It was as clear a mark of the devil standing among them as the smell of sulfur.

As if hearing her thoughts, the crowd thinned between them, revealing Peregrine Fitzroy, Earl Fitzroy, poised as though he owned the world. His sharp features were set in a faintly amused expression as he stood half-turned towards her.

Some of the tightness left her lungs, but a far more complicated feeling began to seize her throat and heart in its fists. Vivid snatches of that ball shoved their way into her mind like a waking nightmare.

The spicy smell of cloves rose in her memory, as well as the slight, mocking curve of his lips as they danced together at his ball. His light blue eyes had been hooded and enigmatic, and her cheeks had burned, fever pitch, as the world began to tilt. She could still feel his arm at her waist, clutching her tightly to him after she stumbled into Grace and Lord Percy, his hand burning like a brand upon her back.

She had been so hot she could not bear to be within her own skin. She had decided to go to the garden and—

Nothing after that. The hole in her memory yawned like a terrifying beast. Charity had been drugged so she would not fight her abduction, and so there was a great deal she could not remember about that night, or the days after.

It had been her friend, Grace, who had explained to her later that Lady Fitzroy had a prodigious medical knowledge of plants. A common headache remedy—henbane—had been slipped into her drink by a maid to make her clumsy in front of the *ton*. After she was taken, her captors had kept her dosed with laudanum to keep her pliant.

Charity's fists tightened until her nails dug into her skin. The flash of pain reminded her to keep her wits sharp. She had lost nearly everything she had been planning for her future that night. *Everything.* And all of this had happened because Lady Marian Fitzroy wished to make Charity's mama pay for slights that happened before she had been born.

It was unjust that so far the witch had escaped punishment. Revealing Lady Fitzroy's role in the kidnapping would have besmirched Charity and her rescuers, too, but their fear of tarnish had only emboldened the woman. Lady Fitzroy had then gone on to commit a different crime—an act of treason during a diplomatic visit from the Swedish Ambassador a few weeks later. That time it was to retaliate against the Crown for the aid the Queen had given Charity. And after that, Lady Fitzroy had fled beyond the grasp of retribution, having escaped to the continent.

Rage edged with fear rooted her to the spot, no matter how much she willed her feet back into motion. If he turned his head only a few more inches, he would see her staring at him as though he had two heads.

Move, Charity, she told herself sternly. *Preferably before he sees you.*

But of course, by then it was too late. Fitzroy turned and glanced lazily in her direction like a great cat surrounded by his pride, surveying his surroundings, sleek and content. As he fixed his gaze upon her, she noticed the way his eyes widened and then sharpened in surprise and recognition.

Then, he had the audacity to lift the corners of his mouth in a faint, mocking smile, the kind that seemed to say he already knew the game and how it would end. Or was it meant to issue a challenge? After everything that Lady Fitzroy had done last year, how innocent could her own son possibly be?

Before Charity could decide which it was, he casually turned away again as though she was beneath his consideration. As if a world of bitter history did not lie between them. He took a glass from a passing footman, the perfect picture of an aristocrat who had every right to be there.

Of course, strictly speaking, he should possess that right. His service had earned him a pardon from his mother's crimes.

Lord Fitzroy should have been stripped of assets. He should have been imprisoned. He should have been horribly maimed when he had been sent to war, or at the least, have come back with a haunted look and shattered nerves. Charity did not know how he had managed such a feat, but it looked as though the man had suffered little from his experience.

The sun shone upon him as though he were a golden god, and people circled him in worship instead of scorn. That smarted most of all—that she still had to put up with the backbiting from overstretched termagants like Lady Pelham, and he was wholly unmarked by the sins of his family.

She glared her frustration at him for a moment, and he turned his eyes her way again, catching her in the act. Shame at being caught staring, coupled with her fury, brought a scalding blush to her cheeks. Damn the man, for that only made his smile widen.

He should have left the country with the rest of his family. The punishment he had gotten… it was not nearly enough. He most certainly should not be standing in Prinny's garden, smirking at her and lifting his glass in a toast.

Abruptly, her anger turned to suspicion, and she pointedly turned her back on him. Why *was* Lord Fitzroy here—at this particular event? What was his purpose? Could it be only to work to repair his damaged reputation? Or was there something else? Given the debacle at the end of last season, one would think he would give people another year to forget his association.

One should not look a gift horse in the mouth, Charity

reminded herself, and the panic that had stifled her breath eased. Truly, his plans did not matter in the end.

Lady Fitzroy, the architect of all her suffering, had spent a great deal of time in Charity's thoughts this winter. Mostly, that had comprised discovering the dowager's whereabouts and formulating a strategy on how to bring her into reach so that Charity could give a little of that suffering back to the entire Fitzroy family.

The solution to both problems, it seemed, might have just been given to her.

2

⁂

"Everyone sees what you appear to be, few experience what you really are."
—Niccolò Machiavelli, The Prince

Prinny's little party was deadly tedious. Peregrine Fitzroy half wished he had never come, but some things had to be reckoned as necessary evils.

Everyone who thought they were someone would have killed for an invitation to this event at Carlton House, and to waste an opportunity to reassert himself triumphantly as a pardoned man in London's *bon ton* after a long absence simply wouldn't do.

Selina had been correct; no one had truly been expecting him to make an appearance. Not even the Prince Regent who had extended the invitation to him, if he had interpreted the man's expression correctly.

That was one of the main reasons why he had let Selina persuade him to come to this specific event. Occasionally, one had to remind the sharp-toothed beasts lurking among the gentry that there were predators in their surroundings more cunning than they, and he was ready to reclaim his place among that more vicious pack.

"...suppose they will welcome you back?"

Peregrine brought his wandering attention back to Lord Tremayne standing beside him. He had not the foggiest idea what the man had been saying. "What do you think?" he evaded, but with a faint sardonic tone, as if the answer should be obvious.

Tremayne smiled faintly, tapping the fine crystal of his glass with a finger. It gave a pleasant ring beneath the percussion. "Well, *I* think that you receiving an invitation says a great deal about the matter."

Ah. Another person who wanted to gossip about him, with him. Fitzroy didn't let the expression on his face change. It was a foolish question, but there was no guile to Tremayne whatsoever, much less malice. No ill intention could be ascribed to it.

Besides, Tremayne was one of the few who seemed to be willing to take the Crown's forgiveness of him at face value. With so few champions to his name, Peregrine was in no position to disdain support from any quarter. Not yet. And no matter how much of a hindquarter that quarter was.

"Has your mother written to you?" was the man's next witless question, drawing curious glances from a nearby cluster.

Peregrine set his glass down on the low garden wall, gripping the young man's shoulders with his hands so he wouldn't do something foolish. Like accidentally show his temper by throttling him.

"Tremayne," he said, clearing his throat. "I cannot think of anything less I would like to discuss so publicly right now. I went to war to prove my loyalty was to the Crown and not my mother, *remember?*"

"Oh!" At least the man had the grace to look abashed at that. "I *am* sorry, Perry. How can I make it up to you?"

"Tell me of someone else's misfortunes, perhaps," Peregrine muttered, picking his glass up again to take another sip. But his voice hadn't been low enough, so Tremayne took him up on that.

"Fine. I was at an event where Lord Gilbert, three sheets to the wind, mistook Lady Moreland's parrot for her hat and tried to wear it."

That was unexpected enough that it made Peregrine laugh, and his sense of humour restored itself somewhat. "I do not believe you."

"I swear it. Ask anyone, and for further proof, I will point out he did not receive an invitation to Carlton House today. It happened just a few weeks ago. Before you—well, just after Napoleon abdicated. There were some rather... outrageous celebrations when the news reached London."

"Well, upon my word." Peregrine chuckled. But as he let his gaze sweep the party again, his stomach soured once more as his eyes fell upon the young blonde woman. One who was making no bones about looking directly at him.

One would think he was the only unexpected face at this soiree, the way the Queen's missing diamond from last season was behaving. Lady Charity Cresswell. Or rather, now Her Grace, the Dowager Duchess Atholl.

This behaviour should have amused him—would have amused him, once upon a time. After everything that had transpired last year, however, it grated. While her kidnapping was an open wound between them, their bitter history went further back. From the moment she learned his name, the duchess had looked down her nose at him, and only the two of them knew why.

It was not that he expected her to be friendly. But how *dare* she look at him with such contempt?

As he leaned casually against one of the trees, he tipped his head in the direction of the young blonde lurker watching him, giving her a bland look to reprove her for her glaring.

Tremayne—curse the man for his sudden power of observation—turned to see what had caught his attention. "Who is that?"

"No one of importance," Peregrine lied, turning his back upon her.

"She is pretty," Tremayne added, obliviously imperceptive. "Do you not think so, Perry?"

Tremayne had all the sense of a sprat whose brains had leaked into his breeches. An ally like him might be worse than none at all. Discreetly, he sidled over and jabbed his elbow into Tremayne's midsection. "Stop gawking at her, you half-wit!"

The man was unabashed as he looked back at Peregrine. "She did not notice. She only has eyes for you, Fitzroy."

"Eyes? Hardly. Daggers, perhaps," he muttered. "Excuse me. I see someone else I must talk to."

That wasn't strictly truthful, but as it happened, he had things to do besides converse with the addlepated. Also things to do other than pulling London's society out of their aristocratic ennui and sending them into a frenzy of speculation about *why does the Duchess Atholl not like Lord Fitzroy overmuch?*

What a little fool she was being.

Peregrine strolled past a large potted plant of some sort or other and out of her sight. As he suspected, he was on familiar terms with nearly everyone here. Of the gentry, only *she* was a relative newcomer, and she still had much of the raw newness of a debutante—wobbling like a foal on new legs, duchess or no. Grasping biddies would see her as prey standing between them and the Queen. But she—and that—was not his problem.

"Fitzroy? Are you skulking? Is there someone here, perchance, that you are attempting to avoid?"

General Rowland Hill's amused tone behind him caused him

to whirl around again, and Peregrine let one side of his mouth turn up in a mocking grin to cover his surprise. "I was attempting to avoid you and my debt, but I see that I failed."

"Ha. That is right, you do owe me a drink, but I don't believe for a moment that I'm the one you were avoiding," Hill said shrewdly.

"Are you quite certain? I seem to recall you threatening to invite me to dinner," Peregrine said lightly. But he said it with a smile, so Hill would take it for a jest instead of the truth that it was.

"You'll give in and become part of the 'family' someday, I'm sure of it." Hill winked.

Not bloody likely. After he had found himself under Rowland Hill's command, Peregrine had vowed he would rather end up as a prisoner of the French than call his commander *Daddy Hill*.

The general turned, surveying the crowd. "I suppose you're hiding instead from that young lady glaring daggers in your direction, then. Whatever bone could she have to pick with you?"

For the love of God, what was *her problem?* "I stepped on her foot by accident during a ball last season and ruined her shoe. It was, as I recall, one of her very favourite shoes." He lied again, letting it slide from his tongue easily. "She still has not forgiven me, and I believe she wants to remind me of the injury to her toes and her father's pocket."

Hill laughed. "If you need protection from the chit…"

Clearly, Hill had not been introduced formally to his veritable barnacle. To be fair to the man, Hill had spent the last several years assisting Wellington on the continent instead of being part of the seasonal circuit. But Fitzroy still considered the man's studied ignorance unforgivable, especially when such information was so easy to obtain. Surviving society—much like battle—required information.

"That *chit*, General, is a widowed duchess and one of the

Queen's pets besides. Have a care, or the knives she is hurling at me might find a new target."

"A widow, you say? Perhaps you might introduce me?"

"If you are interested in attempting to court her, Hill, I would suggest you have Elstone over there do you the favour." Peregrine indicated the man with a point of his chin.

Rowland Hill was a good man, but he hadn't a chance in hell of convincing a title chaser to give it up just like that. But Peregrine wasn't in the business of disabusing an interested general of such harmless flights of fancy, especially when it might get a millstone off his neck.

He added, "An introduction from me would hardly endear you to her. But you should do it now, before Elstone sots himself."

"Splendid idea, lad. I think I'll do just that."

Hill toddled off, and Peregrine exhaled briefly in relief.

That would serve Elstone and his kith right, too. His cluster of nobles had been some of the ones that waited to see how others reacted to Peregrine, so they could follow suit without coming to their own decisions.

Spineless, the lot of them. But so many members of the *ton* were. Fortunately, cannon fodder had its uses even on these more genteel battlefronts.

Peregrine had learned to play this game of society as soon as he could walk, and he was very, very good at it. That was fortunate for him, because his success in disentangling himself from his mother now depended on this very skill.

He was the eldest male. As earl, he had a seat in the House of Lords, an empire of connections, and had been carefully setting himself up as a political and economical force to be reckoned with even without the peerage to back it. And then all of a piece last season, he was reduced to being his traitorous mother's dupe, and the Crown hovered behind his shoulder, their hands waiting to seize the assets that belonged to him.

Now he was naught but 'Lord' Fitzroy, his address spoken like a jest. Damn his mother and her petty machinations both.

His neck prickled as he felt new eyes fall upon him, and he glanced up across the grass to see Selina watching. The woman's plush lips were twisted slightly, and her eyes sparked with avaricious interest, as if she could sense the weakness of his thoughts. Carefully, he stowed his feelings deep once more.

Prinny and his ilk might consider themselves Kings of the proverbial jungle, but only because those with real power knew better than to tip their hands so thoughtlessly. One such, for example, being the Dowager Marchioness Selina of Normanby, who was more of a shark swimming in unknown depths than she was an idle social lioness.

It was wise never to forget that, especially while she stood in a cluster of women that included the Countesses of Hertford and Bessborough.

The marchioness flicked her eyes towards the foreign prince's party, indicating that she would like to approach, and Peregrine inclined his head a bare inch.

Checking his watch, Peregrine then casually circled towards the hedge wall. As he turned the corner, he glanced back at the way he came… and caught the Duchess Atholl watching him. Again.

Immediately, Fitzroy turned back in Selina's approximate direction. Seeing her eyes swing his way, he tapped his chin with a single finger, as though thinking. *I need a moment.*

Selina lifted her eyebrow but tilted her head, and Fitzroy spun on his heel then, locking eyes deliberately with the duchess. Imbuing the moment with a wealth of meaning, he pointedly stepped into the hedge maze.

It didn't matter if his little saddle burr had the guts to follow him. If she shied away, the problem was still resolved.

Prinny's hedge maze had two entrances, and sure enough,

light footfalls entered the maze from the far entrance, as if she planned to confront him discreetly. A laugh. Though he had intended to slip right back out and lose her, Peregrine changed his mind. Instead, he navigated to the first turn from her direction, and caught her unawares.

She muffled her yelp of surprise with a hand over her mouth. He latched onto her free hand and tugged her deeper into the maze. The object of his annoyance was taut with shock at being manhandled, but by the time he found one of the alcoves nearer the center, she began to struggle.

"Why, hallo there, Duchess," he purred. Then he smiled as she stiffened again, this time in outrage at such a casual address. Good. It was beyond satisfying to repay some of the irritation she had given him today in spades. But then she *clawed* him, the little wretch.

Inhaling a soft curse, he gave her hand a little shake. "I would be quiet, were I you. Else we will be answering some very awkward questions."

When she went still in furious compliance, he stepped away slightly, circling around to face her.

"How dare you put your hand upon me!" she hissed.

He had meant to give her a polite lecture, but this woman was an unrelenting plague upon his patience. He leaned in, not touching her, but near enough to intimidate, and her brief tremble almost made him feel like a lout.

Almost.

"Are we trading rules, *Lady Diamond*? Then I have one of my own. Relationships of all kinds require both give and take. That means if you want something from me—civility, for example— you should make sure you do not deny it to me in the bargain."

Her blue eyes, huge in her face, flared. "Civility," she breathed. "Like that at your little party last year, where I was given a draught in my punch and then held against my will?"

Almost against his own will, his mouth quirked at her overly sarcastic timbre, his annoyance souring into something a little more bitter. "I will thank you to remember it was *my ball*, and not a silly little party. And that it was my mother's doing, not mine. I understand your memories of the night may be a little muddled —" he paused and lifted an eyebrow when her face became a rictus.

"Muddled," she repeated after a pause. And then she *shoved* him, if one could believe that.

Peregrine caught her wrists in his hands, his thumbs gliding along the soft, bare skin beneath her gloves. She tried to wrench away, but he held her firm, forcing her to meet his eyes.

"I told you not to touch me," she growled.

She was rattled. And so was he—if he was being honest with himself. She was not the sweet, delicate newling he remembered flirting gently with last season. Not anymore. The differences from his memory were jarring.

He set his jaw. "Mark my words now, I will not be bound by rules you do not intend to follow. You had best comport yourself, Duchess. I have no reasons to spill your secrets to the *ton*. Whether you choose to believe me or not, I do not care. But if we quarrel, people will start guessing as to the reasons why, and if that happens, even if I keep silent, eventually it will not matter a whit."

He let her go then, and she rubbed at her wrists, her breast heaving once in ire before she turned her face away, forcing her expression back in a tense sort of order. Finally, she looked at him again. "I will *never* forgive you for your part in what your mother did to me. You chose her side. I am going to do everything in my power to see your life burned to ashes."

"More powerful people than you have tried," he shot back impatiently, stepping back from her. "For now we should leave. But whatever you do in the future, O perfect one, perhaps you should take care that you do not catch yourself in the conflagration."

His hair certainly might catch fire from the stare she leveled his way, but she gave a rough nod, and began to step past him. Peregrine inhaled, trying to find his calm again, and the cloying smell of rosewater filled his lungs.

She had changed her scent since the previous season. Last year, she had worn something more delicate that smelled pleasingly of citrus and sweet floral nectar. Orange, perhaps.

Before he realised what he was about, he thrust out his arm across her path, and she jerked to a stop. "By the by… the rosewater does not suit you," he added.

The look she gave him was pure disbelief compounded by insult. "What?"

"The scent you wore last year was much lovelier. I thought I would let you know."

"Orange blossom is for innocence and joy," she said flatly, her face losing colour, and with it, the fight that had seemed to animate her. "Excuse me… I must find the princess."

3

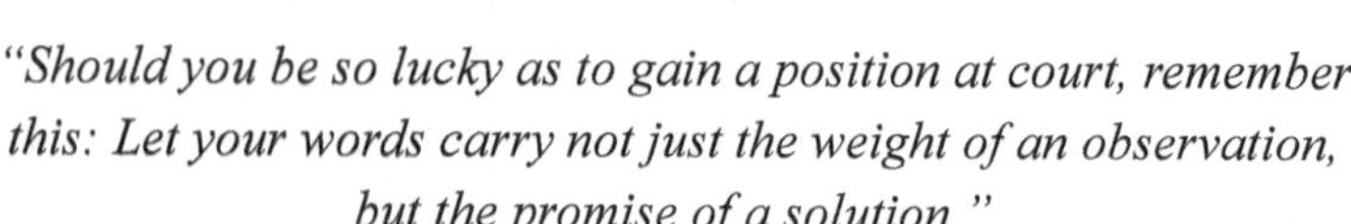

"Should you be so lucky as to gain a position at court, remember this: Let your words carry not just the weight of an observation, but the promise of a solution."
—Reflections of Grace: A Guide to Etiquette

Bright *smile, dear.*

Her mother's voice echoed through her mind. Never had Charity worked so hard to keep her emotions from showing on her face. Her smile was as brittle as the bones of her spine, but she dared not let it slip. The shards would slash what little was left of her composure to bits.

Instead, as she counted the turns until she reached the far end of the maze, she fought to keep hold of her anger. Anger was an emotion she had discovered while in Scotland. Wholly hers.

It had taken her some time to identify it, for all she had been taught by her mother was acceptance. Accept your place, the marriage arrangements, your wifely duties.

Acceptance saw her drummed out of London. And it would

never help her settle the score with Lady Fitzroy. All acceptance could do for her would be to snuff whatever light remained in her soul.

She picked up her pace as quickly as she dared, exiting near a side entrance into the royal residence.

Charity should be looking for the princess. She was derelict in her duty, and who knew what manner of trouble the girl might be getting into? But what if there was some mark—some sign—of her encounter with Lord Fitzroy?

The bands around her chest began to constrict once more.

Hoping she did not already look mussed, she sought the nearest servant, who directed her to the retiring room set aside for women's use. It was blessedly empty.

Charity closed the door and drug a chair in front of it. She spun around and came face to face with her own reflection. A pale, bloodless face stared back, but one fortunately unmarked.

She had expected some stain of his touch to linger. It seemed impossible that there was no trace. Not when she could still feel the hot press of his ungloved fingertips on her face and wrists.

The rosewater does not suit you.

The light, mocking echo of his voice in her thoughts made her feel exhausted.

He preferred what she wore last year? Well so did she, but little right did she have to wear it. She was a washed up widow, and had no man to fight at her side for even the smallest things, much less her own happiness.

She reached for the bar of soap and jug of water, lathering a cloth, and then scrubbed the rose scent from her wrists.

No. If she was to be honest with herself, what she was really scrubbing off with the linen cloth was the feel of his touch. She rubbed until her skin reddened and pain cleared her thoughts. Then she tossed the cloth aside and took another, dipping it into the cool water before wrapping it around her wrists to soothe them.

She forced her gaze upward until she again met her reflection. *Be stark. Sharp. Hard as a diamond.*

Slowly, as cold logic took hold, the pressure in her chest eased and her breathing grew less ragged.

No matter how much she hated Fitzroy, she had only herself to blame for this awkward confrontation. She should not have been caught by surprise by his return to England, even though she was only barely returned to London herself. And who could have expected he would so brazenly show for the season?

Well, matters were easily put to rights. He would not catch her off guard again. With a few whispers in the right ears and coins in the right hands, she would make sure she had word of every step he took. And then she could form a new plan.

If he thought to avoid retribution for what he and his family had done to her by claiming ignorance, he was as mad as his mother was cruel.

Charity unwound the cloth, relieved to find her wrists once again a healthy pink. She pinched her cheeks and bit her lips until they bloomed with colour as well.

All that was left was to address the soap smell still clinging to her. Castille had a mild scent, not unpleasant, but rather earthy. Beside her, a riotous bouquet of fresh cut flowers caught her attention. After careful consideration, she plucked a petal from a crimson carnation and lifted it to her nose.

Spicy yet sweet, it reminded her of cinnamon. To give a cluster of carnations was to show admiration. Every flick of her wrist would remind all around that she was someone worth admiring.

She plucked a few more petals and slid their silky soft surfaces across her pulse points. She tucked them into her corset, nestling them against her heart. Blue eyes glittered in the mirror with a glint both calculating and alluring.

She slid the chair back into place and flung open the door as though she did not have a care in the world. Skirts swirling about her ankles, she strode back into the sun.

Time to find the princess. With any luck, the Queen would not notice how long Charity was away. Unfortunately, today did not feel as though it was a lucky one.

But perhaps her fortune was improving. She spotted the princess straightaway—although she was keeping questionable company. Indeed, as Charity watched, the princess raised a hand to her lips and tittered at some joke the man told. Nearby, a cluster of eavesdropping debutantes blushed in embarrassment. She sped her pace toward the fountain where Princess Charlotte stood with a glass in hand, and Charity peered suspiciously at the princess' companion as she approached.

Lord Ravenscroft.

"Did you lose your grip on the leash of your charge, Your Grace?" he asked indolently. "I found her wandering alone near the Prince and thought someone reputable had better mind her until you caught up."

Charity's jaw dropped at his audacity, but the princess let out a small giggle, not offended by Ravenscroft's suggestion that she was being paraded like a pet dog, and she quickly closed her mouth.

She knew *of* Lord Ravenscroft, and had been introduced to him briefly at some other event, but she always avoided speaking directly with him. He was Prinny's creature, and he had a reputation for being a rather shocking philanderer among women old and young despite his age. Apparently his charm and rugged good looks helped ladies overlook his... less sterling qualities.

"You thought that reputable person would be *you*, Lord

Ravenscroft?" Charity said politely, but her stiff lips made it clear what she thought.

"Lord Ravenscroft? Harm me? Don't be absurd, Your Grace," the princess said with a breezy wave of her hand. "I see him regularly at Carlton House—Papa practically worships the ground he walks on. He is more of an uncle to me than most of my actual relations, and at least he does not lecture."

"—Never unescorted," he interrupted quickly. "Lest Your Grace thinks she must find a sharp object here and do me in with it to safeguard your honour."

As Lord Ravenscroft gave Charity a wolfish smile, she wondered if the Queen and the princess's mother were aware that the princess was so fond of her 'uncle' Lord Ravenscroft. She somehow doubted they were. He did not move away now that Charity was here.

He was a little snoop, but that should not surprise her. She knew he was a favourite of the Regent—he had been in the thick of a murder investigation at Brighton last summer—and Grace had mentioned the Prince Regent called Lord Ravenscroft his magpie. Magpies were a nuisance bird that had a tendency to snatch things that did not belong to them.

Like rich gossip.

Charity decided to ignore him. "My apologies for having stepped away, Your Highness."

"There is nothing to forgive," she said with a sunny smile. "You looked quite vexed about something, so I naturally assumed you were off to settle it. I have been a model of good behaviour in your absence. You may even ask Lord Ravenscroft—he will vouch for me."

"Well, absent I am no longer. I do appreciate your willingness, but I do not want to detain you any longer, my lord. You must have others with whom you need to converse."

"None nearly so beautiful," he replied without hesitation, his voice smooth and practiced. "And none half as intriguing as the princess's lady-in-waiting. You are quite the winsome enigma, if I may say so. Come, Your Grace, Your Highness—allow me the honour of escorting you wherever your hearts desire. Perhaps along the way, I might even earn a fraction of your good opinion."

"May he stay with us, Your Grace?" the princess asked. "He is very good company."

What a horrifying thought. But it was true that there was nothing covetous or sly about Lord Ravenscroft's behaviour towards the princess. Indeed, his posture was actually quite protective.

"I will allow it—if you promise we can finally do our duty to the prince," Charity said. If she denied him, he would likely remain in earshot anyway. But perhaps he could serve as leverage.

"You do not want your grandmama to be angry with the Duchess Atholl, do you?" he added in a whisper, making the princess smile again.

"No, of course not," she replied smoothly, though the mischievous spark in her eye dimmed as she slipped back into the role of poised duty. "You are right—I have delayed long enough. But I would be far more inclined to go if you both accompanied me. A little amusement makes any obligation infinitely more bearable."

"He is a bit dull," Ravenscroft agreed, earning the princess's loyalty. "He is young, though. Virile, I imagine, which is just what an heir requires."

The princess gave the smallest of shudders. "That is what Grandmama says, too. That he will be able to perform well and often, and provide the throne with a bounty of heirs. The whole idea of the task just fills me with… nerves."

"It is rather hard to get to know someone when you have so many chaperones standing about," Charity acknowledged, and Lord Ravenscroft made a sound of agreement before he offered both women an arm. While Charity weighed the risk of saying no, the princess accepted it.

"Come along, Your Grace," Ravenscroft urged Charity, and finally, she took it also.

The trio set off at a meandering pace, slowly passing the other party attendees. Charity took note of which guests smiled at the princess and which ones instead focused on frowning at her and Ravenscroft.

"I am sure Prince William is kind," Charity said, adding, "which you may easily discover should you spend more time speaking with him."

"Kindness is a pleasant trait, but so is a man's visage—or so I have it on authority from the women I have gotten to know," Lord Ravenscroft said conspiratorially. "I say he is… well, he is not too terrible to look at. But that is my opinion as a man, so yours may differ."

Charity cut Ravenscroft a minatory look, but said nothing when the corners of the princess's mouth obligingly turned up again. It was true, the Prince of Orange *was* hardly a man to inspire love poems. He was awkward, tall and slender, his hair a drab mix of blond and brown.

"No, you are right. He is not terrible to look at," she agreed.

"He would not be considered handsome though, would he? Not like a certain *Lord Fitzroy*."

Charity's fingers tightened, digging into Lord Ravenscroft's arm. But the man gave her a devilish look and pointed with his chin at the fair hair and back of the lord in question. He was now speaking with Viscount Sidmouth and a few peers a stone's throw away from the Dutch group. Fortunately, the men were engrossed in some conference and didn't turn around.

The princess let out a brief titter as her gaze landed on him. "He does wear that superfine coat exceedingly well, does he not? What do you think, Your Grace? I could not help noticing you watching him earlier. Such a shame there is not a drop of royal blood in his veins—it would make him quite perfect."

Blanching at the thought, Charity was too horrified to find the words to express how wildly out of the question that was.

"Not a drop of royal blood, fortunately. Alas, that man is not for you, sweet princess," Ravenscroft said drolly. "And you should do well to stay away. Of all the names *I* have earned, fairly or not, 'son of a traitor' has not been one of them."

"As if that is the worst of it. He would toy with your emotions, stripping you of every ounce of value before tossing you aside," Charity muttered. "The prettiest of creatures are often the most vicious, and you should be wary of him."

Lord Ravenscroft's pace faltered as both he and the princess turned their heads her way. Drat. She said that out loud.

"Oh la," the princess flicked her hand with nonchalance, brushing aside Charity's denunciation of Lord Fitzroy. "I am to be the queen of two lands, with two armies at my beck and call. What need have I for protections when the world itself must bow before me?"

They swept by the straggling line of people idly waiting to make the acquaintance of the prince. "You will have no armies at all if you do not heed your father's wishes and marry the man," Charity countered in a murmur. Then she and Ravenscroft hung back, allowing the princess to close the distance.

Prince William of Orange spotted his bride-to-be approaching and concluded his discussions. He smiled honestly at the princess, but his hands were smoothing his lapel in nervous gestures.

"Good afternoon, Your Highness," Charity could hear him say crisply. His English was flawless, though it held a faint hint of a foreign accent in his soft consonants. He bowed, the princess curtseyed, and Charity and Ravenscroft pretended they were ornaments on the lawn.

Princess Charlotte returned the prince's smile, but it fell

quickly from her face as they straightened and then regarded one another in awkward silence.

Charity bit back the urge to save them. Not only would it be inappropriate, it would also do them no good. Every meeting they had so far had gone the same. With the formal engagement announcement looming, Princess Charlotte and Prince William of Orange had to tear down the wall between them with their own hands.

The prince's throat bobbed as he swallowed nervously. "You look lovely, Your Highness."

The princess responded with the requisite demure tilt of the head and responded with something equally safe. The discussion, if it could even be described as such, carried on in fits and starts.

"Perhaps they need a bit of the old Dutch courage," muttered Lord Ravenscroft, unable to bear the awkwardness any longer. "Would you care for a drink, Your Grace?" he asked Charity, but his voice was pitched to carry to the stilted couple.

Charity demurred, and Lord Ravenscroft, seeing the Prince Regent passing nearby, murmured his excuses to leave. But the important task had been done. Prince William, having heard Ravenscroft's suggestion for a drink, signaled one of the footmen who had been assigned to care for the delegation. The footman retrieved an etched crystal decanter with a faintly golden liquid inside.

Removing the crystal stopper, the English footman made a presentation of pouring the liquid into two tulip-shaped glasses, offering them to the prince and princess, before he returned the decanter to the refreshment table.

"This, Your Highness, is Dutch jenever, the pride of my homeland. It is something similar to your gin. Jenever is a symbol of our tradition and resilience—a drink shared in both triumph and alliance," he explained formally. "It is my favourite drink and I hope you, too, will come to appreciate it. May it serve as a token of the strength I hope our future union will embody. To our future, Your Highness."

They both sipped. After a few more words, the prince took a longer drink. "Would Your Grace care to try?" he asked, lifting his voice to include Charity.

She did not, but it was not polite to refuse a prince's offer. "Of course, I would be honoured to be offered a chance to sample a gift of your homeland, Your Highness."

The prince finished his glass, and signaled the footman to return once more. The fluted glass brought the smells of grain and juniper to her nose, and she brought the glass to her lips, pretending to drink with the prince and princess.

After a few more words, they were free to mingle elsewhere. Charity discreetly deposited her still-full glass on a nearby table. These days, she seldom indulged in spirits of any kind.

Princess Charlotte's glass was also still nearly full. She took another small sip from her glass, and then glanced at Charity, pulling a face. "Is it supposed to taste like this?" she whispered.

Charity took the princess's proffered glass and drew in one sip, then another to get the taste. The drink was both warm and malty, somewhat reminiscent of whisky, but with a faint astringent undertone. "I have never tried it before," Charity confessed. "It is not much like English gin, is it?"

"I do not think I care for it any more than I like normal gin," the princess whispered.

"Set down your glass," Charity suggested. "I can get you some wine."

The princess waved her off and began to gossip with one of the Dutch women, and after perhaps twenty minutes, they amiably parted ways with the prince's delegation, the princess heading back towards more familiar churning waters. She marched on ahead, looking for another one of her aunts, leaving Charity to walk behind, beside Ravenscroft who rejoined them.

"Prinny thinks this is the best match, but were you listening? The Dutch seem just as unconvinced as the princess—not to mention the rest of the *ton*."

"I imagine they are no happier to imagine that their prince would abandon Holland than ours are to imagine the princess abandoning England," Charity said softly. "At least they lack the concern that the prince might rule England in her stead."

"Your Grace," Princess Charlotte called to get Charity's attention. "All this time in the sun is positively draining. Will you accompany me inside?"

Charity opened her lips to answer and found her mouth dry as a bone. She coughed to loosen her tongue. "It has been particularly bright today. I will see you to your room and send someone to let your father and grandmother know where you have gone."

"I will take care of that," Ravenscroft assured Charity, but then he peered closer. "Are you feeling well, Your Grace? Your cheeks are flushed. Both of you."

"Yes, I feel fine, but I am a bit hot. Too much sun is all," she assured him, and Ravenscroft nodded, departing.

"Too much sun, I agree. I feel a little lightheaded," the princess admitted. "I think I will lay down for a while and rest."

"A good plan. We are not far from your rooms," Charity nodded. She, too, felt weary, and her eyes felt blurred with fatigue. Just as they reached the upper level, she was forced to reach out a hand to steady herself against the wall. The world tilted slightly, as though she were spinning on the dance floor.

"Duchess? Charity?" The young princess's words brought Charity back to the present.

"I—" Charity tugged at her neckline and dragged in a breath. Another and she remembered where she was. Carlton House, with the princess staring at her. Charity shook her head and the world shifted back into place. "Sorry, for a moment I felt dizzy."

The princess moved closer, looking up at Charity with her wide blue eyes, her pupils large in concern. "I hope you are not ill. Or did you overimbibe?"

"Of course not. I drank only lemonade," Charity assured her automatically. But then she stopped, frowning, as the hazy disarray of the last half hour coalesced into a familiar sense of helpless, muddled fear.

She had drunk only lemonade, except—

The memory of blond hair, standing so near the prince's delegation flashed again in her mind. She had felt this way once before—and the next morning, she had awoken to find herself being held by strangers.

4

As he returned to the party, Peregrine shook off his anger quickly, but some unease remained. He was used to trusting his instincts, and those instincts insisted the duchess was going to cause him trouble.

He could deal with her later. For now, there were appointments to keep. He took care to keep his steps an indolent saunter.

His meeting with Charity had been so brief, gossip rags could speculate on no more than the remotest possibility of a stolen kiss between him and Duchess Atholl. If they did so, he did not care. Baseless speculation was all they would have.

Peregrine might be something of a flirt, but he had no standing reputation as a libertine. Not only because he had been away for nearly a year, but even before he had gone to war, it had been a while since he kept a formal mistress. In the interim, he had seldom indulged in liaisons. And when he did, they were with women who controlled their servants with an iron fist, and thus could manage their affairs nearly as discreetly as the dead.

In fact, the last such woman was prowling across the lawn in his general direction. Selina.

Sina was rumoured to be something of a merry widow, but if she kept a string of suitors, no one knew who they were. Many of the rumours of her promiscuity could be dismissed as petty jealousy and her outrageous flirting. Sina did nothing to quell these rumours, for they served as a useful distraction from what she was really about. Though she was thirty now, she was still a lush beauty, curvy at the top and hips, and with glossy raven locks and piercing green eyes.

Once, he had optimistically thought they might suit, but she had dashed his hopes for something more quite early on. She was the daughter of a duke, and would have never consented to marry a mere earl. But she would dally with one, particularly if he was young and handsome. So Sina had been something of a friend, a lover, and occasionally a useful ally, but she was dangerous in every capacity.

Should he forget that last, he had the reminder from a year before, when her servants had rushed into the bedroom to let her know the Royal Army was on the move, hunting all the members of the Fitzroy family. The marchioness had kicked him from her bed and into the street without a moment of hesitation.

Others might hold a grudge about that sort of thing. Fitzroy let it pass, understanding why she had done so. Machiavelli wasn't the only one who believed that loyalty should only last as long as pragmatism allowed.

But he wasn't about to forget it.

"Why, Lord Fitzroy!" she greeted him, as though they had run into each other by coincidence, when he knew it was nothing of the sort. Sina would have been watching for the duchess's exit, and timed her arrival accordingly. "I have seen you conversing with quite a number of people. Are you having a pleasant time?"

"Most pleasant, Marchioness Normanby," he agreed, allowing a small smile to creep into his face. "Did I not see you earlier with the Regent's mistress?"

Selina's lips curled, and she wrapped her kid-gloved fingers around Peregrine's arm just below the elbow. Obligingly, he crooked his arm as if they were just another chatting pair of old friends, catching up. "You did. Let us take a turn and you can tell me about your clandestine meeting with the Duchess Atholl."

He leaned over, patting her hand. "If I didn't know you as well as I do," he said in an undertone, his lips as near the shell of her ear as he could make it without seeming flirtatious, "I might almost think you were jealous."

"Jealous? *Never*. But I do confess I am perishing of curiosity," the marchioness admitted with a fleeting, sly grin. "Was she not the girl who the new Duke of Northumberland went on a knight's quest to prove himself for?"

"Do you actually expect me to pretend that you do not already know the answer? How boring, Sina. I already thought this party could not possibly be any duller."

"There is still time yet." But Selina let the topic drop, and they chatted about gossip and inconsequential matters for several minutes, ambling through the party at an interminable pace in the general direction of the area where the Dutch stood, along with the many English lords and ladies waiting to exchange words with the man who might be England's leader one day.

When he angled his steps towards the group, Selina tugged his arm.

"Oh! Let us give our regards to Viscount Sidmouth," she said, veering off their path to greet the Prince Regent's Home Secretary.

As if he needed a reminder of what he owed her. Though Sina had abandoned him on that terrible day last year, she had arguably made it up to him by keeping him out of the ignominy of a trial—and his neck from the noose—once it became clear that his mother had escaped.

She had a certain pull with members of the Home Office, and that had come at a price. Sina's discreet favours were expensive, but carrying one debt was a bit better than being dead.

Viscount Sidmouth had been hobnobbing with the foreign secretary, Lord Castlereagh, and Earl Grey, who looked irritated at the interruption. But all three men bowed over the marchioness' hand and nodded their greetings to Fitzroy.

"There is nothing to be done for it," Castlereagh said to the earl, as both men departed the cluster. "The Bourbon monarchy will be restored."

"Grey is… most vocal about Ponsonby's uselessness and the Regent's choice to return France to authoritarianism," Sidmouth explained, his voice dry. "But here, let us talk about more cheerful things. I would not wish to trouble the lady with such drab political talk."

"My dear Viscount Sidmouth," Selina said smoothly, "how can talk of the future of our neighbouring countries be anything but exciting? Peace in France will bring so many opportunities back to us, it hardly matters whether the Bourbon monarchy or someone else ushers it in."

"Truly said, Marchioness. The war has been an unpleasant business for everyone. I suppose you would know that firsthand, Lord Fitzroy, being so newly back from the peninsula? And you were with Wellington, I hear."

"Not Wellington so much as his lieutenant general, Rowland Hill. I was glad to see he has been promoted. Hill was a good commander, and very good to his men," Peregrine said.

"And you survived the Nive," Sidmouth added, giving

Peregrine an assessing look. "I assumed your chances of survival were slim at best when we sent you out, but it seems that God—or luck—decided to let you remain among the living."

Peregrine let his eyelashes fall briefly in respect for the many dead of that battle, deflecting the worst of Sidmouth's savage query. "Both, it would seem. A lot of good men fell under Soult's counterattacks."

Sidmouth made a small noise of agreement. "England weeps. But it seems that you made a mark. I know you were with Hill; he speaks rather fondly of you and your… level head. You appear to be better suited to the task of war than many gentlemen."

"Yes." Peregrine gave Sidmouth a bland smile, careful that no irritation or unpleasantness leaked into it. The Home Secretary, clearly still suspicious of him, was practically dancing around what he really wanted to know: how Peregrine fared following the bloody offensive that shattered many nerves. "I am proud to have been useful to my king and such able commanders."

Likely, Sidmouth hoped he would go to war and find a grave there. There was proof enough he was at least hoping for Peregrine to find a little suffering.

Even if he had, it would be a cold day in hell before Peregrine confessed his private thoughts to anyone. And even if snow fell in those fiery pits, he would sooner call Hill 'daddy' than show any signs of wounds, real or in his head. Wounds were advertisements of weakness. Invitations to strike.

"My lovely marchioness," Peregrine said as he turned to Sina, "since we are so close, shall we give our greetings to the Dutch prince?"

"That would be lovely. Would you introduce me? I have not yet had a chance," Selina said, giving Sidmouth a wide smile of farewell. "Thank you for your time, Viscount."

"Was that really necessary?" Peregrine asked her mildly once they were out of earshot. "I do not need to be reminded of what I need to do."

"It was, my sweet. I know you are a man of integrity. But you are not the only person here who needs their memory prodded regarding matters."

"I shall not ask with whom else you are playing your games, Sina."

"Good," she said cheerfully, fluttering her lashes as she turned her face to look up at him. "Because I will not tell you. Not unless you wish to become one of us. I rather wish you would. We could accomplish so much together."

"Someday, perhaps." Peregrine smiled back at her, not giving any hint of the hard, cold rock in his stomach at the thought. "For now, promise me that the prince will fare no lasting ill."

Selina held his gaze, unblinking, so that he could see she answered honestly. "He will be fine." Taking up her fan, she flicked it open, wafting air at her neck.

He glanced at it, seeing the tiny ornamental vials dangling from the handle. They were so small, they were hardly more than beads.

"He will feel wretched, of course," Selina added in an undertone. "But otherwise it will be harmless to him."

"It is the one we agreed upon, yes?" Peregrine pressed her. "Sina, I am deadly serious. I will turn and leave right at this moment if you are planning more, and if this falls upon my head, I will make sure you pay for the treachery with my dying breath."

"As we agreed. I would happily swear it upon my life, Perry. It is croton, and he will live."

She continued to hold his eyes, no tension in her posture whatsoever, and Peregrine relaxed, believing her. Like most of the others here, Sina knew that predators abided by one another because they maintained certain codes of conduct.

She would never tell a straight lie. Which meant the Prince of

Orange's life wasn't in any real danger—though the same could not be said about his dignity.

Prince William of Orange was about to be poisoned, by Sina's hand, and Peregrine was abetting it.

A favour to be repaid later. That had been part of the terms of the deal for helping influence Sidmouth into sending Peregrine to war. She was calling due now. Unlucky timing for him, to remind her of his existence at the very moment she was looking for assistance in such a perilous task.

Because his mother hadn't raised him to be a fool, Peregrine had set terms of his own. The first had been that this would call their debt quits, since a life risked must certainly be worth a life saved. Second, she must do the deed herself, though he would assist by introducing her and then playing the decoy.

The third term had been the choice of poison. His infernal, backstabbing mother had also taught him a thing or two about that.

He had chosen croton oil, and Sina had agreed. It would suit her purposes admirably by causing the prince to purge himself in an embarrassing fashion.

For his part, Peregrine had chosen it because it was fast, easy to dose, somewhat safe, and easy to conceal, unlike many alternatives. Assuming she did not make a hash of the deed—and Selina's involvement would ensure that she wouldn't—the odds of the prince's vomiting being attributed to poison instead of overindulgence were small. Particularly given his reputation.

And if it was somehow suspected… There would be reasons to look inward for the perpetrator of such a crime. Croton oil was a purgative in many Dutch apothecaries' arsenals, and the prince's physician was not exactly a proponent of their recently-freed vassal nation becoming immediately beholden to England.

Peregrine would take any and all steps to ensure suspicion fell upon the man, if the worst should happen. He did not wish to have gone to war to end up in a noose anyway.

"I hope you understand why I ask," he said softly.

Selina patted his arm, not taking offence to his doubts. Had their roles been reversed, she would be just as distrustful. "I know full well what would happen were I to cross you, particularly in such a stupid way."

They had idled through this party, waiting for the prince to drink in earnest, as he had been wont to do at previous social events, and to judge by the sound of it, he was well on his way. The prince's voice was slurring the slightest amount and had increased in volume.

A throng of people waited nearby to make his acquaintance, waiting politely as the prince animatedly continued his colloque about horse breeding with whatever unfortunate gentleman was facing him. The fact that he could hear every word made Peregrine wonder if the prince's fortitude would sustain him through his drink until they could approach.

"Do you suppose he might cast up his accounts on Sir Wembly's boots?" Selina said, just loud enough that the gentleman waiting ahead of them snickered.

Peregrine did too. "I reckon the Duke of Northumberland would make a wager of it, and he would not need to drink an entire bottle to do so. Let us hope the prince does. It will thin the herd."

As it happened, the procession waiting to greet the prince moved along relatively quickly. Perhaps his well-wishers were being prudent about saving their hearing. But as they drew nearer, an itch began to form at the back of his brain. The prince's colour, which had been unremarkable when they began waiting, was now high.

Something was already wrong with the prince.

Before he could even begin to guess at what his unconscious

mind had already tallied, a memory sprang to mind, and in it was the golden-haired woman who had been a thorn in his backside this afternoon.

In his memory, her cheeks were flushed, and she was fairly glowing with warmth, her hand hot in his. She smiled politely, but her eyes did not focus well. The pupils of her gentian eyes were huge, the colour lost within the darkness. She wobbled. Stumbled and bumped into Lady Grace, forcing him to catch her before she fell to the dance floor.

The Duchess Atholl had rather explicitly thrown in his face the fact that she had been poisoned at his party. Right before she had informed him she would see him destroyed. And before the Prince of Orange began to exhibit many of the same symptoms as one also poisoned by henbane—as she had been.

Swiftly, he turned, tugging on the arm Selina held, pasting a bland smile upon his face. "Marchioness, we may come back to greet the prince in a moment. I see someone else I would like you to meet first. Will you come?"

"But of course," Selina murmured, hiding her confusion well. She held her tongue while they navigated away from the Dutch contingent and had a brief, meaningless conversation with Lord and Lady Braithwaite that lasted less than a minute.

Finally, they were standing in a place outside of easy eavesdropping, but he still left his words vague. "I believe someone has beaten us to the task."

She avoided looking back in the prince's direction, but the marchioness's eyes widened significantly, and then narrowed in hard thought. "I understand your meaning. Are you certain?"

"Do you doubt me in such a matter?"

Selina scrutinised his face again and then shrugged her shoulders. "Very well. I do appreciate you offering to introduce me to the prince, Lord Fitzroy, but I find all of a sudden I am quite exhausted. Perhaps I shall go home to rest. I can meet him another day. Will you call upon me next week?"

Without letting his cheerful expression slip, Lord Fitzroy gallantly bowed to her. "Of course. Your company was a pleasure nonetheless, Marchioness Normanby."

Selina glided towards the exit, making her departure. Leaving him there so she would not be a suspect in any fallout, should it come. And as he let his eyes wander over the assembly, he couldn't help but notice that the duchess herself was nowhere to be seen.

Gone. She had been in the company of the prince not a half an hour ago, some twenty minutes *after she had threatened to ruin him.*

That was the sort of timing that hardly seemed like an accident.

Rage at her perfidy spilled into his veins like burning vitriol. Slowly breathing through his nose, he shoved the emotions back, walling them off to be dealt with later. It took all of his concentration to keep his face from showing anything more than a pleasant, neutral expression while he wrestled with his urge to hunt her down and deal with her at this very moment.

Harming any one of the gentry would be a grave offence, but a foreign prince? That was treason. The sheer audacity of it was stunning.

There was no choice for it. Peregrine had to wait out this interminable party. Should the worst transpire, staying at the scene of the crime might be enough to serve as his alibi. It would also help if he stayed within observation distance of unimpeachable peers like General Hill. Or even the Home Secretary.

The diamond hadn't simply fired a warning shot across his bow. She was engaging in guerrilla warfare.

Unfortunately for her, Peregrine was far more experienced on almost every battlefront she might choose to employ. And now, he had sufficient time and motivation to consider the next move.

5

"I hope all that brings you joy turns to ash within your hands."
– Lady Fitzroy, to Lady Charity

Inside Carlton House, Charity's breath quickened, shallow and uneven, as a cold knot of unease coiled in her stomach. She clenched her hands tightly, trying to still the tremor in her hands. The jenever had been the only drink Charity had touched besides lemonade, and she had not been the only one to drink it.

The princess had, too.

"Your Highness, are you absolutely sure you are feeling all right?" Charity asked, trying to remain calm.

The princess frowned at her. "I—I think so. I only have a bit of a headache and I would like to lie down."

If the bottle or glasses had indeed been drugged, all Charity could do was be thankful the girl had stopped after a few sips rather than following the lead of her future husband and drinking more.

She pulled herself together as best as she could. "Do you have a pitcher of water?"

Princess Charlotte nodded her head and pointed to a side table near the settee. Charity poured them each a tall glass, sipped hers first to make sure it was clean, and then handed the other to the princess. "Drink all of this and then go lie down. I will ring for your maid so she can loosen your stays."

"But I am not thirsty…"

"Your Highness, please, do as I ask. If you are unwell from the heat, the water will help you recover faster." Charity pulled the bell to ring for the lady's maid and then urged the young woman to take a few more sips. All the while, she did the same, going so far as to refill her glass a second time.

The maid arrived within moments, and only the faint dizziness kept Charity from dashing back down the stairwell, all thoughts of departing the event forgotten. But she only got as far as the next empty room when the black, crushing wave of dread overcame her.

Tingling sensations gnawed at her extremities, making her feel as if she was nearly floating, losing her grasp on her own body. Charity clutched the doorframe hard to ground herself, letting her nails bite into the wood, trying to breathe through the suffocating weight settling in her lungs.

In this state, she could not quite convince herself that she was not dying.

She had had fits like this before. Bouts of womanly hysterics, as her physician had contemptuously called it. He had recommended darkened rooms and laudanum, but Charity could not abide by the idea of dosing herself with laudanum any more than she could wine or spirits.

Compose yourself! Such displays are unbecoming of a lady and will do you no favours in the eyes of society.

Her mother's voice was harsh, but it helped her begin to sew herself together. Her mama was not wrong. Hysterics would prevent her from doing what she must. She had to stop the prince —or anyone else—from drinking more of his jenever.

She had to let someone else *know* it had been poisoned.

Take stock of yourself, she ordered her thoughts. *You can breathe if you slow your breaths. You can feel things if you calm your nerves. This feeling of calamity is all of your own making.*

And the feelings began to recede. She was still off balance, but the feeling seemed to be growing no worse. It would have to do. She had to get back to the fête.

But when she reached the terrace, she found she was too late. Lords and ladies crowded onto the stone expanse, making no attempts to hide what they were doing. Titters of gossip filled the air.

"—sick all down his waistcoat!"

"Prinny was right there! Nearly knocked him down when he tumbled over!"

"The man is a disgrace, I say! A disgrace! Not fit for our heir."

Men in their tall boots and top hats blocked her view. She shifted from side to side, searching for a gap in the crowd where she could pass. Duchess though she was, everyone was far too distracted by the spectacle to consider ceding her space.

"Let me pass," she said to the two men in front of her, but in the ruckus, they ignored her.

Strident calls from the far end of the crowd to make way finally forced the throng to move, clearing a small path to the doorway where Charity stood. It was then that she got her first view of the problem.

Prince William of Orange hung from the strong arms of two of his aides, barely upright. Thin yellowish stains of bile traced a trail down the front of his navy coat and across his fine leather boots.

"Step aside, man!" a guard called again to a leering lord more interested in viewing the spectacle than making way for the group to pass. A pained groan from the ailing prince proved more effective than the shouted orders. The gentleman all but leapt backwards to avoid being vomited upon, and many ladies turned away, their hands covering their mouths and eyes in horror as their own faces turned slightly green.

You are too late. Your weak constitution failed to prevent this tragedy.

Charity snarled inwardly and scooted sideways, turning in time to see the Dutch prince pass. His eyes gazed without seeing, the pupils wide. He stretched an arm her way and called for her to help, slurring incoherent words that were neither English nor Dutch, at least not from what Charity could tell.

Her heart longed to answer, but she forced her limbs to still and her face to remain impassive. There was nothing she could do for him except arouse even more attention.

Shouting that he had been poisoned was entirely out of the question. Worse, it could incite panic, particularly when she lacked any proof. And what could she possibly say? That she recognised the symptoms of his malady because she had once been a victim of it?

Still, sorrow tugged at her in the face of the man's obvious anxiety, but she firmed her backbone. Either he would recover with time… or he would not. Either way, there was naught she could do about it.

"Where are you taking me?" he asked, glancing around in confusion and belligerence. Then his knees gave out, and his aides hoisted him higher, carrying him over the threshold and away from prying eyes. The crowd closed ranks behind them, everyone staring until the group disappeared down a corridor.

Charity nearly leapt out of her slippers when someone took her hand and wrapped it around a warm elbow.

"Your Grace. Are you feeling better? You missed the most exciting display of talent for diplomacy," Lord Ravenscroft murmured beside her. "The Prince of Orange managed to empty this party even faster than he emptied his cups."

The crowd outside was rapidly dispersing, people practically planting their bootheels in each other's backs to share their first-hand view of the scandalous behaviour. By morning, there would not be a soul left in London who had not heard of how the Prince of Orange had gotten so foxed after meeting the princess he had to be carried back to his den.

"I am much improved," Charity said automatically as she turned to Lord Ravenscroft, taking a moment to assess herself. Some of the spinning feeling in her head was slowing. Her stomach felt sour, but it was certainly nowhere near as bad as the prince's.

"I should have looked before I asked. Darling, you look like you have been exhumed. Are you haunting me, or is this just your new aesthetic?"

"Never you mind," she said peevishly, and then she leaned in to Ravenscroft. "What exactly... are people saying has happened?"

He gave her an odd look. "Besides the fact that the Dutch prince's aides have the strongest backs in London? That if the Dutch cannot control their heir, getting the gentry to talk favourably of the wedding will be impossible? Or are you asking about the part where it is a terrible insult to the royal family, and so on and so forth?"

"No," Charity said, making a gesture of frustration with her free hand. "Rather something like perhaps he ate something that disagreed with him. Was anyone else ill?"

Lord Ravenscroft let his lashes fall, half-hooding his eyes. "They are saying that the Prince does not hold his jenever as well as his other countrymen, Your Grace. No one else has shown an inclination to redecorate the lawns. Whyever do you ask… my dear Duchess?"

Charity was tempted to brush Lord Ravenscroft off and go in search of the Queen or someone else of higher status. The Prince Regent was not exactly known for being a good judge of personal character, particularly if it involved a gambling hall. However, if the duchess found herself rich in other assets, she was dreadfully poor in trustworthy allies at a moment she was beginning to question her very wits.

She hesitated for a moment, warring in indecision over the best course of action.

"Walk with me?" she finally asked, disentangling herself and heading back indoors.

Lord Ravenscroft shook his head when Charity turned toward the door to a drawing room, instead guiding her to a smaller sitting room off another corridor. He closed the door behind them and twisted the key to lock it.

"There is no need for that," Charity called, already wondering if she had misjudged him.

"Of course I would thoroughly enjoy ruining you, Your Grace, but then everyone would think I am slumming it—and my reputation is already hanging by a thread."

Rather than be offended, Charity was nearly amused. "One would think I could make you more respectable, not less."

"That is exactly what I mean by ruining it," Lord Ravenscroft gave her another wolfish grin. "But never mind that. I demand you stop beating around the bush and explain *why* you are suddenly so curious about the state of other people's constitutions."

Charity wrung her hands again, and finally decided to be out with it. "I think someone drugged the prince."

Lord Ravenscroft did not laugh off Charity's bald statement, or even look amused. "That… is a very serious charge, Your Grace. Are you quite sure?"

"No," she whispered. "I am not certain at all. I cannot prove it, and I cannot be sure, but I believe that it was the jenever he served that might have been tainted."

The older man's eyes were piercing. "How is the princess? She drank it also."

"No worse off than I appear to be. She may have had one or two sips more."

"You drank it also?" Ravenscroft pushed close to where Charity stood, taking her face in his hands as he peered at her more closely. "Your eyes are still somewhat wide, but you are no longer flushed."

"Two sips," Charity confessed. "The princess did not like the taste and asked me if it was proper. I did not taste anything odd, but I was not familiar with the drink."

He let her go then, pacing the room with his hand to his mouth. "How very troubling. What were you going to do?"

"I—I am not certain. At the least, I was going to try to get the prince to stop drinking it. Then… I thought I might tell the Queen and Prince Regent."

"You were going to swing at shadows with an accusation that could see people imprisoned and executed?" Ravenscroft was aghast. "You saw nothing, can prove nothing more than you had a sip and felt a little unwell which could have been the result of any number of things.

"No one would dare poison a drink at a high society event, and the servants at this all belonged to the Prince Regent. They would not dare harm the princess. The prince himself was drinking like a fish. If you level accusations of poison, the first one on the chopping block would be the footman. You *do* realise this?"

She paled. Charity had given no consideration whatsoever to

the servants who might be entirely innocent in the scheme. Now she felt even more foolish about the idea.

When she said nothing, Ravenscroft sighed, running a hand back over his head. "Gracious. I am glad I cleaved to you when I did, before you could blame the prince's state on a harebrained notion like poison!"

"I am still certain it was poison," Charity grit out. "But… I take your point about who might suffer."

The wrong people, that would be for certain, rather than Lady Fitzroy's son, whom she still believed was involved somehow.

"Oh, well. If *you're* certain, then it must be so. Perhaps you would be willing to share with me *why* you are so certain?"

Flames burned in the pit of Charity's stomach at his scathing sarcasm, but he had a point. In order to convince Lord Ravenscroft to take her seriously, Charity was going to need to explain why. Did she dare trust him with the truth of her disappearance from the Fitzroy ball the year prior?

When faced with an attempt against two thrones, any risk to her reputation paled in comparison.

"The sip I took of the princess's drink left me feeling strange. You commented on our flushed cheeks; well, that was just the start. Before you say it was the sun, hear me out. This—this was not the first time I have been exposed to what I think may have been put in the prince's drink."

Lord Ravenscroft's eyebrows rose, but he did not seem to be inclined to argue with her. He waved a hand to encourage her to continue.

"At a ball last year during my debut, I was served a punch that had been laced with a tincture of henbane. It had… similar effects. My mouth was… dry. I was lightheaded. Red-faced. Confused." Charity squeezed one hand with the other, grinding her knuckles against one another so that the slight pain would keep her focused.

There was no sign of Ravenscroft's indolent smile as she told him all that Lady Fitzroy had done to her, from the drugged punch to the kidnapping and the final escape, with the help of her friends.

"This is why the Queen came up with the falsehood about sending Percy on a knight's quest. To save your reputation." Ravenscroft deduced. "And why he was engaged to you instead of that charming little moppet I met in Brighton."

"I owe them everything," Charity said simply.

"You are not the only one who does," Lord Ravenscroft volunteered unexpectedly. "I certainly owe him for my life, at least. Well then, Duchess, perhaps I might repay my debts in part by not being a thorn in your backside like I had half planned on being."

Charity gave him a sideways glance, and he grinned again. "Plaguing the Queen's ladies is one of my favourite sports. Surely you understand. All right. Tell me the facts as you know them, and we can come to a plan of action."

"The prince's drink had been decanted. It would have been easy to tamper with. It was also reserved for him and the princess, as he had brought it as a gift. And Lord Fitzroy was at the event— and near the prince."

"Ah, here we go. Even should the poisoning be credible, Lord Fitzroy's involvement is hardly the sort of thing one could take upon faith."

She resisted the urge to back down. "His mother had a guard murdered at a state affair for the Swedish Ambassador. And she stole directly from the Prince Regent. Her *son*—"

"—Has behaved impeccably today," the magpie interrupted. "I should know; I spent a great deal of time watching him. And I know you did as well, which is why I am reminding you now rather than telling you the truth."

"I am relieved I am not the only one here who questions the presence of Lord Fitzroy," she muttered under her breath.

"Many are watching him with suspicion. Some are no doubt betting on when he will show where his true loyalties lie. But to poison a visiting royal immediately upon his return? He might be daring, he might even be untrustworthy, but he doesn't strike me as the sort of man who is missing half his wits."

"Unless he has no intention of staying in London."

Lord Ravenscroft shook his dark hair. "Wishful thinking, Your Grace. Fitzroy is a war hero now. He had opportunities aplenty to make an escape during the Battle of the Nive, and if he wanted to quit England entirely, that was the time to do it."

Charity hated that the man was right. Everyone had assumed Lord Fitzroy would never return to London. It would be far easier to live a quiet life in the country, or on the continent, than to return to where his family's name had become synonymous with treason.

Lord Ravenscroft crossed the room and laid a gentle hand on her arm. "Look. I believe you were unwell, as was the princess. I will also grant that it is not impossible—nor even improbable, that someone did taint the man's drink. But you cannot start slinging stones without being sure you are not going to hit a friend. I have picked up twitters about his own delegation having some unhappy feelings about the marriage negotiations. An enemy could as easily be within the prince's house as without."

He began to pace again, thinking. "But then again, if the enemy is a Dutchman, we would know straight away. Subtlety is not exactly their strong suit."

"What do you think we should do?" she asked him.

Shifting his weight back and forth as he thought, Ravenscroft finally shook his head. "What is done is done. If he was poisoned, the prince is already feeling the effects. It is too late to stop him. So... now we have to wait. Either he will recover with no harm done, or he… will not, and other factors must be considered. I assume you were given such a common herb instead of something more noxious for a good reason?"

"Lady Fitzroy… told me to my face that I could not suffer if I were dead," Charity said flatly.

"Ah. So we can expect that the prince will likely recover. Assuming, of course, that you are right about the poisoning… and the substance. So there is no harm in waiting to see what transpires, to see if more information makes itself available." Ravenscroft returned to the closed door and twisted the key to unlock it. "Go home, Your Grace, and get some rest. Tomorrow will out the truth. Either the prince will be fine or he will be dead. If he is dead, you can take your thoughts to the Queen after she begins demanding answers to so many uncomfortable questions."

She nodded stiffly and left, saying no more. But a nagging feeling that Fitzroy must be connected to the poisoning lingered. He must be. Because if he wasn't, it meant Fitzroy had taken up residence in her thoughts for all the wrong reasons.

Either way, she thought she might pen a note to the Queen. Just to be safe after all.

6

By midnight, Peregrine was a crucible of half-molten fury. An afternoon and evening of cooling his heels had only tempered his will into steel.

He had waited and watched through the evening hours as the windows went dark in the duchess's house. The final few lights had been extinguished some half hour past, and now anticipation stoked the fire in his soul. He focused it with a purpose, letting it burn hot and clean through his frustration.

Peregrine had been stuck at that blasted garden party all afternoon, waiting on tenterhooks for the prince to fall gravely ill, perhaps to die. But the prince's poisoner had done their job with precision. William of Orange had embarrassed himself by vomiting and being carried off like a common drunk... and that was all.

The storm he had feared had never come. There was no

outcry. As he finally departed from Carlton House, he had been at the end of his tether, sticky with the commingled sweat of relief and worry.

It wasn't the first time he'd been a game piece in society's endless chessboard of schemes. Normally, though, he was the one making the moves. Being an unwitting pawn in someone else's game was rare—and unsettling. And worse still was playing a game where the rules weren't clear, a scenario he found utterly intolerable.

His thoughts ran in circles as he retallied the events of the day, but he came back to the same final deduction.

The fact that the prince did not fall ill enough to garner suspicion made it feel like a message intended for his eyes only. A warning that his life continued at someone's whim.

Only someone who knew the signs would be able to discern that the prince had been dosed. Fewer still would recognise the specific symptoms of the prince's particular toxin. Peregrine knew of only one person at the party who possessed the knowledge, means and motive to employ a stratagem simply to destroy his peace of mind.

And now he stood below that vengeful woman's balcony.

All he had to do was shuck his coat so that his ability to climb was not impeded, and he did so without hesitation. His decency was the penultimate concern on his mind. The last spot was reserved for the reputation of a woman with the brass balls to threaten *him* in such a manner.

No wonder the duchess had been staring at him with hate in her eyes. She had made her opening salvo in a plot for revenge and wanted to ensure he heard her message as clear as a bell, the little wretch.

The part that he despised the most was that she had succeeded in forcing him to question his own judgement.

How much of this had she orchestrated? Had she even gone so

far as to ensure he had received the invitation in the first place? Peregrine's hands briefly clenched into fists at his side before he threw himself upwards, clambering up the edifice.

The truth was like shifting sand beneath his feet. Everything he thought he knew since returning home was no longer reliable. He could depend on absolutely nothing—not his standing with other members of the *ton*, and certainly not their actions towards him. Perhaps even his hard-won redemption had been corrupted by her touch. A laugh to be had by the Queen and her family at his expense.

When Peregrine's mother had fled England, abandoning him to either survive or pay the price for her crimes, he had thought so naively that things couldn't possibly be any worse. But it seemed that anguish was only the merest fraction of what would lie ahead in his future.

Only sheer *need* to see this next deed through was keeping him from going stark, raving mad. He was going to break into *that woman's* room and let her know beyond any shadow of a doubt: If she wanted his attention, she had it. In spades.

If she thought she could hide behind the rules of genteel behaviour, attacking him and then retreating to the safety of her home where she believed he would not retaliate because he was a gentleman, she was about to be disabused of the notion. As he had warned her earlier, he would not be bound by any rule she did not follow herself. And for every slight she meted out against him, he would return it a thousandfold.

If she wanted him to question his own judgement and standing, he was going to take every bloody scrap of peace of mind she possessed. If she wanted him to feel insecure, he would show her how easily he could have her at his mercy.

Some of the most dangerous vipers of the *ton* that he knew were women. He would give no quarter to this chit simply because she was one of the fairer sex.

To ensure his peace, he would go to war.

Within a few short minutes, he found himself standing in the bedroom of the Duchess Atholl. The weather was unseasonably warm, and she had mostly thrown the covers off herself. They lay in a tangled bunch near mid-thigh, and what he could see of her night rail clung to her curves damply. Her blonde locks had been plaited into a simple braid that lay across her shoulder.

He had left the curtains parted to give him enough light to see, and moonlight flooded the room, giving him a clear view of his quarry. She slept like a babe, completely without remorse or trouble.

Entering a sleeping woman's bedroom like this, standing in partial dishabille while he watched her like a voyeur? It was almost enough to make him feel like a scoundrel. Almost. But that brief pang was smothered quickly by thick resentment.

He crept across the room and turned the brass key in her door to ensure that it was locked. Then he pocketed it. Time to cut straight to the final act of her little performance and see the finale.

His blood was up as he approached her bed. Small noises made by his booted feet were unavoidable, but she slept on, blithely unaware of his presence. She didn't even stir when he stealthily set one hand and knee on the edge of the four-posted canopy bed.

Spreading his weight to cause the least amount of disturbance, he hoisted himself off the floor, straddling her prone body. She stirred then, not truly conscious. He held his breath for a moment, and then with the swiftness of a cobra striking, he covered her mouth with his left palm to keep her from screaming.

Her eyes flew open in surprise, and the surge of savage elation pulsing through him was heady. But as she focused on the person above her, her lifted brows slammed together and she shouted something into the palm of his hand. The words were muffled, but he understood exactly what she meant to say.

"How *dare* I enter your room like this?" he murmured, his voice low and edged with mockery as his hand cupped her face, holding her gaze captive. "I *dare*, you gilded harpy. You and I, we need to continue our little chat. And if you thrash, scream, or call for your servants, know that I will tell them you invited me here. It will be your word against mine. Just imagine the scandal."

She was still, malice glittering in her eyes. Finally, he returned his left hand to the feathered mattress beside her ear, sweeping a loose strand of her blonde hair off of her face as he did so. Turning the tables on this canny little witch... it was edifying.

"No? You are not going to shout? What a pity. The thought of being asked to marry you to preserve your honour, all while knowing that you are utterly horrified by the predicament... well, it is the sort of irony I could savour for days."

That finally sparked her voice. "You—you... utter blackguard," she hissed, her words barely louder than a breath as she fought to summon something sharper. "Traitor's son!"

He let out a low snort, laced with bitter amusement. "Oh, come now, O Shining One. Is that the best you can do? I have long since claimed those words for myself. Will you punish me forever for things long past between us?"

"Your mother held a grudge against mine since before I was born. Why should I not carry this one until I can spit upon your grave?"

He wasn't surprised by her words. But he was disappointed by the fact she seemed to overlook the part her own family had to play in their feud.

"Fine. I really do not care if you want to despise me until kingdom come. But your discretion is sorely lacking. I have enough to contend with without being dragged into the messes you insist on making. Whatever this is—your plans, your manipulations—you need to leave me out of it. Stay away from me. Do you understand? Because if you keep pushing things, breaking into your bedroom for a little chat will be the least of what I do, hellion."

Her chin jerked up in defiance as she bared her teeth at him. "You think I cannot imagine what you are capable of? Only a Fitzroy would play games with people's lives."

He laughed almost silently in her face."You two-faced hypocrite. That's bloody rich from the title chaser who played half the *ton* on a merry chase last season, and who manipulated two men into an engagement—"

"That isn't at all what happened!"

Her voice had grown louder as the words spilled from her lips, and Peregrine tapped her soft lower lip gently with the very tip of his index finger to warn her to be quiet. "Whatever you believe happened does not matter. You do not have the *right* to toy with me and my life."

"I disagree," she said, her face growing ugly with hate. "You gave me the right when you watched as your mother tore my future to shreds, and you did nothing. You are as much a monster as your mother, and I will be repeating every word of this conversation to the Queen."

His pulse throbbed in his veins, and his chest tried to heave in shallow, controlled breaths as he froze, warring over his own wounded instincts. He let out a long hiss through his teeth.

It wasn't enough for her to devise a scheme to frighten or blackmail him. She was so consumed by her hatred that she planned to grind him to dust beneath her slippers. Where would this end? What lies would she tell to see that he suffered the ultimate price?

Peregrine briefly closed his eyes, and then he slid his hand into his pocket, withdrawing the intricately carved ivory-handled folding knife he had grown accustomed to carrying since last summer.

He sat back on his haunches, pinning her torso with his weight as he unfolded the blade. The duchess's eyes fluttered, and she let out a small whimper.

Hard as it was to believe, last June—just before he had been shipped to the front and after he had heard about her broken engagement—he had actually felt sorry for this woman. No matter what happened between their parents, she had been an innocent wronged, and while it was true that his mother had been responsible for her kidnapping and not him, he felt a share of guilt for it.

Last June they had both been licking their wounds, preparing to survive a world that would cast judgement on them for the offences of others, and the chance to explain had passed unacknowledged. Rather than send the letter he had begun to write to her, he had drowned his regrets in brandy instead.

He might have earned at least some small measure of forgiveness, and as unlikely as that was, he could not help but wonder if it would have prevented… all this.

Peregrine doubted it. Trust was required for forgiveness, so some things were impossible to forgive.

Casually, he flipped the knife in his hand. And as she stared up at him, white faced, he reached for her right hand, pressing the handle into her limp, unresisting palm, wrapping her fingers around it.

A hard crease formed between her brows, and she blinked at him. "What—what are you doing?"

"Since you are out for blood, let us be done with it. I am giving you my knife, my lovely little luminary. Go on. Stick me with it."

She let out a small, disbelieving laugh. "What madness is this? You broke into my home so you could give me your knife and tell me to *stab* you?"

If he believed the duchess had a prayer of killing him, he would not have put a weapon in her hand. But he wanted to make her afraid to even try. He had to put an end to their open animosity.

"Why not? You believe me to be a monster."

"I do not know what your game is, Fitzroy," she hissed, trying to pull her hand away, "but I will play no part in this. Begone with you."

He held her firmly. "It is so much harder to take a life when you must do so with your own hand, is it not? My heart is here," he told her simply, taking her other hand and resting it over his chest.

She was a coward, prepared to let other people's hands do her dirty work.

"I will not allow you to use the Crown's hands to achieve your ambition. You wish me to die? You will need to drive the knife home yourself. Go ahead, *Duchess*. Do. It."

7

"You may discover that shared affection—or even a well-placed spark—makes certain intimacies far more enjoyable than you were led to believe."
— Lady Grace Percy, Duchess of Northumberland

Charity could feel his heartbeat beneath her palm. It was strong. Steady, if a trifle fast. Unlike her own, which was so erratic that she felt faint. It took her a moment to make sense of his words.

The rage and fear still lurked, but confusion was rising to the surface. The ivory handle of Lord Fitzroy's knife felt slippery in her hand, and she tried to drop it. His fingers tightened again, keeping the knife in her palm, his face lined with tension as he stared into her face.

"No, I will not let you put it down. You have said your piece, and now I am saying mine. This has nothing to do with the Queen —this is about you and me, and you have but two choices. Kill me, or leave me to my own devices."

"I despise you," she informed him, but even to her own ears, the words sounded trite. What she really wanted at this moment was for him and his mother to disappear from the face of the earth so she would never have to hear the name ever again.

"I know."

He thought he had her cornered. The expression on his face was one of grim satisfaction, and it roused Charity's temper enough that she wanted to scratch his eyes out.

"This will be the only time I offer you the chance. Take your courage into your own hands, or we set aside our public quarrel. But I shall not be forsworn, Shining One. If you decide to cross me later, there will be no place on this earth you can hide from my wrath. Not in London, not your own home."

Charity had no idea how he had secured an invitation to Prinny's event, but it must have caused him quite the consternation to find her there. Why else was he so ready to threaten her in her own home, if not to cow her into silence and make her ignore whatever his schemes were here in England?

She must somehow be a threat to his larger plans.

Sneering in his face, feigning more bravado she did not feel, she realised she had to get him to divulge more. "Some might call it a public service if I stuck you with your own blade."

"Too bad you appear to be too craven to earn the accolades. Shall we call it a draw?"

"There is no peace between us. I will not let you keep me silent," she warned him, and then she tried to throw him off balance, arching abruptly so she could get out from beneath him. But the villain was as heavy as a boulder, and he settled deeper, even though he was considerately not sitting on her with all his weight.

He inhaled a breath, leaning forward over her again. His expression would nearly be playful, if it weren't for the set lines at his mouth. "Why, Duchess… are you inviting me to play a different game?"

His weight on her stomach was—she gasped once, then again, trying to stay her panic. Finally she shoved him with the hand still resting on his chest. "You're—suffocating me, you ogre!"

Fitzroy immediately rolled them on both of their sides, the weight of his thigh pinning her legs beneath the tangled bedding. But this was worse somehow. More intimate. For now their faces were inches apart, and she could clearly see the devil dancing in his eyes. "Better, darling?"

Yes.

Charity froze as a new part of her psyche woke up in hot interest. *No!* she shouted at it in her thoughts in horror. In rage, she pulled the weapon from between them and sent it in an arc that would sink it into his exposed thigh.

But he caught her hand before she could complete the deed, halting the path of the blade. "The instructions were for you to kill me cleanly, not *maim* me."

"You do not deserve a clean death," she said, glaring into his face, and he lifted a brow indolently. "And anyway, you are too late to stop me."

The demon might try to look unconcerned, but Charity felt the pace of his heart pick up beneath her hand—God. Why was she still touching him? She tried to pull her hands away, and he let her.

When he asked the next question, she knew she had tipped the scales back in her favour. "What precisely am I too late for?"

"I already sent a letter to the Queen with all the details." She gave him a sweet smile.

His gaze flickered as he searched her face, probably looking for the telltales of a lie. "Did you? I think you are bluffing."

"Unfortunately for you, it is the truth. And Lord Ravenscroft also knows." That was still somewhat true, although Ravenscroft did not believe there was sufficient evidence to implicate Fitzroy.

But her words hit home. His smug, stupid handsome face grew uncertain, and Charity relished every moment of it.

"You took the Prince Regent's magpie into your confidence? And yet I do not appear to be locked in a tower."

With more nonchalance than she felt, Charity hurled his knife into a corner and simpered at him. "I did send her a note late, but did not mark it as urgent. If she did not read it last night, she will surely do so this morning. Don't worry. Once she reads what you did to Prince William, you will find yourself in the tower then."

Fitzroy flinched slightly as his dagger clattered to the floor, his eyes widening in surprise—and then something different passed over his face, so quickly Charity almost missed it.

Fear.

The tension was thick enough to choke on, and with neither of them drawing breath, Charity's manse was so silent she could hear the footfalls of a servant getting out of bed to investigate the noise. Briefly, she glanced at the ceiling before she flicked her eyes back toward Lord Fitzroy's face.

Whatever fleeting humanity she had seen in his expression was gone, replaced with flatness. "Strange. I never imagined the pretty debutante I met last year had such a streak of cruelty inside of her."

Pain thrummed along her nerves, inflicted by his words alone. How could anything this man said to her hurt this much?

"Perhaps that is because *then* I did not have it!" she shouted, forgetting the wandering servant. "Get out!"

Swiftly, he rolled away, off her bed and onto his feet. He stared at her a moment, and inclined his head mockingly.

Then he was gone—disappearing out her window.

Charity kicked her legs free from the bedcovers, which had somehow turned into a knot worthy of a sailor's pride. The guards must be alerted. Where would he go? Fitzroy might already be galloping for the coast—or, worse, toward Buckingham House. She cursed herself for mentioning that infernal note. What would the man do to stay at large? Truly, there was no telling.

By the time she reached the window, Fitzroy was nowhere to be seen, and furious pounding had begun in the hallway. "Your Grace!" The words were male, muffled by the thick wood. "Open the door!"

Only one step towards the door, she realised she was scandalously indecent. "Wait!" she called, "I am not dressed!"

She dashed into her dressing room. The first gown her hands encountered—a faded green affair, a relic from a previous wife, with a pattern that could charitably be described as "early cabbage"—was tugged on over her shift. Corsets were for occasions when one wasn't saving the monarchy from a tedious villain.

Finally, Charity strode back to the door, only to discover it resisted her as stubbornly as an obstinate mule. The knob turned, but the door refused to budge.

"What on earth—" She hadn't locked it. As she jiggled the knob again, she peered at the lock. The keyhole gaped at her like an empty, toothless mouth.

She was trapped.

Panic rose, swift and merciless. Her heart pounded like a child with a new drum. The walls pressed closer. She would die there. Alone. In cabbage green.

Get a hold of yourself, Charity. Her mother's voice scolded from the distant recesses of her mind. *At least die in a more flattering color.*

And then a man's voice, dark and smooth as cognac, pushed her mother's shrillness aside.

You are not trapped, you ninny, the smooth voice of Fitzroy drawled in her thoughts before terror could turn her brains to mush. *Call for the housekeeper's set of keys.*

"Mr Pritchard!" she shouted. "Fetch the other keys!"

His footsteps receded, and Charity began to pace back and forth, slowly dissolving into madness. Finally she dashed for the window, sucking in a breath, and shouted again. "Help!" she bellowed. "Someone help me! I am locked in my room, and the fate of England may depend on my immediate departure!"

A muffled voice called from below. "Your Grace?" A figure stumbled into view in the courtyard below, holding a lantern as if it were a particularly disagreeable cat.

Finally!

"I am locked in my room!" Charity called down. "Did you see which way he went?"

"Who?" the man shouted back, clearly at odds with consciousness.

"Never mind! Wake the house, fetch the spare key, and ready the carriage!" she ordered. The man saluted, nearly dropped the lantern, and vanished.

It took another five minutes, but finally footsteps thundered in the hallway, followed by a chorus of concerned voices. Charity abandoned the window to press her ear to the door.

"Stand aside!" bellowed Mr Pritchard, her unflappable butler, his voice cutting through the clamour. Keys jangled, and with a scrape as sweet as a Mozart concerto, the lock turned. Charity flung open the door to find half the household staring back at her.

The maids blinked, frilly caps askew, and the footmen gaped, their hair in various stages of dishevelment. Charity drew herself up.

"Someone broke into my room!" she announced.

All eyes shifted to the butler's key in the lock. Then back to her.

Her fists clenched. "He locked me in! Now move. I must get to Buckingham House."

Her dramatic declaration had all the effect of a feather duster against a hurricane. It was only when Mr Pritchard clapped his hands like a schoolmaster that the staff scattered. He bowed low and gestured for her to step through.

"If Your Grace would care to pen a note, I will have it dispatched at once. Perhaps you would like a drink while we await the constables?"

"I do not want a drink, Mr Pritchard!" Charity snapped, her composure fraying like an old hem. "Nor the constables. I know the identity of the intruder, and I must alert the Queen. This is a matter of state!"

"Er, of course, Your Grace. But might I suggest we first locate a pair of shoes?"

Charity glanced down and found, to her horror, her bare toes peeking from beneath her gown.

"Shoes," she muttered. "Yes. Fine. That would be lovely."

While her lady's maid laced her boots with record speed, Mr Pritchard returned, his expression grim. "There is an issue with the carriage, Your Grace. Thomas Driver is, alas, too deeply ensconced in his dreams to be of service. I do not believe it to be a natural sleep, I am afraid."

"Damn you, Fitzroy!" Charity cursed, startling the maid into dropping a bootlace. "Saddle my horse. I will ride myself."

"Very good, Your Grace," Mr Pritchard intoned with the air of a man who refused to be surprised by anything. At least, he wouldn't be surprised by anything anymore.

When she emerged from her room, she found the hallway blessedly clear of all but a single footman. He remained at attention when she walked past, standing rigidly with his eyes forward despite the cowlick in the middle of his hair.

The main staircase grew by lengths and bounds, giving plenty of time for the framed portraits of past dukes and duchesses to frown down upon her distasteful ensemble. She had read enough family diaries during her winter in Scotland to know that she was hardly the first member of the family to undertake questionable activities. She was, however, the first to do so with the intention of seeing the Queen of England.

Charity decided to take that as a mark in her favour.

As her boot heels clicked on the marble floors, still dressed in cabbage green and without a corset, Charity could not help but think that Fitzroy had better run fast. Because if they caught him, she might just kill him now after all.

When she arrived at the mews, she found both her horse and another saddled.

Mr Pritchard cleared his throat. "I took the liberty of asking Lewis to accompany you. He is the strongest footman in the house and has plenty of experience sitting a horse." He offered her a boost into her saddle and then waved for the footman to lead the way out.

Charity wasted no time. She kicked her heels against the horse's flank, urging it forward with the same crisp intonation her mother used when reprimanding tardy footmen. The horse launched into a gallop, nearly bowling over an unfortunate servant who dove for the safety of a hedge. Hooves thundered against the cobblestones, the clattering echo bouncing off the silent buildings as Charity hurtled into the night.

Her cloak betrayed her almost immediately, slipping from her head and flapping behind her. Strands of hair escaped her nightly braid, whipping into her eyes and mouth. She spat them out with a growl of frustration, tugging the reins to steer her mount down the correct street.

Behind her, Lewis proved moderately useful, his voice ringing out to clear their path. "Out of the way! Her Grace approaches!"

he bellowed at a cart that was inching along like a slug enjoying its twilight stroll.

The gates of Buckingham House loomed ahead, growing larger with every pounding stride of her horse. The stately residence glowed faintly in the moonlight, its imposing façade framed by the shadow of iron gates and lantern-bearing guards. The latter appeared unimpressed by Charity's midnight dash, their faces set in expressions of mild irritation, as though wondering what sort of nonsense this was at such an hour.

Charity reined in her horse, which skidded to a halt with the enthusiasm of a dancer executing a dramatic final pose. She slid from the saddle, her knees wobbling in protest. For a moment, it seemed they might betray her entirely, but sheer indignation forced her upright. Fury, it turned out, was an excellent substitute for muscle strength.

"Make way for Her Grace, the Duchess of Atholl!" Lewis shouted with such authority that even the guards hesitated. They moved to block her path anyway but didn't bother disguising their curiosity, their gazes sweeping over her windblown hair, askew cloak, and undoubtedly wild expression.

Charity fought the urge to yank her cloak over her head like an embarrassed child. A year ago, she'd stood in this exact spot under eerily similar circumstances. Twice now, a Fitzroy had sent her galloping to the Queen's doorstep in the dead of night, like some sort of nocturnal carrier pigeon.

Not this time. This time, she would see it through to the end. Fitzroy would be dragged to the gallows, kicking and screaming if need be, and she wouldn't leave until his fate was as firmly sealed as the wax on one of the Queen's letters.

With a sharp toss of her head, Charity straightened her spine and strode forward, cloak billowing behind her like the cape of an avenging heroine, to where the Queen's aide de camp stood waiting at the door. Like Mr Pritchard, he refrained from making a comment about her cabbage dress and wind-blown hair. After a half bow to acknowledge her position, he ushered her inside and led her to a sitting room where she could wait.

"I will let Her Majesty know you are here, Your Grace, and return with an answer as to whether she will see you." Before he departed, he nodded his head at something across the room.

Spinning around to follow the direction he had indicated, Charity found a framed mirror hanging on the wall. She made a vain attempt at putting herself to rights, sending a silent prayer to the heavens that the Queen would grant her a second midnight meeting.

She was still wrestling with the unruly strands of her blonde hair when the scrape of the door opening announced his return. She spun around, expecting to see the Queen's butler, but instead found the last person on Earth she wanted to see.

Peregrine Fitzroy leaned against the doorway, with not a stain of dirt marring his dark clothing nor a scratch on his shiny, black leather boots. Every hair was perfectly placed, his face radiating a suave confidence, as if he had never shown another expression to her earlier.

He let his eyes wander down her body, top to bottom and then back up again, and a trace of wicked amusement at her disheveled state lit his smile, causing him to show even white teeth.

"Well hello, Sparkles. Fancy meeting you here."

8

*"Power is the ultimate aphrodisiac, and its exercise is the
ultimate proof of freedom."*
— Marquis de Sade

P eregrine knew he had found the perfect sobriquet for the bane of his existence. The very instant it touched her ears, she looked as if she was ready to detonate.

She was humiliated beyond reason, and here he was with a ringside view of her undoing. The delicate, beautiful, icy meddler who had come here with a plan to throw him to the wolves was instead a complete and utter disaster.

Oh, yes. This agonised, thwarted moment was one Peregrine knew he would savour for a long time to come.

Sparkles. This was as satisfying as the most illicit pleasures— and far, far more entertaining.

"Guards!" she shouted, her hands making fists at her sides. Then she turned to the footman, as if she had already forgotten his presence. "Get the guards and let them know this man is here!"

The footman traded a wary look with Peregrine, who lifted one shoulder in casual dismissal. "Your Grace, er..." the man said politely, trying to act as if their situation were entirely normal. "The guards are already aware that Lord Fitzroy is here."

Peregrine couldn't help himself. He gave her a jaunty bow, grinning ear to ear, which only fueled her temper.

"The duchess is just a little out of sorts from her interrupted evening," Peregrine told the poor footman. "Would you get some tea to help settle her nerves?"

Knowing how the servants were, Peregrine suspected the footman was dying to leave anyway so he could tell everyone about the duchess's state. But the footman gave him a sideways look, as if he wasn't certain it was wise to leave the two of them alone.

"She need have no fear of harm from me," he reassured the servant. "Tea, if you would, good man. And leave the door open a crack. The duchess can shout out to whoever is in the hallway if she finds herself being mistreated."

The footman backed from the room, rushing to do his bidding and tell whoever else was awake what was afoot.

Her eyes widened, as if she suddenly intuited that she was about to be left alone. With him. "Wait—" But the footman didn't hear her.

The Duchess Atholl covered her face with both hands for a long moment, praying for patience perhaps. Or that she could melt into the floor. And as she stood there, her lips moving silently, Peregrine prowled closer, thoroughly enjoying himself.

This was the balm he needed to his soul after finding out she had already enacted her wretched plan to frame him for some form of villainy. At her home, he had hoped that by some miracle he could frighten her into a cessation of hostilities before becoming worse, and he had miscalculated. Badly.

Now, not only did he have to deal with the ignominy of that, he also bore measures of guilt in truth. He had broken into her home and not managed to keep her silent. Worse, she had forced him to harm someone in the escape. After fleeing her bedroom and dropping back down to the lawn, he was forced to contend with her carriage driver.

It was too terrible a risk to let the duchess get to the Queen first, giving the two of them time to take matters into their own hands. He needed to get his own horse in the race, proverbially speaking.

He had needed the Prince Regent. And fortunately, he knew just where to look for Prinny, who spent most of his late nights and early mornings at his latest den of iniquity.

So he had disabled her driver and set off to find His Highness, and both had then ridden here posthaste. A part of Peregrine was still darkly amused—and impressed—that she had managed to arrive before them. Clearly, she had abandoned a great deal of common sense to do so. Her hair was still half in the tangled ruin of a braid. Instead of hiring a hack, she must have ridden here without even bothering to dress properly—and on a horse herself, if the smell could be trusted.

When he circled behind her, the duchess dropped her hands and spun to glare at him. "Are you enjoying yourself?"

"Oh, immensely," he admitted, crossing his arms over his chest casually. "Your dress is very charming. I had no idea that vintage styles were making such a bold return. You are quite ahead of—or perhaps behind—the times."

The little vixen lifted both her hands as if to shove him again... or perhaps throttle him. He provoked her by taking one step closer, inviting her to forget his warnings, and she stepped back, her face falling into grimmer lines.

"One of the former Duchess Atholl's, I imagine?" he continued, trying to vex her. "Surely there was one in a more attractive colour. If my recollections are correct, I think you were the fourth wife? You should have had plenty to choose from."

He had anticipated a flash of anger, a biting retort to match his own. Instead, her expression betrayed the briefest expression of dull pain, her voice low but steady. "One would think so, Lord Fitzroy. And yet, it seems my choices are destined always to bend beneath the shadow of your family's influence. Would that I knew the full breadth of my family's sins. The endless litany for which I must pay again, and again, and again!"

"You and I both, Duchess," Peregrine said, letting a trace of sharpness stain his words.

She then turned her back on him with deliberate precision and made her way to the framed mirror. "By all means, continue mocking the first gown I could grab in my haste to ensure the Queen's safety. I am sure your wit requires a soft target to sharpen your claws upon after so long away from society."

"Safety. Oh for—spare me your melodrama!" Peregrine sneered, suddenly irritated beyond belief as he shifted his voice into a mocking falsetto. "'Oh, woe is me, I must pretend the throne is in danger of Lord Fitzroy's villainy so that my Queen believes my utter nonsense and I may ruin him to exact my revenge.' No one here is in mortal peril, your poor taste in clothes notwithstanding."

The duchess, who had been struggling to undo her snarled braid, stared at him as if he was barking mad, which put his back up even more. But she was saved from replying by the footman's return with a tea tray. And then he bowed low to the duchess. "Your Grace, I hope you do not think me impertinent, but I thought I might also assist by bringing you... a comb."

"Er, that is most helpful of you," she replied stiffly. "Is the Queen expected to arrive soon?"

The footman shook his head. "It may be a while yet. The Queen is in a conference with the Prince Regent, Your Grace."

"The Prince Regent is here? When did he arrive?"

"He came with Lord Fitzroy, Your Grace."

"I… see. We will wait upon their pleasure then. You may go."

Peregrine noted that the duchess looked intensely uncomfortable by that revelation, and his annoyance was abruptly diverted. Did she really expect that somehow she would keep the Prince Regent excluded from these accusations?

The duchess retrieved the comb and began to hack at the snarls of her hair, the swipes of the comb tinged with almost a determined desperation. It looked so bloody painful that even Peregrine couldn't help but give a sympathetic wince, and before he knew it, he strolled closer. As a lady of privilege, she had likely never even brushed her own hair before.

"It will help if you begin at the bottom," he suggested neutrally.

She met his eyes in the mirror, her voice… strange. "I hope you are not giving advice because you are waiting for me to play mother and pour the tea."

He turned to the pot, fully able to manage himself. "Of course not. I would simply rather not stand here and watch you rip out every strand of your hair. You would probably require me to console you afterwards. How do you take your tea, Sparkles?"

She did not rise to his bait beyond a grimace, and instead continued trying to restore order to the long, flowing mass of golden hair. Unfortunately for her, she would be at it long after the royals finally made their appearance. Unbound, her tresses probably fell to her waist. At least she took his advice, and detangling progressed.

"Milk and three lumps," she finally said.

Peregrine fixed her tea, his fingers lingering on the handle of a spoon. He could not pin down the reason for it, but something suddenly was… amiss.

Bringing her cup and saucer to her, he reviewed their biting exchange. This was practically the armistice between them that he had sought an hour ago, and this time she had given it freely. She had not even reacted to his casual prodding, and she was poorly concealing her state.

She was nervous. Uncertain. And suddenly Peregrine was very keen to know why. Forget a penny; he'd pay a pound sterling for her thoughts right now.

"Here," he said, offering her the cup. She helplessly darted a glance down at where her hair hung over her shoulder, holding it in a bunch with one hand and the comb with the other. "Take this and give me the comb."

"But—"

"Quickly now," he insisted, and she gave the wooden comb over without any further complaint.

Before he could think too much about it, he briskly took her hair in his hands, sweeping it back. God, he wasn't even wearing gloves right now. He was shattering every rule of propriety— again—but to hell with it. Decorum had already taken a holiday when he invaded her home.

"Do not read too much into this, all right?" he muttered, using the tip of the comb to deftly pull free the remainder of her braid.

She looked down, and then closed her eyes, surrendering to the necessity of having him help her. "I will not," she said softly, her voice laced with ironic disbelief. And then she took a long sip of the tea. "This is too impossible to take seriously anyway."

This was a terrible mistake in a thousand ways. The thick, heavy cord of her hair was smooth against the palm of his hand, its scent unmistakably hers. Not rosewater, nor some other artificial perfume. Something raw. Real. Salt and starlight mingled with the faint, inescapable essence of a woman.

"Impossible would indeed be a word for it," he agreed dryly, lowering his voice to the point where it could barely carry even to her ear. "Even my education fails to supply the words that would describe this spectacle. Here I am, tending to the hair of a woman who would commit an offence just to see me imprisoned."

Suddenly, she turned to face him, and he lost his grasp on her tresses.

"You think *I* was the one responsible for..." Her words trailed off, eyes open wide and shining with a new light of understanding, realisation becoming a stark fact.

Peregrine's spine turned to stone as he abruptly came to a conclusion that he didn't like in the slightest. With alacrity, he took her shoulders and spun her around again so that he could tie her tresses in a careless knot. At least her hair was no longer entirely a lumpy, disastrous mess.

Then he turned her back towards him, parting his lips to speak, though his wits lagged behind as his thoughts collided. Every assumption he'd made about what happened at the party fragmented and fell to pieces.

But before he could form words, the door standing ajar was thrust open.

Charity leapt backwards, bumping into a side table hard enough to send it rocking. On instinct, she grabbed onto the edge and righted it before it tumbled over. She chanced a look at Fitzroy to see what he had done, and found him doubled over in a deep bow in the direction of the Queen and Prince Regent.

Caught as she was, with a side table at her back and a silk-covered settee on her right, even Charity's mother would have struggled to execute a perfect curtsey. Still, she sank low, giving thanks for the wide skirt of the unfashionable gown that hid her trembling legs.

"Get up, the both of you!" The Queen's voice was at once a godsend and a curse, for it was clear she was not in a forgiving mood. "What is the meaning of this? Have we been summoned from our chambers only to witness the two of you pawing at one another like unsupervised children?"

Charity's mind went blank. For the first time, her mother's voice had nothing to offer. She averted her gaze, focusing on the vibrant red silk turban atop the woman's head, and the matching quilted silk robe on her shoulders. Out of the corner of her eye, she noticed the Queen frown deeper in disgust at Charity's cabbage-green gown.

After a moment, it was Fitzroy who spoke up. "No, Your Majesty. The late hour is my doing."

She had hesitated to speak too long, and now Lord Fitzroy tried to placate Queen Charlotte like a consummate politician, giving her a moment to regain her wits. An unexpectedly charitable act—though it could easily be self-preservation.

But a man acting solely in the interests of protecting himself would not have touched her hair.

For a moment there, when his strong hands had pulled the comb through her tresses with such careful strokes, shivers had run along her spine. No one had ever tended to her that way. In that moment of unexpected kindness, Charity had almost forgotten that she hated him.

Charity blinked, the haze of her thoughts abruptly clearing, only to find every pair of eyes in the room fixed squarely on her. Heat crept up her neck, but he had already thrown her a lifeline. "Yes, he is correct, Your Majesty, Your Highness, and I am as appalled as you—"

"Yes, we can see that." The Queen marched over and plucked a long, dark-gold hair from the front of Peregrine's black coat and held it aloft. "Is this yours, Your Grace? Or shall I conclude it belongs to one of the other blonde-haired young ladies present?"

"If it is, Your Majesty, I assure you it was entirely uninvited,"

Lord Fitzroy spoke up again. "Though I suppose even stray hairs are drawn to me—it is a curse, really."

"You are not amusing, Lord Fitzroy," the Queen said, her voice like ice. "Be silent."

Turning her back on Fitzroy, Queen Charlotte gave Charity a baleful look. "I think I have been apprised of the pertinent information, though it is hard to distill from a note full of baseless speculation and the wild accusations two peers are hurling at one another. Let us examine the notion that you both believe our honoured guest was poisoned. I do not wish *at all* to discuss how you apparently realised—too late—that you were both labouring under delusions as to the guilty party. Together. At this hour."

Unfortunately, the notion and the delusion were related. "We both believe Prince William was given henbane, Your Majesty," Charity confessed.

"Ah." The Queen understood the significance, and pressed a jewelled finger to her lips, considering.

"Mama," Prinny interrupted, swaying slightly. He raised his hand to hide a burp. "Let us all sit and talk. And maybe have a drink."

"No more drinks," his mother replied, giving him the evil eye while she settled onto a nearby chair. After waving for the others to sit, she rapped her son on the arm. "For God's sake! Have a cup of tea instead, Prinny. If there was ever a time during which we required clear heads, it is now!"

Then she turned back to the silent lord. "How *is* your mama doing these days, Lord Fitzroy? I hope life in exile suits her."

A line of pique formed between Fitzroy's brows. "My mother made her plans without so much as a by-your-leave to me. If keeping me informed when my life depended on it did not rank high on her list of priorities, I cannot imagine why you suppose that has changed."

But Charity could. Both she and Fitzroy had begun this

audience at a disadvantage because they had blamed one another, and her mind was racing to try to put together a picture of the larger game at stake.

"I offer a hundred apologies for waking you up and appearing in this manner," Charity cut in before the bickering could grow worse. "It was my error to draw Lord Fitzroy into the situation because we were quarreling over... other past matters. But rather than look backwards, we need to look forward to find the plot. You are right, Your Majesty, I am operating under a great deal of assumption in believing Prince William was dosed."

"But the prince is still breathing," Prinny said, his words only slightly slurred. "He is restless and keeps vomiting, but he has grown no worse."

"A toxin is not always required to be fatal." How well did Charity know this. "What I did not say in the letter to the Queen is that the Princess of Wales was also served from the same bottle. She did not like the drink, and only consumed a few sips. And I tasted it also. We both felt similar, though much milder effects. There is a chance that she may have been the target. Or both of them at once."

"Someone attempted to poison the princess?" Prinny sobered at that statement. "And you did not come to me immediately?"

"I only had the proof of my suspicion, and the princess and I both recovered quickly enough," Charity rushed to assure the royals. "Please, Your Highness, speak with Lord Ravenscroft. He will confirm I considered seeking aid earlier but he convinced me to bide my time until we could see if it resulted in real harm."

"A subtle poison," the Queen grumbled, standing to pace a few steps around the room. "Showing little proof and no sign of the hand that wielded it. I am beginning to understand why you took Prinny's pet's counsel to wait and see. Prinny, *do* check with your magpie and see if he corroborates the duchess's story."

"This does not make any bloody sense," the Prince Regent

said testily. "What is the point in giving such a weak poison to them that it risks passing without notice?"

Both royals turned Charity's way, looking for an answer, and she swallowed hard. "To cause embarrassment to the royal families of both England and the Netherlands?"

"Or to spoil diplomatic negotiations between our two countries," the Queen mused. "If the Dutch knew he had been poisoned, it would cause… problems."

"It could also be a coded threat. One interpreted correctly by someone who would understand its meaning." Lord Fitzroy's face was calculating as he locked eyes with Charity, and she felt a touch sick.

"How do we respond to something like this?" was Prinny's next artless question.

The Queen rounded on him in irritation, and then she turned her hot gaze on Charity. "I take it you no longer believe *he* is the guilty party," she said contemptuously, tilting her head in Lord Fitzroy's direction.

Charity locked eyes with him. She did not believe so strongly he poisoned the prince and princess anymore. But… she wasn't certain enough of his innocence to voice it with conviction. Her kidnapping—twenty years in the waiting to get revenge against Charity's mama—was proof that the Fitzroy family preferred to play the long game.

She let her eyes slide away. "In this? I—no, ma'am. It is improbable, but I cannot rule it out with certainty. Even if he is innocent in this, he might once again be his mother's dupe."

She fancied she could hear Lord Fitzroy's molars grinding from where she stood, and it was shortly about to get worse.

"Your Majesty… I think we should ensure that he is a guest of Buckingham House for a time while we gather more information about what happened. To be sure he does not use his resources to attempt to escape while we investigate his innocence. We… we need to be sure."

"*What!*" Lord Fitzroy fairly shouted at Charity. "You conniving hag!"

"Mind your tongue and tone of voice, Lord Fitzroy!" Queen Charlotte snapped. "Whether you are offended by the notion or not, it certainly would align with your mother's purposes and methods. If you are afraid that questions might expose your guilt, perhaps a confession is in order. And if you cannot bear even the weight of a suspicion, then you should never have returned to court."

Fitzroy took a long breath, but the expression on his face was ugly. "Of course I am not afraid, Your Majesty. Your Highness," he said in a brittle voice, spots of colour showing on his cheeks. "Then I consent to be a guest. A room where I might lay my head for a few hours will be well appreciated."

Turning, Charlotte gave a baleful look to Charity. "You, my diamond, return home at once and put on something more appropriate to your station." The Queen and Prince Regent rose and departed, issuing instructions to the footman on their way out.

Charity stopped the guard who was waiting for Lord Fitzroy. "Can you send the footman who was serving Prince William to my house after sunrise?" she asked.

The guard nodded, and before he could carry on, the angry young lord leaned in to have his final say.

"So I was mistaken about the Prince of Orange. It seems, however, I was not wrong about your venom. You were willing to sink your fangs into me to get your petty revenge after all."

9

"Never compete with someone who has nothing to lose."
– Baltasar Gracián, The Art of Worldly Wisdom

"**H**er Majesty has asked me to take you to the Garden View Chamber," said the footman. The slight man's expression was now studiously blank. "Would you follow me, please?"

Peregrine noted the absence of name and title. This lack of respect was his fault; he had no doubt the servant heard him shouting in the Queen's presence. Still, a bold act for a man in livery. One he did not intend to ignore.

The duchess's duplicity scalded, the burn of it searing far beneath his skin. But Peregrine's anger wasn't reserved solely for her—it turned inward, sharp and unforgiving. He had dropped his guard because for one fleeting moment they had reached an accord about the prince's poisoning. And in that moment, he somehow managed to forget that she blamed him for other miseries in her life.

Idiot.

He didn't normally feel an urge to demand his pound of flesh from servants, but the rude footman had caught him at the wrong moment. He ran his tongue over the sharp tip of his eye teeth, repressing a smirk as the footman walked ahead, and the guard trailed behind. Lazily, he slowed his step, managing to nearly end up side by side with the guard.

The guard was attempting to remain stone faced, but the tilt of his eyebrows showed confusion and discomfort. At first, he tried to slow his step and fall behind, but Peregrine tilted himself slightly towards the man, and reluctantly the guard settled only a half step behind and to his right.

"It has been a frightful night," Peregrine said to the guard, pitching his voice just enough that the footman would hear him clearly. "I imagine at this hour the kitchens are a bit sluggish, but since you are here, do you think they could manage a cup of chocolate? I adore it with a dash of cinnamon, if the chef would not be too put out."

The guard's eyes darted to the footman, whose shoulders had gone up but otherwise betrayed no sign he was listening. "I, er… will see your request passed on, my lord," he murmured.

"Marvelous," Peregrine said. "I am sure it is not a usual part of your duties, but your effort is appreciated nonetheless. Thank you for seeing to my comfort." And then he stepped forward back into place, not wanting to accidentally antagonise the guard—just the ruddy footman for putting on more airs than his narrow shoulders could carry.

The distance they walked indicated the room was quite far away from everything. Peregrine made a private wager with himself. The Queen, vain and spiteful creature that she was, was the sort of woman who liked to make displays of her displeasure.

It was rather hard for Peregrine to act offended when the ploys were so predictable.

And he was right. The room was at the very end of a hall,

lacking the opulence he had seen everywhere else in Buckingham House. It was modest in size, and painted in a washed-out blue. The furniture it contained was well-crafted, but simple, lacking in gilt adornments or carving, and the fireplace was serviceable but small.

It was a perfect, carefully contrived picture of deliberately restrained hospitality, with just enough amenity to avoid being insulting, but lacking the more luxurious touches afforded to an honoured guest.

"Your washstand is stocked, and the fire has been laid. The chest contains a spare blanket, shirt, robe and slippers. The bell-pull is there, should it prove necessary, my lord," the footman said, his voice clipped.

Amused hugely, Peregrine let it show on his face, not caring at all if the footman interpreted it as pleasure with his room. His padded prison. "Excellent. I shall be quite comfortable here."

He shucked his coat, noting with a curse that a few more stray golden hairs clung to it. But he handed it swiftly to the footman. "I suppose you can manage this, I trust. Or else find someone who can. I would hate for the fabric to suffer for lack of expertise. And if someone can come retrieve the rest of my clothes to freshen them, I believe I will need them for tomorrow."

The man gave a shallow bow, "As you wish, my lord."

Prig. Peregrine stared out the single window for a moment as he changed into the nightshirt, seeing only the faint glow of gas lamps.

There was nothing more he could do this night. The Queen was waiting for him to dance to the beat of her drum, and the duchess—well, who knew what instrument she was playing? Suffice it to say, she had a rhythm of her own going, even if he hadn't yet identified the song she was trying to perform.

He was not interested in their coarse manipulations. If they wanted him embarrassed and ill at ease, he would give them a taste of their own medicine. Releasing all the tension in his back and neck, Peregrine hopped into his bed and promptly fell asleep.

~

He slept as deeply as a babe, rousing late—perhaps sometime around one in the afternoon, to judge by the shadows. His clothes rested on the chair, brushed and freshened. Ravenous, he yanked the bell pull, wondering if the servants would respond or if the pretense of hospitality would be entirely cast aside.

But they responded quickly and adroitly, acceding to his whims. He received all that he could want—good food, the papers, even a bath—but no summons came for him, and given the guard positioned in the hallway, he was not intended to leave.

Peregrine idled the rest of the day away, with plenty of time to think about everything.

Someone would get him, sooner rather than later. It would cause too much speculation if he vanished at Buckingham House, so his detainment was unlikely to be protracted. Doubtless, the royal family and that chit were following what few bits of information they had.

They would find nothing that tied to him. Outwardly, he exuded patience, and no small amount of gloating. Not only would they fail to pin the deed on him, they would probably have no firm leads in any other direction either.

And so he expected the knock at the door which roused him on the morning of the second day of his confinement. He washed and dressed as leisurely as he could without being rude, ignoring the fidgeting of the footman who expected him to move in haste to the Queen's private sitting room.

Dappled sunlight filtered through the tall windows of Queen Charlotte's space, brightening the sage green silk of her walls and the florals of her carpet. Peregrine was in no way surprised to find the Regent already seated in an upholstered chair beside his mother, the positioning of the chairs set for an inquiry.

It gave him some small measure of appeasement to see the Duchess Atholl was standing, slightly behind and to the side of the Queen.

"Lord Fitzroy," the Queen said once he finished his bow. "We trust our hospitality has been satisfactory?"

"Quite, Your Majesty," Peregrine said serenely. "I have wanted for nothing. How did your investigations fare yesterday?"

Charlotte's lips pursed slightly as she raked her gaze down him, unsatisfied, and Peregrine hid his sense of triumph.

"We have been as thorough as we dared while trying to remain discreet," Prinny admitted. "The Princess and Prince William have made full recoveries and are no longer experiencing any ill effects. I believe the duchess has improved as well," he added, giving the young woman a quick glance.

Charity nodded, her eyes downcast.

Was that all they had bothered looking into? "What came of questioning the footman serving the drinks to the Dutch contingent?" he asked.

Prinny harrumphed, looking displeased. "Nothing we can act upon with any surety. The footman is one of ours, and he said that the bottle had been corked and sealed when it was given into his possession. And then, as the duchess said, the jenever had been decanted. The prince had been partaking from it all afternoon and seemed no worse for wear until late in the day."

Peregrine carefully sifted through that statement. "Correct me if I am mistaken, but it sounds as though you have verified the drink was tainted."

"With henbane, yes. Or something that acted to the same effect," the Queen said sourly. "When no one showed signs of becoming too ill, we had the apothecary's assistant imbibe what remained. They have agreed with your identification of the drug."

There was a small silence, and Peregrine suppressed the urge to sigh. Would they ever get to the point? "This is all very fascinating," he said at last, his speech polite but edged with impatience. "And I do appreciate your need for caution. I understand. But—and I assume you are confiding in me because you have come to agree with what I am telling you now—none of this has anything whatsoever to do with me. So, respectfully, might I be allowed to go home now?"

The Queen's eyelids flickered with irritation. "Refresh my memory, Lord Fitzroy. Which one of the parties present during our last meeting mentioned that the choice of tincture might be… how did you put it? A 'coded threat'?"

"I suppose I did, but that does not mean that is what it is. It could easily have been nothing more than the weapon that was at hand. I trust your apothecary did inform you of how very common henbane is, which is why *certain parties* who are present now have some passing familiarity with its adverse effects."

The duchess remained silent, not even meeting Peregrine's eyes at that.

Prinny stuck his oar in, leaning on the arm of his chair. "The apothecary believes this the work of an amateur. The right dose of henbane would be fatal. He could not fathom why someone might so deliberately miss the mark when there are better choices to make him ill."

Peregrine lifted his eyebrows, betraying no other sign than polite interest. "There is a possibility he might be right. Alternatively, it would take a practiced hand to accomplish what they did."

"Enough. I am tired of beating around the bush," Queen Charlotte said, cutting the air with her hand. "There are far too many *possibilities*. We have a handful of facts, and too many avenues to pursue. Then the point remains that *if* it was meant to be a message, there were only two people who managed to hear it: you, and the Duchess Atholl."

He laughed out loud. "You think my mother would poison Prince William to send me a note to say 'Hallo son, how is the weather in England this time of year?'" His eyes fell on the duchess, who had finally looked at him. "I am, of course, assuming you still believe it could be my mother."

The young woman's eyes flashed, and finally she spoke out of turn. "Stop acting the fool."

He had been bored by this posturing. Annoyed even. And now sudden anger bit deep. "I do beg your pardon; did you just tell me *I* am the one being a fool? After you impugned my honour and invited me to spend a full day as an unexpected guest of the Queen?"

"I told you to stop acting like one," she hissed. "Do I believe that you are indifferent to what happened at the fête? Not for one moment. Not after you broke into my home, convinced I was the one behind it all. And most certainly not after I recognised the pattern and suspected it had been orchestrated by *you.* You do not believe it is a coincidence, Lord Fitzroy. Do not pretend that what happened does not prey upon your peace of mind."

Peregrine let a smile curl his lips, but it did not reach his eyes. He felt... he didn't know. Hollow and strange. Perhaps this was what it was like to be losing his bloody mind on top of everything else.

"What a rousing speech. Yes, you are quite correct that I will take steps to ensure I am not being implicated in any plot. Perhaps you can see why, given how my loyalty tends to be... rewarded. Whatever else is on my mind, my dear duchess, is really none of your damn business."

"Two things can be true, Lord Fitzroy." The Queen steepled her fingers. "You can be a dangerous man with questionable loyalties, and you can still be the uniquely suited tool we are willing to wield to run our enemy to the ground."

"At the risk of being thrown into a dungeon and forgotten, I do not care to be your *tool*, Your Majesty. If I fail to find the guilty party, someone with a particular grievance against me could ensure I take the blame. And, as luck would have it, that could describe just about everyone in this room."

The Queen's gaze hardened, her pitch threatening. "If you insist, Lord Fitzroy, although let me assure you of this: though the testimony shows you kept your path away from the prince and princess during the party, you know better than most how other hands might achieve your means. I have *no* intention of letting you pursue your own devices. Evidence has a way of being tampered with by those with much to lose—and you, it seems, have more to lose than most."

Peregrine's back teeth ached. "I see I am outmanoeuvred. If I concede and agree to help, will you at least allow me to deal with matters directly?"

Charlotte tittered, a cutting sound. "Oh Lord Fitzroy! As if we would ever let you leave without a safeguard. You are far too clever to be trusted on your own."

Prinny, who had been watching the match of wills between Charlotte and Peregrine with pensive interest, finally volunteered another comment. "Lord Ravenscroft—"

"No." The Queen's voice brooked no argument.

When his eyes found their way to the duchess, Peregrine barked a sharp laugh in helpless disbelief. "*Her!* You want—a mere slip of a girl—to play my nursemaid while I ask around about who might have committed treason? Have your jest."

At least the duchess seemed no happier about this than he did. Were they to swap shoes, he would likely be crowing about it.

The Duchess Atholl's composure broke just long enough for her to take a half step forward before she caught herself. She drew herself up and turned to the Queen, waiting for the woman's permission to speak. Queen Charlotte showed the first hint of approval Fitzroy had seen yet as she nodded.

"Your 'nursemaid,' Lord Fitzroy," Charity said distastefully, "is even less interested in playing the role than you are in having me play it. Already tongues have been wagging. But as much as I would prefer it, I cannot follow my Queen's wishes acting alone —and neither can you."

Truly, generosity was its own form of punishment. He should have let her fly to the Queen, alone and looking like a crazed wild thing, to endure whatever suspicion they might level and then be released.

Prinny stirred. "The Duchess Atholl is correct, Fitzroy. The questioning is moving towards the upper classes, and as that is fraught with delicacies, it would be both unseemly and ill-advised to send her alone. You are not the only ones we have looking into things, but where your mother is concerned, you and the duchess are the... best equipped. Go be useful," he barked. "This is tiresome, and I have a game of billiards waiting for me, so I am of no mind to cross my mother's wishes."

The Queen was slower to rise, though that might have been more to do with her advancing age than anything else. She gazed at the pair of them through lowered lids before finally settling the weight of her royal gaze on him.

"If it soothes your wounded pride in the slightest, Lord Fitzroy, both my son and my diamond are convinced that, whatever your other failings, you are not guilty of poisoning the prince or princess. That is why I permit you to remain in my diamond's company and why you have this opportunity to earn my trust." Then, like her son, she turned her back and left.

As he and the duchess stood there, Peregrine exhaled slowly, the only outlet he allowed himself for his agitation. It was seldom in his life that he found himself in situations where his control of matters was tenuous.

It was… vexing.

"I am sorry, Lord Fitzroy, but perhaps we should assume this… partnership… is for the best. It occurs to me that this might not be a message for you or I—it might be a message meant instead for your mother."

That had occurred to him too. But he was unsure how to take her meaning. He whirled, meeting the duchess's gentian eyes. "And you think it best I cooperate because I need the protection of the Crown, Duchess?"

"I think you see enemies in the shadows, and you have no compunction against striking against them. If you are willing to do so, it would be useful to harness that to our benefit."

"And *I* think that if your Queen has the slightest idea what she is getting you involved in, she is not showing nearly enough concern for your safety."

Being involved in scandal was one thing, but investigating a crime was far, far more dangerous for any woman, much less one only a year past her debut.

"She knows I will be able to open doors you cannot." She turned away, straightening her skirts.

The only person who remained behind was the footman. Once again, he was studiously ignoring Lord Fitzroy. "Your Grace, I shall send to have your carriage brought around."

"Thank you, Branson. Would you also see that Lord Fitzroy's horse is prepared? I imagine he would prefer to refresh himself after his ordeal before coming to Atholl House." She glanced at Fitzroy and added, "That is agreeable to you, I trust? After two days, I suspect a change of clothing might even prove advantageous. I shall await you at home when you are ready."

So it was going to be like that, was it? Fine. She would

quickly find out that he was no tame dog to be held on her leash. Peregrine gave her a bow so low that it was sarcastic. "As you command, sparkling one."

10

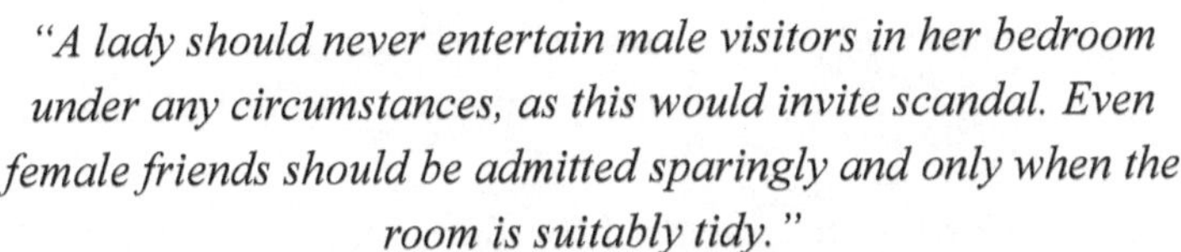

*"A lady should never entertain male visitors in her bedroom
under any circumstances, as this would invite scandal. Even
female friends should be admitted sparingly and only when the
room is suitably tidy."*
—Reflections of Grace: A Guide to Etiquette

Charity had loved Atholl House from the first moment she
had walked through the door. Truth be told, even before
then, for she had often admired it while perambulating around
Grosvenor Square. Spanning five floors, with tall sash windows
that gleamed like polished mirrors and a marble-columned
entryway that echoed with footsteps, the stately home had more
than enough space for its single occupant.

Or at least Charity had so thought before she woke to Lord
Fitzroy staring down at her in bed in the dead of night.

The state of Atholl House now was better described as one of
frenzied madness. The silence was disrupted by the hurried
shuffle of maids and the occasional clatter of dropped crockery.

Her servants were too well-trained to breathe a word of their concern within earshot, but Charity could hardly fail to notice how they dogged her footsteps, standing braced for what she would do next now that Lord Fitzroy—the house's invader—was expected to visit.

"There is no need for you to escort me around the house, Mr Pritchard," Charity reassured the butler, her words almost too bright. "Surely your attention must be required somewhere else."

His eyes were pale and flinty as they scanned her face. Her butler was a man who took duty far too seriously. "Nothing is more important than seeing to your safety and comfort, Your Grace."

"I am safe enough. I would be more comfortable if I could have some quiet time for myself—in the privacy of my chambers."

Her butler had been part of the ducal household since King George III took the throne, hired by the duke's second wife. His loyalty was absolute, and he cared not one whit that Charity had played wife for barely more than two weeks before the previous duke died. The duke had chosen Charity, and that was enough for him to hold her in esteem.

Charity had counted his dedicated service as a point in the house's favour. Now, she was… less sure.

Mr Pritchard carried on, heedless of his mistress's waning patience. "I have personally checked the latches on every window and door on the ground floor, Your Grace. The stableboys will take turns guarding the back gates. A footman will be on round the clock duty at the front door. Mrs Potts has her iron skillet ready, having promised repelling invaders is no more daunting than frying eggs. No one shall enter Atholl House without my approval."

"And Lord Fitzroy—"

"Will be invited inside when Your Grace is ready to meet with him. He is still outside, waiting in his carriage."

Good. Call her petty, but he was due a reminder that this was her home. He shouldn't have taken the liberty of invading through her window. She would decide when he would be allowed in to wait.

"In that case, that will be all, Mr Pritchard. I will ring for my maid when I am up to receiving callers." Charity employed her mother's trick of lifting her head just high enough to remind the servants who was in charge, and then she swung open her bedroom door.

"*Eek!*" A tiny screech slipped from her mouth, drawing a smirk from the man lounging in her sitting room beside the obviously opened window.

Behind her, her butler lurched forward. She spun around and held out a hand to stop him, angling her body to prevent him from seeing into her room. "Silly me! Just a bird on the windowsill. I overreacted. You may go, Mr Pritchard."

The old butler searched her face, but eventually followed her command. Charity scooted into her chambers, closed the door behind herself, and then crossed her arms over her chest.

Combed and polished and looking not at all as though he had been troubled by the idea of climbing into the second floor of her home, Lord Fitzroy smiled cattily at her. As if he was amused that she hadn't told her proud butler all his efforts had been in vain.

She stifled her urge to see him tossed from her home, not wanting to give him the satisfaction of turning her house into a circus again.

Lord Fitzroy was reclining languidly on the pale pink velvet upholstered chaise lounge by the window as though he were some ancient deity waiting to be served. All he needed was a tray of grapes and pitcher of wine at his side, and he could be mistaken for Caravaggio's Bacchus. The pink velvet seemed almost insulted by his rakish sprawl, his muddy boots leaving smudges on its otherwise pristine surface.

His smug smirk was a challenge—a weapon he wielded with infuriating ease.

"Your boots are getting dirt on the velvet," she barked a harsh whisper, choosing to skip straight past any questions as to why he was inside her house.

"So sorry about that," he drawled in a low voice, though he did not move his feet. "You should ask a housemaid to leave a mat near the window so I might clean my boots on my way in."

"Perhaps you might consider using the front door like any other *gentleman* of the *ton*."

"Challenging when the *lady* forgets I came at her own invitation. I did warn you that I am a staunch believer in the Golden Rule, so you have no right to be surprised when I treat you the way you treat me."

Because he was right, abruptly she was embarrassed, and then angry. How did this villain manage to have the ability to set her temper alight with the ease of lighting a candle?

"You wish to follow rules?" she hissed as quietly as possible. "I was trying to impress upon you that this is my *home*. Which was what you had forgotten two nights ago when you entered without an invitation."

He smiled wickedly, which only served to remind her that he had seen her undressed, and she felt her face grow hotter. His voice dropped even lower, a quiet rumble. "I suppose it could be argued that was rather ill-done of me. On the other hand, I did give you the chance to stab me for it. And in my defence, it felt necessary at the time, so I hope you will forgive me if I am not too sorry."

She snorted. "You should be sorry. I cannot believe you thought I was the one to poison the prince and princess. I would have to be... lunatic."

The blackguard actually rolled his eyes at her. "It was a possibility that crossed my mind. Maybe if you had chosen a different time to inform me you were going to burn my life to ashes, I would not have jumped to such an erroneous conclusion."

Then he considered Charity from his position, eyebrows raised. "You thought I poisoned the prince. Did you think that made *me* the lunatic?"

"No," Charity muttered. *Vile mastermind like your mother, perhaps.*

"Dreadfully sorry. I am afraid I did not catch that. Could you say it louder?"

She made her hands into fists. "If we raise our voices, my servants will be beating down this door."

Abruptly he stood, taking two steps to close the distance between them. He didn't touch her—but his body was so close she could feel the warmth radiating from his skin. "Then say your words now," he murmured, his breath tickling her ear.

Gooseflesh pebbled her skin. Part of her was horrified he could have such an effect on her body still. There had been such a strange alchemy between them since they had first met in on a balcony during an event before the season. After they had finally been introduced and she had learned his name, that had immediately ended any hope of an association.

That… had been for the best, or so she told herself. But there was another, darker part of her that was reminded of the way she felt like she had come alive that evening last year. The same part that remembered him looming above her in the dark in her room, and it was growing curious about what it might be like to know a man in the ways that sometimes she heard her maids whisper about.

"No," she said again, and steeling herself, she stepped backwards. Unfortunately the wall at her back only granted her a few inches. "Bent on trouble, certainly. People who are not in control of their faculties would not be so… careful not to kill the prince."

Fitzroy searched her eyes, his breath feathering against her temple. "A curious compliment. I think. Are you finally ready to —how did you put it? Open doors for me rather than throw them shut in my face?"

"Since we must." He was still looming, and it was making it hard to think. She put her hands on his chest to make space between them. "Lord Fitzroy, we have to associate with one another. We are acting in concert for a purpose. I do not want people to think we are friends. And you cannot barge into my rooms like this."

"Then you will mind your manners like a civilised acquaintance in public, and invite me to a parlour like a reasonable host." He shrugged as if this was simple.

"We also cannot keep secrets from one another," she insisted, feeling as though she was losing control over this negotiation.

"If you ask for the impossible, you will only be disappointed. Not all secrets can be freely shared, and you do not have the right to demand I give you mine."

"You consider yourself an honourable man, do you?" her voice was sharp.

"As difficult as it may be for you to believe… yes, actually, I do. As do you, else you would not ask me to abide by rules you think I will not keep. Or I would lie to you and tell you what you want to hear. How about this: I will not keep a secret that might prevent you from finding the guilty party. Or do anything that might impede your investigation."

Though her heart was pounding, she gave that compromise the consideration it deserved. It might do. "Fine."

"Are you done?"

"I have other rules," she blurted in a rush. "You cannot touch me."

He pointedly looked down at his chest where her hands were still pushing him away, and then his eyes moved upwards to her hair, as if remembering the touches as vividly as she did. She couldn't let a man do that again. It had left her feeling exposed, vulnerable—and, to her eternal shame, wanting.

Tracing a line in the air above her hands with one of his fingers, he gave her an impish look. "Sparkles, you are blushing. I wonder what you are thinking about. Are you glad you will not have to tell me your secret?"

He could wonder 'til the sun went cold. She yanked her hands away before he could call her on breaking the rule about touching and slapped them over her cheeks. "You also need to respect my title, Lord Fitzroy. No more calling me that… ridiculous name."

Fitzroy pretended so sarcastically to ponder that she knew there was going to be trouble. "Mmm… no."

The warm wash of pleasure the idea of that gave her was absurd. "You must," she insisted. "It will attract too much attention in public."

"I will do in public spaces what must be done. When we are *alone* it will be a different story."

The emphasis on the word alone made her spine tingle. Charity wasn't sure what expression was on her face, but it amused Fitzroy hugely. "I hope you mean that regarding the name, and not the rest of the rules."

"I did. But if you decide you want to change your mind…"

Heaven forbid. "Joining forces was a terrible idea," she gritted, wanting nothing more than to go back and inform the Queen that she could not work with this flirting miscreant. As the thought crossed her mind, she stopped, narrowing her eyes. The sneaky devil. He was badgering her on purpose so that she would go to Queen Charlotte and do just that.

Charity snapped her focus back to the present. Fitzroy was still watching her, his infuriatingly unreadable expression back in place instead of the libertine leer. His expression had changed so thoroughly, it felt uncanny. A chill brushed down her arms, and she wondered if he had pretended everything.

She dug her nails into her palms to stop herself from smoothing her hair or crossing her arms over her chest. She refused to let him see that he'd shaken her composure.

"Fine. Do as you feel you must when we are alone. As long as you do act appropriately in public, it matters not," she said, her voice brittle. "You agreed to more than I thought you would. Shall I codify our rules on paper and have us both sign?" Charity pointed at the paper and pen she had left sitting on the small table.

Fitzroy gave her a disbelieving look and then he laughed almost silently. Charity's face heated again, but this time she felt stupid instead of… something else. Of course he was laughing at her. If she thought he wouldn't honour a spoken agreement, why would he abide by a written one?

His rapidly changing expressions, not knowing what he was really thinking or feeling, left her feeling like her stomach was hovering more towards her navel. She changed the subject. "I started a list of people we might want to question."

Peregrine released her from her position against the wall, retrieving a scrap of paper from her desk. He unfolded it, allowing Charity to see the swirly loops of her own handwriting. " Viscount de Vries, Lord Musgrove, Sir Harris Wycombe… this reads more like a list of candidates for marriage. I must suggest you aim higher than a lowly baron, Duchess."

"That is my list of suspects," she said, quashing the annoyance that threatened to resurface. "Everyone on the list has quite publicly stated their opposition to the royal match. I will leave it to you to indicate which ones might have a quarrel with either you or your mama."

Peregrine raised his eyebrows and went back to studying the

names. After a moment of silence, he balled it up and tossed it into the fireplace.

"What—wait, what are you doing? You did not even read them all," Charity complained.

"They would make sense only if we lived in a chapbook. Even you believed I might only be bent on trouble. Admit it. This was not the work of an amateur. A real villain would not announce his intentions to the world before committing a crime."

Charity crossed her arms over her chest. "You thought I announced my intentions to you."

He smiled—a real one, however brief. "But only to me, and all works of genius require an audience to properly appreciate it."

Indifferent one moment, warm the next. It was enough to drive her to madness. "I suppose you have a better recommendation of where to start, then? One of your gentlemen's clubs or some gaming hell where I am not welcome?"

"In fact, I do know where we need to start. This door will not be barred against you, but as to whether you will come inside? Well... we will see." He approached her and the door she was hovering in front of, stretching his arms like a cat rising from its morning nap. His chest came dangerously close to brushing against Charity's crossed arms. Somehow, she did not think that was an accident. However, true to his word, he did not touch her. "Shall we go?"

She hurried to stay ahead of him, desperately hoping that they might somehow make it downstairs and out the front door without passing any of her servants. She made it as far as the landing before she crossed paths with Mr Pritchard. He opened his mouth to bellow for help, but she cut him off before he got out a word.

"Lord Fitzroy and I are going out. Would you please let one of the upstairs maids know that there is a spot of dust on the chaise lounge?"

The butler held her gaze for a moment. Charity did not so much as blink.

"Of course, Your Grace. Wait just a moment and I will get your wrap and gloves."

The butler did not need to voice his misgivings. All the voices in Charity's head were in agreement. Riding alone in a carriage with a Fitzroy was a terrible idea of the first order. She hurried across the pavement and climbed inside, flicking the curtains closed while he joined her. When he sat on the bench next to her, she burned him to bits with a fiery glare.

"Apologies. I must have misinterpreted your reasons for wanting privacy." Then he winked at her as the carriage lurched into motion.

Charity rolled through a litany of nicknames, each more slanderous than the last, but could not decide which one suited him best. It had to be accurate and unexpected. She had not yet landed on a solution when the carriage rolled to a stop.

She shifted the curtain aside and studied her surroundings. In preparation for her own debut, she had memorised each important lineage in Debrett's and their holdings. It took her a moment of concentration to recall the name of the occupant. A face swam up from the recesses—it matched the woman who had been parading around Prinny's garden party on Fitzroy's arm.

"You brought me to pay a call on your latest paramour?" She gaped at Lord Fitzroy. He was a madman. There was no other explanation. "What happened to respect?"

"Selina is not my mistress. She is a marchioness and was at the self-same event as the two of us."

Charity shrank into the depths of the cushioned seat, her mind a whirl. It was bad enough that someone might have seen her get into the carriage. But to exit here, on Lord Fitzroy's arm, and walk through the front door of that woman's home?

"No. Just no. There are lines, Lord Fitzroy. I do not care

where you draw them, this particular outing is well beyond the boundaries of propriety."

"Suit yourself. Pull the curtains closed again and sit here until I am done. As I said, Sparkles, the only one barring your entry here is you."

He left with a satisfied tip of his hat, confident he was in the right. Charity could have sworn she had made the correct decision. But when the door swung shut and the latch slipped into place, the world around her grew dark and close.

The space felt oppressive, the polished wood panels seemed to close in with every breath. The faint scent of leather and Lord Fitzroy's cologne did nothing to soothe her rising panic. For all her bravado, Charity was sure of only one thing: this darkness would consume her long before she admitted she had a weakness.

11

In a state of pique, Peregrine stuffed his feelings deep and shut the carriage door firmly, leaving *her* inside to stew. His driver, Hodges, would be able to keep her out of trouble.

If the duchess wanted to act the petulant child, he would be happy to treat her like one. But that would come later. Right now, he had to gird himself for dealing with the Marchioness of Normanby. He needed all his wits on her rather than the pointy Diamond jabbing a sore spot on his arse.

Whatever else she might be about, the marchioness didn't deign to play petty games of superiority with Peregrine. He found himself conducted adroitly to her drawing room, where she was already standing to greet him

"Perry," she said, moving forward to clasp his hand. "Whatever happened after I left? There have been no notices about a royal personage's unfortunate demise, but when I heard you were staying at Buckingham House… I wondered."

There were no servants stationed anywhere nearby, but even if they had been, he wouldn't worry about it. There would be no gossip that he was with her, unescorted. The marchioness valued her privacy, and her servants valued the idea of not having to leave the country to obtain new employment.

"Yes, well. I have been doing a great deal of reflecting myself, Sina, having found ample time to do it." He kept his voice cool. "And I have been pondering whether you have spent any of our time apart looking into the strange matters that landed me in the Queen's claws."

She let go of him, transferring her hands to her hips in a posture of irritation, though no sign of those feelings made their way to her face. "That was your own fault, and from what gossip I have heard, I would assume it has something to do with the Duchess Atholl. Combing her hair, Perry. Really?" The marchioness's eyes danced in amusement, but it contained neither malice nor jealousy. "How positively *scandalous*. You have never brushed my hair, and I must admit, now I feel slighted."

God. How had she found that out? Even the gossip rags whispering about his proximity to the duchess had not heard that choice morsel. But he let an unconcerned smirk rise.

"I shall not ask what whisperer you keep in Buckingham House that brought you *that* particular tidbit, but if it is a footman named Branson, dismiss him. His attitude leaves a great deal to be desired."

"Mmm," she agreed. Sina had deliberately cultivated a purr that put a man's mind to all manner of sinful thoughts—the better to manipulate one. But Peregrine was unmoved. "I know who you are speaking of. Branson is not mine. But to answer your question, yes. I felt it would behoove me to do some discreet investigation of my own."

"I thought as much. So I take it then that your associates did not act independently because they had been anticipating our failure. And judging by your displeasure that afternoon on the lawn, I feel fairly confident that *you* were not the architect of some second scheme."

"You would be correct on both counts. My associates were rather miffed at the notion of someone usurping the event and interrupting our plans to further their own agenda, even if the outcome aligned with our objective. The Prince Regent and the Queen have yet to announce the princess's engagement, no doubt waiting until the whole debacle has faded from public memory."

Peregrine inhaled through his nose, thinking. "That does narrow the scope somewhat, though they were scarcely high on my list of suspects to begin with. *Faugh.*"

"The scope?" Selina arched a brow, resting one elbow in her palm as her fingertip languidly traced her lower lip. "I understand that, somehow, you and the duchess contrived to accuse one another of the crime. However, I must confess—my sources are curiously lacking in detail as to how you arrived at such a predicament."

At least he knew that she was telling the truth. Branson wasn't her creature, else she would have the whole damn sordid tale.

"I am afraid you will have to remain curious, Sina, but suffice it to say, the accusation—and the duchess—led to the Queen putting me on a short lead. I am looking into who might be responsible, and for now, our interests are sufficiently aligned that it suits me to bide my time."

"With the duchess?" Selina's delicate dark brows were high on her forehead, and her face took on one of pure deviltry. "Oh, Perry. Do not tell me—never mind, please do. Is *that* who is waiting out front in the carriage?"

Peregrine allowed a slight smile to serve as the answer and Selina's laughter rang to the ceiling.

"My goodness. Whyever is she still sitting out there?"

He elected to tell the truth. It would serve that little vixen right. "Because she is under the ridiculous notion that my first order of business would be to call upon my mistress and seek solace of a… well…"

"More carnal nature?"

"That will do."

Selina laughed again, dabbing the corners of her eyes with a handkerchief. "Oh my. I cannot think of the last time something made me laugh so hard. Does she believe you were dropped on your head as a child?"

"Knowing the duchess, I would not put that past her," he agreed dryly.

"That must be a most novel experience for you. What a darling little lamb she is! Of all the many words I have heard applied to your character, stupid has never once been added to the list. Oh she is far too amusing. The *ton* will devour her whole."

"Sina," he warned the marchioness as a jolt of premonition struck him. Selina was sure to find the duchess an interesting and important person to become acquainted with. The duchess wasn't stupid—Selina wouldn't bother with her if she was—she was only naive about the circles he and the marchioness ran in. And that was the sort of situation that could be easily remedied.

Lady Normanby wrapped her arms around his neck, whispering into his ear wickedly. "I want to invite her in for tea. But perhaps I should muss your hair first. Or loosen your cravat."

Peregrine reached up and disentangled her arms. "Absolutely not, you incorrigible wretch. Go ahead and try to invite her in if you like, but I doubt she will accept it. It is far more likely she will misconstrue the nature of such an offer entirely."

Selina simpered. "I see no harm in indulging both curiosity and scandal at the same time as I play the gracious host. But shall we wager? I think your duchess is savvy enough a social creature that she knows she will be forced to accept my invitation."

"She is not *my* duchess—" he began, but Sina dashed out without waiting for him to respond.

Peregrine watched through the window as the marchioness strode to the carriage, her knuckles tapping smartly on the door with the precision of someone accustomed to being obeyed. After a moment, she leaned in to say something. It must have been a persuasive argument because within ten seconds, the door opened.

He suppressed a smirk. It was just as well he did not make the wager. Since she had been so obviously waiting in the drive, the marchioness had caught the Duchess of Atholl neatly in the snare of propriety, robbed of any excuse about a pressing schedule.

But as they entered the drawing room, Peregrine halted the train of his less charitable thoughts. When she entered, she moved stiffly, as if each step had to be forced. Her posture was perfect, her expression poised, but there was something just slightly off. Too controlled. As if she was holding something at bay.

Sina seemed to sense it too. "Morton, dear, fetch us all some tea and whatever sweet delights Cook has made today, would you?" she asked her butler. Then she turned back to the duchess. "Please. Sit and relax, Your Grace. It is the least I can do after this oaf left you sitting in front of my house. He should have told you that you were welcome to come in. I have been most interested in making your acquaintance since I saw you two together at Prinny's party."

Already the colour was coming back to the duchess's face, and now she pinkened with a touch of embarrassment. "To be honest, he did. I was the one who did not want to… presume."

Well, at least she did him some credit. "May I present Lady Selina, Marchioness of Normanby? A paragon of wit and charm, as I am sure you will soon discover. Selina, this is… the Duchess Atholl."

Selina was a master of dissembling, and she quite convincingly nattered away for the next few minutes like an empty-headed lady of fashion until Morton returned with the tea tray. And then she served like a good hostess, not even raising an eyebrow at Duchess Atholl's request again for milk and three lumps.

Peregrine's eyelid twitched at the amount of sweetener. But he also noted she ignored the plate of small cakes. He idled, munching on a frosted concoction and drinking tea while the women chatted about inconsequential things like the latest dress styles and tatted lace. Or rather, the marchioness chatted, and the golden-haired virago responded with clipped replies.

As the conversation continued, the duchess gradually loosened her tongue, her answers growing longer. Sina laid her trap barehanded and obvious, like a snare sitting across a rabbit's path, and his shiny nuisance—however questionably versed she was in manners—was completely unaware of it.

Without a doubt, the marchioness was enjoying herself immensely. Peregrine certainly was. He was having difficulty maintaining a straight face as he waited for the inevitable to happen.

It wasn't until she had finally managed to convince the duchess to nibble politely on a ratafia biscuit that Selina let it spring.

"I must confess, Your Grace, you are the very last person I would have expected to find in Peregrine's carriage. Especially after everything that happened last year."

The duchess nearly choked on her bite, and swallowed painfully. There was too long a pause before she managed to echo the marchioness. "What happened last year?"

Selina delicately swirled her tea. "That little... incident at Fitzroy's ball. Such a peculiar turn of events. One moment, you were enjoying a glittering debut; the next, you vanished. It was quite the topic of gossip. I can see why you would nurse a grievance against the Fitzroy household."

The duchess actually gave him a withering look. "You told the marchioness about what your mother did?"

The marchioness took the spoon out of her cup and took a long sip. "My goodness, little lamb."

The duchess's face reddened, and Peregrine relaxed back in his chair, wondering if she would explode. "Why does *everyone* think they can ignore my title and call me by some insulting pet name?"

Peregrine sighed. "The marchioness has two eyes and a mind behind them. You knew already the Queen's excuses for your absence were awful, you kept giving me the evil eye at Prinny's party, and then when Lady Normanby goes fishing with the most flimsy of bait, your hunger for revenge made you swallow the hook whole. I did not tell her. You did—Sparkles."

The Duchess Atholl's red face drained of colour quickly as she realised her error.

"You should be nicer to Perry," the marchioness told her. "Not only is he correct, when it came to your secrets, he was the soul of discretion. Really, you should be mindful of the fact that he is an impenetrable strongbox when it comes to information of all kinds. I should know—I have tried to… pick his lock. Once or twice."

Peregrine rolled his eyes, because now she was only trying to scald the duchess's ears with innuendo. "Sina, do not be vulgar; she was married so briefly, she would hardly understand the meaning of your words."

The marchioness blithely finished her tea, telling Peregrine without words that her mind was working very hard. The fact that they remained in each other's company gave the marchioness's clever brain more to chew upon than he liked. He needed to take control of things, and Selina had a weakness for flattery. They were there for a reason, and it was time he brought it up.

The Dutch delegation was still high on the probability of suspects, but it seemed that the Crown was conducting their own investigation in that direction. Given Selina's earlier statements, all of the men of means she associated with were unlikely to have interfered with the two of them. But there were a great many more who had not been invited, and as Queen Charlotte had pointed out, it would not be an impossible matter to buy or force another person's hands.

"Sina, we rub along because one has ears where the other does not. You know what transpired with Prince William. Let us play a little game. If his sabotage or embarrassment was the aim, who from the list of people who were not invited to attend would you mark for having the means and the motivation? Someone who is not among the visiting Dutch lords and ladies?"

Selina paused, thinking. "Without any proof to lean on? At the top of my list would be the Prince Regent's wife," she said. "Once Princess Charlotte is wed, the Regent will toss her mama out on her ears."

Both he and Selina looked to the duchess to see if she would weigh in, and the woman fidgeted, understanding that her connection to the Princess of Wales might provide helpful insight. "If you are hoping that Princess Charlotte might have heard a confession from her mother, you will be disappointed. I cannot believe she would betray Caroline."

She continued slowly, choosing her words with an excess of care. "But… I think the idea has merit. Not only would it allow Princess Caroline to stay in England longer, it would be just another wicked, scandalous blow dealt to the Regent in their ongoing row."

Peregrine huffed a quiet breath of agreement.

If they were only considering the first two possibilities— breaking up the negotiations, or causing a scandal for the Crown —then Princess Caroline was the only remaining name he had.

Unfortunately, if it was a message, the list of suspects would be considerably longer.

But he would have to examine that possibility later, with the pretty and very vexing little duchess. Sina would not hear a whiff of suspicion about that from him.

"Well, Sparkles, it seems we have our afternoon planned for us. Shall we go call on Princess Caroline?"

The duchess nodded, her brow knotted in thought, and stood up, straightening her skirts.

Selina concealed a knowing smile behind her hand while the duchess wasn't looking and then shook her head. Reaching out a hand, she said her farewells to the duchess. "I expect your opinion may differ, Your Grace, but I feel that if we met on a more even ground, I would like you very much. So I will give you this advice for free. Information is the only currency that matters, and the only one that can buy true power." Pausing for emphasis, Sina continued, "Do not let *others* pick your pockets."

To her credit, the Duchess Atholl considered those words seriously. "Thank you. It is a lesson I thought I already knew but... perhaps I did not understand its meaning as fully as I thought."

The marchioness stood then. "Good. Then I cannot wait until we see each other again."

Both a promise and a threat. It would be interesting to watch and see if the duchess could survive Selina's friendship. Heavens knew sometimes it felt like he barely did.

"Perry..." the marchioness turned to him, resting a hand upon his. "You are skirting unsafe territory. I wish you... luck."

Well, *that* didn't seem sinister or anything.

The duchess remained thoughtful during the walk out to his carriage, and he gave his driver the address as the man helped her in. Of course, she helped herself to the forward facing seat, and made sure she was positioned directly in the middle, so he would have to sit opposite and find a place for his legs.

What a cat. Pleasure rippled through his belly as he briefly considered how to return tit for tat. Finally he slouched into the corner as he faced her, stretching out his long legs. He let his limbs brush against hers as he used the tip of his shoe to nudge her feet to the other side.

"I beg your pardon," she muttered, scowling as she slid to the other end of the bench on her side of the carriage.

"Beg away. I am a soft touch for a properly remorseful woman. And besides, it is an hour's ride to reach Montagu House in Greenwich Park. Why should I be uncomfortable?"

Despite her efforts to lean away from him, every jostle and bump caused his leg to brush against her skirts. He could practically see her blood heating slowly to a boil as discomfort from her position settled in.

Amusement passed quickly. His twenty-seventh birthday was in a month, giving him perhaps six or so years seniority over the duchess, but sometimes her inexperience left him feeling a hundred years older.

"You are punishing yourself more than you are punishing me. You know that, right? All you are going to do is end up with a pain in your side from sitting like that. Relax. There is no one here to judge you for riding with me."

"Except for you and me." But she did straighten herself. After perhaps ten minutes passing in silence, she volunteered a new comment. "The marchioness was not at all what I expected her to be."

"Nothing you could say would please her more."

She studied him through lidded lashes. "You like the Marchioness of Normanby, but you do not seem to trust her. At least, I assume that is why you did not ask her about who might wish to send your mama a message."

Peregrine's habitual, neutral smile became a touch more genuine. "Be careful, Sparkles. If you learn to become astute, I might have to revise my opinion of you."

She ignored the nickname. "Would a better opinion include trust? At least—more trust than now. You could have kept me from walking into her den that blindly," she murmured with only the barest hint of petulance.

Thank God she had amended her question, because he doubted she would like being told no. He couldn't imagine allowing himself to be so vulnerable with anyone. Never again.

"I will never leave you ignorant where it might cause us harm," he temporised. "Some people play for much higher stakes than party invitations, Duchess. But trust is a weakness that few people with ambitions can afford."

12

*"In the game of hearts, let your rival falter with desperation—
grace and wit are the weapons of a true lady."*
—Reflections of Grace: A Guide to Etiquette

Though his words had been more of an evasion than an answer, both he—and Selina, for that matter—had reminded her that they considered information of the utmost value. That piqued her curiosity. By her mama's measure, Charity had already gained everything worth achieving in life.

Fitzroy's taunts hinted at a new challenge. Loathe though she was to admit it, she wondered what possible stakes people like the marchioness played for. The firm set to his mouth discouraged her from voicing more questions.

It probably was unlawful somehow. Jewels and heirlooms weren't the only things that could be stolen or held for ransom.

The possibility of finding out that Lord Fitzroy was little better than a common cheat and swindler disappointed her somehow. It would be like… finding out that the sorcerer in a fairy tale was a charlatan.

She decided to ask something else. Lord Fitzroy seemed to be in an almost friendly mood, and she did not want to disturb the calm between them.

"What can you tell me of Princess Caroline?" Charity asked. "I have not yet made her acquaintance. The Queen and Prinny keep her name off every guest list."

"I am sure you know the reasons for that. She has been unwelcome in polite society for years, which I am sure she took as a blow. Once upon a time she was quite a darling of the *ton*." He let his boot tap pensively against the wall of the carriage. "Now Montagu House is one of those places where people want to be, but not to be seen."

Charity's eyes nearly crossed as she struggled to make sense of his last statement. Eventually, she gave up and asked. "I am not certain I understand what you mean."

"If you are a friend of Caroline's, you are not one of the royal court. You see how it would be impossible to accidentally cross her path, or to say you happened to be passing and saw someone go inside. Those who visit her keep quiet about it. Which brings us nicely to you, Duchess. Do you expect Princess Caroline to welcome the Queen's diamond into her home?"

"I am a dear friend of her daughter," Charity reminded him. "If we can agree to emphasise that connection, I am reasonably certain she will welcome the chance to get to know me."

Fitzroy exhaled noisily, his face wreathed in an expression she couldn't quite interpret. "Let me venture one suggestion. Do not emphasise your commitment to seeing her daughter wed to the Dutch royal. Princess Caroline has been outspoken against the match."

Did he think she had no sense at all? "I only want what is best for the princess, and on that, I am certain her mother and I can come to an agreement."

The carriage picked up pace once they crossed over the Thames. Charity risked pushing the curtains aside. The hustle and bustle of London was gradually replaced by the bucolic rolling hills of Greenwich Park. She studied each carriage that passed, searching for a coat of arms to identify the occupants, though none were so fine. As they turned into the drive of Montagu House, a dark coach rumbled past, kicking clods of dirt and dust into the air.

At the house, Charity allowed the footman to help her down from the carriage and then took a moment to surreptitiously study the grand estate while pretending to smooth her skirt. The tall, stately mansion pleased the eye with its symmetrical layout and prominent central entrance.

Fitzroy did not so much as pause as he exited the carriage. Not to walk with her, nor offer her his arm. Instead, he strode forward to present his card to the butler waiting at the front door. "Would you please ask Her Highness if she is receiving visitors?"

Charity gaped at him—or at his backside, at any rate. It was a backside that presented superbly in the pantaloons he was wearing, but really! The utter cheek! She nearly turned an ankle on the loose stone in her rush to catch up, and once she did, she glared at Fitzroy and grumbled, "You could have offered me your arm."

"You told me not to touch you," he reminded her smugly. "I was only following your directive."

Charity did not slap the man's smirking face, but he would have deserved it if she had.

"Her Highness is available. Please follow me." The butler stopped long enough to pass their hats and gloves to the footman before leading them to a drawing room.

The wallpaper was green, not cabbage green like the dress

Charity had worn, but a deeper green that evoked memories of forest walks in the middle of summer. The colour theme continued in the choice of upholstery and decorations. Wooden chairs and tables cut through the shades of green like branches on a tree, inviting birds to perch upon their edges.

In the middle of the room, swathed in vibrant yellow, orange, and red, sat the estranged wife of the Prince Regent. She leapt to her feet and raised her arms wide, putting the swirling shades of her elaborate gown on full display. The peacocks of Vauxhall would have screamed with envy had one been there to see her.

Her round cheeks flushed with satisfaction as she hurried over to welcome them. As she neared, her blue eyes, sparkling bright, opened wide with curiosity. "Lord Fitzroy, what an unexpected delight!"

Fitzroy bowed gallantly over her hand, and Caroline *tsked* softly. With a playful smile, she drew him closer, rose on her toes, and kissed him lightly on each cheek in the continental style before gesturing for him to sit beside her.

Charity blinked, finding herself standing all alone, forgotten. She stood, uncertain as to whether she should follow the pair across the room or wait for one of them to remember her.

"Fitzroy, you naughty, naughty man!" Caroline cooed. "How many times did I encourage you to come to one of my little gatherings, and only now are you here! Though I suppose I should not complain as at least now I do not have to share your attention with anyone else."

Warmth spread up Charity's neck, tingeing her cheeks in bright pink. Was the princess cutting her dead? She would hardly be the first society matron to sniff with disdain in Charity's direction, but none had gone so far as to ignore her existence entirely.

But perhaps Caroline had not noticed her? She had been rather intent on greeting Fitzroy. And Fitzroy, to be fair, hadn't forgotten her. He turned his face just far enough in Charity's direction to give her a slow wink.

Good God. Was Charity the only woman in all of London who *wasn't* in this flaxen-haired reprobate's thrall?

Charity raised her fist to her mouth and gave a polite cough.

Princess Caroline shifted her attention away from Fitzroy's face long enough to narrow her gaze at Charity. And Fitzroy, damn the man, looked like he might grin fit to crack his face. He smothered the amusement beneath a polite, restrained smile, and then put Charity out of her misery. "Your Highness, might I introduce you to the Duchess Atholl?"

Charity rushed forward, determined to get the awkwardness behind her. "I am a dear friend of the Princess of Wales, and have been most fortunate to accompany her during her debut."

Caroline's expression puckered, the harshness of the lines getting lost in the roundness of her face. "And yet, here I am, banished to the countryside, without the chance to even witness her presentation at court. Do you not find that to be a travesty, Lord Fitzroy?"

"Absolutely, Your Highness," he purred, using every ounce of his despicable charm. "I am sure Her Grace would be happy to tell you about all of the latest events, if you so wish."

"I wish to be there in person, not hearing about my daughter's life second-hand as though I was no better than a lady's maid subsisting on the stories of my betters." Princess Caroline scowled at Charity. "Do you think yourself better than I am?"

Curtsey, child!

Her mother's voice sent Charity dropping into the deepest curtsey in her repertoire, one she reserved exclusively for the Queen. Surely Queen Charlotte would forgive her given the circumstances.

Princess Caroline left Charity lingering in the position so long

Charity feared she would struggle to rise again, but eventually she relented.

"Come, Lord Fitzroy. Let us enjoy a cup of tea and discuss our shared acquaintances." She glanced over in Charity's direction. "You may come along too, Duchess."

Charity glided upwards by sheer force of will, for her legs were trembling. She took great care to keep the ache from showing on her face. She might as well have frowned, however, for the princess had already moved on.

You are accustomed to dealing with royals. Though her logical side spoke the truth, Princess Caroline was thus far exhibiting a whole new level of capriciousness. There was nothing for it but to grit her teeth.

The way the woman was hanging on Lord Fitzroy's arm, you might have thought the floor was slippery with ice. The princess chose a pair of chairs near a bowed window overlooking the gardens, taking a seat without any consideration of what Charity would do. At her insistence, Fitzroy took the other chair, making sure to catch Charity's attention when he did. His light blue eyes glittered, daring her to voice a word of complaint.

With a sudden epiphany, Charity realised he *enjoyed* when she was annoyed or caught at a disadvantage. What a scoundrel!

Now that she understood his measure, Charity would not give him the satisfaction. And neither would she give it to the princess, for that matter. She carried on, choosing a settee a few feet away. She crossed her legs at her ankles and tucked them under the chair. While the footmen poured tea and offered biscuits to them all, Princess Caroline peppered Lord Fitzroy with questions.

"Have you any plans to host your annual ball this season?" She frowned when he shook his head. "How about something more intimate—like a supper and a small concert? You could include my daughter on the guestlist, and invite me to act as chaperone."

"I will give it some thought just for you, Your Highness. You know I was away for the better part of this last year, though. The house is still at sixes and sevens. You will have to grant me some time getting it in order."

"Time is a luxury I am not afforded, my lord. Prinny means to announce Charlotte's engagement any day now." The princess's voice was somehow able to sound even more petulant than her daughter's. "He would have her at the altar and on a boat for the Netherlands before I get the chance to see her again. Who will prepare her for her wedding night? Who will give her advice?"

Charity froze in place, fearing Fitzroy would offer her name, but he did her the kindness of remaining silent. Lord Fitzroy took the princess's hand in his and patted it in sympathy.

Princess Caroline was nothing if not determined. She prodded Fitzroy for information on who he counted as a close friend and whether they might be willing to arrange an event where she could see her daughter. Fitzroy handled her with adroitness that impressed even Charity. Captivated by the performance, she leaned a little too far forward and caught Princess Caroline's eye.

"Your Grace, have you seen my gardens?" Caroline asked, her face the picture of innocence. Charity might have been convinced had she not seen Princess Charlotte use the same expression. Usually, it was a sure sign that Princess Charlotte was up to no good.

Caroline called a footman forward. "Take the duchess on a tour of the garden. Make sure she sees the roses in first bloom before she returns. Go along, Duchess Atholl. You can recount what you see to my daughter the next time you meet her."

Gritted teeth would convey an honest, yet unwelcome, sentiment that served no purpose. Charity did, however, give Fitzroy a speculative look as she left. He wanted to be treated with respect? Now was his chance to prove he was worthy of it— assuming he would tell her what he discovered later.

The garden was lovely, which was to be expected, and Charity had the chance to see all of it, for of course, the roses held a prime position at the far end. By the time she returned, Fitzroy was standing at the front door with her gloves and wrap in hand.

"I hope you are not offended that I said our goodbyes for you. We should be on our way. It is a long drive."

Trying to keep him amicable, she did not complain when he took up three-quarters of the carriage with his splayed limbs. She even left the curtains open, hoping the daylight would remind him that they were not to keep secrets.

"Did you have any luck?" she finally ventured, once they turned back onto the road to London.

"She is not the culprit, but she *is* tiresome," he groaned. "And dogged in her persistence."

"She is a mother," Charity replied, surprising him. "The garden stroll gave me time to reflect on the untenable position in which Princess Caroline finds herself."

Fitzroy cast a sidelong glance at her, his gaze breathing life back into a feeling she had believed long dead. "That is a thought worthy of your name. How is it that you can muster such charity towards her?"

"And so little for you?" the duchess asked laconically, folding her arms over the butterflies in her stomach.

He lifted an eyebrow. "I did not say that, but I reckon it is a fair question."

Charity gave him a small, tight-lipped smile. "You seem to be doing well enough without my pity."

She regretted her words as soon as she said them. He blinked, and in that fleeting moment, the windows to his soul became mirrors, denying her a glimpse within.

"I must confess that I have never heard anyone say no so many times without making an enemy of the person asking," she continued, seeing if a compliment might soften him again and finally explain what Caroline had wanted.

He chuckled absently, his attention back to the window, bracing himself as the road got rougher. "There is an art to it. As we all surmised, she is desperate to slow down the wedding negotiations. Prince William's penchant for being disorderly is convenient to her."

"But what did she say that made you think she was innocent?" The carriage had picked up pace, bouncing its occupants around enough to make it difficult to keep their seats.

"She asked me if I could help arrange correspondence with my mother to beg a favour," he replied.

Charity sucked in a breath, following that line of thought to its conclusion. If she had poisoned William of Orange, it seemed logical that she wouldn't need Lady Fitzroy's help. However, she could just as easily want more help since her first attempt had failed to achieve the objective. Prinny was still determined to see his daughter wed to Prince William. It was worth further discussion.

Charity was about to raise the point but he was no longer paying her any mind. His attention was turned outside of the carriage.

And for good reason. Charity braced herself to save herself from the humiliation of being flung into Lord Fitzroy's lap.

They were close enough to London that the industrial buildings near the docks had replaced the trees and hills. Going as fast as they were, she barely had time to note one building before they passed another. "I say, Fitzroy, has your driver not had proper training on how to handle a carriage?"

"Sorry I need to break your rules, Duchess, but I assure you it is for a reason." Fitzroy's hands gently moved her out of the way enough that he had a clear view through the narrow rear window behind her. Charity spun around, heedless of bumping against his legs, and spotted a pair of men on horseback behind them. Fitzroy twisted around and slid open a panel to allow himself to speak to the driver. "Move to the side and let them pass."

The driver's raised voice sounded irritated. "Can't. We're being paced, and I can't sodding lose them."

"What does that mean?" Charity asked, for from Fitzroy's expression alone she could tell it was not good.

"Turn onto another road," he ordered the driver. "We can take a different bridge across the Thames."

The carriage slowed only enough to allow the turn, sending Charity and Fitzroy sliding to the far side of the benches. Their limbs ended up intertwined in an effort to avoid being a heap on the floor. Fitzroy grunted before grabbing Charity around the waist, forcing her to sit beside him.

"I need to see what is happening," he muttered at her gasp. "And this will keep you from sliding around. Mind your head." He spread his legs and planted his feet, locking her into place at his side.

Charity was beyond complaints about his mishandling. All she could do was bring one arm up, bracing herself and keeping her skull from hitting the wall. But the rough ride threw her thoughts askew anyway, and abruptly it felt like she was back in the carriage that had abducted her on that terrible night, sick and nigh-insensible.

Every crunch of gravel under the wheel emphasised just how much danger they had been in. What if the carriage had turned over? What if the door got damaged and she could not get out? Would anyone think to save her?

Her vision narrowed, and she found it impossible to breathe. Like in the worst of the fits she had before, it felt like her soul had shaken loose within her cage of bones, ready to rise and fly free if she did not keep it within herself by sheer force of will.

Violently, she clung to the nearest thing her free hand could grab, trying to tether herself to the earth.

"Breathe, Sparkles!" Fitzroy's hand was on her cheek and his face was alarmingly close to hers. "You are going to swoon if you don't start breathing."

He was right; her vision was already dim around the edges. She took one gasp, and then another, and the world began to fit itself into place. The carriage was shuddering—no, wait, that was her trembling. But the lord beside her didn't mock her... or even point out the fact that she had seized a hold of his thigh just above the knee in her distress. She had to be hurting him. Her hand was aching at her fierce grip.

As she forced herself to let go of him, she noted that the carriage had slowed to a near crawl. Outside the window, the rippling flows of the Thames soothed her jangled nerves. "Nearly home," she whispered under her breath. She counted masts bobbing on the river to keep her fears of being trapped at bay. "Just a few more minutes."

As if to spite her words, the carriage came to a complete halt.

"Lord Fitzroy, we have problems," the driver called down from his perch. "The road is blocked. Cart overturned on the bridge, looks deliberate. And riders coming up behind us. The same men as before, best I can tell, plus some new friends."

Charity's heart leapt into her throat as she heard the coachman's voice. She leaned toward the window, but Fitzroy's arm shot out, blocking her view.

"Stay down," he ordered, his tone sharper than she'd ever heard it, and then he pushed the cushion aside on the other bench, drawing an officer's dagger from under the seat. "How many?" he called to the driver.

"Four," the coachman replied, a faint metallic click echoing ominously. A sudden crack followed. The report of the gunshot nearly deafened them both. "That there was your warning!" the driver bellowed. "The next one won't miss!"

Charity slapped both hands over her mouth to keep from screaming in surprise.

"Didn't send the rats scurrying. I'll hold them off as long as I can," the coachman told Fitzroy.

There was a second crack that echoed off the water, and Fitzroy sprang to his feet, steady despite the jolt of the carriage shifting beneath him. He wrenched open the door, sending a gust of damp air rushing inside.

"Fitzroy!" Charity hissed.

"Three now. No arms but knives." The driver must have nerves of pure iron to keep talking so calmly to Lord Fitzroy.

"Stay here," he said to Charity firmly, his face shadowed by grim determination.

"But—"

But he was already moving toward the three men advancing on the carriage. They looked like wolves circling prey, their knives glinting in the afternoon light. Fitzroy, however, showed no hesitation.

In the ballrooms, he had moved with the grace of a dancer. Now she could see how effortlessly he slipped between worlds. He was a man equally at ease commanding attention with charm as he was wielding steel.

Charity's breath caught as she pressed her hands to the window. She couldn't look away, even as fear pooled cold and heavy in her stomach. Her view of him was shifting, as though someone had upended the neat little boxes where she'd placed her opinions. Fitzroy wasn't just the irritating rogue who pushed her buttons at every opportunity. There was something else, something dangerous and utterly magnetic about the man facing down three armed attackers without so much as a flinch.

Outside, Fitzroy raised the dagger, his posture poised and ready. Charity's nails dug into the edge of her seat as the men closed in.

13

"Almost all our faults are more pardonable than the methods we resort to to hide them."
—François Duc de La Rochefoucauld

His driver, Will Hodges, had spoken truly on all counts. He hadn't missed. The bullet had taken a brute square in the chest, leaving him motionless and bloody on the pavement. The rest were still approaching.

This was wrong.

An ordinary pack of highwaymen would have cut their losses already when they discovered their prey was armed and capable, not to mention that highwaymen rarely staged their attacks on a London bridge. These men were different, and Peregrine recognized their ilk—violent, expendable tools for hire. Men moving with the kind of confidence born from countless dirty jobs going unpunished.

While Hodges's shot hadn't frightened the others off, it had given them a moment's pause. And then Peregrine's armed exit gave them another.

Foolish of them to hesitate, really. Will Hodges was a seasoned veteran who only needed half a minute to reload both barrels of the flintlock carbine. It was a fact Peregrine knew intimately because they had both been infantrymen who survived the Nive.

On the banks of the Nive, they had stood in lines of two, and many of the men around Hodges and Peregrine had died, little rhyme or reason to survival. The only control over the future that a man could have was taking to heart the idea that every dead enemy soldier was one that couldn't aim his musket your way. Speed and ruthlessness were the only facets they could control, and they leveraged them unstintingly.

That was one of the reasons they endured while so many soldiers broke—a certain, fatalistic camaraderie when faced with impossible odds. This, however, was not the Nive; here, three on two odds were laughable.

And these ruffians had no idea what manner of men they had cornered.

"Lock the carriage doors!" Peregrine said, raising his voice enough that the duchess would hear—and obey, hopefully. She had been so bloody pale, there was more than a small chance she had fainted dead away inside.

Hodges slid off the bench with the gun, staying on the far side of the carriage so that they each covered one entry. Once he finished reloading, Peregrine was certain that at least one more of these thugs would find himself a corpse.

One of their attackers began to circle in his driver's direction, knife in hand. Peregrine paid that one no mind as Hodges could manage himself. It was the others who had decided to circle into the lee side of the carriage, out of Hodge's line of fire, he needed to keep his attention on. They probably thought they'd overpower

Peregrine quickly, flank his driver, and then have their merry way with the duchess and horses.

It was high time to stop acting like a gentleman.

Peregrine let confidence ooze from him, and he laughed with a low, mocking edge. "You should turn around." He brandished his dagger in his right hand, point up. "It would be terrible to be sent home in more pieces than you arrived."

The taller of the two laughed, a rough bark of a sound. "Brave talk for a man about to bleed."

"Perhaps." Peregrine held back and let them approach, welcoming the acrimony bubbling within him like a caldron of black, boiling tar waiting to be poured from the battlements. "But I warn you, it will not be my blood that stains this bridge."

They were watching his dagger hand instead of his left, where he had palmed a large chunk of broken cobblestone he had picked up when he stepped down. And as they closed to a distance of maybe ten feet, Peregrine hurled it with all the strength of his left arm—right at the face of the large one.

The earth seemed to still, his blood singing with a rush of anticipation.

Now was a chance to release the violence that pooled just below the surface of his skin this past year, usually so carefully concealed beneath the polished veneer. To empty some of the endless well of wrath that churned within him, dark and bottomless.

Peregrine's ears told him his aim had been true. The big one roared in pain and staggered back. Watching him from the corner of his eye, Peregrine spun to deal with the shorter man who was lunging at him, knife arcing towards his ribs.

Pivoting, he sidestepped the blade, letting his own slice neatly down the thug's forearm. And then he kicked out with his boot, catching the man's knee with brutal force. Shorty screamed as the bone cracked, and then he crumpled to the ground, writhing and clutching his leg.

In those few seconds, the tall one recovered enough to close with him, snarling, his knife slashing wildly and blood streaming down his cheek. Peregrine deflected the blow in a clash of steel. The force of it reverberated up his arm, but he held firm, gritting his teeth against the pain.

What is one more pain in your life, after all? His inner voice mocked.

Twisting, he drove his elbow into the man's jaw, but not hard enough. His coat hindered him, and the thug recovered from the glancing blow quickly. Using the butt of his dagger like a hammer, the tall man landed a blow to Peregrine's arm that made him drop his dagger, his hand nerveless. And then he grabbed Peregrine by the dangling edge of his cravat, yanking him into his arms.

In a grapple, Peregrine was outmatched. He had height, speed and stamina, but the softer life of the aristocracy did not lend itself overmuch to developing raw strength. He struggled in the grasp of the other man, his right arm pinned, trying to get an angle that would let him do enough damage with his left to get free.

"You think you're a bloody hard case, do ya?" the man muttered in Peregrine's ear.

"I do," Peregrine grunted. "Certainly more than… you're used to getting from a toff."

The man laughed, and then he balled his fist, landing it into Peregrine's stomach cruelly. All the air left his lungs in a rush, and the man let him collapse to the ground, wheezing, before planting his boot in Peregrine's side. Suddenly, the flintlock cracked again, and Peregrine rolled out of the way of the collapsing thug, still struggling to regain his wind.

The driver's steady steps approached as Peregrine flipped

onto his stomach and slowly made his way to his feet. "You only had one man to deal with," Peregrine groused, retrieving his dagger and brushing off his ruined clothing. "What were you doing, Will? Admiring the scenery?"

"Aye." Of his own accord, Hodges was a man of few words and dry wit. "Reckoned you needed the exercise."

Peregrine looked for the third fallen man for hire. "And where is yours?"

"River." Hodges jerked his thumb in the direction of the Thames. His pained grimace suggested he had not come through without injury, but he brushed aside Fitzroy's questioning expression.

Both turned to look down at the two remaining attackers. The short one had tried to crawl away discreetly, but he wasn't making much progress. The tall one, it seemed, was dead.

Too bad.

"The duchess?" was Peregrine's next question, and his driver lifted one shoulder in a gesture of unconcern. He took that to mean she was still in the carriage, probably with her hands over her eyes, which was just as well. She already thought badly of him; she didn't need to have her worst imaginings made true.

"Keep an eye on her and turn the carriage around. And for goodness' sake, keep her from looking out the window. I might need to work for a few answers," he told Hodges, and the driver nodded.

As Will clucked to the horses, guiding them to back the carriage up, Peregrine noticed the silence around the bridge. He looked around to see a few gawkers standing at a distance— largely cart traffic who found themselves inconvenienced—but they stayed far away, fearful.

The only sound was the whimpers and laboured breathing of the wounded thug, clutching his knee. Fitzroy turned to him, his expression cold and unforgiving. "Start talking."

The man glared up at him, defiance sparking in his bloodshot eyes. "You think I'm afraid of you?" he spat. "Traitor's son."

Peregrine sighed, letting his head roll on his neck to ease the tension building at the base of his skull, hopefully before it exploded. Abruptly, he seized the man by his filthy neck, letting his fingers bite deep.

"Do you know the most ironic part?—I mean, besides the truth that I am weary beyond belief of being blamed for my mother's plots," he said, his voice low and biting. "It is that a man like you dares to believe the shadow of my mother's designs elevates you above me. *You.* A man who trades your principles for coin. You pox-ridden, greasy, murderous cur!"

The man gagged, scrabbling at Peregrine's hand, his face turning red at first, then purple. His eyes were wide in fear.

Peregrine dropped him, letting his face take on his usual mask of supercilious boredom. "If you do not answer my questions, I shall leave you here for the magistrate to find. I think we both know what they do to men like you, and I wager I know what you would prefer. So tell me—who sent you to kill us?"

The man stared at Peregrine for a moment, as if he believed himself in the presence of a madman. "A contract through Red Hand. Not to kill," he finally whispered. "Just to rough you up. To send a warning."

A frisson of ice ran down his spine, but Peregrine kept his expression empty. "If you wanted to deliver a message, that could have come as a bloody letter."

"Can't read nor write. Weren't my choice," the man moaned softly, taking his words literally, and Peregrine rolled his eyes. "Had to slow you down."

"Who put the contract up?"

"Don't know. Red Hand probably don't know either. Heard it came through a go-between. Someone with deep pockets. I don't know no more, I swear."

"Get out of here. If you can," he told the short man curtly. "And be sure to tell your employer the message was received."

Peregrine's inner thoughts were ghastly quiet as he considered the few pieces of information, rubbing his aching right arm. Then he jerked his head up, looking for Hodges, who had turned the carriage and was leaning against one of its doors, blocking the duchess's view—and exit.

Will nodded, understanding Peregrine's unspoken message and drew his belt knife.

Peregrine didn't bother looking backward to make sure he was safe from the thug he had let go. He just walked away, leaving the man to either lie in the street or pick himself up and get away. The magistrate or the Bow Street Runners would eventually get interested in what was happening here. It was up to Shorty to decide what was worse—pain, or London's system of justice.

Having been lanced by the battlelust, the festering wound to his soul was now oozing corruption into his bloodstream. He felt tired. Hollow. Like he had been in the grip of some monstrous illness that had drained him of everything vital.

"We have to get the carriage moving. We are not safe here," he told his driver, and Will nodded again, but he split a look between the drawn curtains and Peregrine. Uncertain if he should intervene.

Peregrine lay his own hand upon the handle of the carriage door, understanding Will's hesitation to pull it open. But then he remembered he had told her to lock them. He could hear no sound from inside, so Peregrine knocked.

There was a long pause. "Fitzroy?" The duchess's voice was soft.

"Yes," he answered, keeping his voice neutral, and instead of just unlocking it, the blonde woman actually flung the carriage door open herself.

It wasn't until that moment that Peregrine realised his eyes were downcast. That in the space between his breaths, he had been numb with wondering. What did the duchess think of him now? Was she about to look at him as though he were something truly reprehensible?

All he saw, however, was wide-eyed concern, tinged with fear. "Are you hurt?" she asked, and her eyes raked down his figure, as if looking for blood.

She cared for his well-being. At least a little. She was… afraid, not of him, but for him.

Anger was one of the few emotions he felt strongly. Most times, he felt hardly anything from the rest at all. Ordinary feelings were like conversation heard through a locked door, and he didn't have the key.

But now the spark of surprise lit a warm spot in the pit of his belly. It was… such a fragile bloom of a thing.

A smile—small but genuine—touched the corners of his lips. "Would it please you more if I were bruiised and battered, Sparkles?"

Blinking, the duchess's face transformed from fear to confusion… to annoyance. She scowled at him. "Because you felt compelled to ask me this question, then yes. It would."

Peregrine's smile grew wider. "My ribs are likely to be black and blue by tomorrow, if that earns me any tender sympathies."

"Get in, you lout," she huffed at him, sliding backwards to make room.

With an exaggerated groan, he stepped inside and found his way to the bench, and the duchess shook her head, her voice a trifle shaky. "Stop carrying on. I know you are not that hurt."

"How would you know? I could be hiding grievous wounds."

"You are not. I… watched you fighting with them. And though it was quite terrifying—" her voice shifted upwards, threatening to break. She stopped and her throat bobbed as she swallowed. "I could see that you were… holding your own."

That surprised him. She had watched him acting every bit as vulgarly as the brutes that attacked them? And she wasn't looking at him as though he was a disgrace.

He leaned his head back against the cushion, not wanting to examine this revelation too closely. "Does that ruin my hopes for tender nursing of the lumps and bruises I earned in your defence? A cool cloth, soothing words—but no, you will probably just shove me off the bench and tell me to walk it off."

She leveled a fierce frown at him—probably because the alternative was either to laugh or to weep. Closing his eyes, he let another small bit of truth slip from his lips without censure. "I prefer when you glower at me than when you are afraid."

"You—what?"

They were treading in dangerous territory with such confessions. Peregrine ignored her question and forced his lids open again, watching as her eyebrows pinched together in bewilderment. "Do you have plans tonight? If so, you need to cancel them. I insist."

She twisted her hands together in uncertainty, and then she crossed her arms over her chest in annoyance. "You learned something."

"*Something* would be one way of putting it. Things have become a bit more complicated."

The duchess pursed her lips. Bless her little head, she was thinking hard. Perhaps Selina was right about seeing a spark within her after all. A potential that was trainable, however happily ignorant it was at the moment. He would have to keep the two of them from spending time together.

"You think that we did not get trapped by ordinary bandits," she finally concluded. "That they targeted us deliberately."

God help him, he didn't want to make her fearful again. But she had been the one to demand that they keep no secrets. For whatever other flaws he had, at least he did try to have the integrity of his word. "I know it. Someone wishes us to stop looking into matters entirely."

"You recognised them?"

"Not them so much as I recognised the type of men they were. It was the one I let go that told me we were to be frightened as a warning."

The duchess held her head in her hands. "Why should they worry? We have found absolutely nothing. Caroline was our best suspect."

Peregrine agreed, musing over the possibilities. The Order—which Selina had already vouched for—was now firmly off the list of suspects. Selina and her ilk would never resort to hiring a jackal like Red Hand.

But they weren't the only clandestine forces of power in London.

"Fitzroy."

Peregrine reined in his stray thoughts, looking at the duchess, who looked like she had sucked on a lemon. "Yes, Sparkles?"

"Why do you recognise the type of men they were? What have you had to do with such things?"

Damnation. He really put his boot in this one. "I have... had dealings with some of the less savoury elements of society."

She lifted a slender golden eyebrow imperiously, like an irascible toddler. It reminded him of his sister Lark when she was small. Better... more innocent times. He couldn't help it; he stifled a smile. Which, of course, only vexed the duchess more.

"Secrets," he reminded her, as he shifted with a groan. This one wasn't nearly as feigned. The side where he had been kicked ached like fury. "All I can safely tell you, Duchess, is that the Queen and Regent are not the only powerful factions in England."

"And some are willing to be violent?" she asked softly.

"It seems so, Sparkles," he agreed lightly. "Would that I had better sources to help lead us to the next possibilities. Alas, I had the unmitigated audacity to gallivant across the continent for the last year. Worse, the whole world decided to shift in my absence."

She ignored his barbed comments, looking down at her lap, considering. "I may have someone we should speak with. Someone who, like the marchioness, values information quite highly."

His nickname wasn't bedeviling her anymore. He must be losing his touch.

"Are you referring to Lord Ravenscroft?" he asked her curiously. He knew quite a bit about Prinny's magpie, including that he was quite cagy about giving up his information to others… and that he enjoyed a torrid but illicit love affair with his valet. He wondered if the duchess knew that part.

The duchess was frowning slightly, but her thoughts looked turned inward, as if she had remembered something she hadn't before. "...Yes. Perhaps I need to pay a visit."

Fitzroy sat forward, his bruised parts protesting, but he locked eyes with her so she would know he was as serious as the grave. "Not alone, you will not."

Her eyes slid away, and she waved her hand dismissively. "Carlton House is safe enough. I can arrange to meet him there."

It probably was, but she was hiding something. Some thought. Fortunately he had other leverage. "Going alone would be a violation of your rules, Sparkles," he rebuked her. "And if you are going to disregard the rules, so will I. You look very peaceful when you sleep, incidentally."

Face flaming, she put her hands on her hips. "Stay out of my bedroom, you scoundrel."

"If only there were a way to make that happen…" he mused.

"Fine." She gritted her teeth. "I will arrange a meeting at my home tomorrow at four. But your presence is going to make talking to him far more difficult. I wish you would trust me to manage him. Lord Ravenscroft does not seem to like you very much, and I *cannot* begin to imagine why that is."

The warmth inside Peregrine snuffed abruptly, and he faced the window, noting that they were close to Atholl House. "Like most people who pretend they do not like me, his quarrel is really with my relations."

As though realising the mood between them had shifted, she too looked out her window for the rest of the ride.

14

"When tempers flare, my dear, a soft word and a sharper wit will tame even the most unruly gentleman."
—Lady Cresswell, to her daughter

At the appointed time on the following day, the rhythmic clicks of boot heels on marble floors gave Charity plenty of warning that her guest had arrived. She gave each cheek a quick pinch to ensure they were perfectly pink and then pasted a welcoming smile on her face. She had not been sure Ravenscroft would accept her invitation.

That smile dropped when a tall, blond man waltzed into the room. "Good afternoon, Your Grace," Fitzroy said, letting his gaze linger on the room's extravagant decor. "I must say, it is refreshing to see more of your home than just the bedroom. I was starting to believe that was the only place where the *real* entertainment happened."

Pig. Why had she bothered pinching her cheeks? "We will not

be discussing my bedroom, Lord Fitzroy. Mind your manners, or I will see you escorted off the grounds."

Fitzroy had the gall to lay claim to the most comfortable chair in Charity's drawing room. "Strange. You seem to like me better when my manners are poor. I did not hear a single word about my cravat in the carriage last night."

That was… a different thing entirely. Was it fair to complain about dishabille when they had been beset by armed men?

Charity crossed her arms over her chest and glared down at him, not that it made any difference. Perhaps if she stood long enough he would recall that a gentleman waited for the lady to sit. His expression suggested he knew and was ignoring all propriety. She did not harrumph, but it was a close thing. "You are early."

"My apologies for arriving ahead of schedule, Sparkles. Truthfully, I expected to have to waste time tracking you down because you left me standing on the lawn. But here you are, and here I am. Do you have any tea or cakes? I am feeling somewhat peckish."

"Go away. I need to have a word with Lord Ravenscroft."

"I thought that was the point of this invitation—for both of us to speak with him about what he saw at the event?" Fitzroy cocked his head to the side and studied her, and then he laughed. "Ah. You did *not* warn him I was going to be here."

"You did not send the marchioness any warning of *my* visit," she said mulishly.

Fitzroy's face went bland. "Sina harboured no ill will towards you, as you saw when she ran out and invited you in the moment she heard you were there."

"Fine. But you are friends. I do not know his lordship well enough to go that far. Given what happened to us yesterday, discretion and caution are… warranted." Charity stopped as another set of footsteps echoed in the hallway.

"Behave!" she hissed over her shoulder as she spun around,

appalled at the irony of the situation. She had her archnemesis in her drawing room, ostensibly for a polite visit and tea. Her friend Grace would never believe this. Not a word. Not unless she could see it for herself.

Hurrying over to the doorway, she found it harder to keep the smile on her face as she held out her hands to welcome the other man into her home.

"Lord Ravenscroft for you, ma'am," Pritchard announced, his voice both correct and yet censorious. He turned on his heels and left without asking if she wanted tea.

"You are a vision, Your Grace," Ravenscroft purred, his words gliding forth like silk. "Radiant, as ever, with a brilliance so dazzling it sets all of London frothing in envy and despair."

"I could not agree more," Fitzroy piped up from behind her. "I tell her so rather regularly, do I not… Sparkles?"

Lord Ravenscroft jerked sideways to see over Charity's shoulder to the man now standing on the other side of the room. His mouth dropped open before slamming shut into a grim frown. "What is *he* doing here?"

"How rude. I was invited by the duchess." Lord Fitzroy *tsked*.

Ravenscroft looked confounded. Charity latched her arm through his and guided him back into the hallway. "There is much to explain—" she began.

"Pray, correct me if I am mistaken—" Ravenscroft interrupted in his velvet tone, the words edged, "—but were you not, only three days past, declaring with utmost certainty that this man had drugged both the prince and princess?"

"No secrets!" Fitzroy's voice called from inside the drawing room, and Ravenscroft's eyebrows crawled even higher up his forehead.

Shaking his arm, Ravenscroft loosened Charity's hold.

Charity was losing her grip on the entire situation, and not just Ravenscroft's arm. She stepped in front of him. "*Please*, my lord.

I will explain it all, if you will give me the chance. I need your help," she added, praying that would be enough.

The pause before he responded was so long that Charity was certain he was going to say no. But with a terse nod, he stepped aside to allow her to lead the way back to the drawing room.

Unlike Ravenscroft, Fitzroy was standing at ease, which was a relief. But then she promptly wanted to kick herself. This was her *home*. Why had she ceded all control over it to Peregrine Fitzroy?

Because as the hostess, it is your responsibility to ensure all are having a pleasant time. Her mother's voice, unwanted on the best of days, held all the allure of nails on slate.

This is absolutely not a social call, Mama.

But her mother's rebuke did remind her of obligations as hostess, and with it in mind, she rang for a footman and asked for two trays to be brought in. Tea and cakes seemed a poor choice of weapon, but hopefully the sugary treats would sweeten them up.

If nothing else, the ceremonial aspects of pouring tea and selecting cakes and biscuits enforced the temporary truce. While the men demolished the sweets, she gave Ravenscroft a brief review of what had been learned during the days Fitzroy had been held.

"I confess, I heard some of this from Prinny," Ravenscroft admitted. "Though I did not agree Lord Fitzroy was absolved by the evidence."

"Whatever other mischief Lord Fitzroy may have gotten into," Charity said softly, giving said lord a brief glance from the corner of her eye, "he played no obvious part in this."

The man gave her a slow, cocky smile in return, and Charity's stomach fluttered, suddenly reminded of the *other mischief* that seemed to be suddenly on his mind.

She hastened on, not mentioning the unnerving visit to the marchioness. "We came to the conclusion that Princess Caroline was the next most likely suspect."

Ravenscroft was so horrified he dropped his cake. "You didn't."

"We did." She carried on, telling of their visit.

"You paid a call on Princess Caroline without me? Without even consulting me? You are lucky she only sent you to view the roses and did not have you cast into the thorns! The woman loathes Prinny, the Queen, and anyone with even the faintest connection to them. And you, my dear, surely occupy a rather prominent position at the very top of her list."

Charity did not miss the amused glance Fitzroy tossed her way, and she remembered how the marchioness had wished him luck. "Yes, yes, I know that now. But surely you can see why we suspected her."

"You wasted the trip. Subtlety is not part of her repertoire. And more," he added, "even if she had been minded to do such a thing, she would never take a risk with her daughter. Say what you will of her, but she does love her child. The bond between a parent and child is something special… is it not, Lord Fitzroy?"

It was only because she was watching him that she saw it.

Fitzroy was in the middle of sipping his tea when Ravenscroft's words struck home, but he did not flinch nor sputter. He carried on, seemingly unfazed, but Charity saw the sudden lines of tension in his gloved hand. The tiniest spark of fury in his gaze. If she had blinked, she would have missed it.

How often did he need to repress such reactions? He must be so tired of having the subject of his mother cast in his face.

"Quite," he said simply, pausing to swallow his sip with deliberate calm. "My mother taught me everything I know about the people in our circle, and her words have frequently served me well. You might be surprised to know that she even had a fair bit to say about you, Lord Ravenscroft."

Ravenscroft's face had become hard. "Did she?"

"My mother did have the most uncanny ability to notice the

more… unspoken nuances in people. I wish I had half the knack of it."

Charity had the strangest sense the two men were exchanging threats. Dire ones, if Ravenscroft's face was any indication. But frustratingly, she could not grasp the meaning of it.

She cleared her throat with a polite cough to get the men's attention. "Stop. Please. We cannot make any progress if we cannot work together. If Caroline is excluded, we have to think about who else might have had the means. The footman said that the prince enjoyed several glasses of jenever throughout the party. He did not show any symptoms of the poison until after he shared that drink with the princess."

Fitzroy took a breath and held it for a moment, thinking. "That would mean it was tainted at the party. We may be able to figure out the time in which someone could have poisoned the jenever. It takes perhaps half an hour to an hour from when they drank it, depending on the strength of the dose."

"Does that mean it was high?" Charity murmured, thinking about how she had only had two sips, and Peregrine nodded, understanding her meaning. "Then we are lucky the princess did not care for it."

"You do realise," Ravenscroft added to Charity, "this only increases odds that the princess might have been the target. *And* it makes someone among the Dutch seem more suspicious by comparison. You seem to have a particular luck with attracting poisonous elements, Your Grace. Could it have something to do with the company you keep?"

"Ah, yes, the company she keeps," Fitzroy drawled, giving a sardonic smile. "Speaking of which, let me say that it is a marvel you are still standing, Ravenscroft, given your penchant for your dangerous... associations. One might think you have built up quite an immunity over the years—poisons, *diseases*, all such things."

This time, Charity did roll her eyes. "Oh, for heaven's sake, drink some tea, both of you," she said, her words exasperated. "Perhaps it will remind you what we are supposed to be focusing on. Lord Ravenscroft, you were lingering near the prince's entourage. Did you notice anyone out of place?"

Ravenscroft raised a brow, leaning back in his chair. "Did I? And what of yourself, Duchess?" His voice was a mixture of mockery and amusement. "We were together for much of the time. Their meeting was so excruciating to witness, it nearly put me off my drink."

Charity gave him a sharp look, her voice cooling slightly. "I do not envy them," she said with a pointed edge of reproach. Then, softening just enough to redirect, she added, "At any rate, I was referring to earlier in the event."

Ravenscroft set his teacup aside, shifting uneasily in his seat. "Truly? No, but again, I must remind you that not everyone connected to the Dutch prince is pleased with the betrothal. I overheard a few cross remarks while I was retrieving the princess."

Charity examined the pieces of information she had against that picture. She firmly believed that the choice of henbane was not a coincidence. Someone meant for her or Fitzroy to understand the significance. Lady Fitzroy certainly would be willing to act against the Crown, but she was far away. She couldn't arrange for someone to come after her and Fitzroy on such short notice.

No, whoever it was, they were here, following their actions. It was not outside the realm of possibility that Lady Fitzroy would help someone in the Dutch contingency end the marriage. But if she were involved, would she target their prince? Why would the Dutch want to embarrass, and worse yet hurt, their future king? It would certainly help if she knew who Lord Ravenscroft meant.

It was on the tip of her tongue to ask when what Lord Ravenscroft had just said snagged her attention. He *retrieved* the princess? From a place where he could overhear the Dutch talking about the marriage? She had forgotten that she had found both Ravenscroft and Princess Charlotte standing near the fountain, some several yards away from the Dutch contingent. To hear their dissatisfaction… both of them would have had to be much closer.

Why had Princess Charlotte approached the Dutch on her own without Charity, especially after dragging her heels for so long?

Tea sloshed over the side of her cup, wetting her hand and nearly staining her gown. The pieces fell into place, one after another, until the answer was so obvious she could not believe they had missed it.

Charity's palms grew damp at the mere thought of it, but it was impossible to deny. The princess was not keen on the match. Drugging Prince William into making an arse of himself in such a public place certainly worked in her favour. It would have been but a moment's work for her to drug his decanter.

As for the attack on their carriage, that too likely had a simple explanation. Just as she had thought at the time, it could have been organised by Caroline. Like mother, like daughter.

You cannot tell anyone. Her own mother's voice insisted, spinning together with the logical voice in her mind, repeating the same phrase. *If you are wrong, it could cost you everything.*

Perhaps it was foolish, but she hoped she was wrong nonetheless. She had to question the princess before she breathed a word of it to anyone else. And then… if she was right… she didn't know. She would deal with it later.

Both the Queen and the Prince Regent would be livid with her for exposing such a thing to Fitzroy.

She drew from the reservoir of calm she relied upon when dealing with the Queen and forced her breathing to slow. With great care, she set her cup aside, wiped her hand on a linen napkin, and glanced at the clock on the mantle.

"My word, the time! I nearly forgot our appointment with the princess this evening. Lord Ravenscroft, I am so sorry to have dragged you back and forth, and now we will be late."

"I, errr," Ravenscroft searched her face before playing along. "It is no matter. We will plead for forgiveness so prettily they will have no choice but to agree. Shall I ring for my coat and your wrap?"

He did not wait for a reply before leaping to his feet and striding to the bell pull.

Charity turned to make an excuse to Fitzroy, and found his nose inches away from hers. She let out a small shriek of surprise. When had he moved to sit beside her on the sofa?

"What appointment? Where are you going?"

"I am going to see the princess at Carlton House." She blinked her thick lashes, trying to look unconcerned even though her heart was racing. "I am sorry. I must have forgotten to mention it in all the excitement yesterday."

"Why do I not believe you?" His voice was dark with suspicion.

Because she was lying. That she could not admit. She chose her words carefully to remain honest without revealing her secret. Lies were always more palatable when salted with the truth.

Her hand rose without conscious thought and brushed across his cheek. "Because… we have an ugly history between us."

Peregrine Fitzroy's skin was warm beneath her hand, and embarrassed, she took her hand away. What was she thinking, touching him like that?

"I will be safe, I promise." She rose from her seat with flawless poise, every movement deliberate, as if elegance could somehow shield her from the guilt twisting her stomach into knots. She refused to meet his gaze, refused to let those questions written so plainly on his brow pierce through her composure. "I will send a note to you tomorrow, and we can decide then where next to turn our attention."

"Fine," he said through gritted teeth. "I will see myself out."

~

Ravenscroft studied Charity in the dim light of the carriage, his eyes gleaming with curiosity. "So," he drawled, breaking the silence with his usual lazy charm. "An appointment with the princess. And here I thought I was the only one who specialized in sudden, unexplained obligations."

Charity kept her gaze on the swaying curtain, her expression calm, though her hands were tightly folded in her lap. "It is a delicate matter," she said simply, as though that explained everything.

"Delicate?" Ravenscroft repeated, arching a brow. "That's a very interesting choice of word. You do realize you have left our dear Fitzroy looking as though you kicked him square in the chest, yes? Not exactly the hallmark of subtlety."

Her jaw tightened at the mention of Peregrine Fitzroy, but she refused to rise to the bait. "He is capable of handling far worse than my absence, I assure you."

"I do not doubt his resilience. What I doubt, my dear duchess, is your ability to keep him in the dark. A man like Fitzroy—clever as a devil—will puzzle it out soon enough. And when he does, I hope you have planned for what comes next."

His words raised gooseflesh. "I appreciate your wisdom, but what comes next is none of your concern, Ravenscroft. This… this requires a particular approach, one I must take alone."

"Ah, *alone*. Now I see why our infamous prickle was left behind. You are worried about the Queen's wrath if he so much as looks sideways at the princess."

Charity felt physically ill. "Ravenscroft. Do yourself a favour and stop guessing what I am about."

To his credit, he listened, eyes flickering. "Tread carefully, my dear. The Queen's wrath may be sharp, but a man's disappointment?" He tapped the side of his temple lightly. "That cuts deeper."

At Carlton House, he offered her a hand for her descent from the carriage. The tall Corinthian columns loomed before her, resembling the bars of a jail cell.

Queen Charlotte would flay Charity alive if she knew she was questioning the princess about whether she had committed this crime. The stakes were as high as she could imagine, and Charity could not breathe a single word of this to *anyone* until she had all the facts.

What the young princess needed now was a confidante. The challenge would be convincing her that Charity could be that person. With that in mind, Charity gathered up her courage, tamped down her fears, and entered Carlton House.

She was in luck. The princess was in and agreed to see her. The footman took the lead, guiding her upstairs to the private rooms the royals called home. He gave a polite rap on the door and a faint feminine voice called for him to enter.

"Duchess Atholl, how lovely and unexpected to see you!" The princess was all smiles as she welcomed Charity into her private sitting room. "It has been a few days. Come, tell me where you have been. Father has refused to let me leave the grounds."

"I do have news," Charity said, darting a glance toward the maid stationed against the wall.

Princess Charlotte followed Charity's gaze, and without further prodding, dismissed the servant. "The duchess and I will see to ourselves, Ethel. I will ring when I need you."

The maid curtseyed and exited the room, closing the door firmly behind her. The princess guided Charity to a pair of gilt edged chairs and urged her to have a seat. Her expression was so pure, so lacking in guile, that Charity felt a hint of doubt.

Could this young girl really have poisoned her intended, and herself, to boot? There was only one sure way to find out.

"Your Highness, I bring your mother's regards," Charity said by way of a beginning.

"You saw Mama?" The princess's eyes lit up. "Where? Is she nearby?"

"I visited her at Montagu House, and spent time viewing the roses. She bade me to tell you that they have grown tall and bloomed since your last visit." Charity glanced around, as if checking that they were still alone, and lowered her voice. "She also told me you have told her you do not wish to marry Prince William. Is that true?"

"Of course I have. I have told everyone. I have practically shouted it from the rooftops," the princess said. "I do not care for him, Your Grace. Not enough to leave England."

"Surely, Your Highness, if you shared your concerns with him —or even the Queen..." Charity hesitated, knowing it was likely futile.

The princess shook her head. "I have tried. Everyone gives me sympathy to some degree, but the answer is always some shade of the same colour. 'Do your duty. Happiness is secondary.' I do not want to try to scratch grains of happiness out of the dirt. That is not how it should be. Do you not agree, Your Grace?"

There was so much anguish in her voice, Charity longed to bob her head in agreement. She allowed a hint of it to show when she phrased her next question. "Is that why you put something in the jenever decanter?"

"I—" the younger woman paused for a breath.

Charity grasped the princess's hand. "I know, Your Highness."

"Did Mama tell you? Oh, I knew it had to be her sending me the messages!" The princess's face lit up. "Mama said she would find a way to help me get free of this betrothal. I thought she would have a word in a few ears like she usually does, but no. When the tincture arrived with the instructions, I was shocked, to say the least. But it worked! Father cannot force me to wed a drunken fool. Mama is much more clever than I had hoped!"

The princess leapt to her feet, her laughter ringing out like a child's delighting in a harmless prank. But this wasn't harmless. It wasn't a game.

Charity kept her expression composed, the mask of the serene duchess never slipping, but beneath it, her mind shrank in horror. The princess had guessed it was her mother sending the messages, but even she had been unsure. And Fitzroy—he was certain that Caroline was not guilty. Charity had little reason to doubt his deduction.

What should she say? What could she say? Did the woman understand the risk she had taken?

"Your Highness," Charity said carefully, choosing her words as judiciously as one would choose their steps on a narrow bridge, "did you not fear for the consequences?"

The princess brushed her concern aside. "The man is fine, is he not?"

He was, though Charity could not stop the wave of doubts rushing over her. She grabbed a hold of the princess's hand and urged her to sit again. "Please, Your Highness. You must tell me everything."

Princess Charlotte rolled her eyes, but the fear showing on Charity's face caused her to submit to the request. "As I said, a tincture came with a letter, and I was instructed to put it in a bottle. I saw my chance when you were not waiting at the fountain. For once, no one was paying attention to me. I distracted the footman with a request for a punch and put it into the decanter."

"But what was in the tincture?"

"I have no earthly idea. It tasted so strange—the jenever, I mean. I cannot imagine how he stomachs it. At least, I am supposing that was the jenever and not the tincture."

"Princess!" Charity gasped, stunned at the girl's actions. "You drank it. You let *me* drink it. What if it was poison?"

"But…" the girl hesitated, confusion crushing her face. "Her letter told me it would be safe to drink if I put it in a bottle. Why would my mother lie?"

There was no hint of malice in the girl's expression. She truly did not understand the seriousness of the situation. And she never, not once, doubted that the person writing the letter had good intentions towards her. Charity hardened her heart and took the young woman to task, consequences be damned.

"Princess, I beg to differ. You put us in danger—all of us. Some person sent you a strange liquid, and without any certainty of what it was, you dosed a foreign guest and yourself! If it had been a real poison, we would all be dead!"

Her eyes were huge in her face. "Mama loves me. She'd never do anything to hurt me—she wouldn't!"

"Your Highness, you do not *know* if your mama sent you the tincture. It could have been anyone who sent you those messages. It could have been someone who wished to assassinate the entire royal family." Charity drew herself up and uttered a harsh truth as she only just grasped the staggering implications of what so easily *could* have happened. "Your rebellion could have caused a catastrophe that would throw the entire court into chaos. And if the Dutch thought England responsible… that would be even worse."

The princess reared back as though struck. Big fat tears rolled down the young woman's cheeks, keeping time with her heaving sobs. Charity's resolve crumbled, leaving behind a pile of dust where her stone heart had been.

"I did not want to hurt him. I did not mean for anything bad to happen!" Charlotte sobbed, clutching Charity's arm. "I only wanted not to marry him! I never thought it would go this far." Her voice cracked with the weight of regret—or was it fear?

Hug the poor child. Her mother's voice rang in her ears, sending Charity lurching forwards. Charity's resolve wavered as the princess sobbed, her face crumpling like a child's. Against her better judgment, Charity drew the girl into her arms, murmuring soothing words she didn't quite believe.

The need to comfort warred with the urgency to press for answers. She had to calm the woman down so that she could learn the rest. How did the messages arrive? Did the princess still have them? How long had they been coming?

But before Charity could utter a word of sympathy, a pounding on the door caused the princess to shriek in fear.

15

"Those who don't know history are doomed to repeat it."
—Edmund Burke

Peregrine watched the duchess disappear into Carlton House, the bile in his throat so sharp and caustic it felt like it might burn a hole clean through his chest.

Focus, damn you. Think. Bloody think. Your life depends on it —again.

He shoved his bruised pride and simmering resentment into an imaginary box, slammed the lid, and shoved it into the farthest, darkest corner of his mind as he considered how to salvage this ruddy disaster. Throughout their talk with Ravenscroft, he had progressively worked through everything that they knew.

A gnawing suspicion had been festering during their conversation with Prinny's magpie. Peregrine had sifted through every scrap of information, every word, and a pattern was beginning to emerge, one he hadn't wanted to see. They'd suspected Caroline and questioned her. But they'd been so narrowly focused on the idea that the enemy was outside the walls that they'd overlooked the rest of the royal family entirely.

That had been a mistake. A monumental, bloody stupid mistake.

The one person they had dismissed from consideration, a person who had both the means and the motive to sabotage this delicate union, was the princess herself. She had long, loudly, and rather publicly lamented the notion of tying her fortunes to William. And now, the pieces began to fall into place, forming part of a picture that was… rather unpleasant to consider.

Peregrine had intended to share his suspicions with the duchess—that they ought to question Princess Charlotte, delicately and thoroughly—once they'd sent Ravenscroft off to amuse himself elsewhere. But as he watched her face shift like the tides, every flicker of thought plainly written for those sharp enough to see, he realized she had already reached the same conclusion.

He should have known better—should never have forgotten—where her loyalty truly lay. It was bound fast to the Queen, with not so much as a scrap left to spare for him.

And the crowning insult, the cherry on top of this whole damned disaster? Trust. Or rather, the lack of it between them.

Instead of confiding in him, instead of pooling their knowledge like rational allies, she had effectively kicked him square in the balls and sent him packing. She thought she'd left him dumb as a post, empty-handed, and clueless.

But she underestimated him once more. How and why she kept underestimating him, he hadn't a notion.

What a little idiot. Just as her foolishness had laid bare the truth of last year's ball to Selina, the duchess's hasty flight to Carlton House hammered suspicion into cold, bitter certainty.

And the worst part? She had no idea what she'd done.

If she went in there and uncovered that the princess herself had poisoned a visiting foreign prince, what then? If she, in all her reckless righteousness, confessed the truth to the Queen?

Peregrine could only hope that the duchess's pretty little head was as vacant as a ballroom at dawn. The alternative—that she knew she might be selling him out—was a truth too bitter to swallow.

Again. You were sold out again, that detestable, feminine voice whispered in his mind, sharp and mocking. *You will never know peace unless you lose yourself in the wilds of Nova Scotia.*

Get back in your box, Mother, he snarled silently.

But the voice wasn't wrong. History had a nasty way of repeating itself, and here he was, scrambling once more to patch together his neck before the noose tightened. He'd have to track down Prinny again and arrange for another tête-à-tête with the duchess. All the while hoping against all odds, that the Prince Regent could grasp the stakes of this situation.

Yes, Princess Charlotte was an important thread, but no tapestry ever depended on a single strand. Her actions, however dire, didn't give a sense of the larger design. There was something far bigger unfolding in London, something with consequences that stretched far beyond a petulant princess and her ill-fated marriage. And whatever it was, it boded ill—not just for the nation, but for him most of all.

His steps carried him to the front door, the weight of the moment pressing down until he let his bitterness consume him, if only for the solace of its burn.

Once he gained entry, Peregrine was conducted to the Prince Regent, who was busy lounging indolently in a quiet corner of the card room, jeweled snuff box in hand. "Fitzroy," Prinny greeted him casually. "I have a dinner I must dress to attend shortly, but I will make time for glad tidings. Any word to the good about the, er… unpleasantness in the gardens?"

"Good? Well, I will let you be the judge of that." Seeing no one near, Peregrine, fists clenched behind his back, gave the meat of his suspicions in clipped, deliberate words, careful not to let the edge of his frustration boil over. As he spoke, Prinny's smile faded, replaced by an expression of mild distaste, as though the words themselves were an unpleasant odour.

Standing up with a speed that belied his girth, Prinny adjusted his waistcoat, casting a sidelong glance at Peregrine. "I should let you know, it is difficult to be on terms with someone possessed of your knack for ruining my evenings."

Cynically, Peregrine gave him a shallow bow, watching as Prinny ruminated like a bad-tempered steer, fiddling with the snuffbox in his hand.

At last, the Prince Regent exhaled sharply, the sound as much irritation as resignation. "Yes, she despises William—I know that well enough. But to think her capable of poisoning the man!" He gestured broadly, as if swatting away the absurdity of it. "Oh, her impetuousness, that I can believe. She has always had a flair for melodrama. However, the planning, the execution..." He let out a bitter laugh. "I could fill a book with all the questions I have about how such a thing might be done by the princess with no one the wiser!"

"You will fill it with nothing but speculation unless we ask her," Peregrine said urgently. "But as to the many questions about the how… in short, I doubt she is the mastermind. The princess is clever, yes, but this reeks of manipulation. Someone else is guiding her hand, and we must find out who. Your mother will, of course, move to shield her—and rightly so—but the longer we wait, the more likely it is that whoever stands at her shoulder will vanish into the shadows."

Prinny's expression darkened. "Then we shan't waste another

moment dithering," he growled, his voice thick with irritation. "If anyone is to confront the girl, it will be me. Come, Fitzroy—better a firm hand than a bloody calamity."

Peregrine followed the Prince Regent into the room where Princess Charlotte and the Duchess Atholl were seated. Both women shot to their feet, the princess wiping a hand over her face to dry her tears.

Peregrine couldn't quite help himself. He leveled a fierce glare at the duchess, letting her know that in no uncertain terms he was wroth with her. But they could hash out their grievances later.

Princess Charlotte, sensing an income battle of wills with her father, crossed her arms, her chin lifting with a regal air no doubt perfected since birth. The duchess tried to radiate icy calm, but she let her gaze slide to the side only a second after meeting Peregrine's eyes.

Guilt. How dare she pretend remorse about her actions now!

The Prince Regent, whose face was already red with temper, didn't bother with pleasantries. "Charlotte Augusta," he barked, his voice sharp enough to cut glass. "Did you mean to poison the Prince of Orange?"

The bluntness of the question hung in the air like cannon smoke. "Father, it was not supposed to happen like this," the princess said, her face tear-streaked and her voice very small. "I thought—I never thought this was dangerous."

"So you did. This is no time for excuses," Prinny cut in, his voice sharp enough to draw blood. "Do you understand the gravity of what you've done, Charlotte? You risked everything—everything—for what? A tantrum? A moment of defiance?"

The princess's tears began anew. "Stop raising your voice to me! Her Grace already told me I could have killed everyone, including myself! Do you not believe that I feel terrible enough already? But I would never have done it if you had listened.

You *never* listen, Father! Even now, you do not ask me why I did it."

"And what is there to listen to?" Prinny barked, his face reddening as he stepped toward her. "Another of your tiresome complaints about how life is unfair? The survival of this family—this nation—requires sacrifices. Or have you forgotten that in your endless self-pity? Duty, Charlotte. Duty! I did mine with your mother, and so will you!"

"Duty? Duty is your excuse for everything! Is that what you call what you and Mama did to me—duty?" Her voice broke, and she pointed at him, her finger trembling. "Do you even know what it is like, being caught between you and her? Your shouting, your insults, your games? Maybe if you had not been forced to marry her, you would have been happy, and I would not have been born to grow up in the shadow of your misery!"

Ignoring the royal family's mortifyingly personal bickering, Peregrine turned to Charity, his face a cold mask that showed nothing of the molten fury threatening to burn through.

"I assume you had a reason you did not think to include me in your plans?" he asked, his voice low but laced with anger. "A reason, I hope, that somehow justifies your actions once you extorted a promise from me that I would keep no secrets that hindered the investigation."

The duchess waved her hands at the argument. "I wanted to handle this alone so it could be done… delicately. Instead, you decide that involving the Prince Regent was the prudent thing to do."

Peregrine let out a sharp, bitter laugh, stepping into her space. "Had you simply been honest with me, as we both agreed, I would not have had to go to Prinny. This mess is entirely of your making."

"Do you ever take any responsibility for the things that happen around you?" she snapped back, her demeanor cracking.

She sucked in a breath, as if realising what she had said, and hurried to add, "The situation was complicated, and I thought it would be better if you were not involved."

He stared at her, speechless, his heart bleeding. Sometimes, this woman acted like she could not give a fig for his life. "Tell me truthfully, Sparkles. You came expecting to hear an answer, and you expected you would have to report it to the Queen. Did you give one thought to what might happen to me then?"

Queen Charlotte wasn't the sort to wring her hands and wail over family guilt. No, the Queen would never allow blame to settle on her precious granddaughter. She'd find someone else to bear the weight of the scandal. Someone expendable.

And Peregrine, son of England's most notorious enemy, had an excellent chance of ending up at the top of that list.

The duchess's face paled slightly, her blue eyes growing shadowed. "I—I didn't…"

Finally, the princess threw her hands up in exasperation, breaking the tension between them. "Enough!" she shouted, silencing them all. Her cheeks were flushed, and her breath came fast as she glared at her father. "You want the information. I will give it to you and then you can all leave me alone!"

She turned on her heel and stormed into the adjoining room, slamming the door behind her. The sound of objects being thrown and crashing against walls echoed back into the parlour.

Peregrine sighed, stepping away, and the duchess began to wring her hands silently. "Fitzroy—" she began.

But before she could say more, the door flew open again, and Princess Charlotte reappeared, clutching a bundle of letters in her trembling hands. She marched back to the table and slammed them down.

"There," she said, her voice shaking with anger. "I wish I knew who sent me these, because I would go to them now. This is the only person in this wretched world who seems to support me."

The argument between them forgotten, the duchess stepped forward first, her face aggrieved as she picked up the top letter. "What are these?" she asked quietly.

"Read them," the princess demanded, sinking into her chair. "See for yourselves."

Prinny leaned over the Duchess Atholl's shoulder, frowning as she unfolded the first letter. Peregrine moved to her other side, scanning the words as she read aloud. It looked like a woman's penmanship, and the paper was of quality, but there was no address.

The first few letters were sympathetic, consoling Princess Charlotte about her dissatisfaction with the plans for her betrothal to the Prince of Orange. But the tone of the letters soon shifted. By the third, there was subtle encouragement to act against the betrothal. By the fifth, the writer was openly suggesting ways to sabotage the union.

Peregrine's brows knit as Charity reached the final letter, dated a few weeks prior. "This one is… chilling to see it put so plainly," she said, her voice unsteady.

She read aloud: "The vial enclosed contains a tincture. It is safe to drink as long as it is added to a bottle, not a glass. Retire to your chambers when you begin to feel tired, and all will proceed as planned."

Prinny's face was bloodless. "This… this is treachery," he growled.

"Who sent these?" Peregrine asked the princess, his voice sharp. "Where did you send your replies?"

"I thought it was my mama. But now… now I do not know," The princess hesitated, biting her lip. "I left them under a bench in Hyde Park. The first Tuesday of every month. I never saw anyone."

Peregrine ran a hand through his bright blonde hair roughly. "Amateur work," he laughed shortly, remembering the apothecary's words. "This is the work of no amateur. The princess's correspondent is someone with close access to the palace—or once had it," he said. "She chose her target with care, cultivating trust so that she could exploit the princess and avoid detection."

And someone who had some of the acumen of his mother, knowing how to acquire the henbane from an apothecary, and how to use it as a weapon.

Feeling the weight of the duchess's gaze on him, Peregrine lifted his eyes. She looked so worried and unhappy that he knew her thoughts were also on his mother, but at the moment, he was too angry to care.

Prinny slammed his hand on the table, making them all jump. "Such speculation is not as helpful as a name," he declared. "We must find out who was writing to the princess. Can we lay a trap at the bench?"

"Pointless," Peregrine muttered. "The usefulness of the correspondence was at its end the moment the princess found the vial. Whoever left it would not risk being caught returning to the scene."

"So what do you think we should do?" the duchess asked him. The irony that she would ask this now, of all times, was thick.

"*We* shall do nothing. *I* have one final lead to follow," Peregrine said crisply.

"But—" the duchess protested, her voice taking on an angry note.

"—Absolutely not," he interrupted, lifting a hand toward her face to stop her. Instead, he began to address his words towards Prinny, who looked shocked and confused by his coarse treatment of Charity. "It would be highly inappropriate for the duchess to assist me. She will find her way *home*."

Red Hand. He had to see if he could discover who had been so interested in stopping them from looking into matters. Not many would be willing to poke the belly of the underworld beast to send a message.

Two spots of colour appeared high on her face. "Your Highness," the duchess said, "might I impose upon you to have a footman send for my carriage?"

The princess's eyes grew round as she divided a look between her father, the duchess, and Peregrine.

"Do not be silly. There is no need to trouble His Highness with that, Your Grace." He forced the honorific out, though it felt like salt on his tongue. "As I am on my way out as well, you may ride with me. I would be *happy* to make sure you arrive home safely."

16

"Desperate times force us to confront the truths we've been avoiding."
—Anonymous

Charity did not utter a word as they made their way through Carlton House. Between Lord Fitzroy's anger and the listening ears of those around them, saying anything would be the height of foolishness. Outside, she stood demurely at Fitzroy's side, waiting for a footman to flag a hired hackney. He didn't look at her, his stony countenance keeping its own counsel. But she knew better; she had seen the wound that lay beneath.

Guilt and shame ate at her. Of course, her Queen would likely want to make him a scapegoat.

But on the other hand, her thoughts had been wholly consumed by the significance of putting such dangerous questions to the princess with only a suspicion to justify it. Finally, they took their seats inside. For once, he kept his legs well clear of her space and stared out the window. Really, he was almost being petulant.

She had to explain. At least, she had to try to make him understand why she had done it. She took a calming breath and forged ahead. "Fitzroy, I had not thought far enough ahead to worry about the aftermath, and what would happen if the worst were true. I just knew I had to be careful—so careful about asking. What if I said something so terrible and I was entirely wrong? It would have been just as catastrophic for you to be involved in questioning the princess."

"Agreed," he said shortly.

If he agreed he could not question the princess with her, then why was he so angry? She glowered at the man from across the confines of his carriage. "Is that all? You have nothing more to say?"

"You are… a most backward, deceitful creature," he said, with all the heat he would address a stubborn cowlick in his hair.

Her mouth dropped open, and her small gasp of outrage finally forced him to look at her. "Surely not more so than other certain women of your relation!"

"Ah, there it is. Is it not just the most peculiar thing? No matter how far we come, when we are quarrelling because *you* are in the wrong, you will always, *always* use the fact that Lady Fitzroy is my mother as a weapon against me."

His words were edged in truth, and they cut to the bone. She was coming to understand how much he despised when people looked at him and only saw his mother, and she had brought it up for that very reason. But— "How can you say I am wrong for not bringing you? You just said you agreed—"

"You wanted no secrets between us, a rule that you blatantly ignored when you set off for Carlton House without telling me the real purpose behind your visit."

"I told you as much as I could, Fitzroy. I did not tell Lord Ravenscroft my suspicions either, if that is any consolation—"

He tossed back his head and barked a laugh. "You looked me in the eye and lied, and you did that for the same reason you will never let the subject of my mother go—because you do not trust me. You… simply don't want to."

"No, Fitzroy, that is not true—"

"Stop. *Spare me* your pathetic attempts at justifying everything. You asked me if I ever took responsibility for my own actions. *Do you?*"

Charity pressed a hand to the sharp pain at her breastbone. How could she possibly make this right?

"You are right. I should have explained my suspicions and why I wanted to speak with the princess alone," she said in a low voice. "And… I did lash out when I realised how wrong I was to do so. I was wrong to do all these things, but please believe the truth in what I say. My silence was not because I thought you were untrustworthy. Not once did I ever consider not telling you if she was guilty."

He raised an eyebrow, his voice cool and biting. "Is that an apology? Because if it is, I must have missed the part where you said the word sorry even once."

She looked him in the eye, feeling the ache linger in her chest. "Would it fix everything if I say it?"

He leaned forward, closing the space between them and commanding her full attention. Suddenly, the realization struck her like a bolt. He wanted to be seen. Not as a shadow cast by his mother, but as his own man.

Why had it taken her so long to notice, when she had wanted the same thing? She had wanted to be seen as a duchess. A lady-in-waiting for the Queen herself. A person of power—and not a broken creature who needed the protection of Roland Percy.

Whatever else he was, he wanted to be seen as Peregrine. *Not* just the son of Lady Fitzroy. Everything was shaped by that need, and she, who should have known better, had spent all this time together ignoring it.

Peregrine. She sounded the name out in her head. It was unwieldy, long, and formal, but somehow it suited him, too. *Perry*, the marchioness had called him.

All of the Fitzroys had been named after birds, including his sister Lark and his father Robin. Falcons were a hunting bird—graceful, precise, and worthy of respect. And so was he.

But his eyes danced with malice, unaware of the rearrangement of her thoughts. "I suppose we will never know until you try."

She had earned this, and she swallowed hard. "You spoke every word true," she said softly, "and I understand why you would believe I was motivated by a lack of trust, but I—"

Charity stopped trying to explain, cutting herself off. "Never mind, the reasons do not matter. I am sorry for everything I did today. I did not intend to slight you."

Peregrine was still watching her, and she said nothing more. She let him hold her gaze, willing him to see the bare truth of it, but his eyes were flat and empty, and she could not guess what he was really thinking.

It seemed that he would not let go of his anger today, which was only to be expected. Feelings did not change at the drop of a hat. Even she did not know if she would ever be able to find it within herself to trust him in all things, without limit. Not after what Lady Fitzroy had done.

Perhaps that was unfair, but… Charity could not quite forgive that it had been well within his power to find the missing diamond —if only he had looked.

She did trust him, at least, in helping to find who had poisoned the prince. Maybe if she extended a small piece of trust they could begin to mend things somewhat.

"Whatever you are planning next," she said, "be careful. I know I cannot go poking around in the darker corners, but at least take someone with you—someone to watch your back."

His eyelids flickered softly, and he sat back.

The carriage jerked to a halt and Charity was startled to see her own front door outside the window. Fitzroy swung open the door on his side of the carriage and leapt down after a cursory glance at passing traffic. She slid across the seat, determined to stop him from stomping off, forgetting he was not at his destination.

He was standing outside her door, looking anywhere but at her, offering a careless hand to assist her with her descent.

She sighed, but took his hand and squeezed, compelling him to look her in the eye, but he did not indulge her. He offered a stiff arm, doing the bare minimum expected of a gentleman, and the coldness of it made her bones ache.

Where had the defiant man who called her the most disrespectful names gone—the one who snuck into her bedroom and splayed across her chaise? How was it that somehow she missed him?

They crossed the distance to her door in seconds. He deposited her there, pulling his arm free of her light hold. "Tonight has been... educational, Your Grace. Good evening." He executed a stiff bow and did an about face before she could reply.

The door opened behind her. She walked through, her mind and attention still on the man walking away outside. A gruff, guttural voice sounded from inside her home.

"Guv didn't say what a beaut' this one is. We'll have some fun before we slit her throat."

Her head snapped around. A bald, hulk of a man, dressed in a stained coat and rough trousers grinned at her with yellowed teeth. He shifted forward, crushing the broken shards of an ancient Greek vase that had stood in her entrance hall under his feet.

Terror closed her throat. Someone stepped out from behind the door and jerked her inside. As the door swung shut behind her, she was shoved against the bulky, smelly, torso of the bald man in front of her. He wrapped his arms about Charity, and his onion-scented breath made her gag.

It was enough to pierce through the fear-induced haze that had stolen her voice. Without conscious thought, she screamed a single cry for help. *"Perry!"*

~

Peregrine had barely taken three steps when the scream reached his ears. It pierced through the evening like a dagger, driving straight to his core.

His name reverberated in his chest, momentarily robbing him of thought. Then, as if a match had been struck, a jolt of heat surged through his limbs, igniting every nerve on fire. Spat with the duchess forgotten, he let himself be consumed by purpose. He turned on his heel and sprinted back to Atholl House, blood pounding in his ears.

Reaching the door, he grabbed the latch. It had been locked. Not wasting any time, he braced himself and kicked it open with his boot. The wooden panel crashed back against the wall. The force rattled the nearby chandelier, but he couldn't care less about the damage to the house.

For as quickly as he had been set ablaze by the need to take action, the scene inside chilled him. The duchess stood with her back arched painfully, a hulking brute holding her hair in one fist, yanking her head back. A worn but wicked knife gleamed in his other hand, the blade hovering ominously close to her throat.

Charity's face was pale, her wide eyes fixed on him, and her captor's yellowed grin widened, revealing crooked teeth as he leered at Peregrine.

"Boss, lookie at who came back," the slatternly man who held her sneered, his voice low and gravelly.

Another man, smaller but wiry, stepped around the broad bastard holding Charity. His face was weathered, his dark eyes gleaming with a cruel kind of intelligence. Peregrine's stomach soured as he recognized the man.

"McGrath," Peregrine said, his voice steady despite the sudden urge to do violence.

The wiry man inclined his head slightly. "Ah, so you remember me, my lord. Always gratifying to make an impression and revisit past glory, but I'm afraid this isn't a social call."

Peregrine's gaze darted between the two men, his mind racing to consider his options. Charity stood stock still, her breaths shallow and quick, her face as colourless as linen. The man holding her tightened his grip again, making her wince.

"Easy," Peregrine muttered, raising his empty hands. "Let us talk about this like gentlemen."

McGrath laughed, and so did his jolly giant friend. "You always were a funny lad when you wanted to be. Unfortunately for you, we ain't got much to talk about, Fitzroy. Our orders were clear. Send a message. And, well, nothing screams louder than a duchess with her throat slit in her own home, all of her servants helpless to do anything about it."

"Don't do this." Peregrine wanted to avoid provoking them further. "Turn around and walk away. No one has to die tonight."

McGrath shook his head. "Ah lad. You fancy this one, do you? *Ach.* No wonder she was chosen as the price of such a sinister bargain. Sorry about that, love," he told her, stroking her cheek with smudged fingers.

"This is bigger than you, yer lordship. Bigger than her. And you should know better than to play the Crown's lapdog. Be careful with that leash around your neck… it'll strangle you someday. Maybe even tonight, if you don't walk away and let us do what we came here to do."

His world felt like it was spinning on its axis, and he gritted his teeth to keep the sense of vertigo at bay. "If you kill her, you will not make it out of this house alive," he promised.

McGrath chuckled darkly. "Don't take offence to this, but I think I'll take my chances, lad."

Sensing a fight about to happen, the bald man shifted slightly, his knife hand dropping and his grip loosening on the duchess's hair just enough that it gave her a head a fraction of movement.

She cast her eyes to the side table where a heavy brass lamp sat. And then she locked eyes with him. His stomach turned at the risk of it, but he gave her a fractional nod.

Charity collapsed bonelessly, feigning a swoon, and the brute holding her cursed, trying to hang onto her as McGrath turned from her to lunge at Peregrine with his knife.

Peregrine sidestepped the reach of the blade. Then he shoved himself against McGrath's overextended arm, trying to pin it against the wall. McGrath's henchman tried to keep the duchess's dead weight from sliding to the floor, but finally, he gave up and let her go so that he was free to help his boss with Peregrine.

Finding herself released, Charity staggered but she caught herself on the table, grabbing the lamp with both hands. Before he could stab his blade in Peregrine's direction, Charity swung the lamp with all her strength, smashing it into the side of his head.

He also hit the floor with his skull. Rather hard, too. But Peregrine had no sympathy.

Though he was rather awkwardly pinned against the wall, McGrath still had a grip on his knife, and he was trying to shove Peregrine off by sweeping outward with his right arm. Peregrine had his right hand wrapped around McGrath's wrist. His left was twisted in the man's short hair to keep him from trying to deliver a blow to Peregrine with his pate.

The duchess lifted the lamp again, trying to swing it at McGrath, but she missed, only hitting him in the shoulder. Still, the force of it caused him to grunt in surprise, slowing his struggle against Peregrine.

Taking advantage of the duchess's distraction and gripped in battle rage, Peregrine slammed McGrath's right hand against the wall over and over until the man finally dropped the knife with a pained cry.

"Look away, duchess," Peregrine hissed at her, not waiting to see if she obeyed before he spun McGrath around and began to knock the man's skull against the wall the same way. Only once the man collapsed did Peregrine release him with a shove, snatching up both men's knives.

McGrath was still alive and would most likely stay that way—for better or for worse. Leaving such a dangerous man breathing in Atholl House was risky, but Peregrine refused to make himself even more like a monster to Charity than he already was. He had to get everyone out before the man regained his senses.

He turned to the duchess, who was leaning against the wall, standing amidst shards of broken antiques, her face tinged with green.

"Are you hurt?" he demanded. His voice made him sound half-mad. It was more than probable he looked that way, too. She shook her head, shaking like a leaf, and trying not to be rough with her, Peregrine spun her around, moving her away from McGrath, deeper into Atholl House.

"Steady, Sparkles," he told her, jollying her along with the nickname. "Where would they hold your servants?"

"T—the cellar," she answered in a whisper. "There is a lock on the door."

She tried to pull ahead of him, but he caught her by the wrist, holding her back. "Stay with me, Duchess. They would not overpower your household with just two men."

Indeed, as they progressed stealthily towards the back of the house, he could hear people rummaging in the butler's pantry. Stealing the good candlesticks, if he had to guess by the clinking. Between the walls and the noise they were making, the fight in the front entryway had gone unnoticed.

McGrath must have sent his lack-witted men to ransack the place and make sure that the servants stayed put, because the thief had left the butler's key ring sitting on the table by the door, the pantry door key conspicuously separate.

Well, that was two men easily taken care of. Pushing the duchess behind him, Peregrine lightly picked up the right key. Two steps, and he slammed it shut on the men inside, locking it even before they realised what had happened.

A scuff behind him, from the kitchen, had Peregrine spin on his heels. One lone thug stood there, muddy green eyes wide as he goggled at the two of them. He was young—hardly more than a boy, really—and had been probably set to watch the cellar.

Hardening his resolve, Peregrine lifted one of the knives he had taken from the front hallway. "Are you and I going to have a problem?" he demanded.

"No milord," the stripling said quickly, his Adam's apple bobbing furiously.

"Then tell me—how many more of your friends are in this house?"

"F-five of us all told, milord."

"Then leave right now. Or… don't."

Peregrine didn't bother to elaborate, but the young man didn't ask for any further explanation. He ran for the door like the hounds of hell were nipping at his heels, leaving the cellar door clear. Pounding and voices on the far side confirmed the duchess's guess; her household had been herded and locked up.

Giving Charity the key ring, he asked her to find the one belonging to the door. She took it from him, but she was still shaking, and the keys were jangling like chimes as she tried to sort without dropping them. As discreetly as he could, he cupped her elbow in his hand, helping her steady it. Finally, she found the right one, and Peregrine unlocked the door, flinging it open to find a very upset butler at the fore.

"Mr Pritchard," Charity gasped as the servants spilled out, hale and safe.

The butler cast a sharp glance at Charity, standing so close to Peregrine's side, before turning his steely gaze on the man himself. "Mr Pritchard," Peregrine said, the slant of his mouth gaining a touch of irreverence.

Before the butler could muster a lecture, Peregrine thrust the keyring into his hand. "There are two locked in your pantry and two more unconscious in the front hall. I would suggest you have the footmen secure those others in the cellar—where they so kindly decided to hold you. And preferably before they wake."

The footmen rushed to do his bidding, but returned with empty hands. The older of the pair said, "The front door was wide open and there was no one there."

Fitzroy cursed under his breath. As a reward for leaving those men alive, he would have to continue looking over his shoulder. He had little doubt they would return. "Send someone to Bow Street to collect the men locked in the pantry. The rest of you can set the place to rights. Her Grace will not be back here for a few days."

As the servants fled, Peregrine turned back to Charity. She was staring at the locked pantry door, her breathing shallow.

"Stay with me," he warned her again, but this time he was more concerned that she was going to lose command of herself. He placed a hand on her shoulder, nudging her toward the door. In a firm voice, he instructed, "Come now, we are leaving."

She nodded, her movements wooden. By the time they reached the door, she looked dangerously close to falling apart.

Peregrine sent Prichard to flag a carriage to meet them around back, and then took Charity in hand. He draped a heavy cloak over her shoulders, steering her toward the mews. As he helped hand her into the hired hack, she froze on the steps, refusing to budge.

"Come on," he said quietly to the suddenly terrified duchess.

"I—" she started, gulping. "I *can't*."

"We are going together," he reminded her firmly, being patient, and she finally moved inside with a lurch.

The hack had only one bench. He spared a single thought for hope that the duchess wasn't going to be fussy about sharing a seat, but she only huddled in her cloak, pressing to the wall as the hack rolled into motion.

Once they found themselves sitting still and no longer fighting for their lives, Peregrine's mind felt free to resume its footrace.

The ride was silent, save for the clatter of hooves and the faint creak of the carriage. For her part, Charity stared out the window as they drove towards the Seven Dials, her hands clenched tightly in her lap.

It was only a matter of time before she collected her wits and began to demand answers. Surely she noticed when he called McGrath by name. She would want to know how they knew one another, and he wasn't sure how he could begin to answer her.

How did one strike up a conversation with a duchess about how his mother's man of business had contacts within London's underbelly, anyway?

This was his comeuppance for being so furious with her. Of course, the duchess could hardly look at him without seeing his mother. Every layer peeled away on the rotting onion of this crime, they found only more and more of her black corruption.

More and more shadows of the past, and more ruins of her neglected empire.

With his mother absent, there was a void to be filled, and someone had just made a declaration of war.

Beside him, the duchess stirred, finally rousing from the inky mire of her distress.

"You came for me," she whispered, her voice muffled, and the sound of it cracked a piece of the wall around his heart.

"Of course I did, Sparkles," he said simply, wrapping her cloak more tightly around her as her shivering increased.

She means you came for her this *time*, his mother's voice gave a low chuckle in his thoughts, and Peregrine shoved the sound of Marian Fitzroy's hateful voice back into the dark hole of his thoughts.

Charity leaned against him slightly, as if she was afraid he would push her away. But he just tucked her beneath his arm, trying not to remember the time last year when he hadn't.

17

"Till this moment, I never knew myself."
—Elizabeth Bennet, Pride & Prejudice

It felt a little like a waking dream, life bent so slightly out of true and not quite real. Outside, lamplight flickered in the gloaming, the shadows blunting the harsher angles of London's face into something more ephemeral.

Charity's thoughts were loose and disordered, and she found herself reluctant to pick them up. To break the fragile peace between them, or to acknowledge the truths that would inevitably splinter them apart once more.

Selfishly, she ignored sense, letting the smell of cloves on him draw her deeper into that uncanny feeling, living the echo of a moment that could have been, but never was.

But then, his breathing changed, and she knew it was over before the hack could even slow to a halt. She moved away from him as the driver alighted, feeling chilled and awkward. The door was opened onto a row of modest brick houses, and she could hear a far-distant clamour of humanity.

He stepped down and held his hand out to her, but his expression was… different this time. Peregrine was watching her with the steady appraisal of his namesake, fixed and preternatural. Not letting her gaze lower, she took his proffered hand, and once she had straightened on the pavement, he reluctantly let it drop.

"Where are we?" she asked softly after the hack moved on.

He glanced around, looking for movement. "My townhouse, near Covent Gardens."

Had he brought her to the home in which the Fitzroy men installed their mistresses? If so, it looked rather dark and forlorn. He beckoned her forward, finally resting his palm on her lower back to guide her silently as she plodded forward.

"But are we safe here?" she asked him, her voice barely above a whisper.

There was a little silence, and she knew he was wondering the same thing. "I think so," he said finally. "Very few people know about it."

Suddenly she realised she knew this house, and knew then it had never seen a mistress here, no matter what others might assume, given its location. It had been one of the places people had searched for her after her kidnapping, but they had found the house mouldering and unused except for the two orphans hiding in the basement.

It didn't smell as musty as Grace had described it, but it was most definitely empty. Perry had brought them through the servant's entrance, and the fireplaces were cold.

When she shivered again reflexively, he stripped his coat, handing it to her. She startled, and he gave her a darkling look. "I am taking it off, so you may as well wear it."

She held his coat like a dullard while he lit a candle.

"How badly were you hurt?" he asked finally, reaching a hand slowly towards her hair like one would approach a frightened child.

She shook her head quickly, stepping away. "It is fine." Really, her scalp ached like fury where the thug had pulled her hair, but she didn't think she could bear to touch the spot.

Peregrine let his hands drop and for a long moment he watched her, rolling up his shirt sleeves over his forearms.

It was uncomfortable to look at him, so she watched his hands. "I cannot tell what you are thinking," she blurted out.

"Sparkles… you really don't want to know." His words were both heavy and guarded. Finally, he turned away from her. "I need to see to things. Consider yourself entirely welcome. There are no servants here… it is just me."

Then he left her, to do… chores. A man of title and his bearing, doing humble tasks like drawing water and tending hearths. It was nearly as hard to add to the picture of the man who had been so comfortable dealing violence. But somehow it fit.

Feeling at her wits' end while he was busy, Charity put on his coat and decided to explore. Or think. Perhaps she could find some way to be useful… removing dustcloths or… something. But as she passed from room to room, she saw the signs of recent habitation, and she filed the mystery away to ask him later.

The parlour on the first floor was empty except for a lone table, and the other room on that floor was a study. The desk was uncovered, but no papers of any kind sat on top of it. The third floor also had only the two rooms—a bedroom and a locked door which would not yield to her.

Charity stood inside the bedroom for a moment, looking down at the covers. It was made, but without exacting care, its maker only having to please himself. And as she looked on, her heart picked up its pace.

With her thoughts at sixes and sevens, Charity went back downstairs to the dark study. She sat behind his desk for a long while, trying to make sense of everything that had happened, and failing miserably.

After perhaps three quarters of an hour, she went searching for Peregrine—and she found him in the kitchen. He was stripped to the waist, scrubbing soot-stained hands and arms over a wash pail.

"Oh!" Charity exclaimed, slapping her hands over her mouth as Peregrine spun to face her. His face was lost in shadow, the faint glow of the light behind him obscuring his expression.

"I—I'm sorry, I did not mean to intrude on you," she stammered, already stepping back, ready to flee, until her eyes caught on the dark mottling curling around his ribs. Her voice faltered. "You did not say you were hurt."

He tilted his head slightly, his words wry. As if he was amused she finally deigned to notice. "The trophy from our adventures yesterday. Surely you remember?"

Yesterday? It felt like a lifetime ago now. "I thought you were speaking in jest. I did not realise you were truly injured."

"Hodges got a few worse than mine—unsightly ones. But bruises heal."

She hadn't even wondered as to why he had taken a hack today. Her face heated.

Peregrine smirked faintly, examining his right arm, on the side above the elbow, prodding the flesh around a small cut, which earned a wince but apparently needed no further treatment. "Sparkles, did no one tell you it is rude to stare? And what do you want?" He pulled his shirt back on, hiding the bruises from sight.

Peregrine was back to making a mock of her—familiar territory.

Safer.

She lowered her eyelashes. "Why did you bring me here?" she asked baldly. "There are inns. The homes of neighbours and friends. The Queen would probably even let me stay. But you...

brought me here. And I cannot help but notice… you have been staying here, too.”

He paused, his expression inscrutable. As if he was weighing how much truth to give her. “Because I feel safer here than anywhere else I can think of. I want you to stay here for a while. Just a few days. I will get Hodges to come play housemaid.”

“You want me to stay here. While you leave?”

In his own sanctuary, where he apparently feels safer than at the Fitzroy estate, her inner voice added, and Charity frowned at that notion.

“There are no more doors you can open for me.”

He wasn’t just keeping her out of the way. He was setting her aside. Abruptly, she was angry. “You promised there would be no secrets!”

Peregrine let out a short, audible breath—just shy of a scoff. “I promised I would not impede your investigation, and that is at an end.”

He had called one of her attackers by name. How many connections to dark places did he have?

“Then what happened with the prince and princess *was* a message of some sort. And the message was meant for you.” It was a guess, but it fit the pattern.

Swiftly, he moved into her space, looming over her like a threat. The faint flicker of light from the hearth caught in his eyes, but the shadows clung to him like a second skin. “It is a dangerous thing, prying into secrets. Leave it alone.”

“No.” Her heart was beating so fast she was breathless. “You cannot intimidate me any longer, Perry. I see who you are now, and I am not afraid of you.”

He hesitated for a long moment, something unnameable hovering in his eyes and on his lips. “Well, that is… something, I suppose.”

The choking sense of unreality tightened on her as he stepped away. He was going to leave her here. Completely unattended. Her entire life, there had always been someone within the reach of her voice or the tug of a bell pull.

Stop thinking only of yourself! He is the one who is going to dangerous places—and he is going to be the one who is by himself. Especially if he sends Hodges to you.

She ran forward, grabbing his shoulder. "Tell me. Who is McGrath to you?"

He turned back to her. "You know I am not going to tell you that." There was no give in his jaw.

Charity lifted her chin, prepared to use the only leverage she had. "Then I will not stay here. I will go home—or wander the streets—unless you tell me what I want to know. You want me to trust you, but I want your trust in return."

"Do not amuse yourself at my expense, Charity," he ground out. "This isn't a game of Question and Command."

She liked the way her name sounded on his tongue. It seemed as familiar as it was forbidden, and made her feel… a little wild.

"Why not?" she dared him, poking him in the chest in a flagrant violation of her rules. "Is that not the point of the game? A secret for a secret? An exchange of trust?"

Something new was waking deep inside of her, and it was as though she only now truly was alive. No wonder Peregrine had enjoyed provoking her. This was so much better than feeling as though she had no power over anything at all.

Peregrine's mood snapped, and he grabbed her hand in his, his eyes flashing dangerously as he let the other pull her against him. "Secrets are never about trust, Sparkles. It is all about *control*."

Charity's lips parted as she suddenly understood. These were the stakes Selina and Peregrine played for. No wonder the marchioness had called it currency. With the right secrets, people could be bought and sold. If you had enough secrets and the right people… just about anything might be possible.

This was the real power, and he was being driven by a need to keep it. She could see it now so clearly that she wondered how she ever misunderstood before.

"Then keep it," she whispered to him, not struggling to get free of his hands. "Keep your control. But do not leave me in the dark."

Now that she had a glimpse of this world that existed… she wanted to know everything about it.

A part of her noted in passing that the voice of her mother was nowhere in evidence, even though she should be shrieking. But Charity was tired of being bound by senseless rules that had no real power to ward off the harm in her life.

She saw his throat move, and she knew it as a sign of victory.

"McGrath is… an associate of my mother's man of business."

Stilling, she considered that. "Does this mean—"

"You are absolute rubbish at following rules of any kind, you know that, right?" He let her go, and her skin felt cold without his hands on her. Peregrine's face, though, had lost some of its hardness. "It is my turn, remember."

Unbidden, Charity felt a smile dig into her cheeks. It was so foolish to find this so funny. But it was the most genuine amusement she could imagine feeling for… far, far too long. "You are right. I do apologise, my lord. Pose your question."

He pursed his lips in thought for a moment and then he smirked. "Did you really take that old codger to your bed?"

Devil. He was either trying to navigate her into choosing command, or he was fishing for evidence that her marriage was a sham. Either way, he was going to be disappointed. "Everything was properly done," she said lightly.

"Yourself included, Sparkles?" he asked, and she couldn't help it. She turned a fiery shade of red as his meaning came clear.

"My God, Perry! Is nothing sacred to you?" she sputtered,

half laughing and half mortified. "And since it wasn't your turn, I will not answer that—now or ever."

"I daresay I will survive the mystery since your face is answering for you."

His voice and expression were teasing now, and Charity felt… a wistful kind of happiness unfurling, chasing away the wretched thoughts and emotions from earlier. Perhaps they weren't irrevocably broken. Not just yet.

"Is she back?" she asked him softly, not really wanting to know. Because… she was already afraid she might never sleep again.

It wasn't until he grazed the corner of her eye with his thumb that she noticed wetness forming there. He didn't even ask who 'she' was. "In England? Not a chance of it. Short of having an army at her back, it would be far too risky." He held his breath a moment, as if he was thinking. "But… my mother's man of business had almost as much ambition as my mama, a thirst for money, and several roots in dark places besides."

Charity nodded slightly, not wanting him to take his hand away, but needing him to. It would be such a mistake between them if she forgot herself. From the very first moment they met, they had been star-crossed in every possible way, cursed generations deep.

"Question or command?" he asked her.

"Question."

He thought for a moment, his expression almost hesitant. "If you could go back a year and do things once more, would things between us be the same?

If she could go back to before they knew one another's name, he meant. Did she have any regrets?

Now, she did. But that didn't mean things wouldn't still be the same. She hadn't expected to find ruin down this path, true, but the other course would have demanded everything from both of them… and then would have left her in a far more permanent state of destruction.

After a moment's consideration, she replied. "Command."

Some of the life left his eyes, but he had his command at the ready. "I want to loosen your hair."

"Of all the things you could ask for, that is what you want?" she asked him, surprised.

There was the briefest hesitation, before his trickster mask fell over his face again. "You seem to think it is such a small thing to ask. But as it happens, I have a terribly unromantic ulterior motive. Several, actually. The first one is I do want to make sure your head is all right. What if the bastard plucked you like a chicken?"

Charity slapped a hand over her mouth at the thought, and then felt at the back of her head, hissing in pain as she poked the tender spots. Then she whirled, granting him the permission to check.

"What else?" she asked him, feeling a lock of her hair fall to her shoulder as he drew the first pin. "You said you had several."

"You are also rubbish at managing your own hair," he muttered as he pulled more pins, and she huffed a laugh. "So really, I am doing you a favour."

Peregrine was being gentle, but now she was worried at his silence. Was there a spot of bare scalp after all? "And?" she prompted.

"I wanted to," he answered, lightly massaging the back of her skull and the hollows in her neck behind her ears as he parted the mass of hair with his thumbs. Her knees grew unsteady, and she inhaled swiftly.

"Oh, you were asking about your hair? It is fine." Then he let her hair go and began to climb the main stair.

"Brute," Charity muttered under her breath, piqued. And then she stood at the stair, looking up. Peregrine had moved out of sight so swiftly it was like he had never been there at all. She began the climb, but slower, more by feel than by the dim light from the windows.

Unlike many members of the *ton*, the Fitzroys were not only wealthy in assets, they had never been short of ready coin. It made little sense that a woman like Marian Fitzroy would be randomly struck with a notion one day to steal from the Crown or kidnap a person. If her man was into dark dealings, one could almost be certain the lady was, too.

It would explain a lot about her means and her ruthlessness. And in her sudden absence, a man of business might see Lord Fitzroy as an obstacle to acquiring everything. Peregrine was in England alone, without an heir of his own.

Charity couldn't begin to imagine the kind of hell Peregrine had stood upon the edge of all this time. How had he managed to keep his soul?

The first floor was dark, and she kept climbing, feeling out of sorts by her sudden abandonment. But perhaps she was being foolish. Maybe he was only preparing the guest room—but no, it was still locked.

Peregrine was in his room, rummaging in his wardrobe and not looking at her. "I know it is not what you are used to, Duchess, but at least it is clean," he said, pulling out one of his shirts. "My brush is on the table, and there is some fruit in the kitchen. I will make sure Hodges brings you more."

He was still planning to leave the house. He was rebuilding the wall that stood between them. And Charity could not think of a way to ask him to stay that wouldn't be entirely inappropriate.

"Question or command," she asked him softly.

Peregrine laughed, the sound bitter. "I think we had better stop playing this game before we both end up regretting it, Charity."

"I already have regrets," she said, her throat aching with it. "You asked me if I would make things different. But it doesn't matter what that answer would be. This… draw between us—it isn't meant for people like us, Perry. Fate would have always torn us apart."

His face, already solemn, turned to stone. Peregrine looked down at the floor for a moment, his face falling into shadow, before he lifted his eyes once more. "Was it fate?" he asked, bringing his fingers up to trail along the curve of her jaw. "It feels more like it was my failing."

Her chest hurt. "Perry—"

"Command," he said softly, cutting her off. "Make your wish, Charity."

What could she ask for? She looked into his eyes, wishing he would show her… something, and she wished she dared ask for just a glimpse of the thing she knew they couldn't have.

"Sleep here? With me? I just—I have never been alone." Not even when she had been held against her will.

He hesitated. "I'll stay downstairs."

There was no furniture. He'd be on the floor, and the memory of his bruised ribs rose in her mind's eye.

"You are hurt. And the bed is big enough for two," she said in a rush. "Especially if I am beneath the covers and you are on top."

Peregrine scratched his cheek wearily. "You really were not jesting when you said you wished to burn my life to ash, were you? Fine," he said finally, his voice resigned. But his gaze lingered on her for just a moment longer, unreadable and too heavy with things unsaid. "But only until morning."

18

"To climb the ranks, to force others to accede to your whim, you must be prepared to use all tools within reach. The sword, the mind—and if need be, the bed."
—Marian Fitzroy, to her son, at eighteen

With the memories in his head and the scents of the woman in his bed, it was no surprise he found himself cast back within his dream.

The cool March night was a balm against his sensibilities, raw with testiness from escorting his sister through events of the little season. Though truly, it was no one's fault but his own that he was at this insufferable event. He could have turned a deaf ear to her pleas to accompany her to Lady Norwood's musicale, but instead he had decided a night away from his club would do him good.

It wasn't until their carriage pulled up to the house that Peregrine recalled Lady Norwood's unfortunate love of performing—despite being tone-deaf. The moment she stepped forward to sing an operetta, he had excused himself, slipping through the nearest door. That it led to a balcony hardly mattered. Once it was shut behind him, the warbling notes mercifully faded.

Would anyone notice if he failed to return? Wishful thinking. Still, a few minutes of peace wouldn't go amiss. He wandered to the far corner, letting the shadows of a nearby oak conceal him.

Just as he resigned himself to returning, the door scraped open. A blonde goddess stepped through. He'd seen her earlier, whispering with his sister—another fresh debutante getting her bearings before the season began in earnest.

As a rule, Peregrine avoided the chits and their marriage-minded mamas. He knew how many saw him—a young, handsome, and rich lord already in full possession of his title, no doubt low hanging fruit ripe for the easy plucking by a pretty young girl. They never even imagined that simpering, empty-headed innocence held all the attraction to him of a goat in a skirt.

But she was alone, and he could still hear Lady Norwood caterwauling like a cat in heat, so he waited for her to go back inside.

Like this, she was pretty, with her head tilted up, and her eyes closed in some silent meditation. Moonlight edged her in silver along her golden curls, high cheekbones, and the bottom curve of her red lips. But she stayed, even though her shoulders, pale as dawn, shivered in the cold.

"You should have bribed a footman to fetch you a wrap before making an escape, my lady."

He tossed in the honorific without knowing if it was due, just to see how she'd react. She jerked at the sound of his voice, her perfect ringlets swinging, and he cursed himself for disturbing her solitude. Unescorted, she could hardly linger on a balcony with a strange man—though he supposed that made him the one who ought to leave.

Instead, she stepped forward, head tilting slightly as if trying to place him in the shifting candlelight from the window. He shifted too, letting the glow catch the edge of his face. Rather than shrink away, she took his measure just as boldly as he had done hers a moment earlier.

"A gentleman might offer a lady his coat, my lord," she said archly.

She was a bold thing, at least. He gave her a slight mocking grin. "What if I am not a gentleman?"

The girl lowered her lashes at his evasion. "Of course you are. I can see your clothing."

"Many men dress beyond their means."

She gave a sly smile at him. "Whatever Lady Norwood lacks in singing ability, she has a gift for coaxing the highest of the *ton* into attending her events. Only those who also boast a title or deep pockets make her lists."

Almost against his will he was curious. Few debutantes showed much penchant for observation and the workings of society. It spoke highly of her possibilities for making a match in her first season—not that she would have difficulty. With her vainglorious beauty, she would have men panting at her feet once she made her debut.

"Far be it from me to shatter your illusions," he said gallantly, shrugging off his coat. "I would hate to prove myself a disappointment."

Ignoring all rules of propriety, she came closer, stopping within arm's reach, and he slid his coat over her shoulders. "Are you not at all worried about being caught here with me?"

She paused for a moment. "Not enough to risk my ears," she said, trying to keep a straight face. Then, she muffled a giggle, hand over her mouth.

And the sound had snared his heart.

How could he let it happen? Even though she had a canny eye, she was too young. Too innocent. But her laugh was so honest and lacking in artifice that Fitzroy found himself wanting to make it happen again.

The chill breeze was like an omen, and before both knew it, the moment was over. She returned his coat to him swiftly before sneaking back inside, and he had spent the rest of the evening with the scent of her in his nostrils, a hint of salt and orange mixing pleasantly with the night and the spice of his soap.

Even though courting was—and should have been—the very last thing on his mind, he couldn't help looking for her again and again. When he finally found her, Fitzroy had made certain to ask for an introduction.

Charity's gentian eyes had been sparkling with mischief to see him again, right up until she heard his name and title. And then he had the privilege of watching how the smile in her eyes died aborning, fading into a polite mask.

No mere earl, no matter how wealthy or connected, was worth more of her time. She was meant for greater things. Until the night of his ball, every now and again, he had caught her looking his way across a crowded room, and knew she had wondered. Still, though, it wasn't enough.

He wasn't enough. And a part of his soul had been adrift ever since.

But this was his dream, and here he could take the advantage of a chance encounter that had, in truth, ended all too soon. To take what he knew they both wanted, but what they continued to deny themselves.

And so, taking himself back to that cold garden, he lifted his hand and trailed his fingers through her shimmering strands of gold. The white satin gloves on her arms disappeared, leaving behind more bare skin. She wrapped an arm around his neck, urging him closer. He burrowed his nose against the warm, soft skin on hers. Her hands played with his hair, coaxing him onward. He dragged his lips up to the sensitive place behind her ear.

God help him. She shivered.

"Perry," she moaned. But instead of melting deeper into their embrace, she stiffened and then jerked backwards. The movement dragged him free of Somnus's hold, and into the stark light of day.

He was in his bed, in his townhouse, with his legs intertwined with none other than the woman haunting his dreams. And this time she was most definitely not happy. He had to blink the sleep from his eyes to identify the exact expression twisting her features.

Was that embarrassment? A bolt of pure male satisfaction raced down his spine. She had called his name. And this time, not because some thug was holding her hostage.

He chose his first words with great care, knowing one wrong move would send her running away—back to her unsafe home, to the confines of Buckingham Palace—anywhere but here.

He reached up and plucked her arm from where it lay across his shoulder. "Did we not have a rule about touching?"

She jerked her arm free and shook it off as though cooling a burn and then scowled at him in return. "*You* are touching *me*." She reached up to touch her neck, where he had nuzzled her in his dreams. "You kissed me!"

It seemed he had, and could not find one single regret— except that he had done it while sleeping instead of enjoying it while awake. Still, he relaxed as if it was of no consequence to him whatsoever. "Do not flatter yourself, Your Shininess. You drool in your sleep."

The sight of her rosebud mouth dropping open in shock was worth the mouthful of goosefeather pillow he got in return. She whacked him again with the pillow, calling him a scoundrel, rake, reprobate, but unlike previous times, her anger lacked any real heat.

He rose on his knees to loom over her. "There are no rules in a pillow war. Swing again and I will not be held responsible for whatever you suffer next."

It was a dare, and he half-wished she would carry on. But she called herself back, dropping her pillow as she scooted out of the opposite side of the bed.

At least she attempted to reduce him to ashes with a fiery glare, and perversely, that soothed him.

He left her then, to wash up and make tea. He had no milk but at least he had an abundance of sugar and some bread that was not too stale. When he returned, tray in hand, the duchess had returned to her bearing... although she looked discomfited. Her hair was twisted into a simple knot and her dress hung loose around her shoulders. Charity stared at the tray and then at him, frowning as if she couldn't make sense of him at all.

"What is wrong?" he asked her.

"I cannot—the buttons," she said, in defeat. "I need your help."

God help them both, for a number of reasons. This was torture no man should be forced to endure, to stand this close to a bounty for the senses, dealing with so many buttons. All so tiny, designed to be done up by the delicate hands of a lady's maid.

He took his time closing them, looking at the smooth column of her neck and back and the stray curls that tickled between her shoulders. All the while imagining working in the opposite direction... if not simply ripping them asunder.

"You are... curiously domestic," Charity murmured. Peregrine had been arguing with himself to remove his hand from the warmth between her shoulder blades now that he had fastened the last button. But likewise, she seemed reluctant to pull away. Lifting her head, she stared at him through her lashes over her shoulder. "Thank you."

"Drink your tea before it gets cold and eat what you will. We must hurry." Fitzroy's words came out harsher than he'd meant.

"You are in desperate need of a maid's assistance with your hair. Let us hope Sina will offer hers."

"You know nothing of styling a woman's hair? Pity," she said dryly.

Maybe there was hope for that truce after all.

~

"Dare I ask how often you have used this entrance?" Charity asked him at the back of the Marchioness of Normanby's home, her voice almost sounding jealous.

He smirked. "Once or twice."

As if in answer, a stableboy caught sight of them and hurried off to alert the house.

The crabby-looking marchioness herself opened the door to what Fitzroy knew was her breakfast room. "You have some nerve showing up unannounced at this hour, Perry—oh." Selina's gaze fell upon Charity, hiding beneath his cloak, and her eyebrows took flight. "*Ohhh,*" she repeated, her voice taking a much more interested and amused tone.

Predictably, Charity bridled. "It is not what you think!"

"The marchioness would accord you far more respect if it was," he informed her, and Selina smiled at her in agreement.

"Perry does keep high standards as well as the most interesting guests." She traced her lower lip with the edge of her thumb, her eyes flickering as she thought rapidly. "We have a great deal to talk about. Little lamb, let me sneak you to my maid."

Peregrine was not about to let her drag Charity off to her den without him. Sina wouldn't be interested in prying out the usual juicy tidbits about their entanglement—or lack thereof. Right now, the duchess positively reeked of 'prey animal,' and Selina would be out to get whatever information she could extort.

He couldn't let her have the chance to get it. Peregrine needed it for himself.

So he followed Selina as she whisked Charity upstairs, knowing that her servants would not even try to stop him unless she asked them to. Good manners were like locks on doors; the privacy it afforded was only respected by honest souls. That would apply to no one who ever darkened the Marchioness of Normanby's doorstep.

Predictably, Selina attempted to shut the door in his face, and he thwarted her with the toe of his shoe. "Perry, be reasonable," the marchioness said patiently. "We are just helping her freshen up."

"Your maid can do that," he agreed. "While she is busy, I would have a word with you downstairs."

Selina cocked her head at him in consideration, and then came back out into the hallway, closing the door behind her. "Surely you do not wish to talk with me without her present. I do not think she would appreciate that. At all."

The marchioness was correct—Charity would hate it. But he doubted it would take much in the way of explanation to sway Charity to his point of view later. She was a little too naive to this world. Not stupid.

"Let me be the one to worry about that," he told her.

"I will wait to talk to you both, then," Selina said, the very picture of amiability as she looked up into Peregrine's face, pointedly rubbing a finger lightly over the stubble on his chin. The expression on her face was one of contemplation rather than flirtation. "It rather looks like your evening was so much less entertaining than it should have been. Perhaps you would like the chance to freshen up yourself."

"I am not in the mood to be trifled with, Selina," he told her, impatience thrumming beneath the surface.

She *tsked,* running her hands down the front of his shirt. "You wound me. The gossip mongers have been hard at work, and if half of what I have heard is true, I thought you would appreciate some hospitality."

"Hospitality, yes," he said, conceding he was in dire need of a shave. He plucked her hands off of him, caressing her knuckles briefly with his thumbs to soften his rejection of her touch. "All other things I will leave to men foolish enough to think you are not looking for something in return."

She smiled, not at all put off. "You cannot blame a woman perishing of curiosity."

Peregrine let a knowing smile curl his lip at that. "You are seldom so lacking in subtlety. Do not let your impatience ruin a deal before we can even come to the table."

"Give me a hint, Perry, if for no other reason than to prevent my mind from wasting its energy running in the wrong direction."

Peregrine shook his head at her inability to wait, but did as she asked. "I need to know about Mr Cameron."

"See, that was not so hard at all. I will play good hostess and let you both be. Take the adjoining suite and I will send Locke to you. Come down to the table for breakfast when you are ready."

It said a great deal about the state of his wits that he didn't anticipate the last card up the marchioness's sleeve. When both came downstairs washed, shaven, and groomed, they were whisked promptly into the dining room and plied with food and drink by the marchioness's unassuming servants. He did not even think to question her absence from the table.

Not until they finished and were escorted to the upstairs drawing room, where three men waited with her. The marchioness had clearly made the most of her time, attempting to summon the bloody leadership of the Order of the Centuriate.

Peregrine did not bother to pretend he wasn't annoyed, halting in the doorway with Charity on his arm. Now he sorely regretted bringing her here at all. "Pembroke. Chandros. How interesting to see you here." He looked at the third man. "I do not believe we are acquainted."

"Mr Goldbourne, meet Lord Peregrine Fitzroy," said the Duke of Chandros.

A bloody banker.

"If Fitzroy is too upset to introduce us, I hope you do not mind if we dispense overly with formalities," Chandros said, leaning casually on the gold head of his cane with both hands before he came forward to greet Charity. "You see, we friends of England have been most eager to make your acquaintance, Your Grace."

Peregrine tightened his grip on her arm just slightly. The polished older man who was the de facto leader of the Order had… vision. He kept his fingers in every pie he could, and would use anything—or anyone—as a lever to bend the world to his satisfaction. A well-positioned woman who sat at one side of the Queen and controlled the heir of a chunk of Scotland would be attractive to him.

He had not had a chance to warn Charity, but fortunately, it seemed she had developed a sense of caution. Her smile was easy, if practiced. She tilted her head just so, as though amused by Chandros's directness. "Friends of England?" she repeated lightly. "How very grand. And here I thought we were merely guests in the marchioness's home."

Chandros's smile sharpened. "Ah, but hospitality and business are never far apart, are they?"

"I take it this is your way of negotiating?" Peregrine said dryly, pulling their attention away from Charity. "Stacking the table before we have even agreed to sit at it?"

"Do not be angry at the marchioness," Chandros said mildly. "We were most… put out by the idea of another faction exerting their will on the throne, and so we were pleased to hear that you were part of the investigation. Violent attacks on peers, however, is a reason for all of us to pay close attention. Take our swift response to Selina's summons at this hour as proof we might be happier to strike a good bargain for information than you believe, Peregrine."

"Was it Caroline after all?" Pembroke interjected, his face spotted with colour. "She should have been cast out of the country long ago."

"No," Peregrine said blandly. "I will tell you who I believe is the architect of the violence and the attack at Prinny's garden party. But I need more information in return on that person, and I think you are able to give it to me."

"I think that seems eminently fair," Chandros said, stroking his salt and pepper beard. But he was still casting sidelong glances at Charity, and it raised Peregrine's hackles. "Tell us who it is."

"A Mr Cameron. He was my mother's agent for many years."

There was a brief pause, and Chandros, unexpectedly, laughed. "The unassuming spider who spun your mother's web. *Horror vacui*, Peregrine. How very interesting."

"Your response is not giving me much faith in your network of information, Chandros," Peregrine said, gritting his teeth.

Chandros sighed, looking genuinely regretful. "It was not until after everything happened last year that we even began to suspect the scope of your mother's resources. We had always kept an eye cast towards Marian's dealings, but what we saw also looked so… small-minded and only with an eye to her finances. Smuggling. Questionable trade. And of course, the occasional petty blackmail."

They didn't know a tenth of what his mother's larger ambitions had been before she had been forced to abandon England. Peregrine's stomach soured, but he kept his face expressionless. "So you paid little attention to Cameron after she left. Do you know if he is working for someone else now?"

Pembroke shook his head. "No. Your mother left quite a bit behind. It was easy—and far more lucrative—to continue with what he had himself. He is not taking new business."

"Some small comfort there," Peregrine murmured. "For a man who prizes information, you keep your nose too high in the air, Chandros."

"Fairly said, Fitzroy," the man bowed his head. "Times… they appear to be changing somewhat, and sometimes the current moves faster than I anticipate."

"As Chandros said, nature abhors the vacuum, Peregrine," Pembroke said speculatively. "A single stitch might be all that is needed to restore order to the situation."

Pressure began to build in Peregrine's temples. "I would hate to think, Pembroke," he said lightly, "that you are implying I am somehow guilty of causing this by being so lamentably absent."

Beside him, Charity was silent, but she was tense, listening and thinking.

"Of course not, Perry," Chandros said obliquely. "He is only suggesting that we have all the pieces here to restore power to where it belongs."

"No," Fitzroy said flatly, not caring how rude it was.

"You cannot blame us for thinking it might be a good solution. What other choice is there, Fitzroy?" Goldbourne asked, finally venturing into the conversation. "Even without a more permanent alliance, we still have interests in common here. We know where Cameron is, would you like our assistance in exposing him? He will hardly confess to the Crown, and you do not have much in the way of your own resources."

"I will bear your offers in mind, gentlemen," Peregrine said carefully. "But as entangled as I am now, I would prefer to avoid making commitments of any kind until I have restored order to my house. Duchess, we need to depart if we wish to keep our appointments. Selina, darling…" he looked in the direction of the marchioness. "I will be in touch."

As they hadn't even taken more than two steps into the room before being accosted, leaving it was easy. Fortunately, Charity was silent and thoughtful as they descended to the stair and out the front door.

19

"Blast. What a waste of time. I am sorry to make you walk, Duchess," Peregrine told her, taking a sidelong glance at her styled hair and freshened clothes. "We need only go far enough to flag a passing carriage."

His words proved true, and in short order they were back within the safe confines of an anonymous black hack.

"That was… rather unexpected," she said slowly, hoping it might spur him to response, but Peregrine maintained a dour silence on the subject of the unexpected meeting. "What do we do now?"

He pressed his face into his hands, looking harassed, and Charity swallowed her sense of hopeless unease. If Peregrine was at a loss, then perhaps Goldbourne's comments about a lack of resources had struck a sensitive spot.

But Charity had some connections of her own. Ones she could trust. "Things seem to have grown beyond us. Perhaps we should go to the Prince Regent for aid."

"No," Peregrine said unconsciously, but then he stopped and reconsidered. "Maybe. But… it might be useful for you to inform the Queen. Alone."

Oh God, the Queen, her mother's voice said in horror. *She knows nothing of any of this yet!*

Charity swallowed heavily. "I think she is going to be… rather upset. Are you sure we should not go together?"

He gave her that fey, half-amused grin, but his eyes were still lined with tension. "I would go with you to hold your hand, Sparkles, but then you might have to hold onto my leg to keep her guards from dragging me off. In seriousness, we have two avenues of information still to pursue that might give us a glimpse of what we need to know. I propose we divide and conquer.

"Talk of money is vulgar, I am sure you were raised to believe —as so many others have. Their cultivated blindness allows opportunities for someone bold and ignoble. There are women within the *ton*, not nearly as privileged in power or finances, who will sell information or small favours for money. And Mr Cameron would know that too."

Charity saw what he was getting at. "The princess's letter-writer?"

"Yes. We have only so much time before he acts again, and if you and I prove too hard to strike, Cameron may turn his weapons elsewhere. That letter-writer is Cameron's own agent in play, and we cannot dismiss her as a dogsbody. We do not know how tight his hold is on this woman."

"So you want me to ask the Queen whose circumstances may have changed. Possibly significantly," Charity said, following that train of thought. "Is that not something that these… friends of England," she stumbled over the words, "would have known? Who are they?"

"They are people who attach a great many strings to their favours," Peregrine snorted. "And that is really all you need to be aware of. There are a great many factions who are bound together by a common zeal. Selina's friends simply happen to be better funded and organised than others."

Charity felt cold at the idea of facing Queen Charlotte's anger alone. "Saints preserve me—but what should I tell her?"

"Ideally, as little as you can. We need to keep her from going off half-cocked. I trust you to navigate it."

That was unexpectedly bracing, and she looked at him curiously, wondering if he truly meant it. "Do you?"

"In this? I do. And not just because I have no other choice— although there is a truth to that part, too."

Peregrine looked drawn. Too little sleep… and perhaps she and the whole world were plaguing him more than was fair. For a moment, he seemed only like a man who wanted to be let alone.

"Perry…" she began, uncertain about what to say. Finally, in cowardice, she said the next thing on her mind. "Be careful. I do not like the idea of you being without someone to watch your back. I will agree to see the Queen on my own, so long as you will ask Prinny for help."

For once, Peregrine did not argue. "When you finish your task, go back to the townhouse and wait for me there. I will meet you as soon as I can."

As the carriage rolled to a stop in front of Queen Charlotte's stately home, Charity realised that trust she had asked about had to go two ways. She had only his word that he would do as she asked.

~

Charity descended from the carriage outside Buckingham House, counting herself fortunate on at least one front. Though she was not wearing a day dress appropriate to the hour, she was also not wearing the cabbage atrocity of her last visit. Progress, albeit small, was worth noting.

Try though she might, Charity was unable to entirely banish the niggling concern from the back of her mind. Was the Queen going to somehow blame Charity for her granddaughter's misbehaviour? Charity had been, after all, assigned to keep the princess from doing anything which might ruin the betrothal arrangements.

One should argue that the Queen herself—and Prinny—bore the bulk of the blame. They had issued the edict that Princess Charlotte would wed without taking into account the young woman's misgivings. Was it any wonder that the princess had accepted help from any quarter?

Of course, to raise such an argument would be the height of foolishness. One did not tell the Queen of England that she had been wrong. On this point, Charity's mother had been very clear.

If the Queen was cross, Charity would accept the blame with good grace, and then turn the conversation toward uncovering the identity of whomever was truly responsible for the crime.

She lifted the hem of her skirt and followed the Queen's butler through the grand front hall, down a corridor, and into Queen Charlotte's private reception chamber. Her Majesty sat on a velvet, gilded chair only a shade less imperial than her throne at St James's. While Charity sank into a deep curtsey, the Queen banished her attendants from the room.

No sooner had the door closed behind them than the Queen demanded Charity rise with a voice like a whip crack. "On your feet. *Now.* And tell me why I have been left to wonder about your whereabouts like some common gossip."

Charity deepened her curtsey in obeisance before returning to standing. "I offer my most humble apologies for not coming sooner, Your Majesty. After we spoke with Princess Caroline, the situation progressed in ways well beyond my control."

"So, you have gone sniffing around that pitiful excuse for a princess? Predictable. Caroline has been a thorn in my side since the day she set foot on English soil."

The Queen carried on, retreading old arguments against Princess Caroline, and leaving Charity ever more baffled. Surely Prinny had told his mother the truth…

When the Queen paused for breath, Charity dared to wade into the gap. "Your Majesty, has the Prince Regent not come to visit you?"

That stopped the Queen's diatribe in an instant. "Why do you ask?" she inquired, peering suspiciously at Charity. "Does he know something I do not?"

Charity's stomach lurched. If Prinny had not spoken to his mother, it meant that the Queen did not know about her granddaughter's involvement in the matter. And heaven help her, Charity was going to have to be the messenger.

Her mother whimpered in her mind. Even the newfound voice of calm failed to offer any advice.

"Well?"

Charity had no illusions about how this conversation would unfold. The Queen would not take kindly to being left in the dark —especially not by those she trusted most. Charity swallowed hard, her voice steady despite the sudden weight pressing against her ribs.

"Your Majesty, I regret to inform you that there has been a grievous oversight," she began carefully. "One that I assumed had already been corrected."

Queen Charlotte's eyes, sharp as the points of a diadem, narrowed to slits. "Spare me the riddles, Duchess. I have neither the time nor the patience. *Speak.*"

Charity inhaled slowly, ignoring the icy fear creeping up her spine. "Princess Caroline is not responsible for the poisoning, though I, too, shared your suspicions." In a calm voice that belied Charity's nerves, she told the Queen about her visit to Montagu House and the subsequent trouble she and Fitzroy encountered on their return.

"Does this have anything to do with why Bow Street was called to your home last night?" Charlotte asked mildly. When Charity's head jerked in surprise, the Queen added, "Word of at least that much reached me. What I fail to understand is why I am only hearing it from you now."

"There is more, Your Highness. After the attack on the bridge, it became clear that something bigger was afoot. Lord Fitzroy and I reached out to Lord Ravenscroft for information. It was in my conversation with Prinny's man that I realised who had poisoned the jenever decanter." Charity steeled herself for the fallout and then forced the full confession out of her mouth. "It is my… unhappy duty to tell you that Princess Charlotte was the poisoner."

For a moment, there was nothing but the tick of the mantel clock and the distant sound of a footman passing in the corridor. The Queen did not move, nor did she blink. And then—

A sudden, sharp exhale. "What nonsense is this?" The words were clipped, incredulous.

Charity pressed on. "The princess confessed yesterday to her father and me. She did not act alone. Someone was passing her messages—guiding her. She does not know their identity. I left the princess in her father's care and departed to search for the identity of the messenger."

The Queen stood abruptly, a rare display of raw emotion. "You mean to tell me," she hissed, each word laced with fury, "that my granddaughter—my own blood—has been dragged into scandal, and *not a single soul* thought to inform me?"

It horrified Charity that Prinny had failed to disclose the information immediately. He was the highest ranking man in England, and yet it seemed even he feared to tell his own mother bad news. For a moment, Charity wondered what would happen if she pointed this out, but just as quickly she discarded the notion. She could ill afford to make enemies of anyone wearing a crown. Yet, her stomach churned as she forced her mouth to form the words of apology.

Charity bowed her head. "I should have come sooner, ma'am. That failure is mine."

"Yes, it is," the Queen snapped, her voice rising. "Yours! Prinny's! And I suspect half of my court, who cower and whisper like frightened mice instead of speaking the truth!"

Charity held firm, though her pulse quickened. "Your Majesty, I swear to you—nothing was kept from you with malice. The situation has been... delicate."

The Queen let out a sharp, bitter laugh. "Delicate! And now you tell me my granddaughter is a criminal!"

"She is a misguided girl who thought she had no options," Charity countered. "Whoever influenced her knew how to manipulate that desperation. If we do not uncover their identity, the damage will only worsen."

The Queen's expression was thunderous, but Charity saw the shift—the calculation behind her anger. Queen Charlotte was no fool. For all her fury, she understood the stakes.

A long silence stretched between them. Then, finally, the Queen lowered herself into her chair, her fingers tightening around the armrests. "Start from the beginning and tell me everything you have learned."

Charity gave a full recount of her adventure, such as it had been. On the carriage ride, she had wrestled with the question of how much she could hold back. In a strange, unpredictable twist of fate, she found herself reluctant to reveal the parts that would connect Peregrine to the villainy.

She explained instead that Caroline had sought his mother's favours—not his—and how he had needed to defend the both of them on the bridge and at her home.

She did not confess that she had begun to think of him in his given name.

The Queen leaned forward in her chair, her interest in the story peaked. Charity dared not let her ask the obvious question. *Where did you stay?* The answer was rife with unintended consequences.

Though he would likely call her foolish, Charity offered the name of the only person in London she knew who would take pleasure in misleading the Queen on such a question.

"The Marchioness of Normanby was most generous," she added. "I cannot imagine I would be here now, in such a calm state, had it not been for the loan of her lady's maid to restore me to order."

The Queen sniffed at the mention of Selina, but as Charity had hoped, did not ask if that was where she and Fitzroy had passed the night. "What of these men who attacked you? Surely you are not suggesting that my granddaughter hired them."

"No, nothing of the sort," Charity replied as fast as she could. She sought her calm again. "Though the encounters were horrifying, they provided us with a key piece of information. Fitzroy recognised them."

"Lord Fitzroy recognised the men? From where?" The Queen's temper was on the rise yet again. "Were they soldiers with him? Acquaintances?"

This was the truly uncomfortable part. Of Cameron and his men, she emphasised he had been Lady Fitzroy's man of business, and most certainly not Peregrine's.

The Queen sucked in air and her face grew arch. "Duchess, *where* is Lord Fitzroy now?"

"He should be on his way to consult with the Prince Regent, Your Highness." Charity prayed he would not make her a liar. "I believe he is asking for help to deal with the man."

Queen Charlotte sat back in her chair. "So," she said, each syllable edged with judgment, "you sent Lord Fitzroy—alone—to deal with Prinny."

Charity hesitated only a fraction of a second before nodding. "Given all that has happened, I felt certain Prinny would accede to his request for aid."

"Still, I could not help but notice your choice of words." The Queen's voice was mild, but her fingers tapped against the gilded armrest. "You say he should be on his way to St James's. That is not the same as knowing, Duchess."

Charity's spine stiffened. "I have no reason to doubt him. I do not believe he would suddenly go elsewhere unless there was a reason for it."

"Mm." The Queen's expression remained unreadable. "A year ago, you would not have trusted him to fetch your gloves from the next room, let alone carry sensitive intelligence to my son. And now, you speak as though you know the workings of the man's mind."

Charity carefully kept her face neutral. "I have come to understand him better, ma'am. He has no wish to be associated with his mother."

"Duchess, you are in danger of disappointing me." A derisive snort. "Distancing oneself from a family member causing scandal is the first action any member of the aristocracy would take, if they are not lacking in common sense. The Fitzroy family excels at applying shame, guile, and charm as their instruments of manipulation. I wonder why you think he might hesitate to use your pity."

That notion disturbed her, for she *had* been moved very much by pity. Could it really be a farce? Surely it hadn't been something he had just... evoked in her because she was not responding well to his other methods.

You assumed a great deal of his thoughts and feelings before he told you anything at all. It would not have been hard for him to dupe you, if that was his goal.

Charity swallowed as doubt sank its cold teeth into her. *It could be true. He could be duping me so that I give him support instead of opposition. But even if it is, I know he had nothing to do with poisoning Prince William, and that is what I need to remember.*

"I have not forgotten a thing, Your Majesty. You are correct, and I remain watchful. But he has no motivation to set such high stakes merely to pretend innocence. I have seen him risk his life."

The Queen was silent for a long moment. Then, she leaned forward. "You have always been a sharp girl, Charity. I would not wish to see you become a fool."

Charity inclined her head. "Nor would I, ma'am."

Queen Charlotte studied her a moment longer, then exhaled, her expression cooling. "Answer me plainly, then. Are you absolutely certain that Fitzroy is loyal to the Crown? That he is not, even now, his mother's tool?"

"Yes." Charity said it without hesitation, her voice steady.

The Queen's frown deepened. Her fingers drummed against the armrest once more. "I see."

Nothing more. No rebuke, no dismissal. But the weight of her scrutiny pressed against Charity's shoulders like a leaden cloak.

For the first time in her life, Charity found herself in opposition to the Queen—not in disobedience, but in belief. And that, she knew, was a dangerous place to be.

20

"God is a comedian playing to an audience that is too afraid to laugh."
—Voltaire

Peregrine directed the driver to continue on to St James's Palace, and then went back to sorting out the too many thoughts occupying the small space in his head. Charity, unfortunately, took up more of it than he could allow.

That way lay only destruction. There was no future with the Duchess Atholl.

For years, he had known—that is, when he bothered thinking of marriage at all—that once he took a wife, she would be someone whom he would need to install in a country house, far, far away from London. *From his mother.* Even if Charity overlooked his title, a life away from the scene would never be in her cards. So no matter what his regrets, it seemed she was right. Imagining any different outcome was madness.

Still, she had asked him to stay with her, tormenting him with a fantasy that would never be.

There was no cruelty quite as savage as women's affection.

Vexed, he pushed his feelings aside once more, trying to connect himself to cold reason. If he couldn't keep his head, he may as well go directly to Cameron and ask the man to slit his throat, and he was certain the man would gleefully oblige.

Cameron probably had been watching him since he returned to London. Was likely watching him still. The man of affairs had made two oblique threats to warn him off with the henbane and Red Hand. But Peregrine had changed the game when he and Hodges had fought back against the hired men.

Before Sidmouth sent him into hell, he had been much like any other aristocrat—without the courage to meet violence with his own. Until last summer, he had kept himself out of the shadowy side of London, preferring instead to use secrets and politics. No one would have expected that he would have killed three of Red Hand's cutthroats during the fight on the bridge. Cameron had likely had to fork out an additional sum in recompense. It was no wonder the man had ordered the retaliatory strike.

God. Charity was meant to be a warning in blood. If he hadn't heard her call him—if he hadn't turned back—she might have died. Or worse.

His stomach nearly revolted at that thought and he snarled at himself. *Focus, you idiot.*

This was Cameron's strategy. This was the test: to warn Peregrine away from interfering with his schemes and cow him with the knowledge that he could not act against Cameron without consequence.

Peregrine was, after all, the legitimate heir to Lady Fitzroy's empire. Whatever remained of her lucrative, shadowy business enterprises was Peregrine's to take. But that he wanted no part of it meant very little. In fact, that only sufficed to drive the businessman harder, to seize it for himself before Peregrine had a chance to dismantle or expose any part of it.

There was a slim chance he could find a way to placate the man's greed. To use his knowledge to set up a bargain that would bring him the peace he wanted, and keep Cameron from tipping the scales.

But to find out if such a deal was possible, he needed to talk with Cameron.

Before Peregrine could even negotiate, he had to ensure he would survive a parley, and Peregrine needed an alternative plan —just in case a truce could not be reached.

That he would make such a strike against either him or Charity said a great deal. At best, it meant the sphere of Cameron's influence possibly extended over the magistrate or Bow Street. At worst, there was a risk that Cameron had found a new master. Peregrine had to be careful, and he couldn't depend on the pompous expectation that lawmen would act on his word alone.

If he couldn't strike some kind of deal directly, he needed to turn someone against Cameron. Someone closer to him—like McGrath, who had plenty of his own reasons now to be difficult. It wasn't going to be an easy task, and he was going to have to pay in a different kind of coin.

Even if they could provide the aid he wanted, he didn't dare borrow it from the Order.

That was the real reason he was headed to St James's Palace now.

As much as Charity was going to be uncomfortable with her audience with the Queen, keeping the two royals divided was a necessary part of the plan. Charlotte would never trust him enough to allow him to work with subtlety—and Prinny was incapable of thinking in it.

Peregrine needed to manipulate Prinny into giving him exactly what he needed… and that was the leverage of generosity from a higher power.

One that would also be able to mete out retribution, if he failed.

As it was afternoon, Prinny was cloistered in the Regent's Closet, holding a different kind of court, which suited Peregrine just fine. The scent of brandy and perfume were heavy in the room, and the Regent lounged in his chair, one hand idly swirling his drink, the other resting on the curve of Lady Vivienne's waist, playing with the ribbons at the back of her gown. She laughed at something he murmured—something Lord Ravenscroft, standing near the hearth, had surely heard.

But the lord didn't laugh. He was busy glaring at Peregrine, his face grim with an animosity that hadn't been there at their last meeting. Prinny's magpie either saw no need to curb hostility in this private space, or he too had heard of what had happened.

His guess was the latter.

With a small, ironic twist of his lips, Peregrine cast a lazy eye over what he could see of the patterned red silk of the wallpaper, the Persian carpets, and the round backside of the woman being held in the sotted regent's lap as he held his bow.

Prinny was making a statement that he could do as he pleased. Fine. Peregrine would play the penitent.

"What do you want, Fitzroy?" the Prince Regent asked, finally allowing the woman to stand and move away.

"I would have a word with you, Your Highness," Peregrine said as he stood, affecting boredom.

"Must it be now, Fitzroy?" Prinny murmured, reaching for his snuffbox. "I do hate interruptions."

"If you would indulge me, yes. It is, of course, your right to decide however privately you wish to have it." Then Peregrine pointedly glanced over his shoulder at Lord Ravenscroft.

"Very well." Prinny's eyes flicked to Ravenscroft, then back to Peregrine. "My magpie can stay. You, my dear—" he swatted Lady Vivienne on her buttocks—"must go."

With a huff, the maligned mistress stalked out of the room and Peregrine stifled the urge to roll his eyes at the dissolute Prince Regent. "Well, then, what do you want?"

"Before you ask His Highness for favours, Fitzroy," Lord Ravenscroft said charmingly, as though butter wouldn't melt in his mouth, "perhaps you might first explain why it is that the Duchess Atholl's home was attacked by common criminals."

The Prince Regent nodded his head slowly at that.

Why did they think? Peregrine was annoyed at how bloody obtuse some aristocrats could be about the lower classes.

"Common criminals—and the uncommon ones, as well—tend to mislike the aristocracy *meddling* in their affairs, which is exactly what we have been doing." And that was no less than the truth. "Forgive me for being one man, Ravenscroft, when it was Your Highness and Her Majesty who sent me toddling with the duchess into the thick of a conspiracy, armed with little more than my wits."

Prinny scowled. "I say, Fitzroy, I suspect that of everyone involved, you were in the best position to inform us that there *was* one afoot."

He took a breath, ignoring the Prince Regent's pique. "To be sure, Your Highness, I can see how it would seem so uncharitable to neglect to inform you. I, however, am one man alone. I too would have also preferred the benefits of knowing I was about to stumble face-first into what amounted to a *coup d'état*, but the fates did not see fit to forewarn me."

"It remains that you still failed to warn His Highness after the fact." Ravenscroft muttered, his usual veneer of amusement absent. "The two men you locked in Her Grace's butler's closet, the ones who ended up being taken by Bow Street, found a most *permanent* silence before they could be questioned by the magistrate. And the only reason she is breathing, I suspect, is more blind luck than anything else."

It was hard to be offended by Ravenscroft's words when the same thought had crossed his own mind.

Prince Regent flicked open the snuffbox and inhaled a pinch. "Yes, do let us dwell on the fact that the mastermind remains at large. I was rather hoping this entire sordid matter would be sorted before I had to explain to the Queen that her granddaughter decided to poison a man rather than be forced to marry him."

"At large, but not unidentified." Peregrine explained who Cameron was and their tenuous connection—though he did not disclose the full extent of what services he provided to his mother.

Both the Regent and Ravenscroft looked grim by the end of his explanation. "I suggest Fitzroy has become more of a liability than an asset to the investigation, Your Highness," Ravenscroft said, the surprise of it rendering the man nearly sober.

"The matter is complicated, to be sure, but—"

"Complicated." The Regent barked a single, brittle guffaw. "Ravenscroft is right. I can guess that you are here for one of two reasons. Either you need my aid, or you are about to explain how you are clearly overmatched. Now that I am aware the guilty party is a creature of the rookeries and not one of us, it seems prudent to dismiss you and send in the guard."

"Dismiss me at your peril," Peregrine warned them. "If you send the guard to ask around for Cameron, he and the worst of his henchmen will be in the wind before the guards even catch his scent. You want to watch half of London burn? You have no idea what sort of manpower he can muster. But that strength can also be turned into a weakness. Cameron is untouchable only for as long as he can afford their loyalty, or as long as his men fear him more than they fear the law."

"Why am I not surprised that you would suggest an immoderate solution?" Prinny's voice was dry.

"I believe Fitzroy is suggesting there is more than one incentive we might dangle to the rabble in exchange for betraying Cameron. He wants the right to grant them protection, Your Highness," Ravenscroft said, his eyes half-hooded as he considered Peregrine.

"A double-edged offer, yes," Peregrine agreed simply. "Protection for any man who turns on him. And the threat of no mercy for those who do not."

Prinny barked a laugh. "You *think* I have the authority to simply absolve criminals?"

"Why pretend you do not have the ability to arrange to see it done?" Peregrine countered. "More importantly, I think you have the incentive to see to it."

"I confess, Fitzroy," Prinny said meditatively, his fingers worrying over the snuffbox. "I see your motivations in this more clearly than I see mine. This Mr Cameron rather seems to have a personal interest in your demise. I wonder why that would be."

"If I had been the mastermind of an exacting plan to manipulate the princess and change the course of the Crown with no one the wiser, and it was both exposed and foiled, I might bear a grudge or two," Peregrine said, omitting the other details. "You sent me to block his way, and so I am the focus of his retribution for now. But Cameron's first blow was aimed at the royal family, and once I am dealt with, I imagine you will become a target again."

The Regent studied him; Peregrine could almost hear the wheels turning in his mind. "Point made, Lord Fitzroy, but you need to move with haste. I cannot have the *ton* thinking that I will ignore the gutter-wretches attacking their betters."

Lord Ravenscroft gave his liege a look of incredulity. "Your Highness, he has barely given you a wisp of a plan. Just how *do* you propose to make them talk, Fitzroy? You, alone, wandering into some squalid drinking den, hoping they will be intimidated by your noble frown?"

"I have my methods," Peregrine said coolly, not bothering to inform Ravenscroft that he was rather near the mark. "You need not concern yourself."

"Well, that is unfortunate for you," Prinny said flatly. "Because you shall have his concern. I want my magpie to go with you."

"Your Highness, bringing another gentleman to negotiations with rough men would be a terrible idea—" Peregrine began.

Prinny cut him off with a languid wave. "I do not trust you to do this properly, and I certainly do not trust you to do it alone." He settled back in his chair. "Also, if you do fail, I will need someone who will drag your corpse out of the stews and remember to report back to me."

Ravenscroft looked like he drank spoiled milk.

Peregrine had gotten what he had come for; there was little benefit to arguing. So he bowed to the Prince Regent and took his leave.

"Er," Ravenscroft split a look between the two men and hurried after Peregrine. "You might have argued a little harder against my inclusion, Fitzroy. What in the hell am I supposed to do to help you?"

"You may always hide in the carriage so that you live long enough to drag my corpse back to His Highness as he suggested," Peregrine said lightly. "That would be useful."

He made a moue of distaste. "Ballocks. What is your real plan? And do not pretend it is to walk in with a hope and a prayer that some henchman will turn traitor just because his conscience has been plaguing him. As cheerful as it would make me, I doubt you are the sort who looks down the barrel of your pistol to be sure that it is primed."

"At this point, the plan is rather simple. I need to parley with Cameron. In theory, he should be amenable—stirring up the aristocracy is bad for business, even in the rookeries. Beyond that, I mean to see what influence can be had among the sellswords he has not bought outright."

"So I am just here to play secretary?" Ravenscroft said, giving him a sidelong look.

Peregrine gave the older man a taunting glance. "Have you grown forgetful in your dotage already? I did not ask you to play any part at all. Go home, Ravenscroft. I do not need the help of a dandy, and your *considerable talents* as a courtier would be all but wasted on these men."

When Peregrine asked one of the footmen to arrange for a carriage to take him home, and the servant scurried off, Ravenscroft leaned against the wall with his hand, barring Peregrine's way. "Doubtless I am going to regret this, but I rather think you are going to be stuck with me, and not only because His Highness commanded it. I have taken the liberty of asking a few questions since our last encounter yesterday. Unless I am gravely misinformed, Fitzroy, I am of the impression you can count your allies on one hand and still manage to have fingers left over."

Ravenscroft was right, and that didn't improve his mood. "Ah, but the allies I recruit grow finer by the hour. It would make for a tremendous comedy. You loathe me, I mislike you, and we have the duchess who hates us both—"

"She is already halfway to adoring me. What is more unfortunate is that I do not believe she hates you nearly as much as she pretends to."

"Thank you. You have already made it clear you think she should hate me far more," Peregrine said dryly, and he pushed Ravenscroft to one side so he could head to the waiting carriage. Then he gave the driver the address for the Fitzroy estate proper, getting inside.

"Be serious, for one moment," Ravenscroft scolded him, and he hopped into the carriage with him, without so much as a by his leave. "Answer me this. If you were your mother's son in truth, I would have a great deal more to worry about, would I not?"

"Make no mistake. I am my mother's son, Ravenscroft," Peregrine said softly. "She was the one who taught me the value of collecting other people's secrets, and the… myriad ways one could use them. I know how to play her game. And just because I have not yet demanded any sort of compensation for keeping your particular secrets does not mean I will not—particularly if I am pushed to desperation."

Ravenscroft slanted a curious look at him. "But however well you know how to play the game, I am beginning to get the impression… you would rather not."

"Are you implying you are starting to believe I am holding the truth of your affairs in reserve because I am actually a *nice* person?" Peregrine deflected, flashing the man a swift grin with too many teeth.

"Well, since you are not a nice person, that would be rubbish. But I might be revising my opinion of you upward to a garden snake with a bit of a soul from where I had you before—the lowest form of the devil incarnate."

"Just as well, because the position of the devil is held by someone else, and frankly, I would rather be left alone to my own devices, idling my nights away like every other wastrel."

Ravenscroft snorted. "Playing cards and mingling at soirees? You would be out of your gourd with boredom within a fortnight. I saw your face at the garden party when you thought no one was looking. Where *are* we going, anyway?"

"Back to my home, so I can write a letter or three and collect my driver. I may make you act as my secretary after all."

"Mr William Hodges, eh?" Ravenscroft said cannily, rocking

back and forth. "A rather competent man with a gun, I am given to understand."

"More competent than *you*, certainly. It has always amused me that the Regent calls you 'magpie.' I always thought you more of a court peacock."

Ravenscroft was unflustered. "Peacocks are a proud and noble bird, with sharp enough spurs. How are your talons these days, Lord Canary?"

"Sharp enough to catch some rats, darling Maggie."

21

*"The arrival of royalty demands the utmost preparation—
households must be set in order, staff drilled to perfection, and
every detail arranged with meticulous care."*
—Reflections of Grace: A Guide to Etiquette

The Queen's keen eyes remained fixed on Charity for a moment longer. Then, with a slow, deliberate motion, she leaned back in her chair, the stiff brocade of her gown rustling against the carved wood. A measured breath escaped her nose—not quite a sigh, not quite a huff—as her fingers resumed their rhythmic tapping against the armrest, a sound as precise and unrelenting as a clock marking the seconds.

At last, she spoke. "You look pale, Duchess. Sit."

It was not a kindness. Charity knew better than to mistake the Queen's commands for concern, but she accepted the invitation with a murmured "Thank you, ma'am," and lowered herself onto the nearest chair.

Queen Charlotte lifted a small bell from the table at her side and gave it a delicate ring. A moment later, the door opened just wide enough for a footman to receive her order.

"Tea."

The command was crisp, unadorned. The footman disappeared as swiftly as he had arrived, and returned soon after. He made quick work of pouring tea and then, bowing, he exited the room.

The Queen studied Charity with an uncompromising gaze and pursed her lips as she blew into the steaming cup. "The only positive news in all this is that the Dutch still have no idea their prince was poisoned. Can you imagine, Duchess, what would happen were they to learn? The matter of the betrothal would be insignificant in comparison to the diplomatic nightmare that would result. Who put my granddaughter up to this? You said there were messages?"

"Months' worth, Your Majesty. Each penned in a feminine hand on fine stationery. Lord Fitzroy and I agree that it must be a woman within the *ton*."

"Fitzroy agrees with you, you say?" Charlotte huffed in disgust. "And why should he not, when that description absolves him of any blame? What would he have me do? Drag all the ladies of the land before my throne and subject them to questioning?"

"Of course not, Your Majesty." Charity clenched her jaw at a fierce glare from the Queen.

"And when the Dutch hear—for word will most certainly get out—what then? They will demand a head on a platter."

"Then let us find one to deliver. I believe the person who passed those messages along to the Princess of Wales is someone who has previously been in Lady Fitzroy's employ. How else would her man of business know to find them?"

The Queen shifted. "I am well aware that some of the less fortunate members of the *ton* rely on less savoury ways to line their pockets. We have always turned a blind eye to such matters. It would be far more convenient to blame Lord Fitzroy."

Fear closed Charity's throat. For whatever other issues they had between them, she did not want him dead. She dared to speak again, playing the only card remaining in her hand. "This is far worse than selling a courtesy, my Queen. This person acted directly against the express wishes of both yourself and the Prince Regent. If they are allowed to escape unpunished, what will they do next?" Charity glanced from side to side, as though checking to make sure they were still alone in the room. Then she lowered her voice and added, "Such an individual might very well help Marian Fitzroy, should she someday decide to return."

The Queen sucked in a breath and her cheeks flamed. "I will not allow anyone from that viper's nest to slide through the shadows."

"Nor will I, which is why I hope you will forgive me for pressing this point."

"I will grant you leniency, but do not make a habit of it, Duchess. Now, be quiet, and let me think." Her gaze turned distant as she tapped one manicured finger against the rim of her teacup. "My granddaughter keeps an insipid collection of women around her, most of them married to one of my sons. Of them, at least, I can be certain of loyalty."

Charity held her breath, sensing the Queen working through a line of reasoning.

"If we exclude them, and yourself, Duchess, we are left with a very short list," Queen Charlotte continued, more to herself than to Charity. "Which one of the remaining has both a need for coin and a lack of scruples?" Her gaze sharpened, landing suddenly on Charity as if she had already come to the answer. "Tell me, Duchess, have you made the acquaintance of Lady Blandford?"

Charity hesitated. The name was familiar, but she had been in the north for much of the year, far removed from the latest scandals and whispers of London society. "I have crossed paths with her, ma'am, but our conversations have never progressed beyond polite niceties."

"Then allow me to enlighten you." The Queen sat forward, her voice edged with cool disdain. "At the start of the year, she claimed to have come into a modest inheritance. No relations were reported dead, mind you, but she appeared at court with new gowns and an air of financial ease she had never before possessed. I did not question it at the time, for I had more pressing matters to address. Now, I find myself reconsidering."

Charity remained still, waiting.

"Lady Blandford," Charlotte mused, tilting her head, "is a woman who likes her comforts. And comforts require funds. It would not be the first time she has sold her services to an interested party, though this is rather a bold leap from the usual indiscretions." Her lips pressed into a thin line. "Yes. I do believe she will answer our questions."

Before Charity could speak, the Queen lifted her hand and rang the bell. The footman appeared almost immediately, bowing low.

"Have the carriage brought round," she instructed, as though it were the most natural thing in the world.

A beat of silence. The footman hesitated, flicking a glance toward Charity before facing the Queen. "Your Majesty… you wish to go out?"

Charity's breath caught.

Charlotte's expression did not waver. "Did I not make myself clear?"

The man gave a hurried bow and all but fled to fulfill the command.

Charity found herself gripping the arms of her chair. "You mean to visit Lady Blandford? Now?"

The Queen settled back, smoothing the fabric of her gown.

"We will catch her off guard. That is how one gets confessions, my diamond. Surely you understand that."

Charity swallowed. Queen Charlotte never made unplanned visits. The weight of her presence was an event in and of itself, something carefully orchestrated and never without intent.

Still, she nodded. "Of course, ma'am."

A small, satisfied smile curled at the Queen's lips. "Good. Come along and I will show you what happens to those who dare to defy me."

The carriage rattled through the narrow streets of London, the steady clip of the horses' hooves echoing against the stone facades. Charity sat opposite the Queen, hands neatly folded in her lap, but her thoughts were far from still.

It was not lost on her how unusual this journey was. The Queen of England did not travel in anonymity, nor did she venture into the city without the full pageantry of rank and status. Yet here she sat in an unmarked carriage, the royal crest absent from the doors, with only the bare minimum of guards shadowing their path. No outriders, no heralding trumpets, no crowd of onlookers pausing in reverence. There would be no one to give Lady Blandford warning of her impending doom.

While the Queen had prepared for their outing, Charity had searched her prodigious memory for what little she knew of the Blandford family. Lady Blandford had once presided over an enviable household, her place in society assured by birth and marriage. But that was before her husband's untimely death, before the title passed to a distant cousin who had wasted little time in ejecting her from the Blandford estate.

Queen Charlotte had not spoken since the carriage set off, her expression unreadable. Charity did not fool herself into thinking

Her Majesty was in a softened mood. No, the Queen was merely sharpening the blade before the strike.

The houses grew narrower as they approached their destination, the grandeur of Mayfair left behind in favour of quieter, more practical elegance. The carriage slowed before a modest townhouse squeezed between its wealthier neighbours. Its painted shutters were chipped at the edges, the iron knocker polished but worn smooth from years of use. A pair of potted roses sat on the front step, their blooms slightly wilted, as though tended by a hand that no longer had the time or means to care for them properly.

Queen Charlotte's voice cut through the stillness. "Let us see what secrets Lady Blandford has been keeping, shall we?"

A trio of footmen had accompanied the carriage. One leapt clear and headed to the door, while the other two took great care in helping the Queen down. Charity, nearly an afterthought, had to descend the carriage steps on her own. By then, the front door was open and the housekeeper was dropped into a deep curtsey that would have been the envy of any woman in court.

Queen Charlotte strode into the house, paying the housekeeper no mind, and went straight into the front room, where she and Charity found Lady Blandford waiting.

The woman in question was so pale that she was nearly invisible against the faded wallpaper, its once-grand pattern of roses now ghostlike beneath years of neglect. She jerked into a curtsey, half rose, then hesitated before dipping into another, as though unsure which instinct—self-preservation or formality— ought to take precedence. Her hands fluttered at her sides, before she pressed them tightly together, as though restraining the urge to clutch at her own skirts.

That could be you if you do not take great care in your interactions with the Queen.

Charity shushed her mother's voice. Now was not the time for such reminders.

"Your Majesty, I was not expecting—that is to say, I am most honoured by your visit—"

Queen Charlotte held out a hand to halt Lady Blandford's torrent of words. "Yes, yes, I am here. Ring for tea, and let us be seated."

Lady Blandford glanced around the room. There was an overstuffed sofa with the fabric worn shiny from years of use, a pair of wooden chairs, and a single wingback with a basket of sewing beside it. She rushed over, retrieved the basket, shoved it under a side table, and then offered the Queen her chair.

"The tea tray?" Charlotte reminded her. "I fear your housekeeper will end up frozen in that position if you do not prod her to rise."

Lady Blandford gasped in horror and excused herself. Harshly whispered orders floated in from the corridor, followed by scurrying footsteps, and then the lady returned. She glanced at Charity, her searching gaze begging for some sort of hint of what was in store. Had Charity felt even a moment of sympathy, she might have found an encouraging smile or a slight nod of her head.

Charity had none, not for the woman who likely betrayed them all for coin. If somehow they were wrong in their accusations, she could apologise later.

Lady Blandford perched on the edge of one of the wooden chairs, her back rigid and her hands clenched in her lap. The housekeeper arrived in the doorway, her arms shaking so much that the cups rattled on the plates. She rushed forward, deposited the tray on the low table in the middle of the room, and backed out with her head bowed. A whimper was the last they heard of her.

"Shall I pour?" Lady Blandford asked in a wobbling voice.

"Not yet," the Queen replied. She settled more comfortably onto the chair, but Charity knew any relaxation was feigned. Queen Charlotte was a lioness pretending to sleep long enough to coax her prey within reach.

Charity wondered how long it would take Lady Blandford to break. The answer was no time at all. The woman lasted two blinks of the Queen's scrutiny before she dropped to her knees and begged for leniency.

"I did not think she would do it, not truly, and I had only her best interest at heart…" she babbled on, her words tumbling out between sobs. "She does not want to marry the prince."

"Silence!" Charlotte's voice boomed, making even Charity jump in her seat. "Do not pretend that this was about anything other than coin. Tell me everything and maybe you will avoid spending your remaining days with a view of Tower Bridge."

Lady Blandford stayed where she was on the floor at the Queen's feet, but she did find the wherewithal to sit up. Her skirts pooled around her, dragging her down with the weight of the expensive fabric. The pearls at her wrist and ears testified to her taste for expensive adornments. In a halting voice, with tears carving tracks down her pallid cheeks, she recounted the entire tale.

"No great harm was intended, my liege. I had only to copy the text of the letters I received, and then ensure my copies found their way to the princess. I thought once of refusing, but then who else might they have hired?"

"Have you still the original letters?" Charity asked gently.

Lady Blandford gave a nod of confession. At the Queen's command, she went upstairs to retrieve them.

"Should we worry she might run away?" Charity asked after several long minutes had passed.

"Where would she go that I cannot reach?" Queen Charlotte replied.

Lady Blandford must have arrived at the same conclusion, for she returned clutching a handful of missives. The hair framing her face was damp from where she had stopped to wash away the salt from her cheeks. "Here they are, Your Majesty."

The Queen flicked through them, skimming the brief lines before passing each letter to Charity. The notes were terse and matched with the ones Charity had seen at the palace.

"Where are the instructions for the poison?" Charity asked after she read the last one of the bunch.

"Oh, those came in the letter of introduction." Lady Blandford hurried to her writing desk in the corner of the room, pressed a latch to release a hidden drawer, and then pulled out a ribboned scroll. "I followed them exactly. She told me exactly which herbwoman I could trust to mix the concoction. I asked again before I took the vial, to make sure no one's life was at risk. Here, you can see for yourself."

Charity took the proffered scroll, the weight of it immediately different from the others—thicker, richer, its creamy-white surface free of smudges or wear. A knot tightened in her stomach. This was no ordinary correspondence.

The world narrowed as she slid the ribbon free, the crisp snap of wax breaking too loud in the hush of the room. For a moment, her eyes refused to process what she saw. And then—recognition struck her like a blow.

The initials at the bottom of the page were unmistakable. Bold, flourished, confident. She knew this hand.

She forced herself to swallow, her throat dry. "Your Majesty," she managed at last, the words tasting of dust. "This is from Lady Fitzroy."

Queen Charlotte swiped the letter from Charity's hands without a word. Only the rising colour beneath her powdered cheeks revealed her growing fury. When she lifted her head, it was to pierce Lady Blandford with her fevered gaze.

"You consorted with a known traitor?" She whispered, as though even she could not believe the signature on the page. She held up a hand to forestall any excuses. "No, save them for the judge. For this alone, I will see you cast from our shores, bound for transport to the worst penal camp they can find."

That was the final straw for Lady Blandford. She went completely white, her eyes rolling back, and she crumpled into an unmoving heap on the floor.

Charity felt the sudden urge to kick her with the toe of her slipper, but refrained out of better judgement.

The Queen rose from her chair, slid the scroll into the pocket of her brocade skirt, and then stepped over Lady Blandford on her way to the door. When she passed the footman waiting in the narrow hall, she instructed him to remain behind. "Lady Blandford is not to move from that room until the guards collect her. Do you understand?"

The footman gave a nod in reply and then turned the knob on the front door. Another footman was on the doorstep, ready to assist Queen Charlotte with getting back into the carriage. He did, at least this time, help Charity up the stairs, nudging her toward the empty bench across from Charlotte. Before he closed the door, he asked the Queen for their next destination.

"St James's," she replied, urging them to move with all haste.

Charity braced herself as the carriage lurched into motion, though in truth she was bracing herself against the torrent of worries washing over her. Like her, the Queen was lost in her own thoughts, staring out the window with a determined set to her mouth.

The name of Marian Fitzroy sounded over and over again in Charity's mind, like a bell tolling a death or a call to arms. The back of her neck itched. Had she somehow slipped past everyone and returned to London?

Suddenly, certain events that had happened these few days

past seemed far more sinister. Was Lady Fitzroy out to finish gaining her revenge on Charity and her mama? What if the attacks had been directed at her for that reason?

She had to find Peregrine. He did not know his mother's hand was directing matters. She feared his plans to talk to Mr Cameron might end up with Peregrine walking into a trap.

22

"To be sane in a world of madmen is in itself madness."
—Jean-Jacques Rousseau

"Sounds like a fool thing," Hodges said disapprovingly after Peregrine explained the bones of the plan. "Hope I don't need to be tellin' you this."

"You do not," Peregrine said dryly. "But better, more expedient ideas seem to be in short supply."

Hodges grunted. His face was a colourful motley of bruises from fighting hand to hand with the man on the bridge, but at least the swelling was down over his right eye now. Hodges's rooms, in a cottage next to the stables, were only slightly less spartan than the man himself, and he leaned against one of the bare stone walls with his arms crossed, mulling it over.

"If he's greedy, you might buy off Cameron," he finally agreed reluctantly. "Stayin' alive long enough to do it…"

"Will be the trick, yes."

Ravenscroft stood near the window, his expression one of

disdainful detachment, as if the mere act of breathing in air so close to the stables offended him. He tugged at the lace cuffs of his shirt with a delicacy that bordered on theatrical, his nose wrinkled against the ever-present stench of horse dung. "We could start by writing him a letter—" he began.

"Not Cameron," Hodges interrupted flatly. "Send a message to his right hand. McGrath."

Ravenscroft blinked, incredulous. "You want to write a letter to someone who is an illiterate thug?" he asked.

"Messenger." Hodges transferred his look to Peregrine, one that patently said, *God help us both.* "Neutral ground?"

Peregrine considered the past. So much of his information from this side of things was out of date. "The Hart and Dagger, if it is still standing."

So it was that they sent the other stableman by horse with a very short list of what old haunts Cameron's men frequented that Peregrine could remember.

"Do you regularly consult your carriage driver on matters of strategy, Fitzroy?" Ravenscroft asked him curiously when they returned outdoors, leaving Hodges to the business of getting the horses together, anticipating success.

"It has been a bit of an odd year, Maggie," Peregrine said shortly. "And I know he knows what end of a blade to stick people with."

Peregrine didn't know how Hodges had found himself at the front, but he had long ago guessed that the man's past before the war was checkered with brutality. It didn't matter what the past had been. Over the months they had been stationed with Hill and Wellington, they had gradually gained just enough respect for one another to watch each other's backs.

After Napoleon's abdication, Peregrine had asked him what business he might be returning to, Hodges had shrugged, saying that there was always work for thief takers and enforcers. The businesslike way he conducted his violence certainly suggested he might be familiar with such work.

On a hunch, Peregrine had decided to offer for him as a trusty, before they even returned to England. Hodges, in the infernally patient way he did nearly everything, gave it about thirty seconds of consideration and then accepted.

And this had been good, because Peregrine needed to clean house upon his return. Not a single person who had been employed there by his mother would he tolerate remaining. He had dismissed the remaining few staff members who had kept the Fitzroy estate from deteriorating after its abandonment—and with recommendations, because he wasn't a monster—and he was still in the long process of replacing them, starting with the barest minimum of essential staff. Which mostly involved caring for the horses.

Finally, Dawson returned as the afternoon was waning. "He'll meet you where you said," he called. "The hour before sundown."

Hodges nodded, checking the position of the sun before rearranging the pistol in his coat pocket. "Get ready, Dawson. We'll take you with us."

Dawson was a big bruiser of a man he had 'stolen' from Lord Tremayne, actually—a prizefighter who had been forcibly retired to more menial work after he lost most of the sight in one eye.

Like Hodges, he worked as a bit of a general hand in addition to the stables for Peregrine now, but he was a good choice for a bruiser in a fight. Hopefully this would remain what Peregrine wanted—just a bit of a careful talk with McGrath. But it would be unwise to not make a small show of force.

Ravenscroft looked uneasy and out of place beside the two servants as Peregrine tested the heft of his stoutest walking stick. "I will come too."

Hodges let out a quiet huff. "Best not. Your clothes might get a little dirty."

"He can come. After all, he promised His Highness he would come running back if I got killed," Peregrine said over his shoulder at the old rake, and Hodges grunted his acknowledgement.

Will Hodges shrugged as if he couldn't care less. "Stay out of the way then."

But Peregrine did give Ravenscroft the walking stick, even though the other man looked like he would be more likely to hit a friend with it than a foe. Hopefully, he would never need to use it for defence.

Like Peregrine's townhouse, The Hart and Dagger sat near the border between two worlds, just far enough away from the rookeries that it could attract men who fancied a taste of danger without actively courting it. It was a dingy thing, poorly lit and ale-stained, perfect for doing business with less savoury elements.

It was a few minutes before seven when they arrived, and the tavern was still relatively quiet; most workers were still finishing out their days. Peregrine's thoughts had kept wandering in the most useless directions for the entire ride, still seeking the duchess out like a moth to a flame. Finally he shoved the whole mass of them away.

The moment they stepped inside, he spotted the men sitting near the front, nursing their drinks and pretending indifference. The stripling he had sent running from Atholl House, however, was among them, and the way his gaze darted toward Peregrine before quickly skittering away confirmed the reason they were there.

McGrath and his giant friend, however, had taken position at the back, lounging with the kind of deliberate ease that suggested they weren't worried about being disturbed.

Fine, McGrath hadn't come alone but neither had they. A brawl wasn't necessarily in the cards, but it did say something about the enforcer's expectations for the meeting. And in the worst case scenario, six on four—or perhaps three, if Ravenscroft was truly useless—wasn't the worst odds he had lived through.

McGrath looked like hell. One side of his face was swollen, his lower lip split, and there was a stiffness in the way he held himself, like every movement had a price.

But what Peregrine wasn't expecting was the way the man tilted his head, taking them all in with a sour expression before his gaze landed squarely on Hodges. Hodges didn't shift, but Fitzroy felt a rising tension radiating from his driver.

"Well, lookie here, Abe," McGrath said to his giant friend. His sudden grin was almost frightening. "If it isn't ol' Will Hodges. I *thought* I recognized you. How long has it been? A year, I think? Didn't expect to see you licking that one's boots."

Hodges slouched casually, resting both hands on his hips.

A spike of fear and doubt iced through Peregrine, and he flicked his eyes over his driver. He strove to keep his expressions in check as he did so. "I take it you two know each other."

"This old sellsword? Oh, aye," McGrath grunted dismissively. "Did some work now and again for Cameron, he did."

"Don't work for the cove now," Hodges said simply to Peregrine.

Peregrine ground his teeth together, wondering if he dared take that on faith, even if he had little choice but to at the moment.

"Oh we know it, and you're not likely to find more such work ever again. Cameron is none too happy about what you cost him with Red Hand's men, and some of the others have thoughts about your lapse of decorum.

"You didn't know, did you?" McGrath smirked at him. "That your man here has been paid to watch out for your sorry arse since before you left London? He's been dipping both hands in the pot since you brought him on. Sorry, Fitzroy."

Hodges kept still, his eyes forward, and Peregrine knew then that it was true.

Peregrine felt mildly sick to his stomach, wondering who held Hodges's purse strings—besides him, that was. However furious the idea made him, McGrath was deliberately sowing discord now to weaken him, and he didn't dare lose sight of that fact.

"If you are going to change your side, Hodges, I would kindly ask you to do it now," Peregrine said, his hands fisted at his sides.

Hodges exhaled sharply through his nose, finally shifting his gaze to Peregrine. His expression didn't change, steady as granite. "You ever do something because it was the right thing, my lord? What was an honourable choice—now isn't."

Good enough, for this moment anyway. Assuming that the matter of Hodges didn't complicate his plan.

"I did not come here to talk about Will Hodges, McGrath. I came to discuss our business and discover what might settle things between me and Cameron."

McGrath chuckled. "Knew it. We had a bet that you were far too soft for this sort of thing, no matter what you did with the lords. And that's why you let little Johnny go." Cameron's enforcer jerked his thumb at the stripling.

Peregrine's eyes flickered. "Of course you knew. My mother's business was always her own, and I never tried to be a part of it."

"So that's your plan? You tell Cameron you're not looking to take over your dear mum's legacy, and you think then we both go our merry way," McGrath asked idly.

"I did not imagine it would be so easily settled. But negotiation requires discussion."

"Reckon that makes some sense. Just what did you come here to offer, Fitzroy? Money? The works?"

Peregrine forced himself to spread his hands in query. "I could offer some of those things. What does he want? Maybe I have it."

The tavern keeper was scowling at them, but clearly didn't

want to interfere. And behind him he could hear his stableman and Ravenscroft shifting uneasily.

McGrath gave a laughing sigh. "Ah, Fitzroy. You might be a man now, but you still got the heart of a boy in there, don't you, lad? You think you've got power o'er your life. A few words and your pocket change are the only resources you need. You keep your fists tight around every move, every scheme, every person, thinking that you learned your important lesson—if you trust no one but yourself, then you can be your own master. Maybe that would work if you're content to be nothing special. But somehow I don't think that's you, is it?"

The words struck home. "I did not come for a debate in philosophy," Peregrine replied. "I wanted to see what Cameron might want to end this quarrel between us."

"Your morals bought you nothing, and you forgot the truth," McGrath said contemptuously. "That if you really want to be your own person, you have to be ruthless enough to beat the wheat from the chaff. All your fearfulness has made you weak. Backed up by a silk-stocking, a tired old boxer, and a hired blade with two masters who serves neither well. We don't need your money, or your interference."

It was going to be a brawl.

The men at the far table surged forward, upending stools and scattering their drinks as they moved to block the front door. Behind him, the barkeep cursed loudly and shouted at them to take it outside, but wisely made no other move to interfere. The few other patrons either ducked for cover or scrambled away, sensing what was about to unfold.

Hodges and Peregrine moved first. With a single, sharp motion, Hodges upended the nearest chair, sending it crashing into the legs of one of McGrath's men. The man stumbled, and Hodges didn't hesitate to drive his fist hard into the cutthroat's gut before throwing him headfirst into a nearby table. Then he spun back towards Abel and McGrath.

Peregrine had never developed a taste for the ruthless violence his mother's darker enterprises needed. But what he had needed to do to survive returning to England had already stained his hands.

So McGrath was wrong about one thing—his morals didn't make him weak. And meeting their violence with his own couldn't cause him to lose his soul, especially if it was already gone.

As the giant charged in, Peregrine seized Abel's wrist, and twisted it brutally backwards, sending his knife clattering to the floor.

Dawson, his stableman, threw himself into the fray with the reckless enthusiasm of a man who had sorely missed a good fight. He poleaxed the first man from the far table with a hard right hook to the jaw and swiped at the next one with his left. The second man pushed the boy in front of him like a coward. But Dawson just shoved the youngster at Ravenscroft and kept moving forward. Ravenscroft yelped as the stripling collided with him, and both went sprawling.

Peregrine had only just managed to kick Abel's knife away before someone tackled him hard from behind, nearly sending him falling forward onto his hands and knees. Seeing Peregrine go down, Hodges shoved Abel backwards with a shoulder, keeping the man from crushing Perry with one of his heavy boots as he began to draw the pistol from his coat.

The giant grabbed a bottle to use as a weapon from a nearby table and swung it at Hodge's head like a cricket bat, forcing him to retreat.

Then McGrath himself finally joined the fight. The enforcer pushed forward towards Peregrine, who by this point had been hauled upright by the attacker at his back. The man had an arm looped around Peregrine's neck and was tightening it slowly, constricting his air.

McGrath's face was mocking as he peered at Peregrine. "By the way—your mother sends her love," he murmured, low and amused.

Everything happened at once. He dimly registered the rush of movement—the sound of the flintlock firing, someone tackling McGrath, someone else shouting his name—but it all blurred together.

The pain came a split second later. The sharp, hot agony of a knife sinking into his side.

23

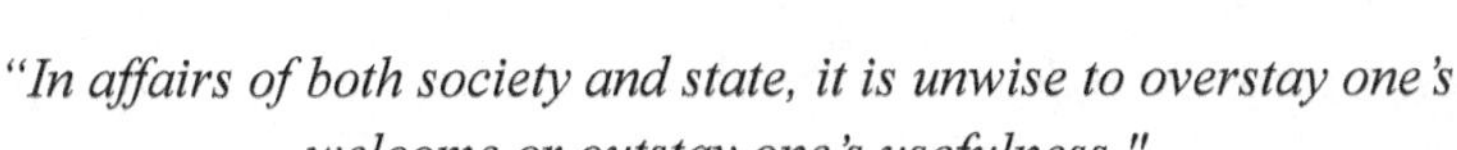

"In affairs of both society and state, it is unwise to overstay one's welcome or outstay one's usefulness."
—Reflections of Grace: A Guide to Etiquette

The silent carriage ride to St James's palace gave Charity far too much time to stir herself into a froth as she pondered the implications of Lady Blandford's revelation.

Lady Fitzroy's words to Charity, on that night she had been there with Roland and Grace demanding an explanation, had been pure poison. She had removed the pretty mask she wore in society, and shown them exactly who she truly was.

And they had still not quite believed what they had seen, because it had seemed too monstrous to be real.

Now, Charity acknowledged what she had seen to be true. Marian Fitzroy had been entirely remorseless for what she had done. The world was her due, and that was how she felt it should be. Lady Fitzroy was incapable of considering another's suffering beyond how it might serve her need for consequence and admiration. If people were moved to please her because they feared her wrath, then the ends were just the same.

Charity couldn't even conceive of how black Marian Fitzroy's soul was. Perhaps she had been born entirely without one, and her heart could only know hate and ambition. Maybe she truly couldn't love anyone at all.

Not even her own children.

God above. If Marian Fitzroy had a hand in things now, how deep did that influence go? What if she had also meant to punish her own son by leaving Charity's broken body for him to find?

How angry would she be at her son for interfering with her plans?

It was almost all Charity could do not to fling open the carriage door while they were moving and hurl herself out to go looking for him.

The shouts of the driver, calling for the horses to slow, signaled Charity and the Queen's arrival at the palace. Though the carriage lacked the royal crest, the footmen must have been recognised.

The guards threw the gates open wide and stood at attention as they passed. At this arrival, Queen Charlotte was greeted with all the fanfare due to her lofty station. Footmen, guards, and maids rushed around to prepare the way. Charity overheard a few grumbled questions of why they were not alerted in advance of her arrival.

Oh, if only they knew the mood of the Queen at that moment, they would all seal their lips shut and bow down, avoiding her gaze as she passed.

Queen Charlotte snapped her fingers and a footman ran forward. "Where is the Prince Regent?"

"He is in the Royal Closet, ma'am. If you will follow me to the receiving room, I will send someone to let him know of your arrival."

"You will lead me to him, posthaste," she ordered, and then added over her shoulder, "Duchess, attend me."

Charity could think of nothing she wanted to do less. But perhaps Prinny knew where Peregrine was bound. Following in the Queen's wake, Charity ventured into a part of the palace she had never been before. Men and women of the *ton* eyed her with blatant curiosity as she passed, but grew few and far between the deeper they went into the prince's private chambers.

Queen Charlotte barely allowed the footman time to rap on the door before she pushed past him and strode inside. All the laughter and chatting came to an abrupt halt at her arrival. The Prince Regent, who had been lounging in a chair with his feet propped on a stool, pushed a woman from his lap and sprang to his feet.

"Get out!" The Queen proclaimed. Even Charity had to resist the urge to run from the room, but she was not going anywhere until she had some idea where to find Peregrine.

Charlotte pulled the scroll from her pocket and thrust it at her son. "Your daughter acted under orders from Marian Fitzroy! Read the paper, and then explain why I have learned all of this from someone else!"

Prinny moved closer to the light of the candelabra, and his mother claimed his chair. She sat with an audible sigh and rubbed at her leg. For a moment, Charity glimpsed the woman beneath the jewelled tiara, a woman fighting a losing match against the march of time. But just as quickly, the Queen straightened, and once again assumed the proud stance of a lady sitting on the throne.

Prinny read the letter twice, as though hoping to find something different the second time around, and then turned his anger onto Charity.

"Why did you not bring this to me?"

"To *you*?" The Queen gasped. "She has brought plenty

enough to you, Prinny! The duchess is *my* lady-in-waiting, lest you need a reminder of her loyalty. Not to mention, *Lord Fitzroy* was by earlier, bringing information to *you*."

Prinny bit back a retort and coughed into his hand to keep from entering a shouting match with his own mother. "Your Majesty—*Mama*—let us discuss this in private."

Charity dared to cut in before she was summarily dismissed. "I beg leave to go in search of Lord Fitzroy, Your Highness. Might you know where I can find him?"

"He and my magpie left something like an hour ago. The footman might have some better idea of their destination."

"With no guard?" Charity had the temerity to ask, trying to keep the censure from her face when Prinny responded in the negative.

Charity glanced at the Queen, waiting for the woman to dismiss her. As soon as Queen Charlotte nodded for her to go, Charity curtseyed and backed out of the room. And then, she ran.

The poor footman had no idea where Peregrine had gone, though he did confirm that his lordship had left in the company of Lord Ravenscroft. He directed Charity to a guardsman, who called over a stableboy. Charity gritted her teeth through the wasted minutes, but eventually she found someone who had overheard Peregrine's instructions to the carriage driver.

He was on his way to his London estate. Perhaps she could catch him there. She girded her loins and asked for use of a carriage for the remainder of the afternoon.

Just the thought of setting foot in that place again caused her to break out in a cold sweat, but she pushed the black tide of hysterics down. *Lady Fitzroy is not there... yet*, she reminded herself.

But when she arrived in a stew, Peregrine was not there, either.

"He passed through briefly," the new family butler had

explained, "but after sending Dawson out with a message, he left again. Dawson and Hodges went with him, so unfortunately I don't know where they might have gone, Your Grace."

He had clearly gone onwards to the meeting—but where? Mr Cameron's offices? She might be able to find him with enough time, but time was something she didn't have. Then she remembered the meeting that had started her day. The promise of additional resources, of help for which they had only to ask.

She opened the carriage door and called out her direction. "Take me to the home of the Marchioness of Normanby."

Perhaps Selina could be persuaded to part with the information she needed—especially if she had ever had any real affection for Peregrine Fitzroy.

"Duchess Atholl! What brings you back to my home?" the marchioness asked gaily when Charity walked into her drawing room. "Have you a need to borrow a gown?"

"I wish it were that simple," Charity replied, shrugging off the woman's catty teasing. She had composed her words during the short ride over, but now doubt coiled tight in her chest.

Peregrine had told her time and again that the marchioness was not a woman to be approached lightly. What if she had misread everything? What if this appeal placed Peregrine in greater danger rather than less? But she had no choice. Hesitation would only be a weakness here. She forced herself to hold the woman's shrewd gaze and pressed on.

"May I speak plainly?" Charity continued on after the woman nodded. "Lord Fitzroy is in trouble."

The marchioness's eyes flickered, but she masked her expression. "Again? Whatever could he be up to this time?"

"His mother is back."

"What?" the marchioness reared back, her voice unstrung with shock for the briefest moment before her expression was brought back under control. "In London? Do you have proof?"

"I—" Charity hesitated. "Not exactly. I only have seen proof that she has been corresponding with people in London."

The beautiful, statuesque woman pursed her lips, thinking hard and quickly as she paced the room. "Correspondence, you say? Giving orders, perhaps? Are you saying Lady Fitzroy had somewhat to do with the... sabotage of Prince William's dignity?"

Charity forgot that Selina would be able to piece that part together, given her previous suggestion about Caroline. "Yes, she did."

"And *that* part you do know for certain? Unlike the supposition she has returned to English soil?"

"Yes," Charity admitted. "I am not able to tell you everything, but it does seem certain now that Marian Fitzroy played a part in the poisoning of the prince."

"You cheeky little devil, Peregrine," the marchioness muttered to herself, looking irritated.

Did she think he was working with his mother? "Please, Marchioness. I do not believe he is in collusion with her."

"Oh, do not fret, Duchess. Perry would sooner dance a reel in his smalls than help his mother. That I have no doubt. It is a valuable—and dire—piece of information you have brought to me, and I am sure that Perry has told you I am a broker in such things. So you came with a purpose. What is it?"

Charity straightened her sleeves and settled into her seat on the sofa across from the marchioness. "One of your... acquaintances said you have resources, Marchioness. I need to know where to find Mr Cameron."

The marchioness's eyes narrowed. "And where is his lordship? Does he know you are here asking for it?"

"I do not know where he is, and that is why I need your aid. I know he was going to seek a meeting with Mr Cameron by other means. But when he left, he did not know about his mother, and I am afraid he might be walking into a trap."

To her credit, the marchioness's expression was quite serious, and she paused before replying. "It seems as though Perry is running out of time."

Confusion swamped her. "I… do not understand."

"Peregrine has been trying to dance on the head of a pin, little lamb," the marchioness said obliquely. "His attempts to remain unattached among the ruling orders have made him weak. He refused to be a player, so he is treated as a pawn. If he does not choose an alliance with someone who can lend him consequence… it will get worse."

"Why must he choose?" Charity countered. She was beginning to understand the challenges Peregrine faced. Everyone seemed to want something from him, but no one was there when he was in need.

Not unless he promised them more than he wanted to give.

The marchioness was calm, even though her face was not unsympathetic. "He must make himself indispensable to someone, otherwise he will be a liability. Liabilities have a rather short life span."

The cold logic of it was chilling.

You are here. That thought calmed Charity's racing pulse. She was not leaving until the woman gave the promised aid.

"Are you going to tell me what I wish to know or not? Lord Fitzroy's life might be on the line if I cannot find him before he gets to Mr Cameron. He needs help. Are you his friend? If so, you will see fit to offer whatever aid you can."

"I already have." The marchioness played with her lower lip idly. "Not just, of course, what you have seen him reject—the promises of aid and shelter under my wing if he consorts with my… friends. I have given him other forms of assistance as discreetly as I dared, so he would not reject it out of hand."

"What is it that you have done?" Charity asked her, uncertain. "Is someone on their way to Cameron now?"

"Duchess—may I call you Charity? And you must call me Selina, of course. Because I spoke the truth before. I believe I would like it if you and I could be very good, very powerful friends."

Charity was not at all convinced that would be a good idea. But she knew one thing—she did not want the Marchioness of Normanby to think her an enemy. So she nodded, deeply masking any hint of uncertainty.

Selina smiled widely, for all appearances, genuinely pleased. "Good. I am so happy you agree. We can speak more plainly with one another, and then I can tell you an interesting story. When Marian Fitzroy fled, your Crown saw an opportunity to be rid of both her… and her bloodline."

Charity blinked, acutely uncomfortable as she was reminded of her own uncharitable thoughts from Prinny's little garden party only just a handful of days ago. How she had been wroth that he had returned unscarred. That he had returned at all. "You believe he was meant to die on the continent."

"Oh no. If I had not intervened, he would have died as a traitor—in a noose, that very week," Selina told her. "Perry bought a favour from me. I called in a great many favours to send him to war instead, and the Crown still did their best to make sure he would never come back."

"Peregrine said your favours are expensive," Charity admitted, and Selina nodded.

"He only knows a piece of it—but from what I hear, the rest is still… working to help keep him alive."

"Your 'friends of England'?" Charity asked, suspicious, and wanting to scream in frustration. It was taking all her years of perfecting her self-control to keep it from leaking out. "Duke Chandros said you were friends of England, but you speak of the Crown as though it is your opponent. Who are they? Some society, like the Freemasons?"

"Oh nothing so tawdry as that little boy's club. My friends are a select group of powerful, influential people who believe that leadership should not be left to random chance. We are the architects of Parliament, the unseen hand behind the ballot."

A creeping unease settled at the base of Charity's spine. She had always assumed the whispers were exaggerations—the mad rumours of idle aristocrats who found pleasure in paranoia. But Selina's expression held no amusement. She was not indulging in speculation. She was stating fact. And that meant there was far more at play than Charity had ever imagined.

"What do your… people want? To overthrow the Crown?"

"Just influence, darling. Nothing so chaotic as overthrowing the king—just making sure we keep a hand on the reins. And we already have it—more than you might suspect."

"I take it you want something of me," Charity said flatly. "My information is not enough to render more assistance."

"For Cameron's location? That is a trifle, Charity. I will give it to you if you like, but even if you send a pack of guards, I do not believe you could help him more than I have already. If it is a trap, as you fear, it will spring before anyone will reach him. But you are correct, I do want something from you. I want you to use all of your power to convince Peregrine it is in his best interest to align with me."

It was so surprising a request that Charity's lips actually parted. "It is… remarkable you think I could manage to convince him to do such a thing when you yourself cannot. Even if I had such sway over his opinion, why would you think I would encourage him to align with you rather than seek more protection from the Crown?"

Selina let her elegant hands stroke over the fabric of her gown. "How much protection do you think they would offer him, truly?"

Little. The voice of the Queen, idly contemplating offering up Peregrine's head to the Dutch, rang in her ears.

The marchioness took her silence as the answer, continuing. "Peregrine Fitzroy knows far too much to be let alone. He is an unattended, loaded gun waiting to be picked up and used carelessly. Ours are the safest hands to put him in—especially if Marian Fitzroy may be planning her return to England."

It made a certain amount of sense, but Peregrine would detest being forced to choose. "I take your meaning, but…" Charity licked her lips. "I do not believe I can convince him."

"He is his own man, of course. All I ask is that you argue our part genuinely."

"And… what if I refuse to plead your case?" she inquired.

"If you refuse, then nothing. I ask you to do it as a favour, as a friend who cares for Peregrine," the marchioness said. "You… are coming to care for him, I think. At least, enough that you understand his thoughts."

But then, her eyes turned opaque. "However, if I find I am forced to use it, evidence of his plans to poison the Prince of Orange will be given over to the crown. I do not want Peregrine harmed, Charity, but if it is the only choice, I will do what I must."

"But—" The breath rushed from Charity's lungs, leaving her momentarily weightless in her seat. "He had nothing to do with what happened to Prince William."

Selina gave her a look of deep pity. "Darling, that is only because someone else poisoned him first. Oh, do not look so shocked. Peregrine had selected croton oil because it would not be fatal. Poor Prince William! He was bound to end up sick in the bushes one way or another that day."

Surprise warred with horror. She wanted to deny it, to argue that Selina must be lying, twisting the truth to suit her purposes. But deep down, an awful part of her recognized that it fit. Peregrine had always carried secrets like armour, had always seemed like a man one step away from destruction. And yet…

A cold sickness curled through her stomach, winding tight. She had known—on some level—that Peregrine was tangled in dangerous affairs. But not this. Not actual treason. Not something so damning that it turned the ground beneath her feet to quicksand.

Her throat felt thick when she finally managed, "Why—why would he do that?"

"Because that was the price I asked for saving his life."

And now that life was being put in Charity's hands.

"What if I cannot convince him?"

"Then you did what you could," Selina's eyes brimmed with sympathy, and then she let her face harden. "All I ask is that you try. I would still enjoy being your friend; however, I would understand if you feel like this is no longer possible. Just know that this is the only favour I would ask of you for so little. If he, or you, want something more, you must negotiate for it, like everyone else." Selina rose from her chair, signaling their meeting had come to an end.

"Do not waste your worry on Perry, Your Grace. A man like him always lands on his feet—until the day he doesn't. And if that day comes… well. That, too, will be a choice."

Her words failed to offer Charity much comfort during her drive to the townhouse near the Seven Dials. She had the carriage drop her off a street over, and wound through the narrow paths between the rows until she found the rear entrance Peregrine had shown her on their way out that morning.

The key was exactly where he had left it. The lock clicked over and silence greeted her when she stepped into the kitchen.

Her thoughts, fears, and worries were her only company as she climbed the stairs to the bedroom. There, she dragged the stool from the dressing table over to the window and nudged the curtains far enough apart to allow her to see the small garden behind.

The night pressed in against the windowpane, cold and indifferent. Her hands curled tightly in her lap, nails biting into her palms as if pain might ground her. Everything felt more uncertain now—more fragile. She had trusted Peregrine, had thought herself a step closer to understanding him. But tonight had unraveled every assumption she had clung to.

She would wait. She would demand the truth. And, God help her, she would have to decide whether she could live with the answer.

24

"The hatred of relatives is the most violent."
—Tacitus

Peregrine gasped, his body locking up at the shock of it, his breath strangled in his throat as the pain seared through him.

The arm was torn from his neck, and the person standing behind him fell away. New hands grabbed him, steadying him, and he blinked blearily up to see Ravenscroft's grim, set face, but he couldn't make out the man's words. His ears were ringing from the flintlock's discharge so close to him.

The brawl was still raging around them, but Abel was dead, and Dawson and Hodges seemed to be beating McGrath and the remaining men into submission. He felt the warm spread of blood under his coat, the dull throb of the wound settling in. He clenched his jaw. The world tilted as he staggered, fighting to stay upright against the shock of it.

Pushing aside Lord Ravenscroft—and it was the stripling lad

who supported him on the other side, of all people—Peregrine took a single step closer to Hodges and McGrath. "Don't make him unable to talk, Will," Peregrine hissed. "Not yet."

McGrath was grinning at him like a fool despite the blood running down his face. "You grew a pair of bollocks while you were off playing soldier. Good on you, lad. A shame you learned it too late."

"What do you know of my mother?" Peregrine barked, in no mood for McGrath's nonsense.

Hodges had the man's arms tied savagely behind his back, and with a backward yank on the enforcer's collar, Will pulled him, stumbling, to his feet. McGrath laughed soundlessly at their efforts.

"She's a right bitch of a woman, your mum is. Isn't she?"

Furious and burning in agony, Peregrine snatched McGrath's bloody knife from the filthy tavern floor and planted it deep into the enforcer's thigh. McGrath shouted in pain, but his cry dissolved back into a choking laughter again.

"Is. My. Mother. Back. In. England?" he demanded of the Irishman, speaking slowly.

"Nay. Not yet. But she will be coming, you can be sure of that," McGrath panted. "Sweet God, you really believed Cameron would have the balls to cross your mum like that? After putting out the contract on her own son?"

Peregrine did not know what expression was on his face, but apparently he could not conceal it well enough, because McGrath cackled. "Aha-ha… you didn't know. Or did you think your mummy would forgive you if you sorted yourself out? Bloody hell, Fitzroy. How much of an optimistic fool are you? Did you think it was some sort of accident that she left you behind after you helped Lord Percy? Who do you think—" he grunted as Hodges twisted his fingers in McGrath's hair—"gave Green your dagger in the first place?"

Since Peregrine's own hand was pressed against his wound, Hodges punched the cutthroat hard in his lower back. "You got a point to make, or are you just getting your jollies in?"

McGrath writhed in his grip. "I had a point, and I already stuck 'im with it. Was just doin' my duty to deliver the message loud and clear to your thick-witted lord, Will. You best enjoy breathing while you have time, too, because you haven't been forgotten neither."

The world had started getting spotty around the edges, but Peregrine couldn't make himself find a chair to sit down. He was irrationally certain that if he did, he might not find the strength to get back up.

"Where does Cameron keep himself these days? Still enjoying the smell of fish over at the docks?" Peregrine asked, trying to focus as Ravenscroft pried his hand away from his flank long enough to insert a folded cloth.

"You're going to have to find that out for yourself—that's assumin' you live long enough to. You don't look too good right now, lad. Maybe you need a bit of a lie down."

"All this gabbing. Dawson, take him to a bench," Hodges said, pointing his chin at Peregrine. "Lord Ravenscroft, you run out and find a hack. I know a doctor who can keep his mouth shut —assuming we don't get held by Bow Street first."

"You didn't stick me well enough to end me," Peregrine said with far more confidence than he currently felt as Dawson guided him to a seat. "And even if you did, I am going to make sure everyone is hunting Cameron before I go. It might take a little longer. That's all."

"Thinking thoughts too small, Fitzroy," McGrath giggled around a moan as Hodges twisted the knife in his thigh. "Yer mum wouldn't do anything by halves. Cameron had his orders, but he's only one cog in the clockwork. Go ahead and find him if you can. Even he doesn't know everything that she has planned."

"Get him to the doctor. I will see to things here," Hodges ordered Lord Ravenscroft, rattling off an address as he shoved him toward the door.

Time seemed to skip, like a stone on the surface of a lake. No, he lost consciousness. Because when he opened his eyes next, he was being hauled out of a carriage, dangling between Dawson and Ravenscroft like a sack of barley.

"Back, are you?" Ravenscroft said sourly from his left side, his arm wrapped around Peregrine's waist so he could hold his side together. "I will never forgive you for failing to bring along a guard to bleed on instead of me."

"Buck up, Maggie," Peregrine said. Or he tried to say. The words seemed to barely tumble out of his mouth as the two of them dragged him onto the doctor's table. "I'll spot you for a new coat. *Nnngh*—!"

The doctor had dumped some liquid—vinegar, to judge by the pungent smell—over his abdomen, clothes and all. It burned like fury, and Peregrine panted through it to refrain from screaming.

"You bloody well will," Ravenscroft snarled, his face pale, and the doctor frowned at him.

"*Bloody* is quite accurate—though vulgar," the doctor told him censoriously, waving something that Peregrine couldn't quite see. "If you can help me move him, I might be able to preserve his clothes."

"Cut them," Ravenscroft told the doctor. "Stop the bleeding. And for God's sake, no leeches. If you bleed him any more, he might run dry."

At least the vinegar and whatever the hells the doctor was poking him with roused from stupor, and with a thrill of terror, Peregrine recalled what had happened. What he so badly needed to do. But his body was not cooperating much with him.

"I need you to find… the duchess. You have to tell her what happened."

"I daresay the Duchess Atholl can wait an evening while I figure out what to tell Prinny about this whole debacle," Ravenscroft retorted. "Or you can send your other man here."

Peregrine snatched at the dandy, grabbing him by his lovely cream-coloured cravat and leaving a great big bloody handprint on it. "The duchess is hiding at my townhouse. She isn't safe there. Go get her and then you can talk to Prinny. I trust *only* you to get her."

Ravenscroft swore a blue streak at him that made even Dawson gawk, and then stomped over to the bucket of water sitting on the floor to wash the red off his hands before he ripped the silk off from his neck and flung it into the corner. Then he came back and had the unmitigated gall to unwind Peregrine's cravat instead, thunking his head once or twice against the table in the process.

"Give me the address," the man said harshly, leaning close to Peregrine's lips for his response. "Doctor, Dawson, watch this idiot, will you?"

Peregrine was both exhausted and half out of his mind. What if it was already too late? He had thought the townhouse he had taken possession of so discreetly safe from the likes of Cameron, but now—now he wouldn't bet on it.

If Ravenscroft could find her, at least he could get her back to the royal family for protection. He had to hope.

He managed only half a thought that they had banked his life on the assumption that Dawson was a loyal man. But then again… if he was another lurking monster in the shadows, perhaps occupying Dawson here as he strangled the life out of him was for the best.

He tumbled headlong into darkness.

〜

Lord Ravenscroft eyed the neighbourhood in suspicion. The narrow townhouses blended one into the other along the dark, dirty London street. He was a far cry from the wide lanes of Mayfair where sprawling mansions stood like grand dames, their carefully pruned gardens forming the flounces of their skirts. Had Fitzroy really brought the Duchess Atholl here?

Try though he might, Ravenscroft could not imagine the elegant woman scurrying down the dirty back alleys so close to the slums, yet if Fitzroy was to be believed, that was exactly what she had done.

"Stop here," he called to the driver. As soon as the horses slowed to a halt, he leapt down from the carriage, his boots landing with a jarring thud that left him groaning. His breath hitched as the bruises on his person ached.

"You all right there, guv?" the driver asked, but Ravenscroft waved his concern aside.

"Stay here. I will return right away."

Or he hoped, assuming Her Grace was hiding away in Fitzroy's bolt hole. He followed the directions exactly, counting gates until he arrived at the third on the left. The latch slid free and the gate swung open on oiled hinges. He scooted in, stepped wide, and stumbled into a pot. The resulting cracking noise was bad enough, the soil spilling across his already scuffed boots adding insult to injury.

"Putain de pot de fleurs! Comme si j'avais besoin de ça..." Ravenscroft hissed as he shook his foot free, cursing more under his breath first in French and then in English. He moved forward more slowly after that, his eyes checking every shadow. There was blessed little light to be found, other than what little glow came from the moon. Not a single ray of light leaked from the windows of the townhouse.

Still, the key was hidden where Fitzroy had said. Ravenscroft unlocked the kitchen door and pushed it open only wide enough to slip inside. The edge of his coat caught on the door handle, jerking him backward, and saving him from a well-aimed frying pan swinging at his head. It came close enough to lift his hair in the breeze before smacking against the side of the door with an almighty clang.

Half deaf, Ravenscroft snarled again in French in his scramble to get free of his attacker. *"Nom de Dieu, quel enfer!"*

"Lord Ravenscroft?" a tentative voice asked. A woman stepped into the doorway—Her Grace, the Duchess Atholl. "What on earth are you doing here?"

"I could ask the same thing about what you are doing with that frying pan, dear Duchess," Ravenscroft panted, clutching his chest with his hand as his splintered nerves began to settle.

The duchess looked uneasy. No, he amended, she was in as thick a stew of agitation as he was. "Why are you here?" she repeated, her eyes darting around. "Where is Per—Lord Fitzroy?"

His eyes narrowed as he still caught that near-slip. When the devil did the duchess start calling Fitzroy by his Christian name? "He is—" Ravenscroft stopped there, unsure what word to use. Fine? No, that most certainly wasn't right. Safe? "He is not far away. He is the one who sent me here."

The duchess calmed enough to urge him inside. She helped him past a table and a tall shelf, and then told him to hold still while she lit a candle. The yellow-orange light flickered feebly, but it was enough to illuminate the dark crimson stains on his white lace cuffs.

"You are hurt!" she gasped.

"The blood is not mine," he replied and then cursed himself again when the duchess stilled. Her face was a mask, but she had paled several shades. "Your Grace, I will tell you everything that has happened. But we need to leave, right now."

Her posture stiffened, and Ravenscroft realised she was both afraid to leave the house—and deeply suspicious. "Why? Just where do you think you are going to take me? I am not going anywhere without *some* answers, Lord Ravenscroft."

What the hell had happened to her since Fitzroy showed up at Carlton house? "We went to meet with Cameron's men and discovered the agent is still working with Lady Fitzroy—"

"—who is occupied with exerting her influence upon England again. I discovered much the same thing." The duchess shivered, the candle wobbling in her hands. "So you already know. I was hoping to find you and Lord Fitzroy but you had left his estate without leaving a note, and I… had no idea where to look."

Ravenscroft took the candle holder from her and set it on the table, then he grasped her delicate hands in his. "You appear overset, and I do not want to press you, but we really do need to leave. I will take you back to the Queen for the evening. Is there anything you want to get before we go?"

She pulled her hands away, reaching for her cloak on the hook, and Ravenscroft rushed to grab it before she could, draping it around her shoulders and snuffing the candle.

The carriage was where he had left it, the horses shifting around under the weight of their harness. He helped her into the seat, pulled a worn rug over her lap, and ordered the driver to set off.

"Someone will see us," she muttered, reaching for the curtain.

"I must be sure no one is following us. Here, pull your hood up, and lean against me, if you like. If someone recognises me, they will assume I am up to my usual cavorting and distract themselves trying to guess your identity. No one will get it right."

She didn't quite lean on him, but she did slouch in his direction. "What happened with Mr Cameron? Whose blood is that? One of the thugs, I hope," she said bitterly.

"We had asked for a meeting and walked into a trap— although given our preparations, I believe both Fitzroy and Hodges expected treachery of some sort. There was a fight, and…" Ravenscroft paused, remembering McGrath's chilling laughter.

His pause caused the duchess's eyes to widen in fear again, and reluctantly, he told her the rest, recalling his abject horror at Lady Fitzroy's message to her son.

"Have mercy," the duchess breathed, sitting bolt upright. "Is he—"

"Alive, but wounded seriously. I left him at the doctor."

"Tell me you did not leave him alone!" she insisted.

Ravenscroft frowned at her. "Of course I did not. I left him with both the doctor and his stableman."

"Turn the carriage. We need to collect him and bring him to safety with us!"

"Your Grace!" he admonished her, surprised at her vehemence. "He is hurt too badly right now to be moved. He has his man—"

"We cannot trust his servant! We cannot trust anyone! Enemies are wearing the masks of friends, and monsters lurk in every shadow. If he is h—" her voice gave out. She mustered her strength and finished her thought. "Right now, Fitzroy is vulnerable. The only people I can be certain not to harm him further are here in this carriage. And if you do not turn it around this instant, I will be most vexed with you!"

Her words made him feel a little bit bad about thunking Fitzroy's thick head on the table when the man had deliberately ruined his fine cravat. Then he frowned, peering harder at the duchess.

Still, her point about betrayals around every corner was well made. Any mother who was so callous about the life of her own son likely had a few more unpleasant surprises in store.

Perhaps it was wise to drop him there as she continued on her way to the Queen. He could remain behind while Antoine was summoned from his place, and then from there, he could report all that had transpired to Prinny. The duchess didn't know his valet, Antoine, but the man expanded her list of people that could be trusted with Peregrine Fitzroy's sorry arse to three. And oddly, perhaps because of their mutual friends, he expected his own arse was safe with Duchess Atholl.

"All right," he told her, knocking on the carriage roof to signal the driver to slow so he could shout the new destination. "Let us go check to see if Fitzroy is still breathing."

He had meant it as a jest, but the duchess sniffled and then buried her head against his shoulder.

Was she actually crying? Over Fitzroy? Ravenscroft urged her back long enough to free his handkerchief and pass it to her. She wiped her eyes, took a ragged breath, and struggled to pull herself together.

What odd duck manner of madness was this? "Duchess Atholl," he asked slowly, the gears in his head turning as he considered things, "are you going *soft* on Lord Fitzroy?"

"I pity him," she retorted, but her words were unconvincing.

Good God, she *was* taking a shine to him. And seen in this light, Fitzroy's insistence made it look like the feeling was reciprocated. Well. Wasn't this a ruddy awful development?

"One does not cry over pathetic creatures, Your Grace. You need to cut these feelings from your chest immediately if you want to remain at court. And with Fitzroy—" he barked a short laugh. "Prinny will think this a grand laugh, but I doubt his mother will."

The duchess shivered again, doubtless imagining the Queen's reaction. "I admit that I have revised my opinion of him, enough to feel sympathy for him, but it is not love. I certainly do not like the countryside so much that I would want to banish myself there."

These words were firmer now, with a ring of truth. Then it wasn't any desperate feeling. Not yet. Just a brutally inconvenient possibility that would take root and damage everything it grew upon if it was given the slightest bit of encouragement.

"What was his condition when you left him?" she asked as if she wasn't able to help herself.

There was no point in lying, not when she was moments away from seeing the truth. "The doctor seemed confident his bowels are intact, but the risk of mortification is high. You should prepare yourself for any outcome."

Her eyes filled with tears again, but this time she wiped them away with a furious set to her mouth. "He will be fine. He cannot let his mother lay him low that easily."

Lord Ravenscroft nodded in agreement with her sentiment and then urged her to lean against him again. If he had to make a wager with himself, he would bet nearly everything he was going to end up being forced to leave her at the doctor's office. She would insist on staying.

And he would let her, because even though he knew this soul destruction himself, he knew it was difficult to resist courting it for the meagre moments of joy.

The *ton* knew that marriage was always meant to be a transaction, and a love match might be supplanted by duty, alliance, and position. But more than most, he and the duchess were keenly aware that acknowledging love was the death of ambition.

It required too much sacrifice to be indulged.

25

—Lady Cresswell, to Charity on the eve of her wedding

"**Y**our Grace?" A man's voice pierced the fog of sleep. Charity's dreams unraveled, slipping through her grasp as she clawed her way to wakefulness. "Duchess, it is morning."

Morning. The word held little meaning. There had been no true rest, only darkness and the aching pull of exhaustion. She scrubbed at her gritty eyes, pushing herself upright. Pain lanced through her spine, stiff and unyielding after a night spent curled on a wooden bench. She sucked in a breath and blinked until the room sharpened into focus.

Lord Ravenscroft peered at her from up close. He backed away at her rousing, revealing the unfamiliar confines of the space around them. The room smelled of charred wood and bitter herbs. A small hearth crackled with freshly stoked embers, casting flickering shadows across a shelf of apothecary bottles. In the corner, a discarded rag—dark with dried blood—lay in stark contrast to the pale wooden floor.

They were still in the doctor's surgery. Still waiting.

The night had yielded no miracles. Charity braced against the surge of frustration. She had refused to retreat to the palace, and made it clear she wanted to stay at his side. But Ravenscroft had forced her to rest—if one could call this pathetic excuse for sleep rest. Now morning had come.

"Lord Fitzroy," she croaked, ignoring the dryness in her throat.

"Has not yet woken," Ravenscroft answered. "The doctor is with him now. I sent Antoine out for rolls and tea to break our fast. Do not shake your head. We must keep up our strength if we are to help him."

Charity rubbed her sore neck and glared at the hard wooden door separating her from the next room. Goodness knew there was little else to see in the spartan space. The only other furniture was a narrow table by the window. The emptiness pressed against her, heavy and suffocating. She took the food Ravenscroft offered, chewing mechanically—not for hunger, but because collapsing from weakness would do Fitzroy no good.

When the doctor finally emerged, she set the half-eaten bun aside, her entire body tensing.

"How is he?"

The doctor did not smile. Did not soften his tone.

"The laudanum should have worn off by now, but he is not coming round." He hesitated. "His temperature is rising."

The words struck like a hammer blow.

Rising. Not lowering.

She forced herself to focus, to hear the rest.

"The wound still looks clean. If there is some sort of infection, it is deep inside. The fever may burn it out."

Or it might burn him away completely.

The room tilted slightly. Charity's fingers dug into the bench, anchoring herself. Fitzroy stood on the threshold of life and death, and all they could do was wait.

No. Not wait. She would not sit by idly and leave this to fate.

Perhaps what he needed was an incentive to make the right choice.

"May I sit with him?" she asked. When the doctor nodded and stepped aside, Charity turned to Lord Ravenscroft. "Will you stay, or have you somewhere to be?"

"I will not depart without your leave—and not until we agree on what to tell the Crown. Prinny will be expecting an update from me before the day is done."

Prinny. Queen Charlotte. The Marchioness. The ever-growing queue of those who wanted something from her. If even one of them had spared a thought for Fitzroy beyond what he could give them, perhaps they wouldn't be here at all.

Charity found the energy to give Lord Ravenscroft a grateful smile and then gathered her nerve to go into the next room. It looked much the same as it had the night before. Someone had added a fresh log to the fire and left a bowl of clean water on the chest of surgical instruments.

From the doorway, Peregrine appeared to be asleep. He lay atop the battered old table that served as a bed, with only a wool blanket beneath to cushion his injured body. His arms twitched and his ragged breaths huffed out far too quickly for Charity's liking. She rushed to his side, brushing damp hair from his fevered brow before lifting the cloth. It had gone warm. Too warm. She dipped it into the cool water, wrung it out, and pressed it gently to his forehead, her fingers lingering for a breath too long.

Her mother would be apoplectic at the sight. Peregrine, bare-chested beneath a thin blanket. Charity, disheveled, her hair mussed, her gown irredeemably wrinkled. Lady Cresswell would demand a wedding before the man even opened his eyes.

The faint smile slipped from Charity's face before it had time to take hold. Stickler though Lady Cresswell was for propriety, she would never consent to her daughter marrying a Fitzroy. Certainly not Marian Fitzroy's only son.

The weak light seeping in around the edge of the curtain cast Peregrine in a strange half shadow. Charity noted a hint of his mother's features in the shape of his brow, not to mention her same white blond locks. He had been cast in her mould, raised by her hand, yet here he was, far, far from his mother's side.

He was just as alone in the world as Charity was, but unlike her, he desperately longed to stay that way. Clawed hands reached for him from every direction, striking out for a pound of his flesh.

How had she ever thought him her enemy?

He had tried to tell her in the maze at the garden party. He had said he intended to leave well enough alone. She had only to keep her distance. She had all but spat in his face. Now, she did not want to leave his side, albeit for a very different reason.

She wet the cloth again and placed it back on his forehead, watching as rivulets of water ran through his hair. He muttered something unintelligible, shifted around, and then clutched his injured side. She pulled his hands away carefully, crooning words in a singsong voice, begging him to lie still, to be at peace.

"You must rest, Perry. Your body needs time to mend, but your spirit is strong—I know it is. Do not slip away. Please… come back to us." She stilled, hoping for any kind of response, but all she got was silence. Yet, even that much was an improvement. She threaded her fingers through his and held on, unwilling to consider anything other than him getting better, even though his feverish skin burned against her palm.

Time blurred into the rise and fall of his fevered breaths.

Shadows lengthened, candle wax pooled and cooled, yet she remained, gripping his hand like an anchor.

Then—three sharp knocks at the door.

Lord Ravenscroft cracked the wooden panel open and motioned to her to come closer. "We need to discuss next steps, Your Grace. Antoine will sit with his lordship."

Before she left, Charity smoothed the sheet that was covering Peregrine's chest. Ravenscroft moved aside, waiting for her to follow, and his valet took up the vigil.

Ravenscroft motioned Charity toward the narrow table near the window where a plate of food and glass of ale awaited her. The curtains had been pushed aside enough to let her see the shoulder of the man who had taken up watch outside. It was a reminder of how precarious their position was, not that she needed one. She had little appetite and told Ravenscroft as much. "I just ate."

"That was six hours ago."

"But Lord Fitzroy—"

"Is in the next room." Ravenscroft pointed again to the table. "Antoine will alert us if anything changes."

Charity glanced over her shoulder at the closed door. "Do you trust him? Are you certain he cannot be corrupted?"

Ravenscroft drew himself up, shifting his stance as though wrestling with something, before he finally huffed out a sigh. "Antoine is—important to me."

Charity searched his face, waiting for him to explain. Of course his valet was important, just as her lady's maid was a key servant. But Ravenscroft's words suggested something more. Something deeper.

Oh. *Oh.*

"So the answer is yes, I do trust him. Should you stay the course with Lord Fitzroy—with *Peregrine*—you may someday find yourself caught in a difficult situation. If no one else in your life understands, you may come to me."

"But the women, the flirting?"

"Ah, well. Variety is the spice of life, Duchess! But... other desires are fleeting. Small mysteries, easily sated with bits of gossip. Like you, I, too, have to be useful. I, too, depend upon the goodwill of the Crown to live the life of my choosing."

Charity mulled his words, her picture of him arranging and rearranging itself until it fit together into a coherent whole.

The question poured from her lips faster than she could stop it. "Is it worth it? All the dancing, pretending, the nights out? Surely you must have had second thoughts, at some point? And what of your title? You must have an heir."

"I am content to let the title fall to my cousin. He is a kind man with four grown sons." Ravenscroft chuckled. "The rest—I have the heart of a hedonist, and it is not nearly as much pretending as you think. I was more fortunate with my nature than many, because otherwise I do not know how I would have been able to play the role society expects."

That was not news to Charity, for she had only to look at her dearest friend Grace to see that love exacted a price. Or Ravenscroft, whose affections saw him shackled firmly to Prinny for his protection.

She allowed Lord Ravenscroft to take her by the arms and guide her to the table. He pushed in her chair and then took the seat opposite.

"The pie is chicken and mushroom from the best shop in the area. Enjoy it, for the ale is more water than anything else. You eat, and I will do the talking."

The aroma rising from the top of the flakey, buttery crust awoke Charity's stomach. She picked up the fork and knife and waved her hand, telling Ravenscroft to continue.

"There is more news I have to share with you. After I sent

Dawson to Bow Street, he brought back word that McGrath—the man who stabbed, err—"

The man's face flashed into Charity's mind from the night she had been attacked, turning her stomach. "I made his acquaintance when he invaded my home." She sipped the ale and took a cleansing breath before returning to her food.

"Well, you do not need to fear crossing paths with him again. He is dead. The prison guard found him in his cell this morning."

"Good." Something about Ravenscroft's expression suddenly left her unsure. "Is that not a good thing?"

"It is a fitting end, though it gives rise to a whole host of new questions. How did someone get to him in a private cell? Someone ordered his death and paid someone handsomely to do it, all on a moment's notice."

"Was it Cameron?" she ventured.

Ravenscroft shook his head. "Bow Street has his office under watch, but there has been no sign of him. He has gone to ground. McGrath said that there was a larger plan, involving others. It looks like he was correct. McGrath's death was ordered by another pair of hands."

Her fork fell from her hand, landing on the ceramic plate with a clatter. Charity raised her hands to her face and covered her eyes. Life, death, more adversaries crawling out from London's underbelly. It was too much to contemplate.

She would start with the most urgent matters. "Does anyone know where we are?"

"As best as I can tell, no, though that luck will not hold for long. The doctor is out seeing patients now, and I have paid him handsomely to keep the surgery closed. But by tomorrow, we will need to move, one way or another. The question, however, is where to go."

"Are you sure the townhouse is unsafe?" Charity asked.

"His mother surely knows of its existence. Same with the

Fitzroy estate. I would offer my home, except I was with Fitzroy at the fight. We need someplace with a lot of guards, few entry points, and loyal staff."

Atholl House met the latter two criteria, but the cutthroats had already made quick work of getting access to it. And Selina's offer was too dangerous to entertain—even if Peregrine hadn't warned her repeatedly that her prices were too high.

"I can go to Prinny," Ravenscroft offered.

Prinny would almost certainly agree, but Queen Charlotte had him wound around her little finger. Not to mention, she would send them all to the devil if they left her out yet again.

No, if they were to approach a royal, it had to be her visiting the Queen.

But the Queen was looking for someone to blame for all that had happened. There was a risk she might see some benefit to despatching Lord Fitzroy, particularly now that they had confirmation his mother was involved. Charity took a few more bites of the cooling food, wracking her mind for a worthwhile option.

"Prinny is the wrong place to start. We need something of value to offer Her Majesty, if we are to convince her that his is a life worth saving. I have the start of an idea, but I am not sure whether it is enough."

Suddenly, the front door crashed open, and Will Hodges entered. Ravenscroft stood quickly, putting himself between the man and Charity, giving Peregrine's driver a wary, hostile glare.

"What do you want, Hodges?" he asked gruffly. "Why are you even still here? You have overstayed your welcome, and you may want to take your leave while Fitzroy is still senseless."

Charity looked from one man to the other. Unlike Ravenscroft, Hodges's face was shuttered. "What has happened?"

"Fitzroy's driver used to be a sellsword, Duchess. Did you

know? And apparently he feels free to accept commissions while pretending to be a loyal man."

"I am a loyal man, Your Grace," Hodges gritted, keeping his eyes on Charity. "My job has always been to protect his lordship. With my life, if need be. That is the order I was given, when the Marchioness of Normanby sent me to war behind him, and that is the oath I follow still."

Charity could feel Ravenscroft's surprise that Hodges would name his other employer so casually. But Charity knew there was nothing casual about the way he dropped Selina's name.

Hodges had driven her to the marchioness's home, and he knew the name would hold meaning for her. The way he was holding her eyes was improper, but it was a telling look. This was a risk. An explanation. Not an excuse.

Ravenscroft sneered at the man. "I suppose you believed this did not divide your interests. Does she know you are here? Did she order you to stay on the doorstep?"

Charity lifted a hand towards Ravenscroft to calm him down. "It is the oath he follows still," she repeated Hodges's words thoughtfully, growing curious. "Does he have any idea what you are?"

"Your Grace, he never asked me for my references. I keep duller knives in my pockets, if you take my meaning. We saw one another at work long before the Nive, and he offered me a position proper."

The man could clearly see the doubt on their faces. "I can see what yer thinking. Well, if you still can't imagine what sort of trouble he thought might come looking for him in London, especially after all this, you're not nearly as clever as the lady or his lordship."

Ravenscroft and Charity shared a glance.

"She is still paying you to protect him here? In London?"

Charity struggled to make sense of it. "Why would you accept her money to do what he is paying you for himself?"

"Hell." Hodges swore softly and paused a moment, as if summoning the energy to speak more words. "If I'm to be damned for it, it may as well be in full and not by halves. Once I got back, I tried to end the contract with Lady Normanby, but she changed her terms for protection. He asked me on as a general hand—and I suspect a guard. But *she* wanted me to make inquiries into the staff and keep away trouble before it could end up on his doorstep, too. That has a cost."

Charity knew nothing about such things. But she had an inkling now of why Hodges might not have felt his loyalties were divided. "And you did it knowing you would be sacked if he ever found out about it."

Hodges grunted. "Aye. I'd do it again, too. I like working for his lordship, but the man has too few people watching his backside. And now he'll have one fewer. He'll want me gone now, and her ladyship won't have no use for me anymore, which is why I'm spilling my guts."

Charity had heard of honour among thieves, but until this moment, she had not fully grasped it. Hodges might have used the marchioness's resources to help Peregrine, but it was clear where both his concerns and loyalty lay.

Ravenscroft flicked a glance her way and Charity gave a subtle nod of agreement. She paused for a moment. "Tell me Hodges. Lady Normanby wanted me to let Fitzroy know she was willing to provide him aid. What do you think about her offer?"

The corner of Hodges' eyelid twitched—which in a way, told Charity everything. "I'd suggest you let his lordship decide."

If only he was hale enough to. But Charity was worried that if —no, *when*, she told herself sternly—he came around, it might be too late to put protection in place. She had to go back to considering the Queen.

Charity was close enough to the woman to foresee exactly what the Crown would demand, assuming they could be convinced to extend their protection. What could she offer that the Queen did not already have?

Perhaps access to Selina's secret society. Yes, the marchioness wanted Fitzroy, but had she not also said she wanted Charity to become her friend? Charity had brushed aside the idea, thinking the Queen would question her allegiance. But now, that played to her advantage.

First, she needed to be certain that the Crown was truly in the dark. Fortunately, she had ready access to someone who would know.

"Lord Ravenscroft, tell me, what does Prinny know of the marchioness and her so-called friends?" she asked.

"I always assumed she was like me," he replied. "A master at using her every resource to gather information, which she passed along to whomever held her loyalty. If it is more, that is far more serious, and certainly warrants further study."

"That is what I hoped you would say." Charity glanced around, searching the space for her wrap and gloves. When she found them lying on a shelf, she sent Hodges out to flag down a carriage. "I must go to Buckingham House, alone," she added. "You should visit Prinny before he is too wroth with you. Antoine and Hodges can remain here to keep up the watch. I will be back as soon as I can, with help in tow."

And she would, though she wished she was more certain about the viability of her plan.

26

"A known evil is better than an unknown one."
—Unknown

The Queen had not yet forgiven Charity for not telling her about her granddaughter. She made Charity wait for more than an hour before granting her a private audience at Buckingham House. That she chose the imposing green drawing room further underscored her displeasure.

When Charity finally gained an entrance, she found Queen Charlotte seated in the middle of the room on a high-back velvet chair, with no other seat in sight. Charity held her skirt to the side, sank low and kept her gaze on the floor.

A queen's indulgence is neither lightly sought nor easily won, her mother whispered as Charity held her deep curtsey. *There will be consequences to this course.*

There would be consequences to any course, Mama.

But only in this one did Charity feel like she had any power to negotiate a deal that could protect Fitzroy.

It took a long time for the Queen to finally command Charity to stand up. "Your Majesty, I seek your justice and wisdom," Charity said gravely, trying to keep her knees sturdy. "As well as ask for the Crown's protection for Lord Fitzroy."

Her Queen's mouth gaped in surprise. "Pardon me, Your Grace, but—*what*?"

Charity was never one to beg. If someone had told her one week ago that not only would she be begging the Queen, she would be doing it on behalf of Lord Fitzroy, she would have ordered them committed to Bedlam. Yet here she stood now, doing exactly that—carefully measuring her words out as she recited what she had rehearsed.

"Since I left your side yesterday, I have learned that Lady Fitzroy is doing more than whispering destructive thoughts to your granddaughter, ma'am. Her involvement with the man of business—the acts against the Dutch—the princess was only one head of a hydra. We have run one head through, and already another has taken its place. I cannot yet guess where the next head might strike—but I know where the last one did. While Fitzroy was trying to parley with Cameron, one of his men passed a message from Lady Fitzroy to her son, and it came at the point of a dagger."

She explained everything Lord Ravenscroft had told her transpired from the moment he and Lord Fitzroy had left St James's palace together. The plan to parley with Cameron. The meeting. The fight, and McGrath's words about Lady Fitzroy sending her 'love' to her son.

The Queen was grave, thinking it over, but Charity did not dare let her think too long on it.

"Your Majesty, Lord Fitzroy has been gravely injured. He lies, fevered and insensible, in a doctor's surgery in the slums—all because Marian Fitzroy considers her son an obstacle to her and her plans. He knows how many of her resources are on English soil. Why else would she attempt to kill her own son, unless she felt he was dangerous? Which means… he is more valuable to you alive, as one of your weapons to be used against her."

Queen Charlotte's eyes narrowed, but Charity felt a small surge of triumph. She had the Queen's undivided attention now, and if anything might help Fitzroy, the knowledge that his life would spite his mother could. "I am sorrowed, of course, to learn of his dire condition, but I fail to see what that has to do with me. If he lives, I would be happy to discuss his future. If he does not, then he is no weapon, is he?"

Charity swallowed, gathering her thoughts. She had held tight to a vain hope that dealing with Marian Fitzroy would be enough. Instead, she was going to have to maneuver through the other trickery she had uncovered.

"My Queen, I am afraid there is more. Lord Fitzroy needs not only your protection, but also your forgiveness."

"Duchess," the Queen finally said smoothly, her gaze fixing on Charity's face. "Why do I feel like you are about to destroy my peace of mind?"

Charity swallowed against the dryness in her mouth. "Fitzroy is entangled in a web that spans from the underbelly of London to the House of Lords. He holds more than his mother's secrets in his head. Others will be competing to either win his loyalty for themselves, or prevent others from gaining it as well."

"You mean his mother is not the only one who will be marking him for death, which makes it far more complicated to keep him alive. But *you* think he is worth our effort."

"For what he knows about his mother alone, I think so, yes. But Marian Fitzroy is not the only one who has dreams of manipulating the throne, and I think her son can expose these factions."

The Queen's eyebrows lowered fractionally, and inwardly, Charity held her breath. The canny old Queen despised the idea of being manipulated by someone—which made it thrice as important that Charity showed no sign she was employing the same tactics against her sovereign.

"Factions like the members of the *ton* who do not like Prince William of Orange and talk about seeing the betrothal talks ended?" The Queen smiled, showing a threatening number of teeth.

This was the part that Charity had agonised over the entire time she was making her plan. Because Peregrine was unconscious, she did not even know if Selina's statement that he had been planning to sicken Prince William were true.

But did she believe him capable? Or that someone might have manipulated him into such a task? Or that the Marchioness of Normanby had the power to level a credible accusation against him regardless of whether he had been planning to do it or not?

Oh, yes.

So Charity was going to tell the Queen that Peregrine Fitzroy was guilty of playing a part in conspiring to poison Prince William of Orange. Because in the end, it did not matter whether or not it was true.

If the marchioness told the Queen before Charity did, it was going to be much more difficult—perhaps impossible—to get his life spared, and whatever the real truth was, it could do nothing more than possibly ease her wretched guilt.

"Not mere talk, ma'am. I fear they nearly succeeded."

"Explain what you mean at once, Duchess Atholl!" she snapped.

Charity held up one hand in temperance, steeling up her courage. *I hope you will forgive me for what I am about to do.*

"I have reason to believe Fitzroy may have been blackmailed to participate in a second plot to poison the prince. At the same event."

The Queen shot to her feet, her face changing colour in a most astonishing way. But what was terrifying was the sudden spectre of death that clung to her cheekbones, just beneath the surface. "How *dare* he do such a thing!"

"Please, Your Majesty," Charity begged her. "Grant me enough time to explain. I do not seek to excuse him. I am not even certain it is true. In his fevered state, he said a great many things. This was one of them. He begged for forgiveness."

Uncertainty flickered on the Queen's countenance, and the light of blind rage left her eyes. "Who put him up to this? Who is responsible for it?"

"Ma'am, I do not know," Charity lied. "His ramblings ranged wide and in his condition, I had no way to direct them."

She had suspicions, certainly, but no evidence. Selina would laugh off any direct questions on the topic. Her friends Lords Chandros and Pembroke were powerful, male, and could simply deny everything.

"This is what you want to beg a pardon for? A wild confession with the unfortunate stink of possibility." The Queen tilted her head.

Charity bowed hers in regret. "I cannot help but think he is a better man than we believe him to be. But because of Lady Fitzroy, Peregrine is caught between the hammer and the anvil, and it would be a shame to waste his steel by letting others bend him to their own designs.

"You have enemies without. He can join with them, unmask them, expose the people who seek to guide England's future from the shadows. Yes, you could see Fitzroy hanged and be rid of the nuisance he presents, but in doing so, you would lose your only means of unraveling the truth. And more importantly, you will lose the only one who knows how his mother truly thinks. All he needs is a safe place to recover, and the care of a competent physician."

She took a step closer, lowering her voice to something near a whisper. "Your Majesty, I do not ask for his mercy. I ask for prudence. You trust me. Let me bring him to heel, and you shall have a hound that sniffs out these other traitors who are trying to stop the wedding. Absolve him of suspicion. Give him to me, and I will see that he ensures your desire in this matter is fulfilled."

The Queen slowly settled back into her chair, but the sharpness in her eyes did not fade. "You ask for prudence, Duchess, and you ask for Fitzroy's life. And in return, you offer me—what? A solution to a minor problem? A finger on a leash you hold until the princess's marriage?" Her voice was cool, assessing. "Unacceptable."

Charity's stomach twisted, but she held her ground. "Your Majesty, if he is made—"

The Queen lifted a single hand, silencing her. "Stop. You have made excellent points for his continued existence. And you are right. I can see how far too easily he could become a danger no matter how much better we think he might be. You will have him spared—but only under my terms."

Queen Charlotte pressed the tips of her fingers together, staring at her just long enough for Charity's breath to catch in uncertainty. Finally, the old Queen continued. "A man's life is worth more than a solution to a temporary nuisance. *If* I grant him a pardon, he will be given a purpose. One that ensures his absolute loyalty."

Conditions. Charity suspected the Queen would apply her own.

"Fitzroy will not be yours to control, nor will you stand between him and my will. I will expect him to do all that I say, even if those orders are delivered through you. He can start by rooting out the very factions that sought to use him, destroying them before they can strike again."

Charity's pulse pounded in her ears. "F-for how long?"

The Queen's smile was slight, but it did not reach her eyes.

"For as long as I have use for him. His pardon is on the condition that he serves me—bound by his life and future to the Crown."

Charity's mouth had gone dry. She had known the Queen would exact a price, but this—this was a collar of iron, a life sentence wrapped in the silken folds of royal favour. "If he... if he survives the fever, I will offer him the choice."

"No, Duchess," the Queen informed her. "I am not offering this choice to him. I am offering it only to you. A tool does not get to choose what hand wields him, and do not think I have missed the fact that you sought to make this bargain for him without consulting him on the matter."

Her smile was slow, deliberate, and all teeth. "For your part, I will insist that you may take no action without my awareness. I expect to be kept better informed than you have done so far. And I expect you to manage Fitzroy."

"So... make your decision now. If you agree to the bargain, I will pardon Lord Fitzroy. But hear me well: I will make you swear to me that he will uphold his part in the bargain, Duchess Atholl. If either of you fail to abide, I will retract that protection."

Charity felt as if the cord were wrapped around her own neck instead of his. She could hardly breathe, and what little she could manage sounded loud in her ears. If he lived, Peregrine was going to be furious that she bartered his life away.

But... at least he might live.

She curtseyed deeply. "You are gracious, Your Majesty."

27

The air was far more sultry than he remembered it as he stood on the balcony of Lady Norwood's home. It was like being in his mother's glassed house for exotic plants, hot, humid and difficult to breathe. But he was cold. He was freezing, actually, despite the coat he wore and the sweat he could feel on his forehead.

Where had she gone? The smell of Charity lifted to his nostrils from his coat. She must have just returned to the ballroom, and he felt oddly bereft.

"You are not giving up already, are you?" she said behind him sternly, and he spun on his heel. The world lurched a bit, and she looked… older somehow. Not worn, exactly, but there was just the slightest bitterness in the tilt of her lips and around her eyes.

Confused, he opened his mouth to ask what she was on about,

but sudden, sharp pain lanced through his side and then everything altered again with a jolt.

Suddenly she was young again, and in his arms as she was in his fantasies. When he imagined things being different.

Her fingers caressed his temple and cheeks with the lightest of brushes. He shifted his head into her palm, wanting more of a connection between them. She rose up on her toes, her mouth a taunting distance from his.

This was heaven, if such a place existed. The fragrance of her hair teased his senses, and he breathed deeper, wanting more of it —more of her. But the scent was… wrong somehow. It smelled of Charity, but it was hidden beneath some floral instead of citrus, clashing with the spice of clove he preferred.

He let her go, pulling away, but he felt weaker now. Like she was some spirit whose touch had robbed him of some of his vitality. She watched him retreat, her eyes shadowed, glittering in the darkness.

"Wake up," she told him.

What did she mean? He was awake—or he thought he was. He went to raise his hand to his face, to rub his eyes, but his arm felt as though it weighed a hundred pounds. The sense of wrongness multiplied, and he struggled against the crushing lethargy.

"There you are," her voice whispered to him, but the sound of it felt as though it was inches from his ear, even though the woman stood yards away from him, watching him so strangely.

Fingers slid through this hair again, wrapping around to the sensitive place behind his ears as the vision standing before him disappeared.

He was losing her again; he couldn't make the moment last.

Vexed by the strange mire that held him, he thrashed his head again and then demanded his body respond the way he wanted. He felt the cool air hit the underside of his arms. It shocked him enough that he flinched. Pain burnt up his side, white hot even against his scorching flesh, and he let out a hiss as his mind finally swam back into consciousness.

His face was wet, and he blinked, droplets from his lashes blurring his vision. Charity's face again swam into view—the older one again, and this time she was close enough he could see the lines of worry on her face. She peered at him intently, some of the weight of her expression finally lightening with relief when his eyes met hers and focused.

"Hallo, Sparkles," he croaked, swallowing to try to generate some moisture in his parched mouth. "Am I still dreaming, or are you brushing my hair?"

Her lips thinned as she tried to repress a smile. He was glad to see it, even though it deepened the circles of fatigue and agitation beneath her eyes. "Perry. Thank God. I was going to try yanking on your hair if you did not finally come back to your senses."

"Don't let my being awake stop you," he whispered, fluttering his lashes at her.

She grimaced. Then her hand left his forelock, and abruptly he wished he hadn't said anything about it. The desperate melancholy from his dream of the past was still sloughing from his thoughts, and he missed the peace of it. The simplicity of that balcony.

What was real was far too complicated.

"How long has it been? Where am I?" he finally asked after she gave him a trickle of some broth to wet his mouth. He glanced around the masculine room, not recognising it. The drapes were drawn, but dim light leaked along the wall. It must have been either early morning or afternoon.

"I suppose that is proof you never skulked around after climbing into my window," Charity said a trifle grimly. "You are in the duke's rooms at Atholl House. The doctor was quite put out by the encampment in his place of business, and we moved you after sundown the day after you were hurt. You have been delirious for a few days."

Picking up a new cloth, she dipped it in the water, wiping down the side of his face and along his neck.

He must be still a bit feverish. The cloth felt like ice, and he gasped at the shock of it, a shudder wracking him. He brought his hand up to arrest her movements as she began to slide it down his collarbone, and Charity froze as the pads of his fingers grazed over her knuckles, her eyes wide.

"This is not proper. You shouldn't be here—nursing me—at all," he said as sternly as he could. Beneath his thumb, he could feel the pulse in her wrist leap. She knew it too. Her butler was probably beside himself.

Tiny diamonds of moisture appeared at the corner of her eyes. "I was afraid… that you would somehow slip away from me while I was absent."

As if he would let a fever carry him away when there was still unfinished business to attend with her. Still—"You do not need the trouble that might come from an accusation I have compromised you."

Her eyes flashed at him. "This is my home. And I am not worried about being accused of being debauched by an insensate man with a gut wound in a house ringed with guards."

Guards? What guards?

He barely parted his lips to ask what was going on when fragments of memories began to piece themselves together. Hodges. Cameron. McGrath.

His mother.

A different kind of sensation lit beneath his breastbone, gnawing him raw from the inside. His mother had marked him for death. And Charity had *brought him back to her home.*

Abruptly he was both furious with her and sick to his

stomach. It took him a moment to even name the feeling: Thick, cloying fear.

Something he hadn't felt in years.

"Why did you bring me here?" he asked, trying to keep his voice even. But his grip on her wrist betrayed him, tightening hard enough to bruise.

Her face was a mask as she endured the pain he caused her, but finally she tore her hand away, looking both uneasy and exasperated. "Why else? To keep you safe while you recover."

Peregrine had to hand it to the duchess. She really knew how to unman a male. This was a bloody uncomfortable way to have a long-due reckoning—flat on his back, where he felt utterly helpless. Pressing his arms down into the mattress, he began to force himself into a slightly more upright position.

"Perry, you should not move too much," Charity protested, putting her hands on his shoulders to keep him from raising himself too far. "We had to move you more than was wise already."

"How could you be so foolish as to bring me here?" he snarled at her, and she dropped her hands, tears springing to her eyes. Abandoning the attempt to sit straight up, he ignored the pain in his side as he rolled to face away from her, attempting to slither to the edge of the bed. He would crawl out the bloody front door on his hands and knees if he had to.

But Charity circled the foot of the bed quickly, throwing her arms around his shoulders.

"Stop, please," she breathed into his ear as she held him fast. "I know you're not angry. You're afraid. But you don't have to be. You're not alone in this, do you understand me?"

Beneath her hands, another shudder wracked through his fever-sensitive body, lightning quick. His soul keened, wanting to pull her closer, even though he needed to thrust her away.

"You don't have to deal with your mother alone," Charity whispered, pressing her forehead to his.

She didn't understand a damn thing, and not since he was a child could he remember ever being so close to weeping for the utter frustration of something. "This—is a mistake. Let me go. Give me space."

She pulled away and gave him a look that hurt, but without her touching him, he had the strength to shove those feelings down. He tried to tell himself this was better.

"What happened with Cameron and McGrath?" he asked, trying to wrest their conversation to safer places.

"Nothing you need to concern yourself with any longer," the duchess replied coolly, a mulish set to her lips. "It is being handled."

"God *damn* it, Charity," he ground out. "Do not act like a petulant child."

"I am not; I am striking bargains for information. A trade for a trade. You want what I know, Fitzroy?" She leaned down to peer in his face again. "I want to know why you are behaving like this."

Fine. She wanted to know? He would tell her. "Because it's *your fault*," he hurled at her. "Not since I became a grown man have I been afraid of anything, but now I am. Everyone knows how they can harm me. I finally have a fatal weakness, Charity— and it's you."

He meant to send her running from the room, but the duchess's face grew lifeless and careworn. "Ravenscroft told me all that McGrath said—he is dead, incidentally, and Cameron is still at large. Someone is cleaning up behind Cameron, which makes McGrath's words about another person working in London credible."

Charity was still for a long moment. "Selina wanted me to try to persuade you to go to her and her people for protection. Is that what you would rather do?"

He flung himself over onto his back again, easing the cut in his flank. "Never. I will not indenture myself for protection—certainly not to Selina and the others."

"Not even if she was threatening to expose your plan to poison Prince William with croton oil to bring you into the fold?"

Peregrine was startled into a brief, low laugh, and he pressed his thumb and fingers into his grainy eyes. "Ah, Sina, you catty bitch."

"Perry, is it true?"

"Will Hodges was her creature, wasn't he?" he said tiredly, ignoring her questions.

"She was the one who sent him to the continent with you, yes," Charity said softly. "But after that… I think he took a shine to you. He says he took Selina's money after that to take more steps to keep your house safe. I think even Ravenscroft believes him, and he was quite annoyed by that.

"But… is it true? Were you going to poison Prince William yourself? She said that was the favour you owed her."

"Those friends of England—they do not want their future queen to get married to that Dutch Prince. I was not going to put it in his cup, but did I help Selina pick a poison that would cause an incident and break off the negotiations?" he finally put his arm down, locking eyes with Charity. "Yes. I did."

He could see her throat working, though her face remained expressionless, and he wondered if this might be the end of his path, after all. "What are you going to do with me now, Charity?" he asked softly. "You have a helpless monster in your adjoining rooms. Are you going to call the guards and see me executed for William?"

"No." She answered so abruptly, he knew she was feeling more emotion than she showed. "Cameron will pay for what was done to William once we find him. Your hand was forced. *You* are not a monster, Perry," she said, sitting on the edge of the bed beside him so she could stroke his cheek with her palm. "I am so sorry for the words and thoughts I had before, and I am so glad you are getting better so I could tell you that—I am sorry."

He closed his eyes again, letting her touch destroy him. "I should have known my mother took you from the ball," he confessed. "I underestimated her willingness to hurt you. But I was... trying to do everything I could to avoid even thinking about you. How the only woman I've ever wanted, in all the seasons I've attended, was going to marry someone else."

The bed tilted unexpectedly, and his eyes flew open just as Charity pressed a kiss to the corner of his mouth. It was a hesitant touch—light, fleeting, uncertain. As though she had meant to kiss him properly and lost her courage at the last moment.

Her breath fanned against his cheek, warm and unsteady, and he felt the way her body had gone still, waiting. Deciding.

A tremor passed through her, so slight he might have imagined it. Then, as if summoned by some force beyond reason, her lips brushed his again—closer this time, still hesitant, still soft, but undeniably a kiss. A real one.

Peregrine wasn't going to miss this chance again. His blood roared in triumph as he sank his hand into her hair, the silken strands tangling around his knuckles as he dragged her back to him. This time, there was no uncertainty. He took her mouth properly, his lips sealing over hers in a kiss that stole the air from both their lungs.

She made a small, surprised sound against him, her lips parting just enough to let him deepen it. He pressed his advantage, but gently—reverently. Widow she might be, but she was so clearly untutored in this. He would not frighten her. Instead, he let her learn him, let her explore at her own pace, teasing her lower lip with his own, tasting the sweetness of her breath.

She hesitated for only a second before responding, her mouth softening beneath his, her hands curling into the fabric of his shirt. The tentative press of her lips turned searching, as if she were committing this moment to memory. As if she were realising —just as he already had—that there would be no coming back from this.

A breathless sound escaped her as he nipped at her lower lip, coaxing her to open for him. She did, tentatively at first, then with a kind of fragile boldness that sent heat thrumming through his veins.

And God help him, but he let himself revel in it. Just this once.

Because for her, this kiss was a beginning. And for him, it was the only taste of a future he would never have. So he clung to her for as long as he dared.

And finally, she pulled away, her eyes huge with want—and guilt.

"I guess you should have had more concerns about being debauched by a sick man," he said teasingly, and her face flushed the deepest pink he had ever seen on her. "Go rest, Sparkles. I think I am on the mend, but I am in need of another nap—and you look like you have been sleeping poorly."

She nodded, crossing the room to a door that opened to the sitting area. "He is awake, and could use some assistance," she said in a low voice, and he could hear stirring from the other room as a man in livery followed her back in, carrying a stack of towels and bedding. And then she departed, leaving him with the manservant who helped to feed him and clean him up.

It was a tiring effort, but Peregrine needed as much time as he could to think and recover. He began to form the bones of his plan.

28

"The appearance of truth, even if it be only an appearance, is essential."
—Aristotle

Peregrine's fever had broken a few hours later, and for the next day, he did what he could to recover as speedily as possible.

He was still not hale, but much of his stamina returned after that first feverless sleep, and the pain in his side dulled to a manageable level with the inflammation under control. McGrath's knife managed to miss everything vital in the fight, and though it hurt and itched, the pain that movement caused was tolerable.

So after every visitor who looked in and went away, he got up and paced silently around his room, carefully studying his surroundings, both inside and out.

Someone had set out a banyan for him, but he also found a small traveling case of shirts and trousers that had been clearly brought from his estate home. At least he wouldn't have to be wholly indecent. The duke's clothing was much too small, but Peregrine had found a dark cloak amongst the items that he would definitely need to employ.

His clothes were too easily spotted, and there were guards, indeed. He counted two men patrolling the outside grounds, and likely, there was another stationed at every entryway. Possibly one or two more in the stables.

Those were just what he could count outside—doubtless, he might find at least one man stationed outside his door, and however many others indoors on the ground level.

There were so many, he was amused to realise no man was stationed below his window. Charity and her royal soldiers clearly reckoned on any threats coming from outside. Or perhaps they thought he was still too weak to worry about him protesting the confinement.

To be fair, all day long he had done what he could to convince them of that charade, eating sparingly and staying in bed. For the last day and a half, he staved off both Charity and her unctuous servants by mostly pretending to doze.

It had been pretending to be deep in sleep when Charity looked in on him that hurt the most. She had visited only twice and stood her ground, standing silently by the doorway for only a moment, as if just to reassure herself he was still breathing. And he wished he had the courage to talk with her, and enjoy their last moments together, but he didn't think he could manage to pretend that nothing was amiss.

He was certain Cameron had someone watching her home, waiting for the guards to be recalled. Or for them to get lax. It would happen, eventually, if Cameron was patient enough—and why shouldn't he be? The guards would become bored, slipping up in their vigilance, and he would have his golden opportunity to strike at one or both of them.

Tonight, he had to leave her four walls before anyone suspected he was capable of doing so.

After the last servant left him alone for the night, he took a piece of stationary from the desk and scrawled a brief note.

C,

Forgive me. I knew that if I did not leave in silence, you would stop me, so this letter must serve as both a goodbye and a plea for understanding. Only one thing could compel me to leave—and that is to do what I must to end the threat against you.

You may have been right about our fate, but I am not ready to concede defeat. Somewhere, some time, we will find happiness. Even if it must wait for another life.

—P

Folding it carefully, he left it on the bed. Then he extinguished the candle, embracing the darkness.

As the guard began to walk past his window, Peregrine readied himself. He would have perhaps a minute to drop from the duke's balcony and hide himself behind the nearby laurel. And as the guard passed by, Peregrine stepped over the rail.

It was agony, hanging onto the bars long enough to drop to the ground softly. But he managed it—just. His boots met the damp earth with barely a sound, knees bending to absorb the impact. The laurel's thick branches swallowed him instantly, the leaves rustling against him as he pressed himself into the shadows and slipped the dark cloak on firmly.

Peregrine stilled his breathing, ears straining for the next guard's arrival, and within a half a minute steps began to approach. The second guard saw nothing untoward. He didn't pause. Didn't turn. Just kept walking, his lantern casting flickering light ahead of him.

Good.

Peregrine waited, counting heartbeats. Five, ten, fifteen. The guard's steps faded toward the gate, and Peregrine moved, strolling out to the main road as quickly and unobtrusively as he could. He waited to pull down the brim of his hat, hiding his eyes, however, until he was halfway to the next street.

It was sooner than he expected that Peregrine could feel wetness seeping through the bandage at his waist. Fortunately, by that point, the shadow on his trail let him know he had succeeded in the first part of his plan. So he didn't linger; as soon as he could, he flagged a carriage and sent them in the direction of the Seven Dials.

It was time to try to make a deal with a devil.

The hired carriage dropped him near his townhouse, and for a moment, he breathed in the brume, smelling of wet cobblestones, refuse, and coal smoke. He didn't turn. Didn't glance over his shoulder. But he could feel the man tracking him still, keeping just outside the lamplight.

Just before he began to walk into the alley, Peregrine turned towards the man in the shadows. "Tell Cameron where I am, and that I still want to talk. This time I am here alone. I think he will want to hear what I have to say."

The large brute waited for a moment, clearly thinking, and Peregrine parted his cloak, showing the growing red stain on his linen shirt. "I will not be running off anywhere. So what does he have to lose? Tell him to come talk, and then you two can decide whether or not to finish the job."

Peregrine's breath was slow, measured, though his pulse hammered against his ribs as he waited for the man to respond. Finally, the cutthroat tipped his hat, and turned on his heel, the soles scraping on the pavement.

Letting himself inside of the servant's entrance, he locked the door behind him, limiting the ways Cameron might try to have his men enter. And then he went upstairs to fetch the smaller flintlock pistol he kept in his wardrobe, placing it in the waist of his pants where his coat would hide it, before he returned downstairs to wait.

Noise outside of the front door sometime after three in the morning caught Peregrine's attention, waking him from drowsing in the chair. He waited as the front door was pushed open, his hands empty and flat on the tabletop to show he was unarmed, his shoulders slumped.

The unassuming man who entered the building was in his early forties, weathered but composed, his mouth curved in a knowing half-smile.

"Mr Cameron," Peregrine greeted him, looking away after just a moment's connection. "It has been a while."

Peregrine knew his mother's man of business, although not very well. Even when he and his mother had been on terms, she had kept him ignorant of the breadth of her commerce, and not for his own sake, either. Marian Fitzroy was a suspicious, selfish creature who preferred being a fearsome enigma to everyone, her own children included. Keeping others unbalanced fed her vanity and sense of self-importance.

He knew that Cameron lucratively invested in a series of expensive gambling hells and brothels—at a remove—which had included the Scarlet Jack before it had burned down. But Cameron was also into smuggling. A handful of times, Peregrine's own 'business' had benefited when he was able to procure certain items that were difficult to acquire during the war for others—such as nice French brandy for the Prime Minister.

When he couldn't acquire them by other means, that had been when he had reached out to Cameron.

Cameron himself stood just inside the doorway, his weight balanced—not quite casual, not quite aggressive, just... waiting. Waiting to see what sort of game Peregrine was playing. And when Peregrine made no attempt to move or to talk further, he shut the door behind himself.

"You look like hell, Fitzroy." Cameron's voice was light, but his gaze flicked once to the dark stain Peregrine had left visible. "Have you been comporting yourself in activities bad for your health?"

Peregrine dropped his gaze and swallowed once, as though he were working up courage. A nobleman, out of his depth, and desperate with it. Let him believe the act. He rose from his seat, but kept his shoulders hunched—non-threatening. "In hindsight, it appears so. What do I have to do to speak with my mother?"

A beat. No reaction. Not surprise, not amusement. Cameron had expected this. Then, with mocking patience, Cameron tilted his head. "Why? Do you need to speak with her?"

Lifting his hands, Peregrine disheveled his hair. "It was a mistake, telling Percy about Matthew. But in my defence, it was an accident. I had no idea she was using him." Matthew's debts had been the noose his mother had tied around Sir David's neck.

"You had found yourself on the register of people who crossed your mother a wee bit earlier than that, Fitzroy. Else you might have been told about Sir David and Matthew Green."

Peregrine knew exactly how he had got here. But playing a lackwit was the edge of the knife that he had to walk. "I know. I made a mistake," he repeated. "I did not ever mean to interfere with her enterprise; I only wanted to find a way to contribute more on my own terms. I was good with people, Cameron. I liked working in the political arena. Matters have gotten too far out of hand, and all I want is a chance to try to explain."

"You wouldn't be the first one to come begging to me, *laddie*," he said dryly, letting the barest trace of his Scottish heritage shine through. But he had come to London when he himself had been young, so his accent was barely there unless he wanted to make it heard. "I understand your sort can't help it. Most people will offer a lot to keep breathing for just five more minutes. But see, you haven't really offered anything to make up for your transgressions, have you?"

"For starters, I can continue with the way things were," Peregrine gritted his teeth. "Collecting secrets and means to extort the lords, of course. We have an opportunity here, Cameron. Many people no longer believe that I am working for my mother, especially after these escapades. The royal family will take me to their bosom, and from there, the rest will follow. Surely that will be useful."

Cameron shook his finger at him, chuckling. "Think you're going to fish for information? I *will* kill you before I let you leave with anything of importance."

"I do not want your information, Cameron, just a second chance to prove my loyalty. The only other thing I would ask is that you call off the dogs you set on the Duchess of Atholl—and only because she is one of my creatures now. She stands at the right hand of the Queen and the princess. I wager that would be closer than whatever lady you blackmailed."

Cameron's face was expressionless beyond the fact that he was clearly weighing things. But he was far from looking convinced. It was time to play his trump card.

"To sweeten the deal, Cameron, consider this—I have been offered the protection of The Order. I can take their offer. And then pass along the roster of all the members once they have brought me into their circle."

"I see." Another long pause. Then, finally, Cameron smiled. It was not a kind one. "Well, I think your mum will want that. But is that all, Fitzroy? Or do you have anything *else* you wish her to know?"

He had to grovel convincingly. It would be his only chance to get a glimpse of the future his mother had planned.

"That I am lost without her. I have nowhere else to go, and I want to… come home."

29

Charity awoke with a start, her eyes open before her consciousness caught up. Her bedroom was swathed in darkness, with only the faintest hint of a breeze coming in through the crack in her window. She lay perfectly still, her breathing slow, while she listened to the sounds of her house.

The antique clock on the wall ticked the seconds off. From outside in the hallway came the light steps of the guard keeping watch. He paced back and forth, with hardly a break, lest he risk falling asleep, or so he had explained. She had chatted with him a few times during the wee hours when she had looked in on Perry —or wandered the grounds, unable to sleep.

Now she was again in her own bed, lying alone beneath her covers. She did not have to work hard to imagine Perry there at her side. She had only to think back on the night that had started it all—when he had broken into her room and forced a blade into her hand, defying her. Daring her to grow a backbone and try to kill him—if she could.

She would give anything to see that same spirit from him now, but he seemed almost eroded by fear and melancholy. Because of her.

The only spark she had seen from him was when he woke up from his fever.

And when you kissed him! Her mother's scandalised voice still rang in her ears.

Yes, Mama, I kissed Peregrine Fitzroy. And believe it or not, I regret not doing it sooner.

Perry had accused her of being a title chaser at the start. And the words had stung, being far nearer to the mark than she liked. But he had not put himself into the market last season, and her own mother had rather gently but explicitly warned her to avoid the Fitzroys whenever possible.

Under those circumstances, what kind of forwardness did he believe a debutante could be expected to display? It had hurt her to acknowledge his name and his unavailability.

But when they had stood, nameless to one another, on that balcony, it had not felt so much like the end of days her mother had threatened, as the start of something else. Something that could be... perhaps a glimpse of what Grace had said she wanted for her.

And now, Charity realised... she wanted that. To seize that elusive sense of the beginning of something that could be truly magical within her own hands. Despite everything she had said to him about their fate. Despite their families.

Yes, there were obstacles aplenty determined to keep them apart, but neither of them was the type to back away from what they wanted. Was that not exactly what had brought them together? The overwhelming desire to claim what they believed themselves due?

Was it so reckless to throw her cap over the windmill and taste this? Could it be possible, if they fought for it?

She nestled deeper into her covers, her eyes closing so she could picture a different life, one with Perry at her side.

But his voice chose that moment to dash those fragile thoughts: *I finally have a fatal weakness, Charity—and it's you.*

Charity wanted to bat away that line of dark thoughts, but it was like trying to cut through smoke. She had taken his power to choose from him when she made the deal with the Queen, and that knowledge twisted around her, smothering her in it, threatening a return of that familiar panic.

He was right. More right than he knew, her own voice taunted.

She had kissed Perry, clung to him, and spoken a few words to him in the day since, but she had not said a single word of her deal with Queen Charlotte. The debt he would have to repay and repay again, until either the Queen tired of him or one of them died. The debt she had remained silent about because she knew how he would react.

She had not woken him from his drowsing to tell him what he ought to know. Because she was a coward, and she was letting the problems of today be put off, hoping she would find the courage tomorrow.

You are not a coward, you are just biding your time. He is unwell, and you must find the right moment so you can explain—

She argued with both herself and her mother's voice again, the same words going round in circles. Would he ever listen to her, would he understand that she had acted only to save him?

I think you know by now he will not. Perry is a man who wants to plot his own course—and not have yet another woman doing it for him.

The thought took hold and any possibility of sleep

disappeared. Charity slid from her bed, the cold wooden floor shocking her fully awake. She tiptoed across her bedroom, to the unlatched door on the far wall. She had used it often enough in the last few days, going into the ducal suite to keep watch over Fitzroy, and then back into her room to catch an hour of rest. Or stare at the ceiling.

This was just like when she had nursed him through the fever, she argued. He was likely deeply asleep, and would have no idea she had peeked through the door.

The handle turned, the hinge swung freely, and moonlight streamed through the wide open window.

It was strange how familiar the space had become in the span of a few days. When she had first arrived in London, she had not set foot in the old duke's chambers. She had turned the lock from her side, barring both the ghost of the man and the future she had avoided with his death.

But when asked in which room to put Lord Fitzroy, she had not hesitated to point them in this direction. Mr Pritchard had nearly swooned in horror, but she had ordered the guards onward, called for the fire to be stoked, and that had been that.

For the last few days, he had slept in the bed meant for her husband. The four poster dominated the space, softened only by the mound of white pillows resting against the headboard.

But the bed itself was empty, the covers rumpled, but clearly made. And with a pulse of foreboding, she knew he had not merely stepped away.

Charity cast any remaining restraint aside and rushed into the room. The crisp edge of the folded letter stood out against the deep blue spread. She nearly tore the paper in her rush to read the contents. Her anguished cry was loud enough to draw the guard into the room from the hallway.

"Your Grace?" he asked, his face turned away so he would not stare at her in her state of undress.

Not that Charity would have noticed, or even cared at that moment. She waved the letter in the air like a flag calling men to arms. "He is gone! Gone!"

"Gone?" the man repeated like he had been hit on the head. "Where did he go?"

The answer was in his letter, and it landed like a blow to her midsection. She crumpled over from the sheer pain of it.

"He went to find Cameron to strike some hare-brained deal for my safety." She glared at the guard, expecting him to respond. "Do you know where Mr Cameron is? Has there been some lead in his whereabouts? Some word Lord Fitzroy might have overheard?"

The guard shook his head, just as bewildered.

"Then he does not know where Cameron is. He strolled out of the house to offer himself as bait," she said bitterly.

The guard stiffened at that, but he was forced to acknowledge the truth. The only way Peregrine slipped out of the house was through the window, and he would have passed the royal guards on the way.

That would mean he believed someone was watching the house—which of course, half the neighbourhood already was. The guards had attracted a great deal of attention these last few days, and no shortage of speculation as to what they were doing there.

"Where would he go?" she demanded of herself. "He is baiting Mr Cameron. I am certain of it. Would he go back to that pub, the place where he got into the brawl?"

The guard's head shook with such fervour that Charity knew she was on the wrong track. "He might have gone to his estate, Your Grace. There are no guards there."

But there were his servants, and Peregrine would not want to put their lives at risk. He needed some place he knew well, somewhere quiet. Somewhere Cameron might already possibly have under watch.

"I know where he has gone. Call another guard and meet me at the stables. We have to go after him."

"We'll go, Your Grace. You shouldn't be out at this hour—"

Charity silenced him with an expression of such arched disdain that he nearly swallowed his tongue. "If Lord Fitzroy is still alive, I am the only person who has a chance of talking him out of this foolish, deadly plan. We will go together, as few as necessary, and pray to God that it is not too late."

Charity was in far too much haste to ring for her maid. She turned to go back to her room, but a memory stilled her. Her mind cast back to the night when she had been rescued from her kidnappers. Her best friend Grace rushed to her aid, wearing trousers under her dress. The pair had laughed many times at the memory.

Now it was to her benefit. Charity strode into her husband's dressing room and rummaged through his few remaining old things until she found something suitable. The man had been old and wizened in his final years, not much bigger than herself. A few rolls of the cuffs and a hastily tied belt would do the trick. She found a dark blue shirt hanging on the rack and appropriated that too, pulling it on over her nightrail and tucking them both into her trousers.

She did put on her own shoes, choosing her leather riding boots, her feet sliding in with ease. Getting them off again was always a devil of a job, but that was a problem for later. Having deemed herself dressed appropriately for whatever challenges the situation entailed, Charity left her room and used the servant's staircase to get outside with the minimum of fuss.

The lieutenant of the guard had gone down to alert the others and her stable. Her poor stableman had managed to equip both her own horse and one of the ones brought by the guard. Apparently the lieutenant had taken the liberty of getting the stableman to also ready her larger carriage. But she couldn't fault him for his forethought; Peregrine might reopen his wound.

Both men spluttered at the sight of her in men's clothing, but again, she glared them into a silent acceptance.

"The carriage will be ready in just a few more minutes, Your Grace," her stableman told her, as the lieutenant handed her the reins of her horse.

"I will be riding ahead. Have the rest of the guards take the carriage to the Seven Dials." She led her horse to a stepping stool so she could climb on.

With that done, Peregrine's foolhardy choices catapulted Charity into another frantic nighttime ride across London. The guard took the lead, clearing a path for Charity to follow, not slowing until they reached the sundial that gave the Seven Dials its name.

"Steady on," the lieutenant told her, getting her to pull to a halt. "We should continue on foot until we can see what awaits us."

"I will defer to you that much," she nodded, directing them towards Neal Street. "Hopefully we will find him alone—but it seems lately our luck has been terrible."

Charity did not know whether to celebrate or gnash her teeth when they got within sight of the house. The curtains of the front window had been left half open, allowing the glow of the candles to cast a pool of light on the pavement. She turned into a narrow gap between two houses across the way and ducked low, hiding in the deep shadows with the guard crouching at her side.

"He might as well have left the door standing wide open in invitation," Charity muttered. She bade the guard to stay where he was, intending to walk past slow enough to glance inside, but he told her to wait. Seconds later, she caught the scuff of footsteps. Her breath caught when a lone man came into view, walking without a care in the world until he disappeared into Peregrine's townhouse.

"That matches the description of Cameron," the guard whispered, rising up.

"You cannot go in after him," Charity countered, grabbing hold of his arm. "He might have a weapon, or others watching. Come, let us find another way in."

She strode off, her steps as confident as any man, heading in the direction of the path between the houses. She had no trouble locating the gate, but came up short when searching for the key. The back door was locked and barred. She took a step back and surveyed the rear of the house, searching for another way in.

The narrow ground floor windows were out of the question. The first floor was the logical choice, but there was too much risk her entry would be heard. Her gaze caught on a rain barrel set near the fence. If she slid it over, she could reach the ledge of the first floor window. From there, with no small amount of determination, she could climb the trellis up to the second floor.

Now, to take the guard or leave him behind? She tilted her head and noticed his hand resting on the pommel of his sword. He would go in swinging—or firing the flintlock in his belt.

Perry obviously had some sort of plan. Until she could figure out the shape of it, she did not want to send the guard running in.

"Go for the others," she said in a harsh whisper. "I will wait here, out of sight, until you return."

The guard did not want to leave her behind, but she convinced him she was safe enough. She waited until she could no longer hear his steps before executing her plan. The barrel was nearly empty, a blessing for which she gave thanks. It took some manoeuvring to get it where she needed it. Then, she climbed on top, checking its sturdiness before committing her full weight.

From there, it was easy enough to make it to the window ledge. She scooted across it until she reached the trellis.

Her arms screamed in pain, her hands growing slick with blood and sweat after only a few halting steps upward. Thorns sliced into her fingers, making her grit her teeth to keep from crying. Yet, she made it up to the dark window of the second floor bedroom. By some small miracle, the window was unlatched.

It took some arguing, but she eventually convinced her leg to pull free from its foothold. She held her breath, and lurched sideways, nearly tumbling through the open window. Heart hammering, she stood stock still, listening for any sign she'd been heard.

No footsteps, no cries of alarm. She gulped in air and nearly choked on the strange smell. The room carried the unmistakable scent of an artist's space—linseed oil and turpentine, sharp and lingering in the air. She spun around, taking the minimal furnishings in at a glance. A half-finished canvas sat on an easel near the corner. A table stood against the wall, lined with bottles and stained with pigment. She grabbed a couple of rags and used them to clean the scrapes on her hands.

She found a single taper lying amidst the brushes. After pulling the curtain, she lit the wick. A stack of canvases, turned to face the wall, caught her eye. This was what Perry was hiding? His painting hobby? She crossed to the easel and studied the work in progress. Wide, bold strokes of black and grey paint slashed across the expanse, a shocking use of colour compared to the landscapes and portraits she was used to seeing. But it was too early in the painting to make out what the background was supposed to be.

Curiosity washed away all hurry and compelled her to see a completed work. She used one hand to turn the outermost painting around, taking care not to drip wax on it.

It was a self portrait of Peregrine, she realised, her hand

shaking so hard that wax burned her wrist. He had painted himself as he had seen himself in the cracked and black-spotted mirror that stood in one corner of the room, including everything faithfully, down to the frame of the mirror and the tools of his craft.

The way he included the frame of the mirror made him look trapped within the looking glass. As though that version of him was not a real person at all.

She dashed the tears away before they could fall and let the canvas settle back against the others. Now was not the time for such worries.

Looking at the locked door, she saw it had a night latch. Unlocking it, she opened the wood panel with great care and tiptoed into the hallway. Across the way loomed the doorway to the bedroom where they had slept in each other's arms. She forced her gaze toward the stairs, moving with a halting gait until she reached the top of it. Two steps down and a board creaked beneath her foot. She froze, carefully sliding her foot to the edge. Her legs trembled with the effort, but she made it halfway down.

On that landing, she could hear the voices coming from the front room.

Perry spoke in a strange voice, pleading instead of his normal confident tone. He was begging for her protection. It made no sense. Was he not there to catch the man and see him imprisoned?

She inched lower still, following the curve of the handrail as it turned, bringing her within sight of the hall outside the parlour. She shifted forward, but a flash of motion stopped her in her tracks.

The guard she had sent off was now coming in from the front door, with another close behind. She waved her arm to get his attention and held up her hand to halt their progress.

"I see." Another long pause. Then Cameron spoke again.

"Well, I think your mum will want that. But is that all, Fitzroy? Or do you have anything *else* you wish her to know?"

That he despised her? That he wished her dead? Whatever she could imagine fell far short of his actual reply.

Peregrine's voice trembled as he uttered the words, "That I am lost without her. I have nowhere else to go, and I want to… come home."

Charity lurched forward without thinking, but the guards were faster. They knocked her aside and barged into the room, shouting for them to hold. Charity stumbled forward, her only interest in reaching Peregrine.

He was standing with his back to her, but his posture was all wrong. His arms hung low at his side, his shoulders hunched, making him smaller. He rocked sideways as he looked over his shoulder, knocked off balance by the sudden arrival of both her and the guards. She longed to wrap her arms around him, but Cameron's angry groan stopped her.

She dragged her gaze away from Fitzroy and saw Cameron lift up his gun.

30

"You should never care for anything that can be taken from you.
And remember: everything can be taken."
—Marian Fitzroy, to both her young children

It was as though time had slowed to a crawl, stretching the moment wide enough for Peregrine to register everything at once.

As the guards stormed in, their eyes locked onto him first. They had heard his words. They thought he was a traitor.

And he sensed, more than saw, the blonde woman entering the room after them. Though she wore men's clothing, her shape was unmistakably feminine. It was as though she filled the room—not just with her presence, but with her authority, her scent, her certainty.

But none of that mattered, because Cameron flinched. A twitch of his arm, the slightest shift toward his hip—Peregrine's full attention snapped to it, and he began moving.

Even before Cameron's face twisted in rage. Even before he reached his own weapon.

Peregrine's fingers slipped into his pocket, closing around cold metal. His thumb found the cock of the pistol, pulling it back as he drew.

But Cameron's hand had begun to rise first—and his gaze wasn't on Peregrine. It was on her.

The duchess stood behind them, still as a doe, staring down the length of Cameron's gun as though waiting for the hunter's hammer to fall.

As the next heartbeat stretched into eternity, Peregrine didn't waste time raising his pistol any higher than Cameron's waist.

The gunshot cracked like thunder, and Cameron's hand jerked open, his weapon slipping from his palm as he staggered back, blood blooming across his lower belly.

The sound was still ringing in Peregrine's ears when rough hands tore his pistol from his grip. Another guard threw Cameron to the ground, pinning him even as the life drained from his eyes.

From the doorway, a sharp voice cut through the chaos. "Bind his lordship. He's under arrest."

Disbelieving, Peregrine's head swung to Charity, who looked alarmed. In the end, all he could manage was a question: "Charity?"

She shook her head firmly, eyes entreating. Whatever this was, the arrest hadn't been her intent. But her folly had earned it for him. Anger boiled, following that initial surprise. She had followed him. She brought these guards here to catch up with him.

What a sodding *mess*.

All of Neal Street was in for a treat this early morning. A public arrest of a nobleman for murder—if not treason—and the scandal that would follow wasn't even the worst of it.

Their best chance of finding out Cameron's accomplice, not to mention whoever else might be working in his mother's employ, was lost. The man of business's minions and contacts would scatter like rats, as people destroyed any evidence of their association. It would be difficult—maybe impossible—to figure out if the contract on Charity's life ended with Cameron's.

And with Cameron dead, there would not be a hope in hell of contacting his mother now, much less pretending to reconcile enough to guess at what she was planning.

Black despair weakened his knees, and he had to grit his teeth to keep from falling to them.

The guard in front of him, no doubt seeing Peregrine's bloodied shirt, interpreted his stagger in a different way. "His lordship's hurt himself again," the guard said, taking him by his arms and depositing him bodily into a chair.

He still put the iron cuffs on him, however.

"Perry!" the duchess shouted, and tiredly he looked up, seeing one of the guards carefully restraining, keeping her from approaching. "Stop what you are doing. This is wrong. I did not order you to do this."

The Lieutenant of the Guard who had ordered him cuffed strode forward and bent down to check Peregrine's side, prying up the bandage just enough to see that while his stitches had torn, the damage wasn't all that severe. "We don't follow your orders, Your Grace. Not too much harm done there, your lordship. I reckon you'll be fine while we bring you back to the palace.

"You—take Her Grace home. Go now. You'll have to hire a hack. And for God's sake, do not address her by name or title until she is wearing something appropriate to her station," the lieutenant told the man holding Charity back, and the man nodded, hurrying her away.

As they left, the remaining two guards bracketed him, picking Peregrine up from the chair by his arms and guiding him towards the front door.

He let them. They were only doing their duty. He was the one who had done the fool thing, leaving Charity the letter in the first place.

His mother had always maintained that most emotions were bloody inconvenient, and could only ever cause them trouble. That showing caring and consideration for another's thoughts or feelings was as good as trusting them with a weakness.

This was a bloody inconvenient way to discover his mother had a point.

~

Being escorted by three armed guards to St James's Palace in their official carriage was an experience Peregrine Fitzroy could have done without in his life.

Lucky him; he had done something like this twice now. The first time, of course, had been the day his mother left aboard a ship bound for the continent, and Selina had kicked him to the curb with an order to go back to his estate, where half a contingent waited for him, and face the consequences of Marian Fitzroy's actions. Now fortune's wheel was turning once again, and here he was, walking a far too familiar road.

He supposed it could always have been worse. He wasn't being dragged straight to the Tower, after all.

When he had been taken there to be interrogated by Sidmouth that first time, he had been in a swivet of fury. There was still a spurt of that old, familiar anger, but it spent itself before he reached the palace.

Now he simply felt empty. Empty, and cynical.

He was only briefly planted on the bench in the Guard Room while matters were sorted. As befitting his status as an earl, the room he had finally been placed in wasn't a cell, but still, it was decidedly less comfortable than where he had been sequestered at Buckingham House. An officer's quarters to judge by the cot.

He wouldn't turn up his nose at such basic accommodation and demand better, as was his right. Indeed, he couldn't really bring himself to care. He blandly followed every order and request put to him by the guards and the pinch-faced butler who had asked him to surrender his bloodied outer clothes.

He lay back, barely twitching when the royal physician came to examine his injury, except for when it was bathed once more in alcohol. And then he allowed himself to be rebandaged, not speaking.

After the physician was finished, he lay back on the cot, half-naked and exhausted, waiting.

He hadn't expected to be able to sleep, but his body, still healing, had other ideas. Sleep snuck in like a thief—this time dark and dreamless, pulling him under.

They let him sleep until late in the morning, and by the time he was roused, he found the satchel of his own clothing that had been taken to Charity's house waiting for him. He was prodded into dressing, and then escorted to the throne room where both the Prince Regent and the Queen waited imperiously without looking at him, their faces grim.

He dropped into the customary deep bow, holding the position while both of the royals ignored him.

After a long minute, Prinny began to inspect his nails. "Is that it? A bow? Not quite the gesture of supplication from a man about to face a second accusation of treason, is it, Mother?"

It was one thing to show him a lack of courtesy in the room he had been kept in for a few hours. This was intended to be a deliberate humiliation. Even peers who were under suspicion would not normally be treated like commoners supplicating their betters, and Peregrine could feel his cheeks heat with rage.

He paused stiffly, and then carefully dropped to a kneel. The colour he could feel rising in slashes across his cheeks would speak volumes about Prinny's pettiness, but he kept his eyes half-lidded so that he wouldn't be tempted to glare in return.

"You kneel quite prettily, though I must say, you do look rather… resentful," Prinny commented. Peregrine breathed through his nose, trying to seek the mocking calm he would have used to deal with this—as he had everything—before his life had been shattered within a span of less than two weeks.

"Enough with the theatrics." Queen Charlotte's voice could cut glass. "Get up, Fitzroy, and explain to me whether you are a fool or a traitor."

Peregrine couldn't help it. He laughed. This was like a grand farce.

It was the Queen's turn to colour this time, and Prinny shifted uneasily in his seat.

He couldn't remember ever feeling such a storm of emotion. At the moment, he could muster no sense of respect for the Queen and Prince Regent at all. Did it even matter what he uttered? They had likely already decided his fate, so he was finally going to say his piece.

At least, whatever part of it he managed to say before he was cast into a gaol and forgotten.

"All my life I have been offered choices like this, Your Majesty," Peregrine said defiantly, before they could demand an explanation for his laughter. "Choices that really are not fair options at all. So I will say I am neither a fool nor a traitor; both your selection and your imagination are too limited."

"You dare—" the Queen hissed.

"I do dare, yes. Because you see, last year, I decided what other people were offering me was inadequate. I had been driven for decades along the roads mapped by other people's ambitions. It was high time, I decided, for me to make my own choice to explore the paths that were *not* being offered to me by my mother.

Which is a part and parcel of how you ever came to lay hands upon me last season to accuse me of treachery *in the first place*."

The Queen leaned forward on the throne. "Your words are boldly spoken, Fitzroy, for someone who was overheard begging to return to kneel at your mother's feet. I do believe the exact words related by my guard were 'I have nowhere else to go, and I want to come home.'"

"Those were the words, yes. But is that what truly happened, ma'am?" he shot back. "Or is that only what you want to believe, because you cannot stand the idea of possibly being wrong?"

There was a deafening silence, and Prinny looked between the two of them as though he was reconsidering the wisdom of his presence in the throne room entirely.

Perhaps Peregrine *was* a fool. Because he could not stop venting his spleen.

"I am tired—so desperately tired—of proving my loyalty over and over again simply because of my own name. No matter what I do, what grudging respect I earn, the moment my mother makes a move, it is abundantly clear that I will become the whipping boy. I object to that, Your Majesty. Most strenuously, in fact.

"*Yes*, I put my life on the line. It was the bait I possessed—the ability to draw Cameron out of hiding, when both you and Bow Street would have had to wait, possibly until Kingdom Come, hoping he would make a foolish mistake and expose himself.

"And *yes*, I debased myself. I told him every single thing he wanted to hear for a chance to glimpse the design of my mother's plans. I should not have to warn you, Your Majesty, that there *is* a design.

"My mother wanted to sabotage a wedding between England and the Dutch, and not once—*not once!*—have I heard anyone ask themselves what the purpose of such an action was. My mother is a spiteful enough creature to do such a thing for a lark, it is true, but she would never do it for only one reason, and I promise that reason is not for some sort of misplaced sense of national pride."

The Queen, for all her other faults, appeared at least to be thinking over his words even though she was in high colour. "Bring in the duchess," she said, not bothering to direct the words, and immediately the throne room's doors cracked open to admit Charity. She must have been standing outside, waiting for admittance.

Peregrine couldn't help himself. As Charity moved to stand beside him, holding a curtsey like the willing penitent he could not force himself to be, he let his eyes stray to her like a moth to the flame.

"I have a simple question. Were you informed, Fitzroy, that the Duchess Atholl sought a pardon for you?" the Queen asked him unexpectedly, nailing him to the floorboards with her gaze.

Beside him, Charity startled.

"No, your highness," he said shortly, his mind spinning in a circle as he wondered what Charity had sought a pardon for. "Charity, did you ask for a pardon for last night?"

"Not for this, Perry," she said in a low whisper of supplication, tipping her head slightly to him.

"I find it a curious coincidence that you are questioning your mother's intent in sabotaging wedding negotiations with the Dutch, Fitzroy," the Queen interrupted them, tapping her fingernails on the arm of her throne. "I wonder if they might be at all similar to the reasons why *you* were attempting to do the same."

"*Ah,*" he said tightly, his stomach sinking in upon itself.

He had nearly forgotten that he had confirmed Selina's words to Charity—that he had been involved in a second plot to poison the Prince of Orange. She must have told the Queen. And it seemed darkly ironic that even though he was no longer the enemy of the Duchess Atholl, she was a well-meaning Diamond as cursed as the French Blue.

Fate would always tear us apart, he heard her voice whisper to him.

Rather than answer the monarch, he turned his head to her. She was lovely. This light in his life.

His ruinous star.

"Well, Your Majesty," he said, taking a deep breath to compose himself. "I can try to explain the whole situation."

The Queen, however, waved her hand at him irritably. "The duchess has already explained everything she needed to convey to me. But it is most apparent that she has explained *nothing* of the terms of her agreement with me *to you*.

"Despite your impudent words to me, I find I am no longer quite so wroth with *you*, Lord Fitzroy. Indeed, I would have granted you my permission to embark upon this plan—had you come to us to request it."

A black suspicion was growing in Fitzroy, and he glanced at Charity, who nearly looked as if she was trying not to weep.

"Your Majesty, I beg your forgiveness. He only regained consciousness the day prior, and I thought he was still too ill—"

The duchess had struck a bargain with the Queen that involved him. Without him. And it was clear from her posture and intonation that she knew he would have *never* approved of it.

His heart shattered into pieces.

The Queen gave her diamond a look that cowed her into silence, and then she turned her implacable stare upon him.

"The Duchess Atholl begged your pardon because she believed your loyalties could be bent by both your mother and some sinister group. She offered up your life, your loyalty, and your servitude to me, promising that you were valuable, and would run England's enemies to the ground both within and without.

"On that agreement, I granted the pardon, and agreed to provide you with protection against your mother and anyone else who might want you dead. I was most vexed because that was a conditional offering, Lord Fitzroy. But you could hardly show the proper deference if you were not made aware of the conditions, could you?" The Queen shifted the full weight of her gaze onto Charity. "Well, my diamond, why did you fail to tell him?"

31

The Queen's focus was unrelenting. No mercy would be offered. Dressed in dark velvet, she sat tall and still upon a gilded chair, her pearl-adorned fingers steepled in quiet judgment.

But it was Peregrine's expression that undid Charity. His mouth parted, his upper lip curling as though he had bitten into something foul. A muscle in his jaw twitched. His usually unshakable posture—so often poised, ready to deflect or attack—had stiffened, his shoulders locked as if bracing for a final blow. His gaze flickered between her and the floor, searching for an escape that did not exist, as if he could not bear to see the face of his betrayer and yet could not look away.

"Your Grace?" the Queen repeated.

Peregrine tilted his head toward the Queen, allowing Charity a clear view of his expression—which looked chillingly like it had in the painting. The man from the mirror.

That was how he saw himself—the person he would rather be trapped behind glass, far from any future. Her agreement with the Queen, however well meaning it had been, might take him farther from that idyl still.

Her heart pleaded for her to fall to her knees and beg him for forgiveness, but her steel will kept her upright. What had she been thinking? Her Majesty was never going to consent to letting him go. It was foolishness of the highest order to even imagine such an outcome. But she had to hold onto that foolish desire, because Charity was his only hope of ever getting free from this obligation.

Perry, she thought desperately, *this was the best of our bad choices.*

But she could hardly say that aloud. Keeping the Queen happy—having her remain confident of Charity's loyalty—was of primary importance right then. Charity schooled her features into an expression of pure obedience and, without so much as a glance in Peregrine's direction, she gave her answer.

"I did not tell him before now, because he had been so ill, and I was certain he would react badly. I did not want to jeopardise his recovery, but I miscalculated how quickly he would try to act. Your Majesty, we need his help most desperately. I still believe he is our best hope for capturing his mother—even more so now that Marian Fitzroy may have revealed her hand. That is, I think, our paramount concern. Any information we gain about this… Order will be the crowning touch on our eventual success."

The Queen's nostrils flared in dissatisfaction, but she did not outright frown.

The force of Peregrine's stare, however, pulled her back

around. "You sold my life to the Queen, and promised her I would hunt my mother and the Order in return."

He did not ask it as if it was a question. If she hadn't learned to understand him better, she might have thought his face expressionless. But what she saw instead… it destroyed her.

She gave the Queen one fleeting glance beseeching her patience and then Charity shifted her stance and appealed to Peregrine. "I lived in terror for three days, thinking you might die, Perry. And I still fear for your life." The words came in a rush, unguarded, raw. "You know you are a threat to too many people. They—" she bit her tongue, mindful that she had not been entirely honest with her Queen about Selina and her secret society— "well, your mother at least, would rather see you dead than risk you slipping from her grasp. I had to make a choice. The Queen and Prinny were the only ones I trusted to protect you. Surely you can see—"

"I do beg your pardon!" the Queen interrupted, waving aside anything else Charity hoped to say. "It hardly matters now why you struck the bargain you did. The only thing that is important now is that you both acknowledge the bargain and the parts I need you to play."

"*Respectfully*, Your Majesty," Peregrine turned and used the most neutral voice she had ever heard from him, "I do not recognise this bargain. The duchess bartered with something that was not hers to give."

"Lord Fitzroy, you may interpret my words in any way you see fit," the Queen leaned forward, enunciating carefully. "I do. Not. Care."

Peregrine looked past the Queen, to where the Prince Regent stood silent. "Your Highness, you are the ruler—are you not? Can you truly look me in the eye and say this is a just outcome?"

Prinny shrugged his shoulders, uncaring, his heavy-lidded

eyes glassy with wine and disinterest. The heavy embroidery of his waistcoat strained against his stomach as he shifted lazily in his chair, a king in all but title—and effort.

"Justice must make a bow to what is reckoned to be necessary, Lord Fitzroy," Prinny murmured. "If it is as you predict, what is the freedom of one man when compared to the safety and welfare of the nation? What sort of patriot would deny this call?"

A muscle jumped in Peregrine's jaw, his breath coming sharp and short. For a moment, it seemed he might spit a retort, but he swallowed it down, his hands curling into fists at his sides— knuckles whitening with the effort to remain civil.

Charity longed to throw herself into his arms, to remind him that she was on his side, but she fought against the impulse. Right now, her help was the least welcome of all.

The silence stretched until Peregrine broke it again. He spoke again to Queen Charlotte. "Your Highness makes a most excellent point," he said, his voice coloured with only the barest trace of sarcasm. "Your Majesty, though your patience is no doubt waning, I must raise one last consideration. You are demanding no less than my total fealty. How will you trust that I will keep my word?"

Charity's breath hitched as she studied the Queen's expression. To even hint at such an outcome could result in Peregrine taking up a permanent occupancy in the Tower.

The Queen smiled. "Should your nation's needs be insufficient to motivate you to task, then of course, you have the right to decline to accept the terms of the agreement. But you still stand guilty of conspiring against both the Prince of Orange and the Crown, twice over since you were overheard by the royal guard conspiring with Mr Cameron. You will be charged, stripped, and the promise of protection rescinded, which I expect to be sufficient motivation to earn your fealty. But *trusting your word*, Lord Fitzroy?" she said delicately. "That may never happen."

"Your Majesty—"

The Queen sighed heavily at his words, signaling her patience had reached an end. "Make your choice and make it now. Swear your loyalty to the Crown or accept the consequences of your actions."

Charity could not turn away from Peregrine. She scanned him from head to toe and back again, searching for a clue as to his next move. "Don't let your mother win," she whispered, barely moving her lips.

Peregrine exhaled sharply, his hands clenching and unclenching, as if grappling with the weight of his choice. "I will swear to the destruction of my mother, Marian Fitzroy. But the Order—you will likely never find them all, much less bring them to heel."

The Queen smiled faintly. "One problem at a time, Lord Fitzroy. Right now, the one I require to be brought to heel is you."

Only Charity stood close enough to mark the faint quiver in his shoulders—like the tension of a bowstring—before resignation settled over him.

"If death is my only alternative, then I will serve. Tell me what you wish. I am yours to command."

Well, you have succeeded in making a Fitzroy pay.

Charity's mother's voice dripped with satisfaction. Imaginary though it was, it turned Charity's stomach. She raised her hand to her mouth and took shallow breaths, desperate not to get sick. Over and over again, she reminded herself that her only goal had been to see Peregrine survive. Surely, once they were alone, he would listen to reason.

His words drew a vicious smile from the Queen. "For now, my command is simple, Lord Fitzroy. Go to the Order and take them up on their offer of protection. Let them think they have won you to their cause, and then you will be in a position to provide us with information."

The muscles in Peregrine's jaw pulsed, but his rigid spine kept him in check. "Is there anything else you wish from me?"

The Queen tapped a single ringed finger against the armrest of her chair, the only sign of her satisfaction. "To remain in touch. Her Grace will be your conduit to us. You may go."

Peregrine spun on his heel, his stride crisp, purposeful—an about-face so precise it would have earned a general's approval. His boots struck the marble floor in measured, deliberate steps, echoing through the cavernous chamber. He did not look back. Not once.

Every step away he took caused another crack in Charity's façade. The air in the room felt stifling, the weight of the Queen's judgment pressing against her like a vice. She could not bear it any longer.

"Your Majesty," Charity turned, barely aware of her own movement, her voice slipping past her lips before she could stop it. "Please—I beg you—allow me a moment with Lord Fitzroy."

The Queen looked at Charity sidelong, but relented enough to wave her off.

The door closed behind her with a muffled thud, leaving her alone in an empty corridor. In a palace filled with courtiers and servants, the barren space had the feel of a mausoleum. It was appropriate, Charity mused, for her hopes of catching Peregrine lay dying.

She gathered her skirt and broke one of the foremost rules of visiting the palace. She ran.

She spotted the back of Peregrine's head as she turned the first corner. "Lord Fitzroy! Peregrine!" she called. His steady gait pulled him further away, leaving her no choice but to make a last desperate attempt to get him to stop. "Perry! Perry, wait!"

He stopped dead, his back going rigid at the sound of his nickname tumbling from her lips. But he did not turn. Charity slowed to a fast walk, letting her skirt fall to the ground so she could hold out her hands to him. She grazed the coat on his back, the fabric smooth under her hand, desperately seeking the connection they had found.

He shuddered once like a fly-stung horse and then became utterly still. Unmoving and unmoved despite the raw ache in her voice.

Charity's hand slid down his arm as she circled around to face him. She stared up at his handsome face, at the chandelier filled with a dozen candles hanging above his head, and remembered someone else.

It had been in nearly this exact spot that she had crossed paths with Lord Percy a year prior. He had borne a similar haggard expression, the same deep shadows under his eyes. He, too, had thought himself facing a grim fate, to be trapped in a future he did not want.

On that occasion she had known just what to say. She had told him of her intention to end their engagement. To free him to marry the woman he truly loved—her dearest friend Grace. Though he had stood in stunned silence, she had witnessed the transformation in his posture as the weight lifted from his shoulders.

Surely, she could do the same again. Peregrine had only to give her a chance to explain.

He kept his nose high, all but ignoring her as he stared at some point high up on the wall. "Did you need something else from me, Your Grace? Perhaps my dignity, so you can crush that beneath your slippers as well?"

A vise tightened around her ribs. "I need a chance to explain why I did this for you."

"Did you?" he asked curiously. "Do it for me, I mean. It rather feels like you did this for your own purposes."

"Of course I did it for you!" she hissed, her voice low. "You are… like a bone, with three dogs fighting over you. Three *very dangerous* dogs."

"I would kill to be a fly on the wall in the throne room when you tell the Queen how you compared her to a vicious canine," he murmured an interruption, his voice light and cutting. "Be sure to invite me for that."

"Be serious! You said you did not trust Selina, and when she threatened to expose you for treason to me, I could see why! And your mother tried to have you killed! The doctor said you were dying. Lord Ravenscroft made it clear that your mother would see the deed done, even if the fever did not."

Charity choked back a sob, barely able to get out her final plea. "I did not want you to die, Perry. I would have done anything to protect you. What else could I have done but go to the one power who I thought would be reasonable? You are up against people who are so powerful—"

"You want to know what else you could do? You might have noticed that I am not so thick I haven't the slightest idea what is going on. I have been doing this dance with these people for years before you ever set foot among the peers, Duchess. If you couldn't have faith in my ability to protect myself, then at the very least, you could have waited for me to admit to my need for help."

"Would you? Tell me the truth, Perry. You snuck from my home in the middle of the night, bleeding and half-dead, to meet with your mother's man of business! Did it give you a moment's pause to think how it would have grieved me to find that letter, and to never see you again?"

Charity's eyes burned, but she refused to be discomposed in public, where anyone could see. "You and I are both prideful, suspicious creatures, afraid to trust others for our own reasons. Nothing makes us more vulnerable than admitting that we need someone else's help. But I trust you now, Perry, and *I need you*," she blurted. "I—needed you to be safe. The Queen… I will try to think of something to fix things if you will just give me a little time."

The corner of his mouth curled up in the smallest smirk, and his eyes finally dropped to hers, the pale blue of them as cold as ice. "By all means. *Try*. I'm not a doll for you to play with, Your Grace. I am a man—however neatly you may have gelded me. I have thoughts and feelings of my own."

She swallowed hard, and Peregrine studied her coldly for a moment. "It is amusing, actually, that you set yourself apart from the others. You, Selina, and even the Queen and my mother—you take my choices, and even the very pretense of them. You are all exactly the same. But heed my words, Your Grace: no matter how you might compel my behaviour, you will never control my thoughts. And right now, I despise you for trying to control me at all."

The words struck her breathless, and she pawed blindly at him, trying to find the right way to beg his forgiveness. "Perry— wait," she whispered.

"Please do not touch me, and on that note, will you excuse me? I am afraid I cannot tarry any longer. I expect I will have a busy afternoon groveling to the marchioness. When—if—I have some word to report about my success, I will write you. Good day, Your Grace." He gave a stiff bow and then stalked past her.

A polite cough from behind made Charity jump.

"Apologies, Your Grace," a footman murmured. "The Queen sent me to find you."

Charity took a deep breath, shuddering as a shiver wracked her shoulders, and then drew her back straight.

Confident steps. Head held high. Chin dipped in perfect obeisance.

Charity took the broken edges of her soul and wrapped them around her spine, shoring it up until it had the strength of forged iron.

Once again the Duchess Atholl, she returned to the throne room.

Epilogue

"A lady who chases a gentleman risks becoming the hound rather than the prize. Better to set the snare and let him believe the pursuit was his idea."
— *Reflections of Grace: A Guide to Etiquette*

The grand ballroom of Carlton House gleamed under the blaze of a thousand candles. The scent of beeswax polish mingled with perfume and champagne, the hum of conversation rising and falling beneath the strains of a lively waltz.

Silk and satin swept across the marble floors as London's finest swirled in elegant formations, their priceless jewels flashing beneath the crystal chandeliers. Footmen in the Prince Regent's livery stood at attention along the perimeter, their faces expressionless as they carried silver trays laden with wine and champagne.

Smile, nod, and listen closely.

Charity stood off to the side of the dance floor, at the centre of a cluster of fashionable women. They tittered as they exchanged commentary on the other guests, their clothing, and their choice of escorts. Charity gave a nod of encouragement now and then, just enough to keep the others from noticing her silence. She had little interest in the attendees thus far. It was in anticipation of new guests that she kept watch over the entrance.

A hush fell over the room as a footman at the doorway lifted his staff and struck it against the marble floor, the sharp crack echoing above the music.

"Her Majesty, Queen Charlotte," the footman announced, his voice ringing through the ballroom. "His Royal Highness, the Prince Regent. Her Royal Highness, Princess Charlotte of Wales."

At once, the guests turned toward the entrance, sweeping into deep bows and curtsies as the royal party made their entrance. The Queen, resplendent in royal blue velvet and diamonds, led the way, her sharp gaze surveying the gathered assembly. The Prince Regent followed, his coat embroidered within an inch of its life, a hand resting lightly on his rounded stomach. Behind them, Princess Charlotte, dressed in a soft green pastel, wore an expression of polite interest—though anyone watching closely might have caught the flicker of unhappiness in her eye.

As the royal procession moved forward, the hush lifted, giving way to murmured admiration and the rustle of shifting skirts as society's elite awaited their cue to rise.

"As you were," Prinny pronounced, mostly so that he could leave his mother's side to ask his mistress for a dance and supper, not necessarily in that order.

The Queen continued on, aiming for the trio of velvet chairs set aside for the royals' use. Charity did not miss the way the woman's attention drifted around the faces of the guests, acknowledging them with a smile or a frown. The worst were those she did not acknowledge at all.

Charity had not sunk that low, but she was still a hair's breadth away from truly falling into disfavour. With that in mind, she excused herself from the ladies and hurried to intercept the princess.

Do your duty with a serene heart and a steady pace, her mother admonished.

"Good evening, Your Highness," she said when she reached the young woman's side. "Your gown is exceptionally gorgeous. Is it new?"

The princess preened under Charity's admiring gaze but then her shoulders sank. "Papa only ordered it because he heard it is the Prince of Orange's favourite colour."

"Oh dear," Charity murmured, before biting her lip. This was to be her dance for the night, to sway between sympathy for the young woman and her orders to ensure the princess behaved.

The engagement was still very much on. It was hard not to see it as punishment, given what Charity now knew of the princess's sentiments. Poisoning one's future husband was not near enough to stop a wedding, if one was in the royal family, but it did not exactly bode well for the Prince of Orange either.

Once, she had dreamt of being a princess. Now, she could imagine no worse fate. That was what made her ideal for the task of accompanying Princess Charlotte around for the rest of the season. At least with Charity, the princess could be honest about her concerns. It made no difference that they were equally unable to do anything about it.

What Prinny and the Queen declared would take place. The futures of the English and Dutch thrones would align, setting up the possibility of a great empire. No one, not the couple themselves, and certainly not Marian Fitzroy, could put a stop to it.

But tonight, the princess seemed to be in good enough spirits. She agreed to promenade past her intended, and to trade the requisite curtseys and bows. She even engaged in a few minutes of conversation. When, as always, the royals ran out of inanities,

Charity whisked the princess away with the promise of a glass of punch.

They arrived at the refreshment table to find a beaming man awaiting them.

Lord Ravenscroft twirled his arms in a flourishing bow before pressing a kiss on the princess's outstretched hand, even though his gesture was more avuncular than flirtatious. "Your Highness," he murmured, letting the words curl like smoke, "what a relief to find something worth looking at in this dreary assembly. I was beginning to despair."

"Was Her Grace not enough?" the princess giggled, nudging Charity forward.

"Oh! I do beg your pardon, Duchess Atholl. I was so blinded by this vision, I did not see you there," Lord Ravenscroft purred before giving Charity a wink. "Will you forgive me long enough to allow me to escort you both to the supper buffet?"

Charity longed to remain within sight of the main entrance, but she could not abandon her charge. Besides, Lord Ravenscroft might have some word about the man whose presence she sought.

"All right. Just this once," Charity replied, slipping her arm through his. The princess took her place on his right, and the trio made their way to the next room where long tables nearly bent under the trays of food.

A footman stepped forward, a plate in his gloved hands, ready to serve the princess. "Would Your Highness like something from the fish and game table? Perhaps a slice of the roast venison with Cumberland sauce?"

The princess wrinkled her nose and commanded him to follow while she perused her father's offerings. Charity and Lord Ravenscroft wandered into a nearby alcove, one where they could keep watch over the princess but speak privately.

"Has our mutual friend been in touch?" he asked, studying her face. "No, I see he has shown us the same silence. Pity that, I was just coming to like the canary."

Charity fought to keep her face from showing any outward sign of the pain that lanced through her, half expecting her mother to chastise her for it.

You may feel as deeply as you like, so long as no one ever sees it, her mother's voice responded primly.

"Give him time," she said, when she noticed she had been silent longer than she should.

Ravenscroft barked a laugh. "Ahh, apologies, Your Grace, but for a moment, the irony of our conversation became too much to bear. A mere two weeks ago, I advised you to practice patience. Our situation has reversed in more ways than one."

They paused to nod at a passing lord and lady, and to flash a smile at the princess, before resuming their conversation.

"Was the princess properly cowed by everything that happened?" Ravenscroft asked in a low whisper.

"We are not nearly so lucky," Charity murmured. "She is still a bit rebellious. But at least now she is wary of wolves in sheep's clothing. She will pick her allies more carefully from now on. And I would still wager that her mama is doing whatever she can to aid her daughter's cause. If the princess leaves England, they will both lose."

"Yes, well, on that note," Ravenscroft drawled, adjusting his cuffs with deliberate nonchalance, "duty calls me back to the dance floor. Though my feet may give the impression of executing a perfectly respectable country reel, rest assured that I am, in fact, kicking over stones to see what unfortunate creatures might scurry out."

"Should you get the chance, ask Lady Pelham for a turn. I am curious to learn what venom she is spitting now," Charity suggested before she wished Lord Ravenscroft luck and then rejoined the princess.

The evening was deadly dull, the usual bowing and scraping of those keen to win the princess's favour. A few brave men asked her to dance, and Prince William even took a turn—while he was still sober. It seemed he too had learned something from the events of Prinny's garden party, but somehow Charity did not think the lesson would stick for long.

When the princess pleaded for a rest, Charity escorted her to the chair beside her grandmother and then asked to be excused.

She passed under the arched entryway, in search of a quiet place, when she heard the footman welcoming a very late guest.

She lurched to a halt, her breath caught in her chest, though she could not say whether it was hope or fear.

And then, there he was. Lord Fitzroy. All in black, the only relief a crisp white cravat at his throat, as stark and unyielding as his expression. And on his arm—Selina, Marchioness of Normanby, a vision in violet silk shot through with silver. Charity did not miss the way Selina's grip on Peregrine's arm tightened when she spied Charity. The catlike smile on her face, however, was one of ownership, not affection.

A sharp breath caught in her throat. Her palms itched to smooth her skirts, to reach up and check her hair. She forced them to stay at her sides, tight against her gown. Lord Fitzroy and the marchioness came to a stop a few feet away.

Peregrine met her gaze with a flat stare, but he did not cut her dead. He gave her the merest inclination of his head, as due her station, and murmured a polite greeting. And then, he looked away.

Selina released him with a silken command. "Run ahead, Perry, and catch Lord Sidmouth before he retreats to the card room, will you, dearest? I want to have a quick word with the duchess and then I will catch up." Selina shooed him off, leaving him no choice but to obey.

Then the dazzling woman turned back to Charity, her painted lips curling in amusement.

"Darling, I am so pleased to see you again. How have you fared these last days? Has the… excitement been settling down? You seem far more relaxed than you did at our last encounter."

"Quite, Lady Normanby," Charity said with a slight smile of her own.

"Please. Do call me Selina. We are friends! I must admit, I did not hold out much hope you would be successful in your endeavours to send him to us. Perry can be rather stubborn when he has a mind to be, especially against his own best interests," Selina said smoothly. "Though I am sorry that sending him my way… seems to have caused the two of you to have a falling out."

Selina was most certainly not Charity's friend. But Charity only smiled blandly. "I cannot say I blame him for being upset, it was a bit of a tumultuous experience."

Selina's expression softened—only slightly. She lifted a gloved hand and rested it lightly on Charity's arm.

"Love and hate are two sides of the same coin, Your Grace," she murmured. "They are both bound together by interest. He will come around in time; our relationship is proof of it. And for now, you can sleep well knowing he is protected."

Selina dipped into a shallow curtsy and glided away, leaving Charity with only her thoughts.

Charity could not help but wonder if the marchioness knew her statement was false. Peregrine might outwardly pretend to ignore the wrongs done to him, but Charity knew he marked them well, and kept it in his internal vault of debts, one day to be reckoned.

But Selina was correct in thinking he would come around, at least in one manner of speaking. Like so many things, he had little choice but to speak with her eventually. That was, after all, what the Queen had ordered.

Though they had managed to thwart two attempted poisonings, and had eliminated one of Lady Fitzroy's hired hands, she did not delude herself into expecting peace and quiet. Between the Queen, the Order, and Lady Fitzroy, life was certain to remain interesting, to say the least.

In the meantime, Charity would bide her time and put together her own plan. She was not at all ready to concede the fight for Peregrine's heart—and his forgiveness.

Will Peregrine forgive Charity for tying him to the Crown? Can they survive Lady Fitzroy's efforts to see them killed?

Their journey towards happily ever after continues in Shadows and Splendour - Book 2 in The Diamond of the Ton Regency Mysteries. Keep reading for more details - or head on over to Amazon to order it.

Shadows and Splendour
A Diamond of the Ton Regency Mystery

He's a spy facing a conspiracy that could bring England to its knees.

London, 1814. Lord Peregrine Fitzroy survived war, a contract out on his life, and now the betrayal of the only woman who has managed to find her way into his heart. Pressed into service as a double agent, he is trapped between the throne and a secret society pulling Britain's political strings.

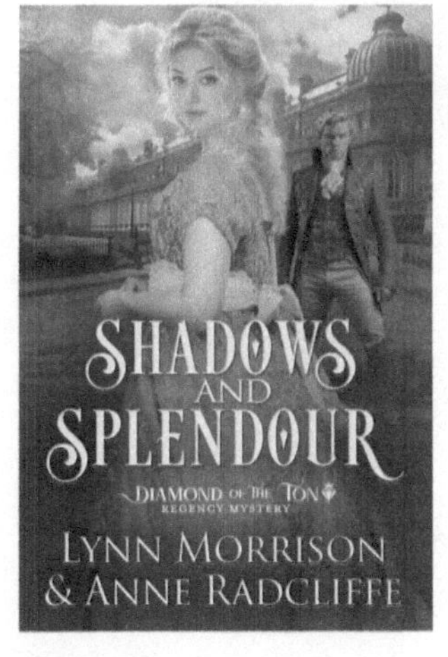

She's a widow who believed fate would have always torn them apart.

Charity, the Duchess Atholl, never expected to fall for Peregrine. With his life on the line, she begged the queen for aid. He survived, but her bargain cost him his independence and stole his trust. With the queen demanding they work together, she has a chance to earn his forgiveness. But will that be enough to ensure a second chance for these star-crossed lovers?

Intrigue at court. A battle fought not with steel, but with wits.

Escalating scandals threaten not only the royal wedding, but also England's political future. Peregrine and Charity are the only people with the knowledge and resources to find a saboteur hiding in plain sight. However, the shadows at court hold more than mortal danger. Working together will make them expose their own secrets… and reopen wounds of the heart that never fully healed.

Can they unmask the traitor before his next strike? Or will England's splendour crumble into chaos?

Find out in **Shadows and Splendour**. Order now on Amazon.

Historical Notes

Princess Charlotte of Wales made her official debut during the season of 1814, starting with a presentation to the Queen and then attendance at major social events. Like other debutantes, she was there for the purpose of finding a husband, though her shortlist of candidates was quite different.

Her father, the Prince Regent—aka Prinny—had already determined that a close alignment with the newly restored royal family of The Netherlands was in England's best interest. Prince William VI of Orange, was of a similar age to the princess and well-known to the Crown, making him the best candidate.

There were, however, two major problems. The first was that the Dutch prince did not make a favourable impression on the young princess during their first meeting. She saw him at her father's birthday party in August of 1813, where he and many other guests drank themselves into a stupor. This particular incident provided us with inspiration for the poisoning at the garden party at the start of the book. The second problem was that of their eventual home. Was it to be in the Netherlands, far from everyone Charlotte knew and loved, or in England?

You might think that Prinny would want to keep his daughter, and her eventual children, close at hand. But he had an ulterior motive for seeing her gone. If she went abroad, he would have no one there to stop him from kicking her mother—-his estranged wife Caroline—out of England as well.

To say that Prinny and Caroline did not get along would be a vast understatement. The two barely managed to tolerate one another long enough to see the birth of their first, and only, child. Their relationship grew into outright animosity, eventually seeing Prinny accuse Princess Caroline of having given birth to an illegitimate, secret child. The so-called "Delicate Investigation" saw the Prime Minister, Lord Chief Justice, and the Home Secretary take testimony on the subject, and eventually rule that she did not birth the alleged illegitimate child. Although Prinny was not able to use this as reason to eject her from England, he did offer it as justification for barring Caroline from seeing their daughter during the investigation, and later curtailing her to a single, weekly visit.

As you can imagine, Princess Charlotte was well aware that her mother and father did not get along. If she left the country on the arm of her new foreign husband, her mother was likely to pay a high price. However, telling the Prince Regent and the Queen of England that you do not want to wed the man they selected is not an easy task.

The matter dragged along from December of 1813 until June of 1814, when Princess Charlotte finally officially broke off the engagement. As to why, you could look it up in the history books.... Or you can stick around for the rest of this series and let us tell you our theory.

As for William VI, Prince of Orange, eventual King William II of the Netherlands, don't worry too much about his future. After his misadventurous engagement with Princess Charlotte, he went on to marry Grand Duchess Anna Pavlovna of Russia, the youngest sister of Tsar Alexander I of Russia. He got an alliance with a major power anyway, even if it was not the one he originally intended.

There are plenty of other real people who peek into our story. No spoilers… but as the plot thickens, the political faces might be seen again! Viscount Sidmouth, who became Home Secretary in 1812, is also a returning visitor from Grace and Roland's series, The Crown Jewels Regency Mysteries. Viscount Castlereagh is the Foreign Secretary and leader of the House of Commons, and in 1814, Earl Charles Grey (yes, tea drinkers, that Earl Grey) was not an unfamiliar face in politics, though he stood in opposition to the Prince Regent because of Prinny's refusal to make concessions on Catholic emancipation.

The Countess of Hertford was Prinny's official mistress sometime between 1807 and 1819. She was a source of considerable influence over Prinny—some would say a restraining influence— and she was politically aligned with the Tories. The Countess of Bessborough on the other hand was Whiggish, and her sister, the Duchess of Devonshire, even more so. While not a mistress of Prinny, she also moved heavily in influential political and social circles.

In the military side of things, everyone knows Wellington, but Rowland Hill was also very much a real person, and believe it or not, yes, he did like treating his men like family, and he did encourage the use of the nickname 'Daddy Hill.'

The Battle of the Nive took place during the 9th and 13th days of December in 1813. Wellington had pushed the French out of the peninsula, over the Pyrenees, and into south-west France. Marshal Soult had fallen back to a defensive line south of the town of Bayonne along the Adour and Nive rivers. On December 13, 1813, Rowland Hill held off the attacks of Soult's 30,000 soldiers and 22 guns with his 14,000 men and 10 guns. It was a very bloody fight, but Hill reputedly fought with great skill and "was seen at every point of danger, and repeatedly led up rallied regiments in person to save what seemed like a lost battle ... He was even heard to swear."

The Nive, and the reinforcement by Wellington, was a major loss for Soult, who had to retreat into Bayonne. By January France was being attacked on all sides. Austria, Russia, Prussia, and Great Britain bound themselves together by the Treaty of Chaumont, and brought their allied armies to Paris on March 30. Parisian authorities decided to treat with the allies, and Napoleon found out that Paris had capitulated when his forces had only reached Fontainbleu. Finally, he abdicated on April 6, 1814—but historians will note that Napoleon wasn't done just yet, just biding his time.

Acknowledgments

As always, we owe many thanks to Ken Morrison and Zoe Burton for guiding us through the editing process. Brenda Chapman, Lois King, and Anne Kavcic beta read the full book and gave us useful feedback on where the story needed more work.

We owe a shout-out to our fellow authors Eryn Scott, Intisar Khanani, and Suzannah Rowntree for helping us fine-tune our opening chapters.

Kim Killion at Killion Design Group took on the challenge of creating covers for this series and wowed us with her work. Thanks, Kim, for the amazing cover designs!

Mary Fields at The Merry Assistant helped us with promotion for this book, and provided much moral support with her cute kitten photos.

Thanks to my ARC team for reading and reviewing the book before we released it. Those early forms of social proof are such a big help!

Last, but never least, many, many big thank yous to the people who hang out with us in our Facebook group and to our newsletter subscribers. You remind us why we keep writing.

About Anne Radcliffe

As an American Expat living in Ontario with a husband and teen son, Anne Radcliffe spends a lot of time editing or writing in order to avoid having to become a Maple Leafs fan. Anne loves a great story no matter the genre or medium - books, graphic novels, TV, movies or video games. You can find out more about Anne on her website at AnneRadcliffe.com.

BB bookbub.com/authors/anne-radcliffe

g goodreads.com/anneradcliffe

a amazon.com/stores/author/B0D1VMVDZ1

About Lynn Morrison

Lynn Morrison lives in Oxford, England along with her husband, two daughters and two cats. Born and raised in Mississippi, her wanderlust attitude has led her to live in California, Italy, France, the UK, and the Netherlands. Despite having rubbed shoulders with presidential candidates and members of parliament, night-clubbed in Geneva and Prague, explored Japanese temples and scrambled through Roman ruins, Lynn's real life adventures can't compete with the stories in her mind.

She is as passionate about reading as she is writing, and can almost always be found with a book in hand. You can find out more about her on her website LynnMorrisonWriter.com.

You can chat with her directly in her Facebook group - Lynn Morrison's Not a Book Club - where she talks about books, life and anything else that crosses her mind.

facebook.com/nomadmomdiary

instagram.com/nomadmomdiary

bookbub.com/authors/lynn-morrison

goodreads.com/nomadmomdiary

amazon.com/Lynn-Morrison/e/B00IKC1LVW

Also by Lynn & Anne